a novel by m.c.miller

HELF SELP

SELF HELP

A Journey From Far To Near

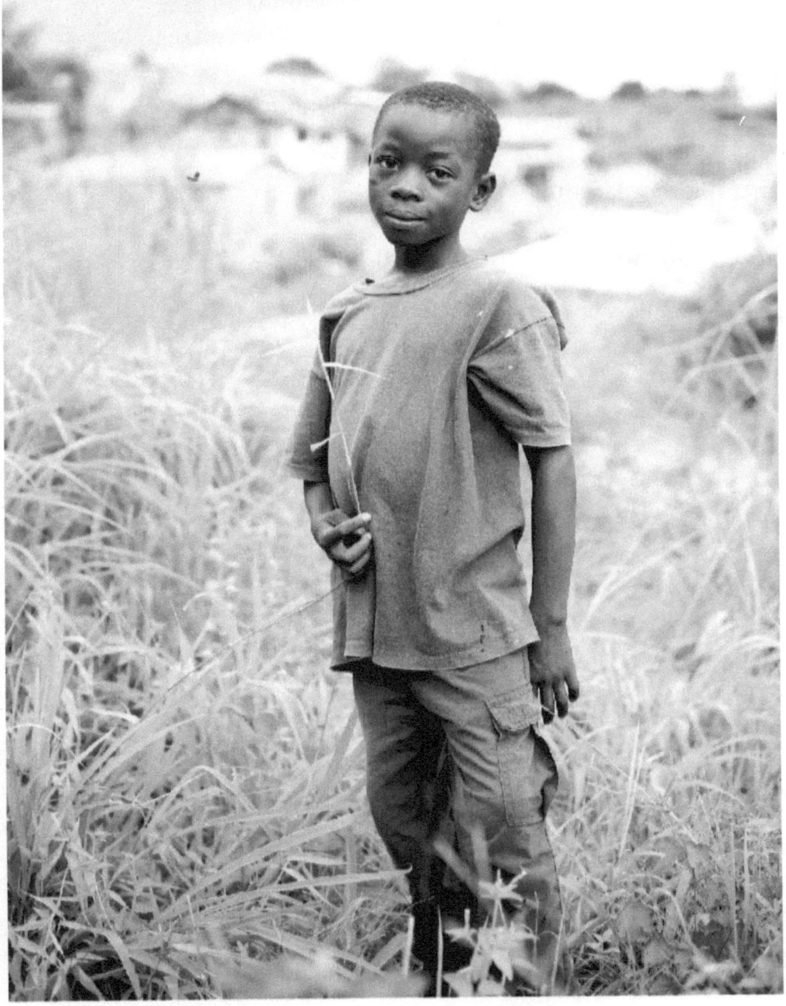

M9D9

This book is a work of fiction. Names, characters, businesses, organizations, government agencies, places, events, and incidents are products of the author's imagination or are used fictitiously. Any resemblance to actual events or locales or persons living or dead is entirely coincidental.

Copyright 2012 © by M.C. Miller

Published by M9D9 Enterprises, LLC
Issaquah, WA 98029
www.mcmillerbooks.com

ISBN: 0982930550   EAN-13: 978-0-9829305-5-7

First Edition

ALSO BY M.C. MILLER

To All The Special Ones Among Us.
You Know Who You Are.
Now Let The World Know.
It Needs You More Than Ever.

HELF SELP

A Journey From Far To Near

a novel by m.c.miller

PROLOGUE

At sunrise on a summer's day
a boy was born on the African plain.

Like all new life, energetic and undeterred,
he had no choice but embrace
the possibilities that life offered.
With his time just beginning,
with so many vital instincts commanding his attention,
everyone assumed he was oblivious to the challenges he faced.
And yet, even if no one noticed,
there was something different about the boy.
He was not like you or me—even if we are not like anyone else.

If anyone had the foresight to really listen to him,
they might have heard the concern and compassion in his cries.
If they had, no doubt they would have explained it away,
a mere projection of their own feelings and nothing more.
After all, for anyone witnessing his birth,
there were many reasons to cry.

The labor was traumatic; a baby didn't cry and then a baby cried.
The underweight boy nearly didn't make it.
His village was poor, the poorest in one of the poorest countries.
Before the year ended, his father would succumb to tuberculosis.
More critically in the moment, his mother had died giving him life.
As his cries became forceful and clear,
hers faded then sighed away to nothing.
His grandfather, sweet and kind and well-intentioned as he was,
was also a mystic, too preoccupied to focus on responsibilities for long.
He was also too naïve about babies to be an adequate substitute.
Not for a mother's love.

Except for the gift of life, there was little to celebrate in the moment.
So much had aligned against this boy
and any chance he'd have a good life.

But there was something in those loud and strong cries,
something that sensed what was well and not so well
about the world around him.
Those fragile first wails came from a remarkable place of mature feeling,
a place that somehow understood without knowing how it had.
No one discussed how this was possible.
Demands of the moment and their preconceptions wouldn't let them.
And even if they could, none would have ever imagined
there was anything to make of it.
Maybe the cries of *all* babies are sage,
echoing the wisdom of life itself.
Birth was life in its purest, exalted form.
A new life, fresh with nature's perfect imprint.

We can't be sure.
That's just the way things are.
And things are never as they seem.

As we grow, we are told such things.
So much more we tell ourselves.
Emerging patterns of life appear so clear
in light of the design and intent we learn to place on ourselves.
Self-fulfilled clarity becomes automatic;
our worldview assured, the illusion complete.
And yet, gifted with a change of perspective,
so much is discovered without ever knowing we've been searching.

A toddler three years later,
the same boy ran and played in a field of tall grass.
His grandfather hobbled after him,
then eagerly crouched and whispered in his ear,
"The closer you move, the more is revealed."

The story of a boy born at sunrise
on a summer's day is quite like that.

Just a whisper in the ear.

"I've come too far for this!" The murmur barely passed the lips.

Gianna Chase clutched a phone to her breast as if holding it close might make a difference. Still too stunned to wipe away the tears, she stood statuesque on her master bedroom balcony and faced a restless ocean. She had held that phone for hours. All the while, darkness had fallen over her posh island estate.

Somewhere behind her an intercom buzzed. She didn't hear it.

Trade winds quivered the lacy edges of her silk camisole and yoga shorts. Gossamer pastel curtains performed a ballet behind her but their soft distraction offered no relief. She searched the dark horizon for any trace of saving grace, something to set things right or make it all seem real.

Any hope of either had long since disappeared with sunset and the twilight phone call. It was a call her common sense expected but for her heart it was out of the blue.

"This can't be happening!" Her cry became a muttered refrain.

Again, the intercom buzzed in the bedroom behind her. She ignored it.

Somewhere in the dark beyond the curtains, white-capped waves pushed in and pulled out. She paced into the room and back then flung the phone onto the bed. There was simply no way to stem the tide of anger crashing on hurt. Nothing was left for her wounded heart to do but sink into the pain or find the firmness of spirit to stop the tears.

One way was giving up and the other, in the moment, felt impossible.

She promised herself; she'd refuse to let it beat her. Even if this time the tears were real. This time he meant it. He was gone, taking his love with him. It was final between them as only a woman's heart can be sure.

Pacing by the dresser, Gianna halted by a photo staring up at her from its beveled frame. It took everything in her to hold back the impulse to throw it.

The group photo was taken a year before, back stage at the Grammies. In it he was at her side, smiling with the others. Looking at that photo had always made her heart sing. Now it was remote, a false echo of another place and time, a tortured lyric with one verse out of rhyme.

She turned away and faced the bed. They had made love in that bed. She turned away again and the anger rose up fresh and hot. He had been everywhere in her life. She couldn't keep turning away without turning away from life itself. That she would never do.

There was no escaping the irony. If nothing else, others might say she still had tears to cling to. They were the same tears she sung about, the kind of tears that fell so dramatically and so often in her songs. Those were the songs that had made her famous and rich.

Like many of her songs, doted over by millions of fans, honest tears laid bare the truth for all to see. The conceit was so seductive. Put together the right thirty-two bars of melody, a verse, chorus, and bridge and anything could be worked out.

But crafting a song was simple. The feel of real tears falling was not.

Life wasn't a song no matter how much the lyrics implied it was.

How would she ever stop her tears before tomorrow at 8am? How would she be strong enough to get into that limo and let it take her away? The impact of the news was so near and new, recovery seemed out of question.

The buzz of the intercom sounded a third time. This time, it startled her. On impulse she pushed the button and forced strength and calmness into her tone. "What is it?"

The maid's voice was apologetic. "Excuse me, ma'am, but Olivia Platt is here to see you."

Gianna paused, her finger wavering on the button. She had sent for Olivia but now wasn't so sure she was in any shape to see anyone. Regardless, Olivia was her business manager and longtime friend. Gianna needed to face her. Some things had to get done no matter if the world had crashed in or not.

The time had come. A decision needed to be made about the tour.

Gianna took a deep breath. "Send her up."

"Yes, ma'am."

Waiting on the open-air terrace of the downstairs living room, Olivia Platt strolled across white marble tiles, pass the Steinway grand piano, then stood transfixed by the red and green running lights of a boat far offshore. As always, she had dressed for 5th Avenue, even if everyone around her had gone island style.

Olivia was always professional, never flustered, although this particular occasion made her nervous. Such a condition was a rarity no matter what confluence of fubar nonsense happened to come her way.

More than nervous, she was annoyed. There was enough unpleasantness in the entertainment business without allowing someone like Jacob Ferrère to spike your highball with emotional Armageddon. To top it off, the hard body bastard couldn't have picked a worse time.

Unfortunately for Gianna, this was obvious to all. And he knew it.

"Ms. Chase will see you now."

Olivia turned and followed the maid upstairs. It was an effort to keep pace with the young woman's duty-driven vitality. Olivia's middle-aged legs had their limits. She also had to be honest with herself; she wasn't looking forward to this. No wonder she was dragging.

The maid paused at the landing to wait for her. Olivia was unfazed. The things she had to do for friendship and a ten percent commission.

With motherly reproach, she waved the woman off. "I know the way."

The maid retreated as Olivia pressed on. At the bedroom door she knocked and a faint but snappish voice invited her in. After a hunt through the expansive master suite, she finally found Gianna, lost in the deep end of a wide, walk-in closet. A certain familiarity was commonplace between them. Added to the situation, it was enough to dispense with normal hellos.

Gianna plucked blouses from a drawer and considered them as if it mattered. "I'm always going somewhere or coming back. It never does me any good to try to pack until the last minute. I always change my mind."

Olivia saw through the busy work and came closer. "You doing OK?"

Gianna caught her breath. "No," she confessed. "But there isn't a goddamn thing I can do about it." What began flippant turned intense. A flood of emotion caught in her throat.

Olivia stepped into a hug, letting Gianna release the worst of it over her shoulder and out of sight. Olivia knew when to be quiet. There was little that wasn't expected and the unexpected would do no good whatsoever.

One couldn't help but be overwhelmed watching a friend suffer. Olivia felt a wave of sorrow flow through her. Needing to deal with it, she pushed the feeling away, even as she held onto Gianna tighter.

"We'll get through this." The statement was made as much to bolster herself as to comfort Gianna.

Gianna pulled away. She tried to recover her composure but the effort backfired. She turned, losing it, and slammed a wardrobe door shut as she shouted. "Why now? He knows the concert tour starts tomorrow! Wasn't it enough to stab me? He wants me cut open for the whole world to see!"

Olivia took a step back. She knew her place. She needed to listen. Afterwards, she would need to keep both of them on topic, moving forward.

Embarrassed by her own outburst, Gianna stormed out of the closet. En route to her escape, she made strides past the dresser and spun the Grammy photo face down with a glass-crunching thud.

Olivia followed her out onto the balcony, then down to a wet bar and seating area at the far end. Gianna poured wine for both of them and busied herself pacing and sipping. She left it to Olivia to collect the second glassful if she so desired. Of course she did.

Gianna gave a flip to her brunette curls and strutted here and there, quick to go nowhere. "It wasn't enough to destroy what we had together! No! He wants to devastate my career!" Her shouts weakened, overtaken with dread. "Jacob knows me. He knows I can't go on stage like this!"

Olivia had heard her worst fear. It was time to be the voice of reason.

"If that's what he wants, why give him the satisfaction?"

"Don't lecture me," snapped Gianna. "I know all about living well as the best revenge. No doubt he and his heiress paramour intend on proving it to me."

"Heiress?" Olivia's heart sank at the thought she had misspoken on the phone with Gianna earlier that night. "I thought she was a fashion model, the darling of Fashion Week in Madrid."

"Right continent, wrong conquest. I don't think you know her. Not yet. You'll know soon enough. The press will chew on this night and day."

"Pardon me for pointing out the obvious," began Olivia, fast on her game, "but as your friend and manager for almost ten years, it occurs to me that emotion cuts both ways, especially in the business you're in."

Gianna turned to the ocean. "What are you talking about?"

"I'm always to the point, practical to a fault; you know that. Call it a personality flaw or the reason you picked me as your manager."

Gianna was both teased to distraction and annoyed beyond belief. "When you're not making sense, you are always scheming."

"Hardly. You may hate me for saying this, but if you could put all of this emotion on stage, into your songs, it would be a phenomenal thing."

Gianna laughed as she cried at the absurdity of it. "Oh my God! You have no clue. You'd actually try turning this around like he did me a big fucking favor?"

"I'm serious…"

Gianna poured herself another one. "I know you're worried I might cancel the tour but don't rub sugar in the wound, for chrissakes."

"Your songs, your performances play to emotion. Your fans will get it, believe me."

"How transparent. This is *not* about milking other people's sympathy. That's pathetic."

Olivia's ire came up. "You had 2.8 million downloads of *Make The World Well Again*. Why? Because you're in the emotion business. Emotion is the way you connect. There's no point acting like this is such a dirty little secret. The more you connect, however you do it, the better it's going to be. Especially for your career. It's what you do! It's what people want!"

Gianna stepped up to confront her. "Are you *that* worried about money that you'd actually try to spin rainbows into this?"

Olivia compelled herself to be calm and direct. After ten years of working together, she had earned the latitude to be frank but it only went so far. "If you want me to talk you into it, I'll do it. You know I can. That's my job and you wouldn't want it any other way."

"Of course! That's why you came over here tonight."

"One of the reasons, yes. As friends, the other should be obvious. As far as talking you into anything, I don't think I have to. I think you've already talked yourself into it."

Gianna stood defiant. "Talked myself into what?"

"Going ahead with the tour. As planned. No cancelled dates, no histrionics in between shows, no breakdowns backstage, no cave-ins onstage. You know it's the best thing for you, going forward."

Gianna turned and strutted to the railing overlooking an expanse of darkness. The crashing of the waves kept even time but the pace of her racing heart quickened.

Olivia stepped after her but was careful to leave space, respecting the limits of where and how she could push. Her voice softened. "Gianna, I get it. You hurt. We don't need to cover it from all angles. We don't need twenty takes. I heard it clear enough on the phone when you called. When you first told me, it hit me deep enough. I understand that with one call your life exploded. But now it's time to let the debris come back to Earth. Like it or not, it's going to anyway. Why not take back your power and chose where it falls?"

Gianna stood with her back to Olivia to hide newly fallen tears.

Olivia moved closer. "I want to help you. I really don't care about anything else." She threw up her hands. "Do the tour or don't do it. It's up to you. I personally think you'll feel far worse if you don't do it."

"It's too much...I need some time alone."

"And how will the press chew on *that*? On tour, you'll have the love of your fans. You'll have the perfect way to vent all of this. You'll be doing the thing you love to do."

Gianna lowered her wine glass and left it on the railing. She looked down and gathered strength. For a long while there was silence between them.

Olivia turned and stepped back to the wet bar. Her demeanor relaxed; she was prepared to accept whatever came next. She set down her empty glass.

Gianna turned around. She leaned back on the railing. "It's easy to say what others should do."

Olivia took her time turning around. She smiled. "I just want to save you from a lot of expensive counseling. Standing in front of thirty thousand of your fans is all the counseling you're ever going to need."

Gianna's body language was noncommittal.

Picking up on it, Olivia persisted. "I know it doesn't seem like it now, but chances are, we have many soul mates. Look at me; I've gone through four husbands. Two of them even survived and are still alive."

The comment got a look from Gianna but no smile.

Olivia shrugged. "As a matter of fact, some claim everyone's connected."

Gianna looked away. "You don't have to tell me there are other men in the world."

Olivia strolled back. "Listen, dear, what I wouldn't give for your voice, face, and body. There are three billion men on this planet. I guarantee you, every one of them would walk through hot coals and do feats of strength to be next to you."

Gianna finished her wine with one gulp. "All except one."

"That's right. Olivia nodded. "All except one. My point exactly."

Standing tall and stoic, Gianna wiped her cheek dry. "It's not easy losing this. I've invested so much."

"You invested in *yourself*, your experience. You can never lose that."

"And what about love?"

Olivia shrugged. "Love is the way you live, not something you barter."

"So your solution is: don't worry about love. If the tables were turned…"

Olivia interrupted, "I'd have a good cry and move on. The main thing now is to love *yourself.*"

Gianna closed her eyes and let the thought flow through her.

Sensing it was time to close the deal, Olivia stood her ground. "We're scheduled to fly out tomorrow. In two nights, we open in Tokyo. I know it's a lot of traveling but it's only ten dates in three weeks. It's only the teaser for the larger tour this summer."

Gianna laughed. "Am I supposed to feel better because it's only ten dates? Like it's no pressure? You know very well they're top-mark cities otherwise they wouldn't be scheduled."

"It is what it is. I hate unnecessary pressure but a lot of people need to know what comes next. It may seem like messy, shitty details, I know, but that's the game we're in. So do we have a tour or not?"

Gianna sat down. Everything that was involved in the whirlwind, four-continent concert tour flooded through her mind. It was overwhelming, even if part of her felt it was necessary. She felt too fragile to decide. It was an impossible choice between what she wanted and needed.

She wanted to sing but she needed to heal. It wasn't certain she'd be strong enough to find out if one led to the other. A shake of the head is all she could offer, along with a whisper.

"I don't know."

Nursing a deflated smile, Olivia finally sat down. "All right. We'll take it one step at a time." She paused and questioned her judgment on the best way to proceed. It would have been better to secure buy-in from her superstar client before going any farther. But it all had to come out sooner or later. Gianna hadn't left her a choice.

Olivia resigned herself to a candid approach and sighed. "As long as we're working through this, there's one other thing that's come up we need to go over."

CHAPTER 2

Gianna leaned back in her chair and with a flip of a toe crossed her legs. "What other thing?"

"Don't worry," started Olivia. "It's manageable. I have a workaround in the works and people chasing down the rest."

"You're talking with your hands," noted Gianna. "It's always a dead giveaway you're nervous about something."

"I know this is abrupt but I just found out earlier today." There was no pleasant way to ease into it. Olivia couldn't help but pause, even if it added weight to what came next. "Hannah has decided to leave the service."

Memory jogged, Gianna jumped up, her concern drawn somewhere else. "Oh my God! Suah! What time is it?"

Olivia waved Gianna back down. "It's all right. I checked. After you sent Paige home early, the maid saw Suah to bed. Everything's fine."

Holding a hand before her mouth, Gianna snapped back to a broader consideration of time and place. "I always tuck him in…"

"He'll live. I'm sure this one time will be OK."

A wave of guilt furrowed Gianna's brow. "He may not understand."

"Gianna, it's not the end of the world."

"Maybe not to you. It's hard to know how he might take it."

"He's a bright little boy; that's part of his specialness."

Gianna settled back down. "I think he had fun today going through his clothes, helping Paige pack them up." Her thoughts flashed back to the problem raised by Olivia. "Now what about Hannah?"

"I got news from the au pair service this morning. Hannah has left their employment effective immediately."

"Why now?" Gianna's concern included an air of disbelief.

"Apparently, she's pregnant and going to get married. We need to find a new au pair for going on tour."

"Hannah's been with Suah since the adoption. That's four years of trust he has in her. On the road, he knows only her and me."

"What about Paige? He's known her almost that long."

"Paige lives here, on the island. She made it clear a long time ago; she wants no part of going on tour. That's never changed."

"Yes, I know. I talked with her earlier."

"You talked with Paige? What about?"

"About coming on tour and taking care of Suah. You're right; she won't do it. Forgive me for taking the liberty but I thought if I could solve this before I came over, all the better."

"The teaser tour isn't that long. Didn't you offer Hannah something more, something to stay on at least three weeks?"

A sly grin passed over Olivia's face. "You say that like you've decided to go on tour after all."

"I haven't decided but I don't see myself going if Suah can't go with me."

"I've checked. The au pair service says they may have someone who can fill in temporarily until you can screen a permanent replacement."

"No." Gianna was adamant. "I won't place him with just anybody. Especially on tour."

"I understand. Hannah worked out well; the hectic schedule, the traveling, even last minute changes didn't bother her. But she isn't the only nanny trained to care for special needs children."

"It goes beyond training. Suah's known her for years. She knows his quirks. More importantly, he knows hers."

"Well, you're not going to get that kind of mutual experience off the shelf. No matter who you pick as a replacement, they're not going to know Suah until they meet him."

Gianna folded her arms. "I have no doubt we'll find a replacement, eventually. I just don't see how it can be done before tomorrow morning."

"Like I said, the agency has a candidate. She's a bit older than Hannah but she's had extensive experience. They say she even worked for a while with a boy in Johannesburg."

Gianna raised her voice. "Suah is not from South Africa and even if he were, what the hell does it matter? Nine-year-old boys are not interchangeable."

"But certain conditions and symptoms *are* the same. Whether someone is autistic or a savant or just dyslexic, care providers learn how to deal with these things."

"I hate those labels. Don't label him! The doctors have tried to do that, and they've never been able to. I won't have anyone doing it now."

"All am saying is, these behaviors are not a challenge to someone who's been exposed to it professionally."

"*Exposed* to it? You make it sound like Suah has some kind of disease."

"Hold on. That's not what I mean and you know it. You've been through a lot today but don't go hair-trigger on me. You know very well that we *both* love Suah and we both want the best for him. That's why you should consider approving the agency's temporary replacement."

"How do we know she can handle herself on tour?"

"We don't," admitted Olivia.

"Can she adapt, keep up, and in the middle of all the craziness still manage to hold focus on what Suah needs?"

Olivia gave her head a slow shake. "That's not a fair test and you know it. Anybody you get, even the permanent replacement, will have to go through a period of adjustment. No one off the street is prepared for the craziness of a concert tour. You know that."

Defiant, Gianna stood and turned to face the ocean. "Since he was five years old, Suah's gone on tour with me. Every one of them. If there are two constants in all of this, it's him and me."

"Having the au pair on tour has also been a constant."

Used to getting her way, Gianna turned back to face Olivia. "I could take him. Maybe I don't need an au pair. Not for this teaser tour."

Olivia jumped up. "You can't be serious."

"You said it yourself; it's only three weeks."

"How are *you* going to keep focused on what Suah needs while you're in the middle of things? Especially after what happened tonight."

"He's older now. He's used to touring. He's used to traveling with me."

"I'm not talking about him."

"I'm only on stage for what, three hours? We can set up some place for him to watch."

"You don't actually think that level of stimulation would be good for him, do you?"

Gianna turned her back on Olivia and faced the surf. "It'll do us both good. He'll have his mother instead of a nanny."

"And you'll have a shoulder to cry on. Oh Gianna, don't do it. Don't put all of that on him. Don't you think he'll pick up on the way you're feeling?"

Gianna paced. "You make it sound like abuse."

"He may be older but he's been sheltered."

"So now I'm overprotective."

"All I'm saying is, for the most part, he's not used to being on his own or out in the regular world without a qualified escort."

"Maybe it's time to open that up, give him room for growth."

"He's used to a limited, predictable routine, even on tour. Don't upset that right now."

"Ask his doctors; even they will tell you. He needs a safe environment with people he trusts and the right kind of stimulation."

"Yes, he needs proper care and development but there's no way you can do that alone, on tour."

"Then we *do* have a problem. Because I can't see going without him and some last-minute temporary replacement for Hannah will not get on my plane tomorrow."

Olivia was driven to break the impasse. She took out her phone and checked her messages. "There's always a third option."

"Such as?"

"You go on tour and Suah stays here with Paige..."

Gianna shook her head no as Olivia finished her thought.

"...He could join you just as soon as you approve the new au pair."

"I can't leave him behind. No."

"If you want to open up his routine, give him room for growth, this is just another way." Olivia persisted. "He's been with Paige for years; they know each other's quirks as you call them. She's trained for his special needs. As far as a safe environment, this is his home. You won't be away that long."

"Paige won't do it," announced Gianna. "She's expecting to go on vacation for three weeks while we're gone."

Olivia turned her phone towards Gianna, showing a text message. "Plans change, remarkably so with a large enough incentive."

Gianna drew near and read the text. It was from Paige, tentatively agreeing to terms. Gianna wavered. "That's not final."

"Of course not. But she's willing to do it. She's waiting for word from us on what it will be—vacation now or in three weeks."

"You promised to shift her vacation?"

"You told me when the tour ends you wanted to take some time off. It'll be the perfect chance for you and Suah to get away and do something together. I've even penciled it in on my calendar; here, look—*Gianna and Suah Chase, incognito on important business.*"

Gianna was unconvinced but marveled at Olivia's deviousness. "Look at you, always onto the next thing."

"I told you I had a workaround."

"You also said you had people chasing down the rest."

"Yes, we're feverishly looking for replacement candidates for Hannah and you're absolutely right; that won't happen by 8am tomorrow." Olivia held up Paige's text message again. "But this *can* be in place as soon as we send her an answer. It's up to you, of course; you're *the star*."

Olivia grinned in a way that usually teased the mischief out of Gianna. This time it fell flat. "I don't know. And don't lecture me—I'm fully aware it's going to have to be decided. Right now, I want to go see Suah and make sure he's OK. I'll be back."

Olivia followed Gianna into the bedroom. "I suspect we're done here— except for the laughing or crying. I'll wait on the terrace downstairs."

As Gianna made her way into the closet, Olivia took a stroll to the stairs.

Gianna threw on a silken robe and hurried down the hall. Careful to be quiet, she opened Suah's bedroom door and crept inside.

A soft nightlight lit the room barely enough to see.

Stepping forward, her gaze locked on the form of a boy under the covers. He was lying half on his back and half on one side. Next to him on the pillow was a small toy, a kaleidoscopic viewer, the kind that dazzled when it was turned by hand and pointed at a light.

Gianna stood awhile, content to watch him sleep. On his face had settled such innocence and peace. The look was captivating, capturing an enchantment; one she marveled at.

That level of contentment had always seemed just out of reach for her.

A surge of elation mixed with jealousy welled up. If only she could escape the way she felt and the things she had to do and find the same serenity that rested so naturally on this little boy's face. What dreams must he be having, what a wondrous place must he have gone to, what a full appreciation he must have found to arrive at such effortless bliss.

The stillness of the room, the low light, the soft breathing of Suah—the tranquility of all of it surrounding her was soothing. She sat on the edge of the bed to drink it in, eager for relief from cares of the moment. There was something about the glow of a child fast asleep that gave hope to those who had to stay awake in the world.

She tried hanging onto that hope but her mind wouldn't stop racing.

Having hope was all well and good but longing alone wouldn't make anything so. Unreasonable hope could drag a person down, set one endlessly yearning for something forever lost. Or it might let a person pine away, wishing for something they never could have simply because it could never exist. Desire, even in love, could become a melancholy pastime. And no amount of money or fame would quench the desires of a soul.

Her tender-to-the-touch mood couldn't take it. Tears returned to her eyes but as fast as they came she blinked them away.

It was a hopeless choice. How could she accept the worst thing imaginable while agreeing to do the impossible? She couldn't imagine leaving Suah behind and the thought of facing the crowds, the interviews, the entourages of hangers-on felt out of the question, not possible, at least not now, not for a while. Olivia's words about her errant lover, Jacob Ferrère, came back to her: *if that's what he wants, why give him the satisfaction.*

Too much had happened in one night. Gianna was left defenseless and engulfed. Her heart sank with the weight of not knowing what to do. But just as her disquiet reached a crescendo, Suah stirred.

Gianna watched his eyes blink open. Lazily they searched the space above him and quickly settled on her face. His rustling stopped once he saw her. Only his eyes moved as they followed her.

She smiled but the squint of it made a tear fall and she tensed. The last thing she wanted to do was call attention to the way she felt. She tried ignoring it but it was too late.

Suah's gaze held an expression of simple but pure comprehension.

She wanted to tell him something, anything, but she couldn't form the words. What should she say? She didn't even know what to tell herself.

She reached out and took hold of his hand and squeezed it. In response, he smoothed his other hand on top of hers. Slowly, lightly, he patted her hand with long, sliding touches. He did this for a while.

He did it until she could speak again.

"Sweet dreams Suah. I love you."

She stood and kissed him on the forehead. Content with her loving attention, he closed his sleepy eyes and turned his head back into the pillow.

Gianna stood and watched him drift back to bliss before retreating to the hallway. There she closed the door behind her and rested against it. Taking deep breaths, she shut her eyes and concentrated on the soothing air rushing in and out. It was time. She knew the way it had to be. She wanted to believe she had known it all along but she also knew that wasn't true.

The momentum of her life had its own pace. It would carry her along.

She made her way to the downstairs terrace and found Olivia. She was sitting lost in thought with a gaze fixated on the expanse of dark ocean.

Gianna settled onto the facing couch and crossed her legs through an opening in her silken robe. Her announcement came as a pleasant surprise and set Olivia in motion. "I want Hannah's replacement a top priority. Suah will join us on tour as soon as we make a selection. You can send the message. Tell Paige her vacation starts in three weeks."

CHAPTER 3

The next morning came quickly. Gianna got little sleep.

"I'll sleep on the plane." She strutted into the kitchen while talking to Ava, her tour handler, through a hands-free earbud. "I don't care who you promised; no interviews in flight. It's nearly eight hours to Tokyo. Most of that time I intend on being unconscious."

Gianna stopped at the kitchen's granite-top island and gave a smile and a wave to Suah as he sat in his pajamas, finishing his breakfast. Looking up with a grin, he chewed and wiggled his fork back and forth in hello.

"All right," Gianna concluded. "Listen, I've got to go. Remember, tell Sanchez I want to see what he's got for social networking. OK, see ya."

Gianna ended the call and stepped around to squeeze Suah's shoulders from behind. "How are you doing, big guy?"

Suah leaned his head way back to look at her. "You look pretty."

Gianna perked up. "Well, thank you."

Paige, Suah's resident nanny, stood nearby at the sink. "Suah's not used to seeing you all dressed up this early in the morning."

"That's right," agreed Gianna. "No pajamas for me this morning." She pulled out a stool, sat cattycorner to Suah, then praised him. "You're very observant!"

Paige finished with cleanup of the breakfast food prep and turned back to the central island. Her blonde hair was pulled back in a braided ponytail and she wore a painter's smock-style top over harem pants. Next to the kitchen's wide range top and double oven, her petite frame looked undersized.

"Is everything all set?" asked Paige.

Gianna nodded and checked the time on the microwave. "The car should be here any minute."

Suah took a gulp of milk. "When do I get to be on TV?"

Gianna leaned back his way. "Tonight's the night!"

Suah rolled his eyes and looked over at Paige then back. "Whoa! Will I see myself?"

"Sure, maybe Paige will record it and play it back for you."

Paige confirmed, "I think that can be arranged."

Gianna verified, "You've recorded webcams before?"

"No problem."

"I'll try to get online about nine o'clock your time."

Paige nodded as Gianna leaned in closer to Suah. "It's fun when we get to try new things."

"Like a new adventure. Our adventure starts today," asserted Suah.

"Yes, we've never talked to each other over the TV before."

Suah's eyes got big as he chuckled, "Not all the way from Tokyo!"

In the doorway behind them the maid appeared. "Ma'am, the car is here."

"All right…" Gianna took a breath to steady her nerves then stood and swiveled Suah around in his stool. "And you, Mr. Chase, are to have a good day."

"I know," grinned Suah. "And don't do anything you wouldn't do."

"That's right. I've got to go now so I can get busy getting everything ready for you to join me."

"It'll be ready really soon…" added Suah with matter-of-fact confidence.

It was a relief hearing him faithfully parrot back what she had told him before breakfast. But it was the only relief to be found in a stressful morning. Leaving him was still tugging at her. She gave him a nod then smothered him with a hug and a kiss. "Mommy loves you. Have fun and be good."

On her way out of the kitchen, Gianna paused and whispered to Paige, "Maybe a little trip out someplace new on the island would be good for him. You know, keep the adventure thing going; get his mind off me not being with him. Tell him it's exploration."

Paige was reserved but attentive. "Certainly."

Gianna added, "And thank you. I hate these last-minute things but this time it couldn't be helped."

Paige forced a slight smile. "No problem. Have a good trip."

With a wave and a turn, Gianna was gone. Suah toddled into the entrance hallway then out the open front door with Paige in tow. Standing in his pajamas, he watched as Gianna ducked into the limousine with a final wave.

He was still waving as the car drove down the estate's private road. He stood awhile watching until the car was out of sight.

Paige slung her arm around his shoulder. "Are you all finished with your breakfast?"

Suah nodded and stared into the distance.

"All right then, I think it's time to get some clothes on. We can't go out if you keep wearing those pajamas."

"Where are we going?"

She rubbed her chin. "I'm not sure. We'll have to think about that."

"Is it a surprise?"

"You might say that. It'll be a surprise to both of us. And I've got another surprise for you."

"What?"

"Because you're starting your adventure today, I'm going to let you pick out your clothes, whatever you want to wear. It'll be *my* surprise. When you're all finished dressing, come back down to the kitchen and show me what you picked out. Sound like fun?"

Suah perked up and nodded.

Paige gave his back a gentle guiding push. "Then off you go."

He scooted back through the front door, across the entrance hallway to the staircase, then took the first steps with determination. With a playful bounce from side to side he climbed. By the time he was halfway up, his steps slowed. A new sense settled around him. It was the feeling of the house without Gianna in it.

By the time he reached the second floor landing, his playful bounce faded with a shuffling stop. Wrapped in silence, he paused to look back, down the stairs, but there was no one there. He turned towards his room then hesitated and looked the other way.

On impulse, he sauntered towards Gianna's bedroom.

At the doorway, he stood looking in. He had never been in his mother's bedroom alone before. That fact and the enveloping silence at first held him back. But only for a minute. He drew forward anyway; the need to somehow be near her overpowered his fear.

He missed his mother but just how much only now occurred to him. Maybe if he spent a little while being in her space, close to her things, he'd find reassurance that she was only away, not completely gone.

Braving a few, halting steps forward, he found himself surrounded by reminders of her. On one side, the silky gauze of her bed canopy rustled in the breeze. On the other side, the scent of jasmine and plumeria wafted from her dresser. From the closet, traces of her perfume still lingered. Everywhere he stepped, another suggestion of her being near got outlined by the sense of things she kept around her.

He stood at her bedside and smoothed his fingers into the pillow impression where her head had rested while she slept. He wandered back through the maze of her closet and marveled at the wall of shoes positioned in pairs on slant racks. One particular high heel caught his eye; it was a four-inch heel with straps studded with small, clear crystals. Carefully poking his finger into the open toe, he wiggled it back and forth and watched as glints of color fired off from the facets of the crystals.

Playfully, he whispered, "You like that, don't you?"

Wandering farther, he exited the closet on the sitting-room side of the bedroom. There he passed Gianna's makeup table and lighted mirror and found himself in a sitting area. Off to one side was a bookshelf and entertainment center. Scattered on the counter nearby lay a half a dozen jewel cases holding compact discs. One of the discs was Gianna's latest album.

Seeing her photo on the cover, he was attracted to it. He picked it up and gazed a long while at the glamorous way she was posed, her carefree smile, and the other-worldly air of rapture engineered into the surrounding artwork.

Opening the case, he found it empty. Looking up, he considered the CD player before him and without hesitation pushed buttons until he found Play.

All at once, the room filled with the opening notes from the first and title song from the album. Pleased with his discovery, he sat cross-legged on the floor in front of the CD player and was soon rewarded with the sound of his mother singing to him. It was as if she was in the room, singing a private concert, pouring out all of her love and emotion for no one but him.

The lyrical verse led to a chorus and then a choir joined in the background as Gianna laid out all of her passion into the refrain.

"If we only mend our hearts, love will make the world well again...make the world well again...make the world well again."

Rocking back and forth, Suah tried to keep time to the music. Ever so often, he would mumble and then interject his own out-of-tune echo.

"...well again...well again...well again."

A floor below him, Paige sat at the breakfast nook sipping coffee and considering the view. A vibration in her pocket signaled an incoming call. Before answering it, she checked to confirm who it was.

"Well, hi there," she smiled. "Aren't we the anxious one."

The voice on the line was deep and strong. It belonged to Diego, her long-time lover. "Is she gone?"

Her smile faded. "Quite gone."

"You're alone?"

"Well, the maid is working in the guest house, doing something."

"So what are you doing?"

Her annoyance was plain. "What do you think I'm doing?"

"Where's the kid?"

"He's around."

"Aren't you supposed to be watching him?"

"He's special; he's not a two-year-old."

"He might as well be."

"Don't be an ass. The kid is smart, too smart at times; he just has a different way of relating to the world."

"Not *this* planet."

"So why are you calling this early?"

"Well…" Diego shifted tone. "I set my alarm, expecting to start a vacation with someone right about now. So now I'm up."

"Yeah, yeah, rub it in." She took a quick sip of coffee.

"No, really. I'm ready to do something. Got any ideas?"

Paige leaned back in her chair. "What do you want from me?"

"You know what I want. Can't you come by?"

"This is my job and I sure as hell don't want to lose it. I couldn't very well say no to Gianna, now could I?"

"Hmmm, I guess not. I'm supposed to understand, but what are we going to do?"

"What a stupid question. What *can* we do?"

"Well, one thing's certain: I'm not going to be able to change *my* time off. You get yours, when, three weeks from now?"

"Yeah…"

"That's a shame 'cause I'm off now, ready to be lovin' somebody. I was hoping that was going to be you."

"Give me a break. Local girls know your game and you're too lazy to pick up a tourist."

Diego sighed, "Is that so? Well, if you know me so well, you know I need something to do with all this energy I saved up for our vacation. Can't you get away at all?"

"Oh sure, I'll put the kid in the tub and let him play for a few hours."

"I'm not talking about locking him in a closet, although the idea's crossed my mind. Just long enough so we can take our time…doing the sweet nasty."

Paige smirked. "Your mouth is going to get you in trouble."

"You seem to like my mouth quite well."

"Shut up, fool. You know I can't get away."

"So what are you doing today?"

Paige's mood soured. "Oh, Gianna got it in her head: she wants to trick the kid into not missing her so much."

"How the hell is she going to do that?"

"You mean *how am I* going to do it."

"That sucks. She left it up to you?"

"Some of it. She's got this webcam thing she's going to do with him and some other stuff. Mainly, the whole idea is to make a game out of her going away."

"Sounds like a shitty game."

"Yeah, but he's special enough not to realize it."

"I thought you said he was smart, *too* smart at times."

"It's a different kind of smart. Smart in only some ways."

Diego laughed and dropped into a Forrest Gump accent. "I guess *smart is as smart does...*"

"It's called Splinter Skills, things that stand out from the overall level of functioning. It's typical in one kind of savant syndrome."

"*Calling Dr. Paige...*" Her clinical explanation was over his head.

"Shut up."

"OK, so what is it you have to do?"

Paige gazed through the window into the view. "That's why I'm sitting here. I'm still deciding. She wants me to take him out someplace, exploring; tell him it's part of the adventure."

"Great. If you're going to be out and about anyway, swing by. Being with me is always an adventure."

"He's been to your place. She wants someplace new."

"Let him kick around with Blake again. School's out; he's home."

"Excuse me, but your son doesn't want to babysit Suah; that was clear when we tried it before."

"Blake will do exactly what I tell him. He just got his license and loves driving around in the old Datsun."

"I thought you got rid of that thing."

"Hell, no. It's been in the garage. Just needed a battery and new gas and oil."

"You put Blake on your insurance?"

"Yeah, why not? He knows better than get into a wreck. I'd kill him."

"I don't picture Blake behind the wheel."

"He knows it's a privilege; one I can take away at any time. I guarantee you; he'll kiss my ass to keep the keys. He's got the power now; he takes himself to all the prime surf spots."

"He takes his board?"

"Oh yeah, he straps it down on the roof. You know he's having some fun escapades, driving around, exploring. You might call it an adventure."

"Hold up." Paige caught on. "You're not suggesting…"

"Why not?"

"Having him watch Suah in the backyard is one thing. Driving him around the island is just too risky."

"What's risky about it? I just told you, Blake is on his best behavior. He doesn't want his wings clipped."

"But shit happens. Besides, I'm not convinced he knows how to interact with the boy."

"What does he need to know? It doesn't take a PhD to let the kid tag along. You saw the way they got along before; Blake did his thing and Suah said nothing and watched. How hard can it be?"

"I don't know…" Paige started to drink her coffee but it was cold; she set it down.

"Don't you think it'd be an adventure to go watch the surfers for a couple of hours? Suah could sit on the beach. Blake could surf. Blake wouldn't have to entertain him but he'd get entertained anyway. The setup's perfect."

"I don't know." Paige stood and stretched. "I'll think about it."

"If you're going out, at least swing by and say hello."

"Yeah, OK."

"What time do you think you'll get here?"

"I could be there in an hour. It shouldn't take longer than that to get the kid dressed and out the door."

"Sounds good…sounds *really* good."

"OK, later." The line went dead.

Paige stood at the table, looking out to sea. The temptation was there to do as Diego suggested. After all, it was lousy the way Gianna had sprung the change of vacation on them at the last minute. Why not make the best of it? Then again, did she really want to trust Blake to babysit Suah again?

Blake would certainly resent having Suah assigned to him as a chore. But who cares? Life was like that; kids did chores all the time whether they liked it or not. Especially if they wanted to keep driving around on their own.

Paige dumped her cold coffee in the sink and put the cup in the dishwasher. Behind the silence of the kitchen she heard another faint sound. It was music coming from upstairs.

She asked herself, *whatever is going on up there?*

A quick climb and a march later, she followed the melody into Gianna's bedroom. Making strides to the sitting area, she found Suah cross-legged on the floor with his eyes closed. Drifting trancelike, he rocked to his mother's music and talked to himself like he was talking to someone else.

"I know…I know…And just as much with you…I know. If you want to, we can try. You can try, if we want to…I know."

"Suah!" called Paige. Her surprise was tinged with irritation. "I thought you told your mother you wouldn't do anything she wouldn't do. Would she sneak into somebody's bedroom when they weren't there?"

As soon as Paige heard herself, she tempered her annoyance with consideration and lowered her voice. "I'm surprised to find you here."

Suah sat still and looked up at her.

He was oblivious to any wrong he had done.

Paige drew near. "I thought you were picking out your clothes. You were going to surprise me. It was part of your adventure."

Suah nodded but remained seated and said nothing.

Paige looked down at the CD cover and the picture of Gianna positioned on the floor squarely in front of him. "Your mother is near when you play the music, isn't she?"

Suah paused then pursed his lips and shook his head no.

Paige sighed. It was no use reasoning with him or being patronizing. He had his own way of seeing things through. The best thing was not to interrupt his process. The main thing was to move the day along.

She rubbed his shoulder and let the music play. "I'll be back with some clothes for you—so you can keep listening. OK?"

Suah nodded then dropped his gaze to his hands. In time to the music, he rubbed one hand over the other, then switched to rub his hands the other way.

Paige patted him on the shoulder then headed out to get the clothes.

After she left, the last song ended and the music stopped. Suddenly, the room was full of breezes and nothing more. But Suah continued to rock and hum to himself as if nothing had changed. From somewhere, he still heard the music and his mother's voice.

Pretty soon, his hums began to mumble.

"I know…I know…Well again…Well again…

I know…I know…Well again."

CHAPTER 4

The paved highway became a gravel road. Before long, the ribbon of rock narrowed as it wound into the sloping foothills on the island's west side.

Turning off the crunch of gravel, Paige steered her car along a dirt path and headed for a custom-built house. It was Diego's place, a sprawling one-story hodgepodge of open rooms and wide patios with few neighbors.

Diego had cleared and leveled the pad for the place himself. It took him over two years to complete the structure, most times working alone, other times getting buddies to help out with tasks that needed two men.

Paige pulled up next to his dusty pickup truck and shut off the engine. The stark quiet of the open foothills was all around. In the silence, questions swirled. Paramount among them, was she comfortable with Diego's plan?

Suah was familiar with the place and the people, which was a plus. Many times she and Suah had stopped by when they were out on outings for 'sensory enrichment' or just to run errands. Most times the visits were short. A couple times, Diego's son Blake had babysat Suah on one side of the house while she and Diego had made quick love on the other side.

But Diego's plan today was taking it to a whole new level.

Unclipping her seatbelt, she looked over at Suah. "Let's say hi to Diego; then we'll go exploring."

Detached from her drama but agreeable, Suah got out of the car and followed along a path of stepping stones that led to double front doors. Before they could reach the porch, one of the doors swung open.

"Ah, there she is!" smiled Diego with open, muscular arms. He ushered them inside. "Welcome to my humble abode."

"You've never been humble." Paige gave him a hug.

"I never claimed to be. I was talking about my *abode*." Barefoot in shorts and a sleeveless T-shirt, Diego retreated to the main patio with Paige sauntering after him. Looking around, she surveyed the place for changes.

Suah stepped along. Suddenly invisible to the loving couple, he kept out of the way and held his motions to a minimum.

Diego returned to his seat on one of the chaise lounges. Nearby, a lethargic old German Shepherd dog drooped his head out from a low-slung hammock. Without raising his head, he considered the new arrivals with passing interest.

Paige smirked. "Scroto doesn't look too happy. What have you been feeding him?"

Diego unfolded a paper wide on his lap. "I don't feed him. He catches his own food." He returned to his paper as if he was serious.

Paige strolled to the edge of the tiles to inspect the yard but glanced back at Diego and what he was reading. "What's so interesting?"

"I'm checking out maps of the other islands. I thought it might be fun to fly over sometime and see parts we haven't been to."

Paige laughed, "What brought this on?" Wanderlust was out-of-character.

Diego looked up. "You and all your talk about exploring."

On mention of the topic, Paige glanced back at Suah. He was standing off to one side, intently watching Scroto watch him. Paige turned around.

"Suah, don't stare at the dog. Dogs don't like that."

Diego looked up. "He likes his chew toy."

Suah's stare shifted to Diego.

"Which one is that?" asked Paige for Suah's benefit.

Diego peered out in the yard. "Well, this week it's the rubber chicken. You can't miss him. He's got flames on his shorts and he's wearing glasses."

Paige scanned the area then pointed. "I see it." She turned back to Suah. "You can go get it. It's right over there."

Suah glanced between them then shuffled to a nearby seat and sat down.

Diego looked to Paige, showing her a derisive grin, but the humor was lost on her. He should know better. Trying to explain or justify the way Suah acted shouldn't be necessary. It didn't help to mock the situation.

He turned his attention back to his map, unfazed that she was peeved. "Have you thought any more about what we talked about on the phone?"

Paige took a seat on a lounge across the way from Diego but hesitated to answer. She never could be sure how much Suah would understand from adult conversations. It was best to err on the cautious side.

"You mean certain escapades in the Datsun?"

"Yeah, how 'bout it?"

"You mean today?"

"Why not?"

"I didn't think you could arrange it so soon."

Diego shrugged. "What is it? Nine? Nine-thirty? The party in question should be rolling out of bed any minute. I'll let him know. No problem."

"How do you know he's going out?"

Diego popped a few nuts in mouth and chewed. "It doesn't take a savant."

Paige grimaced at the reference but he talked over it.

"I checked the surf report. There's a bitchin' northwest swell. That means plenty of double overhead sets with some peaks pushing triple. The standout spots should be strongest mid-day."

"I don't know. It's out of the blue; no warning. Is that the best way to drop it on him?"

"He's a sixteen-year-old kid. He thinks he's a man of the world for chrissakes. He should be able to take it; otherwise, I'll remind him he's acting like a kid and kids get treated like kids."

Paige hugged her knees. "How long are we talking about?"

"As long as we need. Of course, longer is always better."

"How long does he usually surf?"

"Oh, three or four hours. He gets the munchies pretty hard by then."

Paige shifted her gaze to Suah. He sat captivated, a docile spectator of all the spiral metal whirligigs hanging from the edge of the patio's roof.

"If we do this, you'll tell him to call us if anything gets out of hand."

"What do you think? Certainly."

Paige stared into the yard as reason to pause. "It just makes me nervous."

Diego set the map aside. "Don't be. It's not that complicated. It's sitting on the sand. It's watching surfers." He tilted his head towards Suah to draw attention to how engrossed he was with sunlight catching the whirligigs.

"Look at him. He can sit for hours engrossed in something. You know there's nothing like the motion of the waves for doing that."

Paige turned her head and watched Suah held spellbound by the repeating motions shifting stronger and weaker and reversing in the breeze. He really was easy to manage if he had something to occupy his attention.

More to the point, it was easy to weaken when she sat this close to Diego. He was right; this should have been their first day of vacation together. If one could, why not enjoy the best of both worlds.

"All right. We'll try it this one time, see how it goes."

Her acceptance of terms brought a smile to Diego's face. He jumped up and gave her a kiss on his way into the house. "I'll be right back."

Paige knew where Diego had run off. He was going to break the news to his son, Blake. It was a one-sided confrontation she was glad would happen out of her sight. Meanwhile, she had her own concerns.

How should she break the news to Suah?

She stood and strolled over to sit next to him as he watched her approach. Either he was unaware or undisturbed by the social dynamics playing out around him. He neither read between the lines nor considered the many options of what might be about to happen to him. He was simply in the moment, biding his time, enjoying the effortless inputs of his senses.

She couldn't tell if he had forgotten he was promised an adventure or merely had the patience of a saint while waiting to begin his explorations. A direct approach was best; the right words, crafted to the facts at hand.

"Ready to go exploring?"

Playing with his fingers, he nodded.

"Your mother said you're starting something today. What is it again?"

"Adventure." He looked up for a moment, then back at his hands.

"Ah, that's right. Adventures are exciting, very bold. People on adventures can do extraordinary things, new things, things that sometimes might be a little scary at first. But they're not really scary at all."

Suah looked up and considered the open yard in front of him.

Paige couldn't tell if any of her message was sinking in but she had to try.

"Your mother has adventures all the time. One of her biggest adventures is getting up on stage and singing for thousands of people. To do something like that would be very scary for most people. But not for your mother. She loves it because she knows it's an adventure."

Suah set the record straight. "Singing isn't scary."

"That's right," agreed Paige. "Most things aren't scary when we let ourselves enjoy them. Going on a wild, new adventure can seem crazy at first, but really, it's not so crazy. You'll see."

Suah looked to her oddly, with some surprise, but said nothing.

"How would you like to go to the beach and watch real surfers ride the waves on their surf boards? Would that be fun?"

Suah thought about it. After a long while, he nodded.

Relieved, Paige took his hand. "That's just one of the adventures you get to go on. I wish I could go with you and Blake but I have some things to do first. As soon as I can, I'll try to join you and we'll both watch the surfers. Is that a deal?"

Again a nod. Before Paige could say more, Diego returned to the patio with a downcast Blake in tow.

"OK, we're all set," announced Diego.

Blake stood groggy in board shorts and a tank T-shirt and frowned at the sight of Suah in his house. Resigned to his fate, Blake slumped in his posture and waited for last marching orders from his father.

"Remember," ordered Diego. "After the beach, the two of you get some food. I want both of you fed and entertained when you get back here. You got that?"

Cocking his head, Blake nodded.

"Good. Now get the hell out of here. Adventure is waiting!"

Blake turned to go.

"Hey," snapped Diego. "Where are you going? You forgot something."

Paige stood and guided Suah towards Blake. "You go along now and have fun. You can tell me all about your explorations a little later. OK?"

Suah looked at Blake and froze but the surfer had no patience for him.

"Come on, let's go," growled Blake.

Paige walked Suah to the Datsun and got him settled in while Blake checked the strength of the lines holding his surf board to the roof.

"I'll see you in a little bit," promised Paige.

She waved goodbye as Blake got behind the wheel. Riled by his situation, Blake wasted no time driving away down the dirt path.

For Suah, a queasy feeling hit his stomach when they turned onto the gravel road. Leaving Paige behind was another level of transition, only this time turned inside-out. Earlier, he had waved goodbye to his mother as she drove away. Now, another layer of comfort was gone as he watched Paige wave to him and *he* became the one who was driving away.

The feeling he was having couldn't, it shouldn't be fear. And even if it was, there was no reason for it. Paige had explained all about it. There was nothing scary about an adventure. Exploring was fun. His mother loved her adventures, loved them so much she wanted Suah to have his own.

Another voice chimed in; it was a voice that was with him always, a part of him. It told him if this was what Gianna wanted for him, it must be something good. He might not be able to see the fun or joy in it yet but like surprises, some things were better when you went along and let them happen.

The dented white Datsun rumbled onto the paved road. Suah couldn't help but answer the call of his thoughts and go everywhere they were going. He started to mumble out loud to himself. A dreamlike conversation with the other voice emerged through the fog of feeling that had made him queasy.

"*I know...I know...We see what you see...I know.*

If you want it open, we can try. You can try, if we want to...I know."

Blake couldn't ignore Suah any longer; the mumbling got in the way.

"What the fuck are you talking about?"

Suah fell silent. His glance at Blake was halting.

"It's bad enough already; I don't need to hear any of your stupid shit."

Preempting any more nonsense, Blake switched on the radio and let the music blare. They rode along for a while with nothing but the sound of the wind through the open windows to compete with the repetitive boom through the car speakers. Then Blake became the one mumbling to himself.

"…why am I stuck with this?" He turned the radio down and turned his head to Suah. "Where's your mother?"

Suah sat unflustered. "Singing…on adventure with me."

Blake broke out in a laugh that shot spittle to the dashboard. "What the hell is that supposed to mean?"

Suah had no other definition for what he saw as clear. So he said nothing.

The burst of mocking humor loosened Blake up. He considered his passenger as a rare and curious specimen. "You're from Africa, aren't you."

Suah nodded and watched the scenery go by.

"My dad read about you in one of those fan magazines. You're adopted."

With no response, Suah's blank expression and unblinking eyes got misinterpreted by Blake as disbelief at the news.

It fed his impulse to say more. "Yeah, Gianna's not your real mother. But I guess you know that. I mean, it's clear as black and white." Blake giggled at his own inflated approximation of his cleverness.

But Suah sat unruffled. Blake assumed his cleverness had not registered with his passenger and regrouped, determined to try harder.

"So what exactly is wrong with you? Like, did you get dropped on your head or something?"

Suah said nothing but Blake wouldn't let it go.

"They took you to doctors, didn't they?" Blake got a nod back from Suah. "What about loony bins? Where else did they take you?"

"School," answered Suah.

"No way. You're home-schooled. The fan-mag said so."

"In my village."

"In Africa?"

Suah nodded.

"You're a fucking liar. They don't send kids to school at five years old in Africa. Most kids don't even go to school."

Suah sat mute, his serene attitude implying the truth of what he had said.

"OK, if you went to school in Africa, tell me something you learned in class. Go ahead…"

Suah thought for a minute.

Blake was eager to be right. "You can't do it, can you?"

Facing front, Suah closed his eyes and began rocking from side to side.

"I don't know why I'm talking to you anyway," added Blake. "You don't know what's going on. You're as dumb as a rock."

Blake shook his head and sucked in a breath to say more.

But a soft hum got louder. It was coming from Suah.

Blake hesitated and the hum became singing. With the singing, Suah clapped his hands in time with each rock from side to side. His eyes stayed closed and the chant-like song came out strong and clear.

"...*in the lion den,*
  got to pray to the Lord;
...*in the lion den,*
  gonna walk with the Lord;
...*in the lion den,*
  just to talk to the Lord;
...*in the lion den,*
  got to wait on the Lord;
...*in a weary land,*
  got to pray to the Lord;
...*in a weary land,*
  gonna walk with the Lord;
...*in a weary land,*
  just to talk to the Lord;
...*in a weary land,*
  got to wait on the Lord;
...*in the lion den,*
  got to..."

Blake blasted the radio and drowned out Suah's soulful chant.

Suah startled, as if coming awake, and cringed wide-eyed at the loudness.

Blake turned the sound down. "What was *that* all about? You didn't learn that in school."

Suah nodded which only provoked Blake's disdain.

"That's not school. That's some holy-rollers teaching you bull-crap. Can you sing *that*? Go ahead and sing it, '*I'm full of bull-crap.*'"

Blake waited but Suah said nothing, leaving Blake's last words to float on the air as a boomerang lyric. It only made him mad. He couldn't abide the impertinence of the kid.

"You're a pathetic little turd. I don't like driving turds around in my car.

It stinks up the place, you know what I mean?"

Suah innocently returned to watching the scenery go by. Blake took it as being ignored. He slowed the car but grabbed the steering wheel tighter.

"No way am I going to babysit you all day." Blake began talking more to himself than Suah. "I can't show up with some jackwad hodad retard. There's got to be some way to bail on this."

The car rolled to a stop at a stoplight on the edge of town. It was a small, seaside tourist trap, little more than a narrow main street bordered by shops and restaurants and a seawall that offered views of anchored boats in the picturesque, scalloped bay.

As Blake waited at the light, he checked out the pedestrians in the crosswalk. It was easy imagining Suah being pushed out of the car and left to walk away with a herd of tourists.

It gave Blake an idea. When the light changed, he pulled the car off the road into the dirt by a beat-up van that doubled as a food truck. It was the van's regular spot selling churros and funnel cakes, kettle corn and shaved ice. Blake threw the car in park but kept the engine running.

He turned to Suah and unbuckled his seatbelt. "All right, here's the deal..." He leaned over and grabbed Suah by the arm. "Right here, this is your spot. I drop you off, I pick you up right here. You get it?"

Suah looked back at the food truck but said nothing.

"You got any money on you?" Blake checked Suah's pockets but found nothing. "Good. If you ever want to eat again, you be back here at four o'clock." Blake took off his watch and put it on Suah's wrist. "You know how to tell time?" Suah nodded but Blake explained anyway. "When this number here is four, you better be back here. I'll take you to get something to eat."

Suah seemed willing which was a relief to Blake. He didn't want any scenes in front of pedestrians or the food truck guy.

"Until then, you're on your own," added Blake. "Wander around town, sit in the park, look at the boats, I don't give a shit what you do. Just stay out of trouble and don't tell no one who you are or what you're doing. Comprendo?"

Agreeable to just about anything, especially to getting away from someone who didn't seem to like him, Suah gave a nod and reached for the door handle.

Blake's impulsive plan was still coming together. He thought of more to say and held Suah's arm back. "And when we get back to my place, you better not say a word about this. If you do, I'll beat the shit out of you. You understand?" Another nod. "If Paige or anybody asks, you went to see the surfers today; you had fun on the beach. Get it?"

Suah's habit of nodding didn't give Blake much reassurance.

"Tell me—where are you going to be at four o'clock?"

Suah pointed to the ground outside the car.

"Are you going to tell anybody about this?"

For the first time since they got together, Suah shook his head no.

"When you get home, if anybody asks, where did you go today?"

"To see the beach surfers."

"That's right." Blake breathed a little easier. "And what time do we eat?"

Suah pointed at the watch on his wrist. "Four."

"All right. Well, what are you waiting for? Get out of here."

Blake reached past Suah and opened the passenger side door. Suah got out and Blake pulled the door shut. He threw the car into gear and rattled back on the road and was gone in a streak of flying dust.

Suah stood for a couple of minutes just looking around.

Another level of transition settled in.

The last layer of comfort was now gone; he was alone.

And yet, the queasy feeling in the pit of his stomach was gone. He was reminded he was not quite alone. Between him and the other voice that was with him, he was the one most surprised at what had happened.

But that was OK. Adventures were like that.

CHAPTER **5**

Passing pedestrians never suspected that Suah was a world traveler.

Not if they bothered to notice him standing there with nowhere to go. They couldn't have imagined he had been everywhere on five continents. At least everywhere with stadiums big enough to attract the attention of his mother on tour.

No one would have guessed that the waif standing alongside the road had a passport pockmarked with ink. And yet, even with the variety of his travel in four years, there was one thing Suah had never done.

He had never decided where to go or what to do for himself.

His traveling nanny, Hannah, had once called him *a bright little trouper*. From the age of five to nine, he had been to more places and done more things than most adults in a lifetime. And yet, anywhere he went, it was always a highly structured day with trained and competent adult supervision.

He had ridden the London Eye and had his picture taken at rush hour at Tokyo's Shibuya Crossing. In Singapore he had attended a celebratory dinner on a floating *tongkang* on Clarke Quay. Holding his mother's hand, he had stood on the observation deck in the skybridge of the Kingdom Center Tower in Riyadh, Saudi Arabia. And with nanny Hannah, marveled at fireworks at Darling Harbor's Hoopla Festival in Sydney. One afternoon in Paris, he even managed to flummox a street mime by out-staring him.

Everywhere in the world he had gone, he never went alone. But starting that moment standing next to the food truck, that all changed. His greatest adventure was at hand. The chance to explore was wide open.

He turned towards the food truck and stared up at the menu board, just a scrawl of colored chalk on a blackboard. Part of him wanted to read the words but the handwriting made it hard and he found it difficult to settle on one thing. The excitement of the situation wouldn't let him.

He turned the other way to watch the traffic and then got distracted by the laughter of children with their parents farther down the street.

It was a curious feeling but it crossed his mind. Freedom could be a paralyzing thing when you tried to go everywhere at once. So many directions invited him to come their way. To be so completely on one's own in some ways at first was like the free fall of his dreams. In free fall, nothing ties you down or holds you back and yet, as fast as you may be going somewhere, you find you simply can't move yourself anywhere.

He turned back to the truck and caught the eye of the hefty woman working food prep. She was doing something with her hands but took the time to peer out the pass-through window.

"You want something?" she asked.

Suah looked around then realized she was talking to him.

She leaned near the window. "Speak up, I've got the fan and the fryer going in here."

He looked back to the blackboard menu. The handwriting was a jumble of colored lines but one fragment came in focus. It was printed, not written. He tried matching it with one of the pictures painted on the side of the van. Finding a picture that matched would be a good bet but nothing caught his eye. He stepped closer to the window and announced his selection anyway.

"Cunnel fake."

"Funnel cake?" she corrected. "You want a funnel cake?"

The distinction was lost on him. He nodded.

"What flavor?"

The question was daunting. How many flavors were there and what were they? Were they written on the menu board? If so, how long would it take to read them all? He could think of many flavors; maybe he could ask for anything. Better yet, could he have them all? That's what he really wanted.

"All of them," he announced.

She grimaced. "You want all of them…"

He nodded, his confidence appearing impish.

"For you and who else?" Her patience was wearing thin.

The question might have been sarcastic but Suah considered it for real.

The answer was obvious. "Hawa."

"What?" The woman had just about enough.

"Hawa," repeated Suah.

"Sorry, I don't know that language. Go get your parents or come back when you've figured it out." The woman went back to work.

Suah turned and sidled away. He wasn't sure what had just happened but it was clear the conversation was over. He didn't give it another thought.

He stepped to the corner where the stoplight had just changed. The traffic flowed by him. Some of it headed inland; the other half rolled towards the water. He had once been in this town a long time ago with his mother. He knew there was lots to see and do by the water. He turned down the sidewalk and followed the traffic headed towards sailboats in the distance.

The farther he walked, the more commercial the area around him became.

Pretty soon, souvenir shops and boutiques and little cafés lined both sides of the street. As he started to pass one, something going on inside captured his attention. He stood and waited to see what happened. Moving on past, he came to another doorway, then a window display, and then a conversation of strangers that held him rapt and motionless once again.

It took a long time to go the first two blocks.

At one café, a young waitress tended tables on a small patio bordered by a low wrought-iron railing. Suah stood at the railing quite a while, watching the diners but more specifically, watching the waitress in all her busyness.

For Suah, there was a marvel about her. She was quite competent at a hectic pace and yet so much at ease. She was so casual and friendly with everyone but switched to be matter-of-fact about the chores of business. The contrast of who she was and how that changed in the moment was fascinating. People-watching was always one of Suah's great delights.

In time, the waitress took notice of the little boy watching her from the railing. He seemed innocent enough and she eventually smiled and from a distance gave him a little wave.

Suah waved back with a quiet flutter of fingers. His grin was slight. It froze in the middle of his surprise to find that he was not just the observer but also the one being watched. Then he was distracted away by a line of talkative tourists passing by. He looked back once or twice but the waitress had hurried back inside and with her gone the patio seemed suddenly vacant.

He moved on at a pace much slower than the foot traffic around him. Crossing a dip in the sidewalk where the road intersected an alley, he glanced to one side. The narrow alleyway retreated into the distance.

In the middle of the alley's path was a paved dip where runoff collected and drained away. Here and there a full dumpster or old telephone pole defined the space as forgotten, behind the scenes, a place tucked away and shunned by the tourist crowd. There was no pedestrian traffic down the alley probably because there was nothing worthwhile to see. But was that true?

Suah paused and turned facing the long stretch of alleyway. There was something about how vacant it was that imbued it with mystery. It was true, there was little chance of him doing any people-watching in such a deserted space, but adventures were all about exploring places you haven't been.

And who said someone might not be hiding down there, like the little people of island lore that shied away from humans. Paige had told him all about them. And while regular people-watching was all well and good, what would it be like to get a chance to watch those little people? No one had seen them in a very long time but they had to be somewhere. What a better place for them to hide than the one place none of the humans wanted to go. With expectations high, Suah set out along the alley in search of hidden places.

If this was exploring, he liked it.

But it didn't take long for fascination with the alley to wane. He walked quite a ways without seeing anything of too much interest. Pretty much, the alley was nothing more than a place to give backdoor access to businesses.

If anything was hidden there, it was hidden well.

The sound of music was faint through a screen door at the back of one of the businesses. Becoming aware of it, he diverted his attention to listen. As he did, someone inside the shop changed the station. As new music played, it suggested an answer. Maybe the little people were made of the same stuff that carried music through the air and let it play on the radio.

Maybe they were just as real but just as hard to see.

Entranced by the thought of it, he was startled by something touching his hand. He jerked around to find a mutt of a dog licking at his fingers. His jerk of surprise spooked the dog who jumped back and let out a single bark of complaint.

Wanting the dog to come back, Suah squatted down and held out his hands. Responding to the friendly gesture, the dog ran back and let Suah pet him. Suah's hands moved tentatively at first. He wasn't allowed to have a pet, for reasons he didn't understand but he was told they were good reasons.

Any time he got near animals, the adults around him got very nervous. Oddly enough, it was their reaction more than anything the animals ever did that made him skittish of what might happen. That edginess was then sensed by the animals which brought about the very thing the adults fretted about.

Someone once told Suah that animals were unpredictable. It was said as a bad thing. But then another time he overheard his own doctor talk about his own impulsiveness and erratic nature. There didn't seem to be much difference between the two from what he could gather. Did that mean he was like the animals? Was that bad? It certainly seemed to fit. He felt more comfortable around many animals than most people he had encountered.

After a rub got a lick and a smile got a bark, Suah and his new friend continued down the alleyway. Suah talked to the dog but found himself in a three-way conversation with the other voice that was always with him. As he walked he mumbled and the dog trotted around, panting and sniffing.

"Maybe you already told me your name…" said Suah to the dog.

I know…I know…You did not understand it. The voice spoke.

"Maybe I'll give you a nickname…"

He already has a nickname. You should use it.

Suah mumbled to the voice, "What if I can't say it?"

The name is Gris-Gris. Tell him it sounds like 'gree-gree.'

"If he can't say his name, it doesn't matter what it sounds like."

Keep from harm. Say it anyway. It's time to charm.

"Don't be silly. What would Grandpa say?"

He would say I know…I know it's time.

"Why, because you heard the music change?"

There was music before the change. Time is music. We should dance.

"We should play. We'll look for djinns hanging in the air another day."

Don't worry, it's not Du, the bad spirit, within you…It's you.

"For someone who wants to dance, you talk too much."

Look around. It's only you but you're enough.

Suah ran and excited the scruffy mutt to scamper around.

He called out to the dog, "You go exploring all the time, don't you?"

The dog jumped up and knocked Suah back. Plopped on his butt, he sat startled and began to laugh. As he laughed, Gris-Gris got distracted and ran away. Suah jumped up and started to run after him but the dog disappeared around a corner. Suah stood surprised by the sudden departure.

You should have said his name.

Suah sauntered along, his laughter gone. "He had somewhere to go."

I know…I've been to somewhere…I know.

Suah ambled to the end of the alleyway and looked both ways. Gris-Gris was nowhere in sight. But the sailboats were still on the water and the smell of macadamia nut pancakes and breakfast burritos wafted on the sea breeze. The morning sun was warming and bright. Adventure awaited.

Suah tagged along behind an elderly couple making their way down to the one main street in town. The road, narrow but busy, ran parallel to the beach. Others dashed across or jaywalked but he waited at the corner with the hesitant couple. When they finally decided it was safe enough to venture across, he followed them in the crosswalk, keeping pace with their slowness.

On the other side, the old woman took notice of him and looked back and smiled. Suah stopped to acknowledge her. He wanted to smile back but a wave of sadness passed through him. The old man next to her hadn't noticed their exchange but Suah felt drawn to him nonetheless. Suah could tell that the man wasn't well. The two of them didn't have much time left together.

Turning to the seawall, Suah stood in wonder of the view.

CHAPTER 6

Unless one could swim or sail, there were only two ways to go forward once you stood facing the seawall. One way headed north into the heart of town where restaurants and shops were dense with trinkets and tourists. The other way went south where the seawall curved out into a sheltered harbor. It was there where catamarans and other pleasure boats routinely docked.

The allure of boats was not lost on Suah. They were remarkable creations, letting a person venture out where no one rightfully should be able to go.

He stood a long while at the low wall. His eyes fixated between boats at anchor and boats at sail. He was mesmerized by all the small movements of water spread out on what seemed a endless plane of glistening blue.

The enthrallment was complete when he tried to fathom how deep that alien, watery world sunk beneath the tossing waves. Someone had told him the water went down as far as the highest mountain went up. That was hard to imagine. Harder yet was explaining how all of it managed to stay in place.

Keeping water in the tub when he took a bath was hard enough at times. What a marvel it was that all that ocean water magically curved so nicely around the globe while somehow managing to lay so flat.

Floating on top of that watery world and having it all around him would be extraordinary. But even more than that, being on a boat was choosing to be suspended between *two* worlds. Neither one was his.

He was not a bird or fish but out on the ocean, driven by the wind in the open skies, he'd be between their worlds. Really, he'd be nowhere. There'd simply be no place out there to be who *he* was. Between the worlds of birds and fish, he'd have to bring his own place to be with him. That was called a boat. It was bizarrely fantastic. But in a take-your-breath-away kind of way.

So why did the dream of being out there feel so right?

A boat was a miniature world suspended between the vastness of sky and sea. The oddity of it had appeal and mystery, even danger. But being drawn to such an oddity only made the whole strangeness doubly curious.

The possibility of getting nearer to one of those boats was a powerful lure. Suah turned south and followed the seawall's curve by patting his hand on the top of its smooth rocks. They led not only to the harbor but to a lineup of hawker booths selling a variety of boat tours by the hour or by the day.

He ambled down the line, looking at the signs, curious about activity going on around the booths. Some were vacant, either not yet occupied or their ship's captains had already put out to sea. At other booths, sales people set out brochures, baited tourists with small talk, or sat off to one side in folding chairs and waited for business. Behind the booths, half of the slips still had boats moored in them while the other half were empty.

At the end of the row, across from the main line of booths, another booth occupied a permanent spot at the back of a business that was both tour operator and a water sport equipment rental business. The name of the place was *Island Aquatics & Adventures*.

Suah recognized the word *adventure* and was drawn to their booth. If anywhere might be able to tell him about all the ways to have adventures, this surely must be the place. Incredibly, adventure was so commonplace for them, they had figured out how to rent it by the hour.

At first the booth looked deserted. And yet, various brochures were out and a small dive flag fluttered from one of the wood posts. Behind the booth, not far away, the rear door to the equipment rental place featured a sign that dispelled any doubts. *Yes We're Open!*

A sign board above the booth featured a photo of a large catamaran out at sea loaded with beautiful people. All of them were wearing wide smiles, even if they were diving overboard. Everyone was having an amazing time.

Suah had never seen a group of people in real life smile like that all at once but he didn't question it. It certainly seemed to fit since adventures were fun whereas everyday life for most people wasn't an adventure at all.

Suah shuffled around until he discovered a man lounging in a chair with feet propped up on the back of the booth. The man wore flip flops, khaki shorts, a dingy, loose-fitting shirt and had a beat-up fedora hat pulled forward on his head. Light-weight and unintentionally gray, his signature hat gave a modicum of privacy and shade.

Opening one eye, the man briefly checked on the kid spying on him.

Suah stayed in place long enough and the man opened the eye again.

Since the visitor wasn't going away, the man managed to open both eyes.

"You want something?" The question was more confrontation than customer service but the gruffness didn't faze the youngster.

Suah glanced back at the brochures. "You have adventures."

"Oh yeah, I have adventures all the time. My *life* is one big adventure."

The subtleties of sarcasm never registered with Suah. He had always suspected that people said what they really wanted to say, not something else meant to mean the opposite.

"Can you take me along?" For Suah, the question made sense.

To the man it was a non sequitur but amusing enough in a cynical way to warrant a rare chuckle. "Sure, why not."

"When do we go?"

The man threw open his hands. "Right now. Pull up a chair."

Suah looked around. A box of brochures would have to do. And so he sat.

The man pushed his hat back on his head and took an appraisal of the young man waiting patiently at his side. Frowning, the man rubbed his beard's graying stubble. "What's your name?"

"Suah."

"Suah?" the man growled. "What kind of name is that?"

"My first name."

"Geez, a real comedian. What are you doing running around down here?"

"Nothing. Just exploring."

"Yeah? That's what they all say."

"Do you have a boat?"

"No…I have jack squat."

"Maybe Jack has a boat." Suah's delivery was deadpan but hopeful.

Beyond humor at this point, the man lit then sucked on a cigarette. Squinting through the rising smoke, he considered the ocean. "Whatever Jack has, it's more than me."

Suah pointed to a man smiling in the foreground on one of the brochures on display. "Is that Jack?"

"Listen, kid. Forget Jack. Jack Squat isn't going to do shit for you."

"You're the one who knows all about aquatic adventures."

"That's me, but Lucas and Molly own the boat and everything else. I just sit here and tell people all about the great time they're gonna have."

"So what's your name?" asked Suah.

"Mud. But you can call me Brody."

Suah stuck out his hand to shake. "Pleased to meet you, Brody Mud."

The cigarette was left dangling from a corner of Brody's mouth as he looked sideways at the kid. "You're one strange bird." They shook hands.

Suah puzzled, "That's a crazy thing to say."

Brody puffed away. "Get used to it."

"You say crazy things all the time?"

The sarcasm was back. "All the time."

"Are all your aquatic adventures crazy like you?"

"What difference does it make?"

Suah thought. "My mom wants me to have an adventure but my nanny said that going on a wild, new adventure can seem crazy at first – she said they're really *nutzo-crazy*."

"*Nutzo*-crazy? Well, you got that right – not everything is all fun and games. There's lots of crap that doesn't make sense. I guarantee you, plenty of adventures are *nutzo*-crazy."

Suah was wide-eyed. "Have you been on any of those?"

"Holy hell, yes. I'm on one right now." Brody leaned in closer. "Just sitting here with you is a weird adventure, don't you think?"

The thought of it didn't register with Suah. He sat mute.

Brody pulled his feet down from their perch on the back of the booth. Reaching into a rusted coffee can on the bottom shelf, he pulled up a pint liquor bottle wrapped in a brown bag. Taking a quick swig, he found fortification to press on.

"Just think," started Brody. "Of all the people in the world you could have walked up and started talking to – you picked me, the king of *nutzo-crazy* adventures. Now doesn't that tell you something? What does that say about *nutzo-crazy* adventures?"

Suah thought real hard before answering. "They don't need a boat."

Brody leaned back, deflated by the faux finality of it. He nodded, "That's right. You've figured it out. That's why I don't give a shit if Lucas and Molly own the boat. I don't need it, not where I'm going." Brody propped his feet back up. "I can get there sitting right here."

Suah looked around but missed the adventure in their immediate surroundings. But maybe that didn't matter. He didn't see the little people in the alley either. Some things were real even if you couldn't see them. But shouldn't adventures be more than just something you see?

"I don't feel like I'm on an adventure…not yet," announced Suah.

Brody leaned back into his favorite slouch. "You're trying too hard. It's one of those weird things; the more you try to grab it, the faster it squeezes out of your hand. Just give it time. You'll feel it."

Brody pulled the fedora hat back down over his eyes and folded his arms.

Suah was left to sit and wait for something that wouldn't come if he thought about it too much. If this adventure was ever going to start, he'd have to distract himself with something else.

He let his eyes roam over the back of the booth. There wasn't much there and none of it on first glance looked that engrossing. On the bottom shelf, next to the rusted old coffee can, someone had tossed a few brochures, one by one into a small pile. But these were different than the ones on display.

On closer inspection, Suah noticed they had scribbles on them.

Picking up the top brochure, Suah was fascinated. Doodles and scribbles and little drawings filled in all of the blank places. With a ballpoint pen, someone had doodled faces and boats and intricate tiny designs all over the brochure. Suah checked the others in the pile. They too had doodles.

The rustling paper attracted an eye-opening and barked orders from Brody. "What are you doing? Leave those down there."

Suah dropped the brochures onto the pile and sat back down.

Brody returned to his nap but Suah was curious about the pile of doodles. "What are they?" asked Suah.

The hat stayed down over Brody's eyes. "It's nothing; just the trash."

"Did you make the little faces?"

"What if I did?"

Suah paused on the thought. "Can you make my face like that?"

"Why would I want to do a fool thing like that?"

"I'd like to see you do it."

"Showtime is over, kid. It was over long time ago."

Suah stared down at the pile of doodles. "Can I look at them?"

"What for?"

"I want to see more."

Brody shifted into a more comfortable napping position and reset his hat over his eyes. "Oh, go ahead, knock yourself out."

Suah returned to the pile. Scooping it up, he returned to his seat and placed them on his lap. Eagerly, he opened brochures and turned them every which way to see each doodle. Some of the little faces were exaggerated, even cartoonish, which made him giggle.

The giggling got Brody's attention. "What's so damned funny?"

Suah sloppily snorted. "You make funny faces."

"Yeah, well, it goes with the territory."

"Can I try it?"

"Try what?"

"I want to make funny faces."

"Don't look now kid but you already have one."

The insult fell flat, even with Brody. Suah was unfazed by it and Brody was bored enough to be taken in by the kid's genuine enthusiasm.

Sitting up, Brody reached for his ballpoint pen and a fresh brochure from the display above. "All right, here you go."

Suah accepted the pen wide-eyed and held his breath. He sat there a minute, excited but his mind was blank.

"What are you waiting for?" asked Brody. "Go ahead…"

Suah stared down at the clean, empty space on the brochure. "What face should I do?"

"That's up to you. Make one up or do someone you know."

"Can I give anybody a funny face?"

"Hell, yes. Everybody has a funny face."

"Even scary people?"

"*Especially* scary people. So who do you wanna do?"

Suah's fingers tightened around the pen. "Blake."

"Blake, huh. Is he scary?"

Suah nodded and hunched over to begin work on his doodle. He painstakingly pressed pen to paper and made two dots for eyes and a loop for a nose. Taking a breath, he rose up and looked at what he had done so far.

"This is hard."

Brody glanced at the sorry little ink marks and leaned back. "Yeah, but everyone thinks they can do it."

Suah held the pen out in Brody's direction. "Do *my* face?"

Brody rubbed his nose. "That again?"

"Just one."

The negotiation worked. Brody took the pen and brochure in hand.

"All right. Sit still." The sarcasm returned. "If I'm going to do this, I need to capture the true essence of Suah."

Brody went to work. His hand was quick and his eye focused without blinking. He glanced from paper to Suah's face and back and, in what seemed no time at all, showed Suah the results.

Suah was startled, then delighted. His surprise broke out in a wide smile. He chuckled and reached for the doodle. With a closer look, his chuckle broke into a laugh. He threw back his head and rolled it from side to side, letting his delight bubble out.

Brody had drawn a clever but cute caricature full of detail and personality. If this showed Suah's true essence, it was a core spirit full of play and mischief but also contentment and adventure.

Brody snatched the brochure back and started drawing again. "All it needs is a frame around it to make it official."

Suah craned his neck to watch the addition come to life.

As Brody sketched, an ornate frame took shape around the doodled face. Brody showed it off to Suah, "And now we must hang it in the gallery with all the others." With that, Brody tossed the brochure onto the pile by the coffee can.

Suah looked to the pile but Brody distracted him. "Are you serious about wanting to go on a boat?"

Doubly distracted, Suah nodded.

"Have you ever been snorkeling?" asked Brody.

Suah shook his head.

"There's a boat leaving in a little while. I might be able to get you on it. Are your parents around?"

Another shake of the head.

Brody crouched closer and whispered. "That's all right. I'll tell Molly your parents said it's OK. You up for that?" Suah nodded. "You stay here. I'll be right back."

Suah sat on the box of brochures while Brody made his way through the back door of *Island Aquatics & Adventures*. The thought of actually going on a snorkel boat was dreamlike. The idea that sitting on a box of brochures behind a dirty old booth could lead to such a thing was remarkable.

Brody had been right after all—when one tries too hard, adventures can't be found. The more you try to grab it, the faster it squeezes out of your hand. Suah had given it time, forgot about it, and now he could feel it!

Brody returned a minute later with snorkel gear in hand.

"Here you go," offered Brody, handing him snorkel and mask. He pointed. "Head down to slip number nine. Lucas knows you're coming. You're going to have a real aquatic adventure."

Stunned at his quick reversal of fortune, Suah stood wide-eyed holding the mask. His grin was overwhelmed with details of what to do next.

"Have you used one of those before?" asked Brody.

Suah shook his head.

"No problem. Lucas or Gavin will show you the ropes. You better get going or they'll leave without you."

Suah started to go but hesitated and ran back. Dropping down by the coffee can, he snatched up the brochure with his doodled face on it.

Before Brody could protest, Suah stuffed the brochure in his pocket and ran off. For a few seconds, Brody watched him go.

Sitting back down, Brody reached for the pint bottle in the coffee can. He gave his doodle pile a glance. In one hand he held the bottle; in the other hand he still held the ballpoint pen. Tossing the pen on the shelf, he took a swig and settled back into place.

CHAPTER 7

Slip number nine was stuffed with a forty-seven foot long catamaran about ready to get underway. Its twin hulls of white fiberglass gleamed with promises of wind-swept escapades and far-flung voyages soon to be.

As Suah approached, it became apparent that the ship was also stuffed with a motley zoo of vacationers ready to see some fish. Couples and young families crowded the deck and inner compartment. The sun-kissed group varied widely in age as well as demeanor. Everything was on display from impatience to attention deficit disorder.

Suah was wary but interested. The scene, as it was unfolding, had little in common with all the beautiful, smiling people on the photo back at the booth.

A man moved with purpose in the cockpit under a sheltered bimini. He was athletic, tanned but weathered. Another younger man moved about the deck, securing things and directing passengers in shipboard procedures.

Suah shuffled to a stop near the ramp that led onto the boat. He stood in jeans and T-shirt with his mask and snorkel dangling at his side. Looking up, he let his mouth gape wide as he followed the length of mast up until it pointed at the sky.

"You must be Suah."

Suah looked down to find that the younger man had hopped off the boat and now stood before him on the ramp. Somewhat delayed, he nodded.

"I'm Gavin. Come on board; you're just in time."

The younger man led the way until they neared the cockpit.

"Lucas, here he is," Gavin announced.

The older man glanced back from the ship's controls to eye Suah then pushed a button on a mike he held in his hands. "OK Molly, we got him…"

"Roger that," came the reply. "Have a good trip."

Lucas turned to face Suah. "Well, welcome aboard. Do you have a change of clothes?"

Suah looked around and gave his head a shake.

Lucas talked aside to Gavin. "Looks like *the Brody man* is at it again. What the hell is he doing?"

Gavin shrugged. "Must be a last-minute thing. He's friends with the kid's parents."

"And where are they?"

"Who knows…"

Lucas muttered under his breath, "They're all probably ordering shots down at *Sops & Wobbers*."

Gavin led Suah away. "OK, Suah. Have a seat anywhere you like…"

As they got underway, that was easier said than done. Suah sauntered around the boat but mostly all available seats were taken. He finally found a wedge of space back by one of the twin stairs at the fantail. Once he got situated, it wasn't so bad. In fact, it started to be fun. For someone who liked to people-watch, he was at the right place.

Across the way, a young family was in a constant state of flux. The three children fidgeted around as their parents took turns taking pictures and herding their antsy offspring. Near them, a retired couple suffered the distraction. Adjacent to them, three coeds were ready for anything.

To Suah's right, a young couple, probably on their honeymoon, were nuzzled up and doting on one another. To his left, middle-aged sisters were enjoying a rare glimpse of the great outdoors that was somewhat out of their comfort zone. One of the sisters glanced over to Suah. To get her mind off her own nervousness, she made an observation.

"I can tell; you like boats."

Suah didn't expect a conversation but wasn't against it. He gave a nod.

"What is it about boats you like?"

Suah looked around and thought. As the harbor dropped farther behind them, it got easier to describe the feeling.

"I like going out and coming back."

She tipped her head in agreement but with some confusion. "Ah-huh…"

"The water is so open; it has no end."

"Yes, and what about the boats?"

"Boats take me where I can't go."

The woman tried to follow. "Where you *can't* go?"

Suah heard the other voice in his head answer her. It came in such a rush, he had to repeat it. "*I get to go near the far places. That makes the old near-place far. Then they turn the boat around and go back. That makes the new far-place near again.*

"I see…" The woman was kind. "I think I understand."

"The same place can be near or far. But when I try to think about both, I can't go there."

The woman had given up. She repeated, "Near and far…"

Suah concluded, "A boat ride is like Hawa. Hawa is near but far."

The woman had a question on the tip of her tongue but before she could ask it, her sister tapped her arm and pointed out something she had to see.

By the time the boat arrived at their snorkel spot, Suah had been rocked into a reverie of people-watching. Added to that, the open ocean had cast its spell around him. Everyone was so intent upon their own enjoyment, eager to be in the water and about the fun of finding fish, no one but Gavin paid any attention to the fact that Suah stayed on the boat.

With everyone swimming around, Suah sat at the side of the boat and watched all of the flippers and snorkels plying the water.

Gavin came up to him. "You know, you can go on in if you want. Your clothes will dry. No problem."

Suah sat with his snorkel and mask in his lap. "I know. I like to watch."

"All right," concluded Gavin. "Suit yourself. Just have fun."

Suah watched for a while from one side of the boat then switched sides when much of the action moved there. A few times, when he stared directly down into the water, he thought he saw fish swimming together near the boat. At other times he looked up and stared at the thin ribbon of land on the horizon. That was where the harbor was now—so far away.

On the way back to port, the wind came up and gave the ride some seesaw excitement. But not everyone was overjoyed with the buffeting waves, the chilling spray, or the rolling motion. One of the sisters in particular, the sister who had talked to him, started to get seasick.

Everyone had reordered where they sat when they came back on board. No one was sitting where they were on the voyage out. Suah watched from a distance as the sister tried to handle the throes of queasiness and nausea. Since it wasn't safe to try to stand up and heave over the side of the boat, Gavin gave her a bag she could be sick in.

Others near her tried not to be so close which freed up room on the bench next to her. Suah felt squished where he was sitting anyway so he got up and moved over alongside her. As he did, she had another wave of nausea and resorted to using the bag.

Two young boys across the way took note of Suah's move. They thought it was funny that anyone would actually want to reposition themselves closer to the sick woman. Giggling and whispering loudly to each other, Suah and most others on that end of the boat could easily hear their conversation.

"Where is he *going*?" asked one boy.

"Oh yum, let's get some of *that*," laughed the other boy.

"Maybe he *likes* the smell of barf," the giggle came back.

"Naw, he wants the bag as a vacation *souvenir*."

After several exchanges between the boys, their father asked for quiet.

Suah was unaffected. He looked up at the woman and she forced a smile back in thanks for his concern. She reached over and patted his hand. In return, he smoothed his other hand on top of hers. Slowly, lightly, he patted her hand with long, sliding touches. He did this for a while.

He did this until she felt better.

By the time the catamaran got back to the harbor, the sea around the boat was calm and so was everyone on board. The sister was back to her regular self and making light of her ordeal. Her companion couldn't get over how complete was her recovery. Unlike her well-again sister, she had been seasick before and let everyone know she hadn't fared so well.

Once the boat was back in the slip, Gavin secured the lines and helped people disembark. Lucas stood by and wished everyone a good day.

As Suah stepped off, Gavin showed a grin. "Did you enjoy yourself?"

Suah smiled back. "Oh yeah, it was part of my adventure."

"Part of it, huh? Well, wherever you're going, enjoy the rest of it."

Suah happily padded his way back to the booth behind *Island Aquatics & Adventures* but when he got there, Brody was nowhere to be found. A bit shy about going into the store, Suah decided to leave the mask and snorkel on a shelf in the back of the booth.

Stepping away, he checked the watch that Blake had put on his wrist. The time was two-thirty. He had a good wait before four o'clock but he was really hungry and didn't know where else to go. He made his way back to the food truck. Maybe being around food would be better than nothing and who knew, maybe Blake was starving too and would get to the pick-up spot early.

Suah sat cross-legged on the ground next to the food truck for quite a while and watched the traffic go by. The flow of it helped his mind wander and when his mind wandered, time would flow. The food truck lady barely noticed him.

At quarter after four, Blake pulled up in the Datsun. He had already eaten with surfer friends and brought Suah a burger and leftover fries to eat on the way back to Diego's.

"Did you stay out of trouble?" asked Blake

Suah nodded as he gobbled his food.

"What did you do all day?"

Suah tried to collect his thoughts but found it hard in between swallows.

"Never mind," snapped Blake. "It can't be interesting, whatever it was. All you have to remember is what to say when we get back. When somebody asks you what did all day, what do you say?"

Suah was thirsty and his thirst distracted him. He hesitated too long.

Blake threw him a punch to the chest and shouted, "What do you say?"

Suah clutched his chest. "Beach surfers! I watched the beach surfers."

Blake settled back and switched on the radio. "All right. And don't you forget it." In between watching the road, Blake shot glances over to Suah. "And while you're at it, give me back my watch."

Suah slipped the watch off his wrist and handed it back.

Stopped at a light, Blake stared him down. "As long as you do what you're told, we're gonna be good buddies, aren't we?"

Suah nodded.

Blake laughed. "I don't think so, shithead."

The rest of the ride was filled with music from the radio.

Back at Diego's, Paige collected her charge and drove him back to Gianna's estate. Along the way she asked about Suah's day. Suah knew what to say and said it. He seemed reserved and Paige was somewhat concerned.

"Are you tired?"

Suah nodded.

Her conscience was relieved. "Of course that's it. These adventures are all so new, they take a lot of energy. Did you eat?"

Again, Suah dutifully nodded.

Paige turned up the estate's private driveway. "Good. Well, we'll have dinner a little later. You take it easy 'til then. Maybe go in the pool."

The car parked and Suah got out. He was home.

As soon as he got in the door, he scampered straightaway for the refrigerator to get something to drink. Paige seemed tired and took her time following along. He had seen this mood before. It was obvious she wanted to be left alone as much as possible.

With a second drink in hand, Suah headed up to his bedroom to change into his swimsuit. Standing next to his bed, he started to undress. He unbuttoned his pants then remembered to look in his pocket. Grabbing hold of the brochure from *Island Aquatics & Adventures*, he held it out to see.

The doodle of his face in the ornate frame was a masterpiece before him.

It triggered a grin that started a giggle, a giggle that he quickly stifled.

Running to his desk, he rummaged through a drawer until he found a piece of tape. He would tape it up so he could see it every day. But where could he put it? He had to keep it a secret, otherwise Blake would get mad.

Stepping into his closet, he taped it to the back of a wardrobe door.

Later that night, dressed in pajamas, he heard his name called from downstairs. Tracking the call to the media room, he found Paige sitting at a side table in front of a computer.

"Hurry up, it's time!" she prompted.

He padded over next to her and sat down.

Paige shifted over and positioned him squarely in front of the monitor.

"Stay in this spot and watch the screen. You'll be able to see your mother and she'll be able to see you." She leaned closer. "Remember what I said; don't say anything about being with Blake today. Your mother told me she doesn't want to hear anything about him. Got it?"

Suah nodded as Paige paused. She was not quite confident that the little boy at her side could be trusted. She leaned close to him once again.

"You can tell her what fun it was to see the surfers…"

Suah's silence made her hesitate before reaching for the touch-screen controls. Finally, with a tap of her finger, a video link to Tokyo came to life.

A blank screen appeared and then Ava, the tour handler, sat down wearing a production-crew earpiece. Her head and shoulders came into frame. On seeing Suah via the link, her face brightened with relief.

"Great, I see we're online. Hello, Suah!"

Suah waved.

Paige leaned in and reminded him. "You can say hello; she'll hear you."

Suah said nothing and the handler took a moment to check activity offscreen. "Ms. Chase is on her way…oh, here she is…just a moment."

The handler got up and in her place Gianna Chase sat down. Her manner was quick and businesslike at first, having rushed backstage from the concert hall stage. On seeing Suah in frame on the monitor, her face relaxed and brightened.

"Suah, there you are, my love! Happy adventure to you!"

Suah's face brightened. "Hi, Mom! Are you really in Tokyo?"

Gianna let out a frazzled laugh. "Yes, my dear, I'm really in Tokyo."

"Did you ride the bullet train?" asked Suah.

With a smile, Gianna shook her head. "No, not this time. You liked that when we were here together…"

Suah nodded.

"So, did you have fun today going exploring?"

"Lots of fun."

"What kind of adventure did you have?"

Suah paused. A flash of a hundred things flooded his mind. He saw

Scroto and Diego, Blake and the food truck, the waitress and Gris-Gris, the old couple and Brody, the snorkelers and the sick sister, hamburger and fries, and the doodle of his face enshrined in an ornate frame of ballpoint pen ink.

He leaned forward and concentrated really hard. It was complicated pleasing everybody and avoiding what might happen if he didn't. All he had to do was say the right thing and everyone would be happy.

"I watched beach surfers."

"Surfers?"

"Yeah," added Paige. "He went to the beach and got to watch the surfers."

"Oh my." Gianna feigned being impressed. "That *is* an adventure. So, you think you want to be a surfer now?"

Suah shook his head no.

Gianna chuckled but Paige even more so.

"Are you having a *nutzo-crazy* adventure too?" asked Suah.

"Like you wouldn't believe!" Gianna laughed. "I'm in the middle of rehearsals. I gotta get ready to sing for a lot of people."

"You sang for me today."

Gianna was distracted by activity offscreen but waved it off. "I did...?"

Paige leaned in to explain. "He was listening to your latest album."

"Oh," relaxed Gianna.

"He was singing along..."

"Can we sing together?" asked Suah.

"Now?" asked Gianna.

"That'd be nice," added Paige. "It'd be like singing him to sleep."

Gianna forced herself to relax. "Well, I guess so, why not? What song would you like to sing?"

Suah saw himself sitting on her bedroom floor. "The well-again song."

For a moment, the reference was lost on Gianna. "Oh, *Make The World Well Again*...sure, we can do that."

She took a moment to compose herself. This was one command performance she wanted to nail. There would be no orchestra behind her, no staging or light effects, no auditorium full of fans holding up lighters in solidarity, no high-definition dolly-shots framing her in a luxurious gown.

This performance was much more important in its own way and the distance between Suah and her only made it that much more heartfelt.

"OK...ready?"

Suah nodded and leaned a little closer to the monitor.

Gianna stared into the screen and into the face of the little boy who waited

so innocently, so expectantly for his mother's serenade. Singing a cappella
was difficult enough without the flood of emotion that the song mixing with
her circumstances stirred up.

Softly but impassioned, her voice began to sing.

As she sung, Suah rocked from side to side and hummed along with her.

"There's a place in all our hearts
Where everything that's good between us must start.
There's a window in the prison
Where all the things we locked away
Find the light of a brand new day that has arisen.

There's a way to get us through,
And it's all about a new and beautiful view
Of who we are...and what we do,
Of making love...not making do,
Of lending a hand...and pulling through,
No longer wasting away...when it's wiser to renew,
No longer needing to be right...when it's easier being true,
Finding a peace in a time...so long overdue.
A better me...loving a better you.

If we only mend our hearts,
Love will make the world well again,
Make the world well again,
Make the world well again."

As Gianna got to the chorus, Suah's humming turned into words every
time the song said *well again*. As he rocked, he was transfixed on her.

One verse and chorus was all Gianna could manage.

When she finished, she smiled sweetly at the little boy who applauded her
performance as he sat in his pajamas so very far away.

In that moment, the distance between them didn't matter.

He seemed very near.

CHAPTER 8

You never could be certain what to expect while on an adventure. While that was neither good nor bad, it certainly could be one or the other.

For Suah the next day, finding out that his adventure had both predictable and routine elements, that discovery turned out to be *both* good and bad.

It was certainly undesirable to find out that Paige would drive him to Diego's place again. Apparently, Suah had done such a good job at saying exactly what was needed to make everyone happy, everyone decided they wanted a little *more* happiness the following day.

"You have fun," ordered Paige as she waved goodbye.

From the look on her face, it was highly questionable which one of them was more intent on having fun.

And then it was positively objectionable to find out that once again Blake would be his keeper for the day's outing. If the opinionated surfer dude wasn't surly before, he surely was about to go mondo-ballistic over being stuck once again with such a bogus dweeb.

"I have a pet turtle that's smarter than you," announced Blake as he drove and gave Suah a push. "And he just sits around, doesn't do nothing."

Suah could only feel sorry for the trapped creature, although in the moment he felt a bit jealous. At least the turtle had a shell.

And it was certainly disagreeable to be abandoned by the side of the road and endure the indifferent glare of the food truck lady one more time. Especially since Suah still had no money to let him try getting through the process of purchasing of one of her *cunnel fakes*.

Then again, as he stood alongside the road and thought about it, his discovery about the nature of adventures was both bad and good.

Despite all of the nasty parts of his new routine, it was absolutely good to be free again to roam wherever he wanted. It was good to engage the world without nannies or handlers shuttling him forward as if through a maze.

He quite liked roaming around on his own, even if he wasn't sure about all the things he didn't know that he didn't know. Birds in the sky and fish in the water couldn't know everything that smart people knew and yet they got by. Maybe he could get by the same way, the way the birds and fish did.

For them, it wasn't any more complicated than that.

The idea that an adventure could be routine didn't seem to make much sense and so he needed to try it out. He decided to retrace his steps from yesterday and see if covering the same ground felt anything like an adventure. Of course, like Brody Mud had warned him, thinking too hard about wanting an adventure was a sure way of making it not happen. So, the trick was, he needed to retrace his steps but not think about doing it.

But if he didn't think about it, how would he know if he wandered off the routine path? Like his teacher once told him, it was a *contradiction in terms*, one of those things brainy people called a *pair-of-socks*.

Why that had anything to do with it was beyond him.

Maybe absurd ideas came in matched sets like socks. That would explain how people could be right and wrong at the same time. They went out to buy one thing but had to get two things just to say they had the one thing.

It really didn't matter. There was no left sock or right sock.

Suah followed the sidewalk towards the water. Passing by the café with the low railing, he looked for the waitress who had waved at him yesterday but she was nowhere in sight. Moving on, he turned down the alleyway expecting to hunt once again for the little people who hid out of sight.

But that wouldn't work. Not today. Halfway down the alley, a delivery truck had pulled up behind one of the businesses and a man was unloading boxes. There was no way the little people would show themselves with all that activity and racket going on.

Suah moseyed down the alley anyway. If nothing else, he might find Gris-Gris again and have someone to play with.

When Suah got to the delivery truck, he stood back and looked inside. It was amazing how all those boxes found their way to where they were going. For the maid at home, just keeping track of clothes put in the dryer was a mysterious puzzle at times. No doubt, that's where brainy people got the idea for *pair-of-socks* to begin with.

Walking on past, he came to the place where the day before he had heard music coming through the rear-entrance screen door.

Today, only the sound of wind chimes could be heard.

One chime alone would have been music but with so many of them making sounds all at once Suah had to stop and listen to their concert.

There was no way he could hum along with them but he wished he could. There was no way of following the melody but he knew he'd recognize it if he ever heard it again. The voice that was always with him was sure of it.

I know…I know you can. You'll make music like that some day.

He still didn't feel like dancing. So he walked on.

Arriving at the end of the alley, he looked both ways but found no Gris-

Gris. And so, following the pattern from yesterday, he stayed on the sidewalk to the busy main street and crossed in the crosswalk along with two couples and a bicyclist. He didn't stop at the seawall this time. He knew where he wanted to go. Back to the booth where he had made a friend.

Brody was just finishing a rousing description of all the wonders of a night-dive excursion offered by *Island Aquatics & Adventures* to a man and his wife. As the couple turned and walked away sold on the idea, Brody's smile soured and looked like it wanted a refund. A moment later, he caught sight of a small visitor standing off to one side.

"Well, look what the cat drug in." After shuffling brochures, Brody grabbed for his pack of smokes. "Did you see a lot of fish yesterday?"

Suah shook his head no.

"Then you had your eyes closed. From what I hear, they were hoppin'."

Suah had to step closer to keep sight of Brody as he sat back down.

"Do you ever go on the boat?" asked Suah.

Brody blew tobacco smoke at the sky. "Do birds rent bicycles? Nope, you're not gonna get me out there."

"Why not?"

"Why waste all that time when I can waste it here?"

Suah stepped behind the booth and looked for the box of brochures to sit on. Today the box was gone. So much for routine adventures. He remained standing and leaned against the booth.

"Does your job have a name?"

"That's the beauty of it. It doesn't. I simply get paid to waste time. Now what would you call that?"

Suah thought hard. "Time waster."

"There you go. You're a genius and don't know it."

Suah's thoughts carried on. "Whose time is it?"

Brody flicked cigarette ashes into the breeze. "I guess it's my time. I can't waste anybody else's time 'cause they sure as hell won't let me."

"Why would you want to waste your time?"

"I guess because I get paid for it. I get money."

Suah was really trying to understand. "So…money isn't a waste of time."

"Money is never a waste of time—unless it's money you're losing. Losing money is a waste of time."

"You get paid for wasting time. Are you losing money?"

"Don't strain your brain." Brody reached for the rusted old coffee can. After a swig from the pint bottle wrapped inside, he added, "Your mistake is trying to figure it out. When you get older, you'll find out: there's nothing worth figuring out. It's designed that way."

"Is drawing faces a waste of time?"

Brody hesitated. "It's the *biggest* waste of time."

"But you like to do it."

"I do it 'cause I got nothing else to do."

"You could do something else."

Brody showed some temper. "What do you know? You can't even see the fucking fish with a mask and a snorkel."

Suah was unfazed. "Will you let me draw another face?"

"Another one? You didn't even finish the one from yesterday."

Visions of Blake came and went. "I don't want to draw a scary face."

"Look around, kid. They're all scary."

Suah did as suggested and looked around. Across the way stood a portly man with a camera. "He's not scary. Why don't you draw him?"

Raising his fedora hat, Brody leaned his head to one side for a look around the end of the booth. After consideration, he leaned back.

"*That* would not be a waste of time. *That* would be a challenge. I only draw when I want to waste time."

Suah didn't understand. "You don't get paid to draw. That can't be a waste of time."

"You don't get it." Brody slumped in his chair and repositioned his hat.

Suddenly obsessive and compulsive, Suah wouldn't let it go. "You get paid to sit here; that's a waste of time. If you draw him while you sit here, the drawing is also a waste of time. But it can't be. You don't get paid to draw."

"Congratulations…" Brody mumbled from under his hat. "…You've discovered the riddle of life."

Suah felt his heart race. He stared down at the pile of doodles by the coffee can. "Is that a pair-of-socks?"

Brody didn't move. "Beats me, kid. It looked like the guy wasn't wearing socks at all."

Suah watched the portly man. "You don't have to draw all of him, just his face."

"What good is it to have a face without a body?"

"It could be a funny face. You could put a frame around it…"

Badgered to his limits, Brody jerked up and pushed his hat onto his head.

"Geez Louise, alright already. If a stupid funny-face picture of the fat man will get you to shut up, glory bee I'll do it." Brody grabbed a pen and brochure from the shelf. He set right to work on the drawing. "Now, if only porky will turn around, maybe I can get something more than a profile."

Sensing that Brody needed a closer subject more willing to pose, Suah took off and ran across the way and up to the portly man.

"Hello…" The man turned around. "My friend would like to draw your picture but he can't see your face. Could you turn around?"

The man was taken off-guard, not knowing what to think.

Suah pointed back to the booth where a partial view of Brody in his chair was possible from where the portly man stood.

"Draw my picture?" the man repeated.

"It'll only take a minute," assured Suah. He tugged on the man's hand.

Not seeing any harm in seeing what was going on, the man complied.

Back at the booth, Brody hid his embarrassment and anger.

The fat man approached. "The kid says you're drawing pictures."

Brody stood and hemmed and hawed around. "Yeah, well, he ran over to get you; it's no big deal." Brody waved the doodled brochure in the air.

The fat man was confused. "You're drawing on that?"

Brody started to say yes but then Suah handed him a pad of scratch paper from behind the booth. Brody took it but said nothing.

The fat man tensed. "How long will it take?"

Brody groped for answers. "Ah…it's quick; you don't even have to sit down."

Fat man hesitated. "Is this something you just do or do you charge for it?"

It was Brody's turn to hesitate. He looked to Suah and back.

Suah tried to help out. "He gets paid to sit here. The drawing is just a waste of time."

"What?" The fat man stood perplexed.

"Never mind him…" Brody waved off any consideration of the kid. "He thinks he's on a *nutzo-crazy* adventure. I do the drawing. No charge."

The big man relaxed a bit. "Can I keep it as a souvenir?"

"Why not…sure. Just stand there; it'll only take a minute."

The fat man posed and Brody set to work sketching a caricature.

Off to one side stood Suah, smiling.

In what seemed no time flat, Brody signed the work with a flourish and presented it to the waiting man.

The man waggled his head into a grin. "I like it! If I were a cartoon character, that would be me on vacation. Thanks."

Suah hurried around to get a look at the drawing before the man walked off. Suah couldn't help but giggle but Brody was in no mood for festivities.

As soon as the fat man was far enough away, Brody vented.

"What the hell was that supposed to be?" His anger drained the humor out of Suah. "Don't ever do that again." He tossed the pen and scratch pad back on a shelf behind the booth. "How I waste my time is my own business. Don't start bringing other people into it."

Brody slammed a sign down on the booth. *Be Back In Ten Minutes.*

"I'm going for a walk and don't you dare follow me."

Stomping off, Brody left Suah standing next to the booth, dazed and bewildered. He couldn't see what had happened that might have caused such a tirade. It was hard understanding the ways of the people around him. Harder yet was fitting in.

Suah turned back to the booth and considered the pile of doodles on the bottom shelf. Above them one shelf up he saw his mask and snorkel, right where he had left them after the boat ride yesterday. The thought of going far out with a group of people he could watch sounded good right about then.

He grabbed the mask and snorkel and headed off to slip number nine.

Only problem was, the slip was empty when he got there.

Blake had dropped him off later this morning and by now Lucas' boat was already gone. Suah checked the watch that Blake put on his wrist again. It was way later. So much for thinking he could plan his adventures.

With mask and snorkel dangling at his side, he decided to stroll along the slips and look at the other boats, the ones still in port. Who knows, maybe just maybe someone else would invite him to come aboard.

Stranger things had happened.

He walked about halfway down the row of slips when a large cabin cruiser attracted his admiration. He had seen boats like this in pictures but the thing was so immense in real life he had to stop to take it all in.

No sooner had he stopped but motion at his side attracted him to look.

"Gris-Gris!" The stray dog from yesterday had found him this time.

Suah knelt down and gave the dog a good rubbing.

"You're out exploring again like me." The dog panted and wagged its tail. "Yesterday you followed me all the way down the alley," noted Suah. "Today, I promise, I'll follow *you*. You lead the way."

Suah stood and motioned for the dog to go. "Go on…Let's see what your adventure is like."

The dog ran around him and played for a while before trotting off.

As promised, Suah followed.

CHAPTER **9**

The adventures of a stray dog might seem random, even pointless to most people. But to one little boy who had named such a dog Gris-Gris, their afternoon wanderings might as well have been a destined quest of a lifetime.

Even so, so much serendipity is never realized in the moment.

To some passers-by, the sight of a boy and his dog was a living archetype of spontaneity, friendship, and irresponsible play. Many others didn't even notice them or if they did, concluded there was nothing to see.

From boat slip to alley, from dripped spots of ice cream on sidewalks to licking hands at bus stops, Gris-Gris took Suah on a dizzying procession of aimless exploration. Much of it in search of scraps of food and puddles to drink from. It was a tiring trek up and back through town, all of it culminating at the park with the big tree.

At times during the day, Suah had to run to keep up with the busy scavenger who was always in his lead. After one such run, an out-of-breath Suah trotted into the park panting like the dog he was chasing.

"Gris-Gris!" Suah called out but the hapless mutt had a mind, an itinerary, and a schedule of his own. No amount of calling was going to change that.

The tiring game of follow-the-leader took a break when both follower and leader decided to find rest in the park. Suah spotted the dog on the far south side under one of the massive, outstretched limbs of the park's big tree.

Interestingly enough, Gris-Gris had found someone else to befriend. A girl was sitting on one of the shaded benches. As Suah started to walk up, she petted Gris-Gris with a hand that wasn't right.

Suah stood back, taking in the sight. This was something new; he didn't want to rush in without knowing what he was looking at.

The girl was older than him but not by very much, at least not as much as his mother was older. The girl had light yellow hair, a kind of blonde bleached by the sun. She was thin, almost too thin, and wore a plain blouse on top of plain pants. But the thing everyone would notice right away, before anything else, was the way she moved.

She moved her own way, not like anyone else.

Next to her on the bench was a tall walking stick fashioned from a branch of native wood. The top of it was rounded and a curve of tape had been layered over the blunt end until a knob had formed. It was a knob worn smooth from being held for support.

From a distance, Suah followed the interaction of girl and dog. She might not be able to move like anyone else, but Suah could tell she was kind. At least she was kind to Gris-Gris and Suah liked that.

Anyone who was kind to animals probably would be kind to him. He wasn't sure of this but when it came to people other than his mother, there was only so much he could be sure of anyway. The more he people-watched, the more he was sure of that.

Stepping forward, he approached the bench ever so slowly. He had promised Gris-Gris he would follow him and he would. After all the places they had been together that day, a girl sitting on a bench, no matter how different she was, wasn't going to scare him away.

As Suah neared, he caught the girl's attention and could tell how quickly she became defensive, reticent, even suspicious. He could almost hear her thoughts. Who was this boy and what did he want?

Maybe if he called to Gris-Gris again, she'd understand he was harmless.

"Gris-Gris…there you are!"

"Is this your dog?" Her voice was slight, her mannerisms shy. She tried to minimize her movements, as if ashamed of them.

"I've been following him all day. We've been exploring."

"How do you know his name?" asked the girl.

"It's a nickname. I don't know his name."

"Me neither. He answers to anything if you have food."

Suah stepped closer. "You've seen him before?"

"Oh, sure. He comes around the park all the time."

"You like the park?" Standing closer, Suah had a chance to examine the unique walking stick in more detail.

"It's one of my favorite places. I love this tree."

Suah looked up. "Is all of this *one* tree?"

"Incredible, isn't it?

"Yeah…" Holding his head way back, he stared up into the branches.

"If it wasn't here and someone told me about it, I don't think I would have believed it." She looked up and petted Gris-Gris down his neck with a hand curled and twisted.

Suah's eyes rolled to follow the branches. "I'm right here and I still don't believe it. I thought the park had a forest in it—not one tree!"

The girl's chuckle was demure. "I guess you can't see the forest for the tree."

The girl's relaxed humor gave Suah the impression she was more approachable than expected. He edged a bit closer but remained standing.

"You know all about the park. You must come here a lot."

"Every day…for lunch," she explained.

"This is a fun place to eat lunch. You can feed the birds."

"Sometimes I give them a little but they're greedy little monsters. They'd take it all if I let them."

"What kind of monsters?" Suah took a worried glance at the tree.

"No, silly. They're just birds. How old are you?"

"Nine. How old are you?"

"Twenty."

Suah got wide-eyed. "That's a lot more than me."

"Not that much."

"Do you always sit here when you eat your lunch?"

"Yeah, I guess so. I love the ocean." There was passion in her voice.

Suah looked around and then back. He pointed. "You could sit over there and *see* the ocean."

"Right here is fine."

"Here you can see the street. Don't you want to see the ocean?"

The girl's temper flared. "I said right here is fine."

Suah took a moment to process the change in her. People-watching was always much easier than talking with people. People were much more understandable when you simply watched what they did. Right now, the girl was looking away from him, paying all her attention to Gris-Gris.

When Suah was curious about something, he saw no reason to let the topic go. "Would you like to see the boats?"

"Not right now," she snapped.

"No one's sitting on the other bench…"

"Then maybe you should go sit on it." The girl twisted back his way. "You know what's strange? You're walking around a park carrying a snorkel mask. If you like snorkeling so much, why aren't you in the water?"

Suah answered calmly. "The boat's gone."

"So what? You have to carry around the mask? I thought you said you were with the dog all day. Does the dog like to snorkel?"

A grin stretched wide on Suah's face and he began to chuckle. "I don't know; we should ask him."

Suah's giggle melted the girl's anger; she could see he meant no harm. Relaxing, she let the joke sidetrack them both from talking about the bench.

When their laughter and smiles died away, a calm and silence settled back in around them. Gris-Gris laid down and curled up by the girl's feet. They said nothing for a minute and Suah stepped over and sat down on the far end of the same bench. Nearby was her walking stick.

"Is that your stick?" he asked.

Her defensiveness returned. She looked away. "What do you think?"

Suah rarely picked up on social cues, especially from conversation. He took her question as a question and answered it.

"I think it is."

She said nothing. He had no idea she meant the question to be off-putting. He only knew he had never seen anyone like her before. That meant he had no restraint on his innocent curiosity.

"Do you need it all the time?"

She twisted back his way, her eyes watering with hurt. "Why do you want to know? You have something *funny* to say?"

Suah shook his head no. "I've never seen a stick like that before."

"Well, aren't you lucky."

Suah sat still; his voice was soft. "Did someone make it for you?"

The girl gazed out across the park towards the street. "I made it myself."

"Was it too big for you when you were little?"

"I didn't have it when I was little."

"How long have you had it?"

"Two years."

"That's a long time."

"Yeah, a long time."

Suah gazed down at her twisted hand. "Does it hurt?"

The girl looked back to see he meant her hand. "No."

Suah buried his hands between his knees. "It looks like it hurts."

A spike of bitterness came through. "How would *you* know?"

Before Suah could answer, a swell of something hopeful but embryonic stirred within as he heard the inner voice that was always with him.

...I know...I know...

He kept his hands hidden between his legs. "It would hurt if I turned *my* hand like that."

The girl looked over and saw his honest concern. This was not one of the children who laughed at her or made jokes. She could tell he was special, special in many ways. Some of those ways probably got him laughed at too. In that, they shared a common bond.

She tried changing the subject. "So what do you do for fun?"

With a glance down at Gris-Gris, Suah's face lit up. "I'm on an adventure. I go exploring."

"Really," smiled the girl. "You do this all day?"

"Until it's time to get picked up. Sometimes I have adventures at night. Last night I was on TV."

"Wow." The girl played along; she assumed he was in his own world.

"I like exploring," gushed Suah. "I used to think adventures might be scary." He parroted what Paige had told him, "But most things aren't scary when we let ourselves enjoy them."

"You still have to be careful."

Suah looked her way, noting her concern. "Even on adventures?"

"Especially on adventures. Look what happened to me." As she said it, she regretted it. She didn't mean to switch the topic back to her.

Concern returned to Suah's face. "You hurt yourself on an adventure?"

Reluctantly, the girl nodded. "Right here on the island."

"Did you get hit by a car? I was told to always use the crosswalk."

The girl gave her head a shake then gazed away at the trunk of the big tree. "No, it wasn't a car. I did a crazy thing."

Suah's interest was piqued. "Oh, so it was a *nutzo-crazy* adventure."

The girl smiled. "That's *exactly* what it was."

Suah was putting it together. "Did Brody Mud tell you it could be scary?"

"Who?"

"Brody Mud?"

"No, no one told me. Just the opposite. Everyone there was telling me it was no big deal. It was fun."

"You hurt yourself having fun?"

The girl nodded.

A quizzical look came over Suah. "That sounds like a *pair-of-socks*."

The girl hardly heard him. Her gaze was locked on the tree trunk but her thoughts were wandering back two years ago.

"I shouldn't have let them talk me into it. It didn't feel right."

"What did they want you to do?"

"Jump." The word hung in the air. "Jump into the water. We were all having fun. Others were jumping and they were all right. It was about twenty feet down. The surf was pretty calm; that wasn't the problem. The problem was the rocks. When I jumped, I hit my back and neck on the rocks."

Suah's mouth hung open. "You jumped into the ocean?"

A slight nod. "And that's the last time I've been in the ocean."

"Did you have to stay in a hospital?"

"I stayed awhile—until my mom's insurance wouldn't pay."

"Where did you go then?"

"I went home. I tried a free clinic but they only made it worse."

"When *my* mom doesn't like a doctor, she goes to another one. Maybe you should get a new doctor."

"They can't do anything now. It's too late."

Suah was amazed. "They can't make it better?"

The girl could only manage a shake of the head.

"Maybe your mom can get new insurance."

A huff of air became a laugh. "My mom is on the other side of the world. She got remarried and moved away to live with him. Good for her. The insurance wouldn't matter anyway."

"Do you go to school?"

"I finished high school; that was enough for me."

"Do you go to work?"

"I used to be a waitress. I can't do that anymore."

"So what do you do all day?"

"I live with a lady. She lets me stay there if I help out and do some chores. She likes the company, I guess. I'm there a lot or I come to the park." The girl paused and glanced at Suah's interested face. "I don't know why I'm telling you all of this."

Suah shrugged. "Maybe you want to."

Her smile was strained. "So when you're not exploring, what do you like to do?"

Looking down at his hands, Suah brushed one hand over the next and then switched them back and forth. "I like to people-watch."

She eyed the snorkel on his lap. "What about watching the fish?"

"I don't go in the water."

"You don't? Why not?"

"I can't see the people down there. I already know what fish look like."

"How do you know if you never go in the water?"

"I've seen pictures. My teacher showed me movies that had lots of fish."

"That's not the same," insisted the girl. The passion in her voice had returned. "There's nothing like seeing them close up."

Again, Suah shrugged. "I saw them at the aquarium. I've seen them at the store where we get our food."

"But you haven't gone swimming with them, have you?"

"No…"

"That's a whole other world."

"I know. Birds live in the air; fish in the water. But I like to people-watch."

Put off by the fact that Suah didn't share her enthusiasm for everything aquatic, she looked away. "Why don't you find out everything you need to know about people by looking at pictures of them too? You don't have to go out and people-watch. You can stay home and look at pictures of them."

Suah was unconvinced. "People are different."

Gris-Gris became restless. In the distance, something attracted his interest and he jumped up and ran off.

Suah sprung to his feet. The snorkel and mask went flying on the ground.

"Gris-Gris!" Scrambling to pick up the snorkel, Suah turned back to the girl. "I promised him I'd follow. Sorry, I've got to go!"

With that, Suah was off running. Along a diagonal path and then across the dirt and scruffy grass growing under the big tree, he chased the dog to a spot where a pair of children ran in circles and played.

With Gris-Gris occupied nearby, Suah halted, caught his breath, then looked back across the park towards the bench where the girl was sitting. She was still sitting there and he couldn't quiet his wonder about her.

Close by, a bum who frequented the park was scrounging through a trash barrel. Suah marched up to him.

"Do you come to the park a lot?"

The bum looked up, disinterested and annoyed.

Suah persisted. He pointed towards the girl. "Do you know her name?"

The bum glanced in the direction of the pointing finger. "Her name?"

"Yeah, do you know her name?"

The bum went back to his foraging but as he did, he answered.

"Lolo. Wiwi Lolo."

CHAPTER 10

By the next day, Suah was getting used to the idea that adventures, while always different from day to day, in some ways could still be routine.

He suffered in stride the ride in the Datsun with Blake, knowing full well that in a short time he'd be launching into another day on his own. With the food truck as base camp for his explorations, there appeared to be no limit to the heights of excitement he could climb. Just the smell of deep flyers and fried dough in the morning was now enough to arouse his wanderlust.

Flexing his new confidence, he varied the route to *Island Aquatics & Adventures* by not taking the alleyway. Instead, he followed the side street directly to the main street. There he enjoyed being tempted to stop and watch the people milling about as they shopped for bathing suits and all the authentic island wares made in China.

As much as he wanted to stop and watch, he couldn't. Not yet. He didn't want to miss the boat. As carefree as most adventures could be, he was learning there were some parts of audacious exploration that demanded a certain discipline. If he wanted to ride out where the far watery reaches were brought near, he would have to show up on time.

He had memorized what time Lucas' boat left. And thanks to Blake, he even had a way, strapped to his wrist, to help him navigate through time and space, ensuring safe passage aboard.

He was getting used to this Marco Polo thing.

Brody was upselling an all-inclusive package to a gullible group from the mainland when Suah showed up at the booth. There was no time to talk for either of them. Suah knew the drill by now. He snagged the snorkel and mask from behind the booth and trotted off to boat slip number nine.

Suah made strides, convinced there was nothing more invigorating than having the day to yourself with the trade winds in your face and the rising sun shining off the catamaran you were about to board. He got in line with the day's current crop of vacationers and made his way on deck.

"Ready to see some whales?" smiled Gavin.

Suah sat down but his eyes got big. "Real whales?"

"I'm afraid so. It's just about that time a year. It's possible."

Suah looked around. Reactions from other passengers were mixed. Either Gavin was exaggerating or some people aboard saw whales all the time.

With snorkel and mask hanging from the knees of his jeans, Suah enjoyed the trip out of the harbor and away from shore. Some people walked around taking pictures. Others sat back, worshiping the sun. Lucas, as usual, was busy at the helm. Gavin was the proficient assistant, fielding the typical questions from the landlubbers so Lucas needn't be bothered.

Unlike the rest of the passengers aboard, for Suah, the trip out and back *was* the main attraction. While everyone else waited either to get to the fish or get back to shore, Suah had a fabulous time just watching them.

With people, there was no end to variations on common themes. While human nature appeared to be constant, people were different. How amusing.

The current trip was no exception. They were all on a thrilling voyage, just like Suah. They all had their hearts set on fun and adventure. But it became such a delight for him to watch the individual ways such a repeatable thing like a boat trip could play out among them.

Each trip, each day had its own personality, even though there was a predictable, almost comfortable sameness about all of it at the same time.

With each trip, Suah got a stronger sense that he was able to understand people more—and less. It was a *pair-of-socks*. How could his comprehension of them be growing wider but no deeper?

A wide ocean that wasn't deep certainly wouldn't float one's boat.

"You think we're gonna see any whales?" The deep and gravelly voice came from Suah's right side.

Suah looked up at the old man asking the question and shrugged.

"I don't," asserted the man. "I think it's a lot of hype."

"That's OK," countered Suah. "My mom pays people for hype."

"Is that so…"

Suah looked over at the man's pants. "Do you have a change of clothes?"

The man snorted and swallowed. "I don't go in the water."

"You like to people-watch too?"

"People-watch? Hell, no. I'm just along for the ride." He pointed across the aisle. "That's my granddaughter over there with my son and his wife. It's *their* vacation. They let me come along…if I don't get in the way."

"You don't like to look at the fish? Most people do."

"The only fish I like is fried and on my plate." He patted his stomach.

"Blake gives me burgers and fries."

"They're good too."

"I like them warm but the ones I get are cold."

The old man shook his head. "Life is rough, isn't it?"

Suah wondered, "If you were on *your* vacation, where would *you* go?"

"*My* vacation?" The old man took in the gist of the question. "Oh, I don't know. Maybe some river in Wyoming. Do some fishin'."

"You been there before?"

"When I was a kid. That was a hell of a long time ago."

"Would you take your boat?"

"I don't have a boat. Wouldn't need a boat. Just some waders and a rod. You stand right out in the river; let it all flow by. The fish come to you."

"Wow," gaped Suah. "That sounds like fun."

"It is. It's the most fun you can have with your clothes on."

"You have clothes on. When are you going?"

"Oh, I don't know. I get busy…"

"You've got a lot of work to do, huh."

"I'm retired. Been so for a while."

Suah puzzled, "Being retired sounds like work."

"How so?"

"You still get busy."

"There's all kinds of busyness."

Suah imagined the scene. "I'd sure like to stand in the river and have the fish come to me."

"You're young. You should go do it."

"I'd like to—except I'm too busy exploring."

"Exploring what?"

"I'm still figuring that out. I'm working on it."

The old man shook his head. "Well, don't take too long. Life is short. It goes by in a blink of an eye."

"Not when I'm waiting for Blake."

"This Blake character sounds like a real piece of work. Why do you hang around with him?"

"He just drops me off."

"I don't care," the old man declared. "Time is too precious to spend it with people who don't love or respect you."

"I'm spending time with you."

"Vice versa, young man. That's just my point."

"What does *vice versa* mean?"

"It means coming back at ya."

Suah pondered. "I think you're right."

"About what?"

Suah looked out to sea. "About the whales."

When it came time to drop anchor and offload the snorkelers, Gavin and Lucas were busy about the deck. Suah marveled that they still seemed to be having some fun even though they were so busy.

Before long, the old man and Suah were the only passengers not in the water. The old man sat on the side where he could watch his granddaughter try out her flippers and mask with ample guidance from her parents.

Suah moved around to whatever side had the most action. Here or there someone would splash or call out to someone they knew and urge them to come see what they were seeing. At times, a couple would surface and jabber to each other excitedly. Much of the time, as usual, it was quiet.

But halfway through their time at anchor, someone began calling out in a way Suah hadn't heard before. There was no fun in these cries, only panic and desperation. A single mother, swimming with her son, started panicking over her son's struggle in the water.

Spotting the trouble, Gavin wasted no time. He dove overboard and rushed to where the boy's thrashes suddenly quieted down.

The mother was inconsolable as Gavin turned the boy over in the water and tugged him back to the boat. With Lucas' help, they managed to lift the limp body of the boy back on deck and set him down not far away from where Suah was standing.

The mother scrambled aboard. She was shaking and crying and calling out for someone to help her boy. The old man Suah had been talking to hurried to her side to support and console her.

Lucas started basic first aid on the boy. He checked the airway and listened for signs of a pulse or breathing. Unable to detect either, he started chest compressions.

"Get the AED!" shouted Lucas.

Gavin scrambled back under the bimini in search of the defibrillator.

"Where is it?" came the cry. Gavin was tearing open compartments.

Continuing CPR, Lucas yelled back, "Starboard hatch, next to the helm!"

"I'm there! I don't see it!"

Frantic, Lucas had no choice but to run to look himself.

Left lying on his back on the deck, the boy's head was turned to one side. He looked lifeless. The only sounds on deck were of the frenzied search by Gavin and Lucas in the cabin and the prayerful muttering and sobs of the boy's mother.

Standing near, Suah felt pulled to the boy. He knelt and with one hand smoothed back the wet hair from the boy's forehead. Slowly, lightly, he patted the boy's forehead with long, sliding touches. He did this for a while.

He did it until the boy lurched onto his side and began coughing.

Reacting to the sound, Lucas and Gavin returned to the boy. In Gavin's grip was the box that contained the automated external defibrillator.

Lucas dropped to the boy's side and assisted his recovery.

Gavin stood shaken. "What happened?" He looked at the old man.

The boy's mother dropped to the deck, hysterical with joy.

Lucas gave Gavin a glance. "We got lucky."

The old man shifted his stare from Suah to Lucas. "That wasn't luck."

Suah sat back on the deck and watched the boy recover.

Gavin was still stunned. "...he didn't have a pulse."

"Stranger things have happened..." Lucas pointed. "Go get a blanket."

Forced to respond by the order, Gavin retreated into the cabin.

Suah stood up and watched as the boy sat up. Gavin rushed back and wrapped a warming blanket around him. With Lucas' help, they picked him up and placed him in a protected space inside the cabin. The boy's mother followed along, not wanting to leave the boy's side.

The deck was clear except for the old man and Suah. Suah sat down and the old man took a seat not far away.

"I've seen a lot of strange things," remarked the old man. "but that takes the cake. If I didn't know better..."

The old man couldn't bring himself to say anything more.

Suah settled back, relieved but more somber than the man had ever seen him. Somewhere between a mumble and a whisper, Suah could be heard saying something as he took a few deep breaths.

I know...You see what we see...I know...

It's only me but you're enough...I know...I-and-I can dance.

The old man heard the last of it but wasn't sure he had heard it right. He started to ask Suah a question about the whispers but held up as the first of the other snorkelers started coming back onboard. The whole incident had put a damper on everyone's fun.

Suah thought back to Lolo. She was right. Adventures were not all fun.

You had to be careful, even on adventures.

Lucas called out overboard. "All right, everybody back onboard. We need to head back in and get this boy checked out."

In the confusion, the old man got a chance to ask his question. He slid over on the seat and leaned into Suah. "Did you say *I-and-I can dance*?"

Suah rubbed one hand over another. "I didn't say it. Hawa said it."

CHAPTER 11

Suah Chase stepped off the boat with a sensation shivering through him unlike anything he understood. It was slight as it ebbed away, but while it lasted, it was a warm awakening. Some things are different in a special way. They hint at a budding awareness. They resonate in unique spaces within.

Back on dock, he stood off to one side of the action. Holding his snorkel and mask at his side, he watched the scene play out. Lucas had radioed ahead and Molly was waiting with the car to take the young boy to the hospital to get checked out. The boy, shaken but walking under his own power, was escorted to the car by a distressed but thankful mother.

Some passengers hurried off while others dawdled around to witness the drama play out. The old man that Suah spoke with on the boat had a mind to dawdle but the family he was with wanted to be about their day of play. As his granddaughter ran off with parents in tow, the old man straggled behind. His steps were halting. As his head turned back, his eye locked on Suah.

Suah glanced over and watched him go but had no answers for him.

There was no explanation for the sum of things that had no substance.

Whispers of intuition was all Suah had to go on, just a suggestion that, for a few transformative moments, the other voice inside of him had become something more than a voice. Somehow, as Suah had looked down on the boy after they pulled him from the water, the voice and Suah had merged.

It wasn't so much a feeling of completeness as a rush of purpose and a surprised glimpse of a fated resolution. For a few trancelike moments, the fusion of voices had allowed him to flow in a direction that was all downhill. He had been moved merely by the way things should be.

No one noticed Suah ambling away. The weight and consequence of the adult world wouldn't let them. He was an odd little boy who had finished a boat ride. What else did they need to know?

The farther Suah stepped away from the dock the more he discounted that anything extraordinary had happened. Plainly, it was quite an event to be nearby and witness the boy's natural recovery. The high energy of such a thing was most certainly adventure-like. But that was all it was.

Softly but persistent, his inner voice wouldn't let it rest.

That's not all...You know...You know there's more...

Suah shuffled along, mumbling. "You like to pretend big things."

Pretending is rehearsing...Gianna rehearses too...Pretending is good...

"I don't need to rehearse. I'm not going to sing for lots of people."

No...You're going to dance...I know...I-and-I can dance...

Suah started to hum a playful little tune hoping to drown out the voice. He stopped long enough to say, "Don't be silly," then started humming again.

What will it take to let you believe?...You are who you are...I know...

Suah pretended to ignore what he heard and kept strolling and humming.

Maybe if you saw something too perfect...Something that shouldn't be... Just for you, just for me...A coincidence, something only pretending could ever make be...You need to feel the way of the dance...

"All you do is pretend."

I know you know...The power of pretend...Like running in a field with nothing to do but play...I know...You can follow yourself to find the way...

Suah thought no more of it and wandered along the seawall down the main street and back into town. After the crisis with the boy on the boat and a bewildering encounter with his own inner voice, it was reassuring to let go of everything and simply people-watch along the shops and restaurants.

Afternoon business was not as brisk as some days, but it didn't take much to occupy Suah's interest. Before long, a flurry of little things that other people wouldn't ever notice caught his eye.

At a T-shirt shop, he stood a step inside the doorway and watched as a father and son studied the designs that blanketed an entire wall. They took turns finding and pointing out funny or attention-grabbing messages and patterns. Many of the shirt styles they liked and yet they wound up getting none of them. Their search moved on to a spinner rack of hats. As the father spun the rack, the son separated off to try on mirrored sunglasses.

Suah turned and left. The many T-shirt designs were a blur in memory. What lingered was the interaction of man and boy. A sense-echo followed Suah down the sidewalk. It was always beguiling to watch fathers and sons doing anything together. Suah wondered how he would act if he had a dad.

A few steps farther, Suah came to an art gallery. Its wide, open doorway gave ample opportunity for passing foot traffic to be enthralled by artworks. Stretching deep inside, the walls were black but bright spots of light highlighted framed piece hanging on display. Interspersed within meandering aisles, pedestals and platforms held sculpture pieces lit from above.

One piece in particular hooked Suah's curiosity and pulled him in.

His steps were slow. The gallery had no customers just then which made walking into the space a singular descent into another world. All was cool and quiet and ethereal with showcased patches of color and light all around.

The sculpture piece he found so enticing sat in the center of a rectangular pedestal that held two smaller-sized works on either side.

The piece that fascinated was tall and slender, symmetrical and smooth. It was fashioned out of shiny black rock and depicted two lithe forms, joyously facing each other. As they leaned back, each of them raised one arm longingly towards the sky. At mid-thigh, the two forms blended into one cohesive base of rock flowing down and out in all directions.

Suah stood and gazed at the piece.

A sales lady, sauntering around on a floor-check, halted on seeing him.

"And how are you today?" Noting the snorkel and mask at his side, she smiled with humored curiosity.

Suah gave her a glance. "Fine…"

"You like that statue?"

Suah nodded, not talking his eyes off it.

The saleslady folded her arms. With no other customers in the shop at the moment, she might as well pass the time and talk with the youngster. At least so far, he showed an interest in the gallery in a way most children rarely did.

"You have a good eye for art. That piece is made out of a very special stone. It's called Brazilian black soapstone."

Suah's eyes got wide. "It's a big bar of soap?"

The saleslady chuckled. "No, that's just the name. I guarantee you it's solid rock. Go ahead, you can touch it. You'll see. Just be very careful."

Suah inched forward. The last thing he expected was being invited to walk up and touch such a wondrous object. Reaching into the focused bath of light, he smoothed the tips of his fingers along its base.

He glanced over at the lady. "It's smooth! That's a big rock!"

"It takes a lot of time and patience to carve a rock like that."

He lifted his gaze to where the carving separated into two forms. "What happened to their feet?"

The saleslady shrugged. "That's just the way it is. They're together at the bottom but two different people at top."

Suah pointed to a small plate embedded at one end. "What's that?"

"That's the name of the piece; it's engraved in brass."

"The two people have a name?"

"The whole sculpture has a name. As far as I know, the two people can have any name you like. They could be anybody."

Suah squinted and tilted his head; he tried to read the brass plate.

The saleslady saved him the trouble. "It's called *Reaching Far*. You see?

The two people are reaching up and back. As they reach, they're stretching farther away from each other."

Suah looked up at their arching backs made out of stone, their graceful fingertips outstretched and expectant. "Far reaching…"

"It's the other way around," the lady corrected. "*Reaching Far*."

"How long is it going to stay here?"

"For a while, unless somebody buys it."

Suah took a couple steps back. "I'd like to have it in my room."

The saleslady grinned. "That would be quite a display. Is your room big enough?"

"I don't know," wondered Suah. "Maybe my closet…"

The saleslady's grin broadened at the suggestion. Just then, three people sauntered into the gallery together. Distracted by the prospect of paying customers, she took her leave of Suah.

"Look around if you want to. There are many more pieces to see."

She headed off, leaving Suah to stand and admire the work a minute more. Satisfied that he had seen what he came in to see, he returned to the sidewalk and restarted his ramble down the main street.

Two blocks down, he slowed at a corner and noticed Lolo making her way up a side street. Meandering at her side was Gris-Gris. Suah had never seen Lolo walk before. It was a slow and deliberate process, twisted at places and aided by the tall walking stick. It was a struggle made into a routine.

Suah ran up to them and petted the dog. "Where are you going?"

"Going home," answered Lolo. "Lunchtime is over."

"Can I come along?"

"What for?"

"I don't know. Someplace new to explore."

Inclined to say no but not wanting the discussion directed at her, Lolo shifted the blame. "I don't think Lilyana wants any company today."

"Who's Lilyana?"

"The lady who lets me live with her. She works out of the house and doesn't want me to bring people around when she's got clients."

"Why? Do your friends make a lot of noise?"

"I've never brought anybody around. I think she likes it that way; it helps her concentrate."

"On what? What does she do?"

"She works on people."

"What kind of work?"

"Oh, lots of things. Massage and Reiki. Sometimes she gives energy readings. Every once in a while, fortunetelling."

"Wow," pondered Suah. "she knows the future?"

"Parts of it, I guess. At least her customers think so."

"What about your future? Did she tell you all about it?"

"I didn't ask."

"Why not?"

"I've got no reason to ask about the obvious."

"What does that mean?"

"Nothing. So what have you been doing today?"

"I went on a boat ride."

"How did you manage that?"

"Friends of Brody Mud get to ride free."

"Really. And you're a friend."

"I must be."

"Brody Mud. That's an odd name. What does *he* do?"

"Mostly he wastes time. But he likes to draw pictures. He just doesn't like anybody to see them."

"Weird."

"Why?"

"Because if you like something, you don't want to hide it away."

"You like the ocean but you don't like to look at it."

"That's different."

"How?"

"It just is." Her steps slowed. "Here we are..."

The two of them arrived at a little frame house set back from the sidewalk. It was up the block from the town's main street. The house was old, with a step-up porch and weathered wood siding. Two casement windows flanked an entrance hidden behind a rusted screen door. In the small front yard a 4-by-4 post held a hanging sign advertising the homely structure as a place of business.

Lilyana Gorst
Massage, Reiki, Energy Work
Horoscopes & Tarot Readings

Suah paused to check out the sign as Lolo worked her way to the porch. Gris-Gris trotted around a hedge into the next yard and surprised another dog that was sniffing there. The two dogs startled each other into a confrontation and soon were yapping and snapping at each other. The dog fight escalated until Lilyana Gorst came charging out of the front door.

"What's going on out here?" she demanded.

Lilyana was a short but stocky woman with salt-and-pepper hair and not a trace of makeup. She had no vanity about the way her middle years looked on her. Her clothes were simple and utilitarian, a plain cotton dress and nurse's shoes. She met Lolo halfway up the steps but Lolo had turned back, her attention drawn to the dog fight.

Suah scampered to the hedge but froze, not knowing what to do.

Lilyana had enough of the interruption. She snatched a broom off the porch and headed into the yard to scatter the two dogs apart.

"All right you two, enough!" She swiped the broom repeatedly in an attempt to break them up. "Stop it!"

Catching the dogs in the side of their faces with the bristles, they broke apart. The other dog went skittering off down the sidewalk. Gris-Gris was left behind, cowering by the hedge.

Lilyana marched back to the porch with Lolo watching her progress.

"What are these dogs doing around here anyway…"

Lolo looked back in time to see Gris-Gris limping across the neighbor's yard. "They're both strays. I don't think they belong to anybody."

Lilyana put the broom back in place and surveyed the aftermath from her elevated perch on the porch.

"Dumb animals. Fighting about nothing." She caught sight of Gris-Gris. "Look—now *that* one's hurt." She watched as Suah followed then caught up with the dog. "Who's the kid?"

Lolo worked her way up the steps. "Just a boy I met in the park."

Lilyana stepped closer to one side of the porch to get a better look at Suah. "Don't be bringing strangers around. I don't mind your friends, but you can't be too careful."

"He's all right," commented Lolo. "He just tags along."

Lilyana watched as Suah knelt down and got Gris-Gris to sit and raise his wounded front paw. With gentle strokes of the hand, Suah passed over the injured area time and again with a steady and single focus. As if mesmerized by the attention, Gris-Gris sat perfectly still.

"What is he doing now?" asked Lilyana.

Before Lolo could look back and hazard an answer, Suah stood up and petted the top of Gris-Gris' head. The dog scampered around as if released from a command to stay and now expected to play.

"What was that?" The question was studied reflection as Lilyana stepped down off the porch and into the yard. She walked up to Gris-Gris and checked the injured paw. There was blood on the fur but the bleeding had stopped. The dog's mood couldn't have been brighter and the limp was gone.

She turned to Suah. "Did you do something to this dog?"

Worried he might get into trouble, Suah shook his head no.

"You did something," Lilyana asserted. "How did you do that?"

Suah shrugged.

Lilyana reached out for him. "Let me see your hands."

Suah complied. Lilyana took his hands in hers and held them a long time. As she held them, her breaths came deeper, then quicker.

"Your energy is different. Where did you learn to do that?"

"Nowhere," insisted Suah.

"It had to start somewhere."

"It's the way it should be." As much as Suah tried to hold back his inner voice, he felt it rising to the surface.

Lilyana glanced back at Gris-Gris trotting around and sniffing the hedges.

"Is that something you've always been able to do?"

Suah tilted his head in doubt. "Maybe." As soon as the word was out, he felt his inner voice come through him. From somewhere between an after-thought and a daydream, he started to mumble.

A part of I-and-I is near…A part is far…
Only fingers and heart touch them both.

To Lilyana, it sounded as if Suah was reciting something he had learned.

"Who told you that?"

Suah pulled his hands back from hers. "Maadoops."

"Maadoops?" she repeated. "Where is Maadoops?"

Suah glanced at the watch on his wrist. "At GeeJam."

Lolo called from the porch, "What's going on?"

Suah looked to her. "I have to go. It's almost pickup time."

"All right," said Lolo. "I'll see you at the park maybe."

Lilyana took a few steps after him. "Come back some time. I'd really like to talk to you some more."

Suah gave a short wave and toddled off with Gris-Gris following after.

Lolo made her way inside. But Lilyana stood and watched the boy until he disappeared around the corner. Something had happened, something she had always imagined would be easy to explain. To her surprise, it wasn't.

CHAPTER 12

That night, Suah dreamed about a boat ride on a crystal blue ocean. Everyone on the boat was having a splendid time. No one paid any attention to the fact that the boat was half full of water that was slowly rising.

People chatted and laughed. Either they didn't notice or weren't worried that water had risen above their ankles. For the captain, everything seemed routine until he noticed something strange on the horizon.

Far out in front of the boat he saw land, just as it should be. But then he turned and discovered that no matter which way he looked, he could see land outlined on *every* horizon. In all directions, the horizon was covered with land. How could that be?

Desperate to discover what was going on, the captain revved the engines and powered the boat forward. As he did, the land on the horizon got closer—but not just in front of the boat. It got closer all around the boat. Incredibly, the crystal blue ocean had become a muddy lake and the lake was shrinking.

Anxious to reverse the ominous trend, the captain ordered everyone on board to hurry up and bail water out of the boat—not to save the boat from going under but in a desperate attempt to fill the ocean back up again.

As fast as they could, they tried. The efforts of everyone onboard were valiant but ultimately paltry against the tide of massive contraction closing in on them. In short order, the land on the horizon had moved in so close that the gigantic lake became a pond. Soon, the pond turned into a watering hole too shallow for the elephants to bathe in. In no time at all, the boat was left high and dry. The ocean was gone. The boat was useless.

All those aboard the boat were stunned; they stood as silent statues under a cloudless sky. What had happened and why? How could this be?

Whatever would they do now?

They expected the ride and all their fun to go on forever. And yet, somehow they hadn't left room for the one thing they needed most but took for granted. Even if they cried the rest of their lives, their tears would never fill the ocean back up again. Some things when lost are simply gone forever.

Suah awoke with a sad feeling lingering from the dream. He knew if he told anybody about it, they'd try to make him feel better by dismissing it as a nightmare. He didn't see any difference between dreams and nightmares except one of them you really would rather not have.

No matter what anyone said, he couldn't tell if the dream world was real or not. Sometimes, given the way people acted, it was hard enough to tell if the *awake* world was real or not. From what he saw from either of them, both were equally hard to understand.

Of course, whenever he had nightmares, most adults told him not to worry because dreams and nightmares were not real. But how could that be true if they *felt* so real? He also felt things when he was awake but no one told him *those* things weren't real.

Only one older person had ever told him to cherish and respect his dreams as something to embrace and learn from. That was his grandfather. But his grandfather wasn't with him now and there was no way he could tell him about it. Still, Suah couldn't help wondering what he might say.

Rubbing sleepers from his eyes, Suah wandered into his closet to get dressed. With the gloom of the dream still around him, he opened his wardrobe door to let Brody's drawing of him on the brochure brighten his mood. Sensing he might need the same support throughout the day, he took it off the door, folded it neatly in half, and put it into his pocket. That way, whenever he needed a little pick-me-up, he could take it out and look at it.

Sitting in Paige's car a little later on the way to Diego's house, Suah looked down and counted on his fingers. This was the fourth day since Gianna had gone on tour and the fourth time that Paige was making use of Blake's babysitting services.

At Diego's, Suah wished he could go directly to the Datsun and sit and wait for Blake. It was not pleasant being around Diego that morning. He and Paige started arguing about something. Diego had tickets to go somewhere and Paige was trying to beg off and not go. He didn't like being stood up but, even more, he hated the fact that she left it to the last minute to tell him.

As proof that grumpiness rolls downhill, a crabby Diego spawned a grouchy Blake for the ride into town.

"Another day you get to play in the alley, you little freak." Blake was glad to get away from Diego but still needed to let off steam at someone.

Suah knew to acknowledge him but do little else.

"Yeah," Blake continued. "A friend of mine saw you in the alley. What do you do back there? Dig for lunch?"

For Suah, it was not necessary to answer. The conversation was meant to be one-way. They had left early and Blake enjoyed the realization that he had extra time to entertain some mischief.

"Maybe you should see someplace new. That food truck is way too close to your favorite alley. We should mix it up a little. Would you like that?"

If Suah answered, he'd only provoke Blake. If he didn't answer, he'd get hit for ignoring him. Approximating something in between, Suah shrugged.

Blake grinned. "You're supposed to be on the beach watching the surfers anyway. So let's go to the beach. It doesn't have to be *my* beach."

When they got to the corner where the food truck was parked, Blake drove on past. Several streets beyond, he turned right and followed a narrow, curving road that ended up straddling the beach. Blake pulled the car over.

"OK, dufus, there's the beach. You can go sit on it." He handed Suah his watch. "Just be back by the food truck by 4 o'clock."

Suah got out and closed the door.

Blake rolled down the passenger side window and pointed with a thumb.

"The town is *that* way, in case you can't figure it out."

The Datsun spun into a U-turn and sped off, leaving Suah standing.

Suah turned to look at the beach but there were no surfers to be seen. He'd rather go back into town anyway but it would be a long walk.

A half hour later, Suah reached the south edge of town, just a couple blocks from the park with the big tree. He rambled along a walkway into the park and up to the bench where Lolo usually sat.

But she wasn't there. It wasn't lunchtime yet. Lunchtime was hours away. He sat down and looked up at the limbs of the big tree. Morning birds were chirping away in its branches but without Lolo to talk to, the park felt empty.

It felt good to sit and rest but he didn't stay long. There was so much more he wanted to do. For one thing, after the dream the night before, he wanted to go on a boat ride. He needed to check and make certain that the ocean would stay wide and deep for at least a little while longer.

Walking up to *Island Aquatics and Adventures*, he could tell right away that Brody was nowhere in sight. Even his folding chair was folded up and leaning against the back of the booth. Suah wanted to ask Brody the boat schedule for the day but now he'd have to go into the store and talk to Molly if he wanted to know that. She might tell him he couldn't go at all. It'd probably be better if he just went to the boat and found out for himself.

He turned and grabbed his snorkel and mask from the back of the booth and headed straightaway for slip number nine. There he found Lucas busy at work on the boat but he was alone. Gavin was nowhere in sight. More surprisingly, the dock and the deck were devoid of passengers looking forward to their chance to swim with the fishes.

Lucas turned to pick up another one of the ice chests stacked on the plank and waiting to be loaded onboard. With one foot on deck and the other on the dock, he glanced up at Suah.

"Not today…sorry," he explained. "I have a charter."

Suah didn't understand. "Is the boat going out?"

Lucas stopped only to answer but then decided to take a break. "Yeah, it's going out but it's reserved."

Interested, Suah stood his ground. "What's a charter."

"It's when a person or a group or family hires the boat for the day, just for themselves and no one else."

Suah was amazed. "The whole boat for one person?"

Lucas took off his gloves and took a couple steps to stand next to Suah.

"That's right. One person. This guy is rich and famous and he's got the boat all to himself and his family—all day. Nobody else gets to go."

"Not even Gavin?"

"He wants a small crew, so…not even Gavin."

"He's famous? Who is he?"

"I can't tell you that. He doesn't want a lot of people to know."

"Why?"

"I guess he wants peace and quiet."

"That's easy if he's the only one on the boat."

"He doesn't want a lot of commotion coming or going either."

"So where are you taking the boat?"

"Oh, we're going farther out, across to one of the other islands, to another spot for good snorkeling. It should be private. No one takes the trouble to go way over there."

"Whoa!" gushed Suah. "All the way to another island."

"It's not like anything is happening there. The island's deserted."

"Nobody lives there?"

Lucas put his gloves back on. "Nothing but birds and lizards."

Suah gazed out to sea. "That sounds far away."

"Yeah…" Lucas started loading the rest of the supplies. "That's the idea."

At the end of the seawall, a black town car appeared. It turned towards the boats at dock and slowly made its way past the higher number berths.

From the front passenger seat, a girl's voice called out, "Which one is it?"

Settled in next to his wife Claire in the back seat, Jaxon Muse dipped his head to have a look out the tinted windows. "It's slip number nine."

"Which one is that?" The question was loaded with teenage flippancy.

"I think we're about to find out," answered Jaxon, unruffled.

The girl rolled her eyes. "Well yeah, I guess so."

Claire spoke up but sounded tired. "Hailey, give it a rest."

Jaxon leaned into her. "You doing OK?"

Claire nodded and braved a smile. "Sure, just a little drowsy. You know how I get, driving in the back seat of cars."

Jaxon held her hand and squeezed it. It was brave of her to come along despite the effects of the chemo. Her courage brought to mind one of his seminars and something he always reminded his audiences. It wasn't enough to want the life you deserved; you had to live the life you wanted.

"The day is ours," he reminded her with a kiss on the cheek.

"Let's do it." She bravely squeezed his hand back and thought of something that would make him feel better. "I'm living proof of one thing you kept saying in your new book."

"What's that?"

"When you really live in the moment, life is too short for anything less."

"You know, I'm going to have to get you up on stage with me."

"Oh no," Claire chuckled, pulling away. "None of that…"

The driver stopped the car at slip number nine and got out to open the rear door for Mr. and Mrs. Muse. Lucas was watching for them but his attention was drawn somewhere else.

Sixteen-year-old Hailey was first to get out; she didn't need anyone to open the door for her. She sized up the catamaran with her carry-on tote slung over one shoulder and a beach cover-up hinting at a bright green bikini underneath. Her raven black hair was cut dead even across her shoulders and she donned sunglasses as if she had an endless prescription refill on cool.

She strolled up to the dock where Lucas waited.

"Welcome aboard," he smiled.

Hailey struggled to smile then pulled it back. "Does this boat have boom netting?"

"Ah, no," admitted Lucas. "Just the regular netting across the bow."

Hailey sighed. "Is there any way to rig it up?"

Lucas gave her a shake of his head. "Sorry, not without more notice."

Right behind Hailey came Jaxon and Claire. Grateful for the diversion, Lucas turned his attention to the one person who was paying for the charter.

Lucas extended his hand in welcome. "Mr. Muse, welcome aboard."

Jaxon Muse shook his hand then turned back to introduce Claire.

"And this is my wife Claire."

Lucas bowed slightly. "Pleased to meet you."

Claire smiled and held her hat on with one hand while offering the other hand to get help stepping onto the boat.

"And it looks like you've met my daughter Hailey," added Jaxon.

"Yes, sir." Lucas welcomed her onboard while sizing them all up.

As a family, when one discounted the snazzier clothes and the fancy-car arrival, they didn't seem any different than the regular troupe of tourists that came and went each day. Lucas' first impression was typical. The parents held their posture and the teenager had an attitude. What was new about that?

Lucas had heard all about the famous Mr. Muse from his wife Molly. She was on a self-improvement kick and had read a couple of his books and watched one of his TV specials. From the way she talked about his stuff, Lucas half expected to have to bow and genuflect to some New Age Buddha. It was a relief that so far the man appeared to be a regular guy.

Jaxon Muse had a worldwide reputation as motivational guru and spiritual adviser. He was a man of wit and intelligence and endless positive energy for all things that made people successful at being the best of who they were.

He was clearly intent on living what he preached. He took good care of himself for a man sailing through his late fifties. Trim and tanned, he had long since given up on the vanity of dying his hair. He now kept a ring of silver closely cropped to his head above the ears. To some of his fans, no doubt, it must have seemed like a halo.

He was clean-shaven and looked better that way. He had made the switch not long after a new beard on the dust-cover photo of his last book garnered snarky reviews. Some egghead journalists thought it'd be fun to deflate the rarified air around the hallowed man of everything *genuine* and *actualized*. Little did they know what a sensitive spot they had hit.

Success, it seemed, even for a man who had wisdom to spare for every-one, could still be a challenge at times. News that his wife Claire had been stricken with a rare form of cancer came as an especially hard blow. Not only did he have to contend with what it meant to his relationship and family, it had to be extra difficult knowing that everyone would be watching to see how the man who had endless advice for everyone else would follow his own positive path.

Claire, through all of it, had retained her grace and charm. She had always been something of a transcendent woman, preserving enough of her privacy and all of her dignity in the face of constant media interest and scrutiny.

It was no secret; she was the bedrock that held together the Muse dynasty.

She was the one who kept Jaxon grounded and on course. Only she could tell him the truth about himself and have him not only listen but act on it.

The thought of losing her must have shaken Jaxon's worldview to the core. No wonder everyone was curious if he would manage to save himself. Could he not only survive losing her but then find a way of living out the bright and simple principles so beautifully described by his philosophy?

If he could, he would personify the single most important validation of his many books and seminars, bar none. If there was anyone who ever needed to take his own advice, the world knew it was Jaxon Muse.

As Hailey toured the boat, Claire found a comfortable spot out of the sun to settle into. Standing off to one side, Jaxon and Lucas bonded as shipmates, trading questions and answers in setup for the day's adventure.

Jaxon stood in shorts and collared shirt. "I just want to take it easy; take our time. No rush, let's enjoy the day."

"Sounds good," Lucas confirmed. "Are you more interested in cruising or snorkeling?"

"Claire and I just want to get out and tour around one or two of the other islands. Hailey is the one who wants to snorkel so if you know some good spots, we should definitely spend half of the time at anchor doing that."

"Great," confirmed Lucas. "I have a couple places in mind…"

Jaxon interrupted with a tilt of his head, "Do you know him?"

Lucas turned to look and spotted Suah standing back from the dock. His undivided interest was on the preparations for getting underway.

"Sure, he's just a local boy who likes watching the boats."

Jaxon's brow furrowed. "Then why is he holding a snorkel and mask?"

"He's kinda different, if you know what I mean," chuckled Lucas.

"You mean…special?"

"Oh, you know, sort of an odd duck. But he's a good kid."

"So why does he walk around with the gear?"

"That's kinda funny," admitted Lucas. "I've never seen him without it. People tell me he carries it all around town."

"Does he ever ride on the boats?"

Lucas tried shifting cargo in hopes of diverting attention away from an interruption he'd rather not have as a complication. "Sometimes he rides on regular runs."

"On this boat?"

"Yeah, but it's no problem. I told him the boat is chartered for the day."

"It looks like he expected to go along with us…"

"He never knows if he can go until he gets here. It's a hit or miss thing."

"Hmmm…" Jaxon thought about it. "It's a shame to disappoint him. The boat is large enough for fifty people."

"And that's exactly what he likes. He likes people-watching so today wouldn't be much fun for him anyway."

"Oh, I don't know," smiled Jaxon. "I've read in many publications that watching the Muse family can be *quite* entertaining."

Lucas gave a nervous laugh. "I wouldn't know about that…"

Jaxon felt a surge of optimism. He loved finding chances, wherever they might be, to act out in a charitable and egalitarian way.

He slapped Lucas' arm. "Go tell him he can come along."

Lucas hesitated. "Are you sure? We're gonna be gone all day…"

Jaxon turned and stepped back to Claire. "Honey, there's a boy over there who was expecting to ride on this boat today. I say we should let him. What do you think?"

Claire offered an easygoing smile. "Why not. It's not like it's cramped in here." She looked to Lucas, "Are you sure it's OK with his parents?"

Jaxon turned to Lucas for confirmation.

Never one to argue with a man who paid for a rare, all-day charter, Lucas resigned to telling the truth. "It's never been a problem any other day."

Jaxon brightened up even more. "Then that settles it. Go get him!"

Suah had met a lot of rich and famous people in the last four years living with Gianna Chase, but he didn't recognize anyone on Lucas' boat. Any one of the three passengers on board could be famous. Perhaps they *all* were. Maybe they were the first family to go into space together or something equally out of this world.

Suah stood back, content to find out what a boat charter looked like. After three days of the boat being stuffed with happy wanderers, it was peculiar watching such a large catamaran getting ready to cast off lines with hardly anyone aboard. Even more perplexing, why was Lucas getting off the boat?

Lucas walked up to him. "It's your lucky day, kid. You can come along."

"On the charter?" Suah felt he was being invited into a private world.

Lucas gave him a pat on the back. "Yeah, come on, let's go."

Suah didn't need a second invitation. He made strides for the dock and like the regular passenger he was, climbed right aboard.

Jaxon Muse was there to greet him. "Hello there, welcome. My name is Jaxon. What's yours?"

Suah stood in a respectful place not far from his first steps on deck. If a charter meant that the whole boat was reserved by the famous man, then it was anyone's guess where Suah could sit or even stand.

"Suah," he answered.

"Well, Suah, we're going take a cruise around an island or two, do some snorkeling. We'll be out most of the day; is that something you'd like to do?"

Suah's nod came with a caveat. "I have to be back by four."

Jaxon glanced at Lucas. "That's perfect. We're planning on being back about 3:30. When things are right they work out, don't you think?"

Suah nodded and looked around. His eyes stopped on the woman resting in the cabin.

Jaxon turned to her. "That's my wife, Claire."

She waved and smiled. "Hello, Suah."

He raised his hand and wiggled his fingers. "Hi."

Jaxon turned the other way. "And my daughter Hailey is around here somewhere. She's probably found a place to work on her tan up by the bow."

"Is that your whole family?" asked Suah.

"Not quite," admitted Jaxon before he grinned. "We had to leave Shiva at home. Shiva is the family cat. He hates water so a boat ride might be considered cruel and unusual punishment for all the little claw marks he's made in our dining room table."

"I like his name."

"It fits him. He's a little destroyer."

"He's also a creator, preserver, concealer, and revealer."

Jaxon was taken aback. "Are you Hindu?"

"No. Is Shiva?"

The question was a surprise. Jaxon couldn't believe the little boy actually intended a philosophical double entendre. Then again, Suah had asked it with such conviction, it was puzzling. Jaxon saw the issue two ways and smiled.

"That's a good question…"

"Where can I sit?" asked Suah.

"Anywhere you like." Jaxon swept his arm around.

Lucas added, "I'll have food and drink set up after we get underway."

"I'm curious," added Jaxon. "Where did you learn about the nature of Shiva?"

Suah crossed to his favorite seat and sat down. "At home."

"Your parents taught you…"

"No. I saw it on TV."

CHAPTER 13

Half an hour into an all-day cruise and Jaxon Muse thought he'd be relaxing. Too restless to focus on any one thing for long, he lowered binoculars to his side then crossed the deck to hand them to Suah.

"Would you like to take a look?"

Suah brightened as he took them. "Thanks. Did you find anything?"

"No…" Jaxon gazed back out to sea. "Wasn't really looking for anything. I just like seeing what's out there."

"Me too," agreed Suah. "It's always the same but always different."

"Like a lot of other things," murmured Jaxon.

Suah adjusted the focusing wheel. "These are heavy…"

"I had a pair of binoculars as a kid," shared Jaxon. "At the time I thought they were the most amazing thing. I couldn't figure out how a couple pieces of glass could bring far away things so near."

Suah stared down at the lens. "Yeah, it really reaches far. Way out there."

"The way it works seemed too simple to be real." Jaxon's mind wandered.

"It's like being here and there at the same time."

Jaxon chuckled. "And that's hard to do."

Suah pulled the binoculars up to his eyes. "I know…*I know*."

Jaxon strolled back into the cabin and sat down next to Claire.

"He's an interesting boy."

Claire watched Suah observe a distant shore. "He sure isn't a rabble rouser. He hasn't moved from that seat since we left."

"Yeah, well, Lucas said something about him being *different*."

"You mean…" Claire's inference trailed off.

"Maybe so."

"If that's true, I wonder why he's allowed to wander around by himself."

Always the optimist, Jaxon struck a more comfortable pose. "I wouldn't worry about it. He seems to know people down at the docks and in town who watch out for him. It's probably like an extended family."

"All the same," countered Claire, "letting *any* child wander around town by himself is questionable."

"He likes watching the boats. Who says he wanders around town?"

"You said people in town watch out for him."

"People in general. I didn't mean all over town."

"It still strikes me as odd. He's out here with us but do his parents know?"

"Lucas said he gets rides on boats all the time. It's no big deal."

The stress of feeling bad was wearing nerves thin. Claire tensed.

"Pardon me, but I don't like my concerns discounted."

"Who's discounting them?"

"All worries are not the ridiculous yammerings of lost souls who don't know any better. Kneejerk positivity is just as deluded as anything else."

"Why are you getting upset? I asked you what you thought of bringing him onboard and you said 'why not.'"

"I also asked about his parents." Claire blinked and held her eyes closed as she sighed.

Jaxon rested a comforting hand on her knee. Her doctors had told him the pain and where it was located in her brain might cause uncharacteristic mood swings. If anything, the energy behind them only proved how hard she was fighting against the disease as it advanced.

"There's no sense arguing about this; he's with us now."

Claire reacted to his touch. "I don't intend on arguing about it. Who would ever dare argue with you." She forced a calming breath.

"What does that mean?"

"You know very well. You are a wonderful man but you can also be insufferable. Sometimes there's nothing as aggravating as living with a man who makes his living dispensing wisdom."

Jaxon grinned and leaned into her. "Since when have you ever listened to anything I said."

"I don't have to. If I have any doubts about the right thing to do, I can read it in one of your books."

He smoothed back her hair. "So what's the right thing to do now?"

She smoldered a moment then melted. "I suppose I should kiss you."

Jaxon let a look of wonder pass his face. "My, how wise you are."

She smiled and they pressed lips together, if only briefly. She reminded him, "Our very first kiss was after a boat ride."

Jaxon thought back and took issue with her. "That wasn't a boat ride; that was a near-death experience."

"Why did you ever pick whitewater rafting for a date?" she laughed.

"Rehearsing for the ups and downs of life, I suppose."

"You were so funny…"

Jaxon reminisced. "You saved the day with that ridiculous song of yours."

"It's *not* ridiculous! I sang that song as a Girl Scout. It's a perfectly good song. It got us laughing, you have to admit that."

"Oh yeah, it got our minds off the fact that we were going to die!"

"It wasn't that bad; it only seemed so at the time. I bet you don't remember the whole thing."

"Why would I?" asked Jaxon.

"It's fun. Come on, sing it with me."

"Oh, no. Not that."

"I'll give you another kiss if you do…"

Jaxon thought back. "You mean just like that day, up on the bank?"

"Even better," promised Claire.

"OK. You begin…"

Claire gathered her strength and put her arm around Jaxon. Looking out to sea, she started to sing softly. As she sang, Jaxon joined in.

"Did you ever see a fishie on a hot summer day?
Did you ever see a fishie out swimming in the bay?
With his hands in his pockets and his pockets in his pants.
Did you ever see a fishie do a hoochie-coochie dance?"

Claire waited for Jaxon to solo the end of the refrain.

"You never did - you never will!"

Jaxon turned to her. "OK, time for that kiss."

She held her fingers against his lips. "Not so fast! Second verse…*not* the same as the first!" Again she started to sing with Jaxon joining in.

"Did you ever see a fishie on a cold winter day?
Did you ever see a fishie out frozen in the bay?
With his hands in his pockets and his pockets in his pants.
Did you ever see a fishie do a hoochie-coochie dance?"

This time, Jaxon waited for Claire to be the one to solo.

"You never did - you never will!"

Jaxon could wait no more. He leaned in and claimed his kiss.

Just then, Hailey came bounding around the corner from the bow. Her ponytail jostled from a bedazzled baseball cap. The few parts of her not covered by a lime-green bikini were slathered with low SPF sunscreen.

"Geez," she moaned. "Already with the PDAs?"

"OMG back at ya," quipped Jaxon.

"Don't bother. So what's there to drink?" She perused the offerings, pausing near the beer and wine but reaching for a soda.

"How's life on the other side of the boat?" asked Jaxon.

Hailey sidestepped from beverages to food. "It could be better. This thing could have a boom net."

"We're going too fast to get towed through the water."

"He could slow down." Hailey glanced back at Suah and frowned. "What's with the kid? Did you put him in time-out or something?"

"No, he just likes that spot."

She grimaced. "Apparently."

As Hailey moved around the food table, the back of her came into view. Always one to push the limits of what was acceptable, she wore her bikini bottoms as low as she could. She said it eliminated tan lines for when she wore her low-slung pants.

Jaxon was used to her testing his nonjudgmental, enlightened view of life. He even expected some rebellion out of her but he wasn't prepared for the severity and form it had taken this past year. She had started acting as if establishing her own identity meant rejecting everything positive and affirming in the messages he gave to the world in his daily work.

Jaxon was optimistic enough to believe that every life had a way of working itself out. With Hailey, he was prepared to show by example and not press her too much. But something new at the middle of her bikini briefs in back was pushing it.

"Is that a tattoo I see…?" asked Jaxon.

Hailey feigned an air of scandal. "Why are *you* even looking *there*?"

"You know very well why. What did we say about tattoos?"

Lifting a sandwich wedge in hand, she worked hard at making light of the topic. "We said it was probably better to wait a few years to make sure it was something I really wanted to do."

"So what happened?"

She shrugged and bit off enough to chew and still talk. "The whole idea of *probably* seemed so uncertain. I *know* I like it so why not?"

Jaxon looked to Claire. "Did you know about this?"

Claire shook her head. She was more disgusted than angry.

"Is that thing permanent?" asked Jaxon.

"You taught me nothing in the world is permanent."

"Can you wash it off?" he persisted.

"It would take a lot of rubbing."

"How much?"

"Let's just say it would be considered physical abuse." The corners of Hailey's mouth curled into a grin, one she turned away from view.

Jaxon waved his hand. "Come over here; I want to look at it."

From a distance, Suah watched the confrontation between father and daughter. He was glad he was alone with his ocean view.

Hailey stepped on over and turned around. Jaxon could see that the small tattoo was comprised of two oriental characters centered at the spot where her butt cheeks began to diverge.

"What are they? Chinese?"

"Yes," confirmed Hailey

"What do they say?"

Before Hailey could answer, Claire answered for her with a sigh.

"It says *perfect*."

"Really," snapped Jaxon. "Is that something you're striving for or do you think you've already attained it?"

Hailey was coy. "I don't know; I've been told *parts* of me are perfect."

"Perfect for what?" Jaxon's insinuation was as frank as Hailey's attitude.

"Perfect for what God intended." Her voice was gentle; the intent anything but. Anyway she could, she would find a way to twist objections to her behavior straight to the heart of everything free and natural.

To call her out too much on anything would be turned into an indictment of enlightenment. Victorian-style discipline was caught in a double-bind. Not invoking parental authority was surrender but applying it would come across as nothing more than remnants of ego-greed, a desire for power, or clueless illusion. In other words, why go there and gather such bad karma?

Jaxon settled back. "Is that the only one or do you have more?"

Hailey stepped back to the beverage table. "That's it. Honest."

"Would you tell me if it wasn't?"

Hailey rolled her eyes. "It's not like you won't find out. The next time we go to that nudist resort, you can do an inspection and see for yourself."

"It'd rather hear it from you."

Hailey turned to Claire. "Mom, do something."

"Don't look at me. I'm disappointed too." Claire shook her head.

Hailey picked at her lower lip. "Why are you guys freaking on this? The thing is so little. No one will even see it most of the time?"

Claire leaned forward. "We're just surprised, that's all. You should have told us. Parading it in front of us was just asking for an argument. Well, you got the argument you wanted. Now it's over."

Jaxon stood and stepped to the food table. "Your mom's right. If you wanted a reaction, you got it. Now I'm going to have one of these sandwiches."

With the turmoil suddenly diffused, Hailey turned on heel, grabbing food and drink, and headed back to the bow of the boat.

Aware of what was going on, Suah glanced over and watched as father and daughter parted ways. It was interesting how their argument wound up on the word *perfect*. Someone so rich and famous as Jaxon Muse might be thought to have the perfect life. Suah sat baffled.

Perfect must be a sporadic thing, like sun breaks on a mostly cloudy day. That might explain how so much around the edges could remain so flawed within a perfect life. It reminded Suah of how his mother Gianna had been so sad and anxious on the night before she left on tour. Despite her wealth and all of the fans who loved her, the perfect mom hadn't been happy.

A little while later, Lucas slowed the boat as they approached the other island. Jaxon and Claire came out on the aft deck to get an unobstructed view. For the next hour, they were treated to a cruise close in to shore.

Suah watched the waves crashing on the rocks and became curious. He got up and padded his way into the cabin and up to the helm where Lucas was at the wheel with his daydreaming on autopilot.

"Well, hello there," Lucas greeted him. "What's up?"

Suah looked up at him more serious than anyone had a right to be on a pleasure cruise. "How do you know how close you can go?"

"How close to the beach?"

Suah nodded. "There's lots of rocks."

"There's no secret to it," boasted Lucas. "I know because I have lots of experience…" He paused to sucker Suah in, then pointed at an indicator on the instrument panel. "…and because I have this little gizmo right here."

"What does it do?" Suah craned his neck to see it more clearly.

"It tells me how far down the bottom is."

"How does it do that?"

"It shoots a signal down through the water. When the signal bounces back, this thing measures how far it went."

Suah was amazed. "Wow. It's like riding on a boat…"

"A boat?" puzzled Lucas.

"Yeah, a boat brings far places near by going out and touching them."

"Yeah, I guess you could say that."

Suah pointed. "So that thing says how *far away* the bottom is."

"That's right."

Suah laughed. "It'd be funny if you had to have another one of those things to tell you how *near* the bottom is."

Lucas half-grinned at the silliness. "I could do that—but I'd only have to look at one of them."

"Why is that?" An unsure curiosity replaced Suah's smile.

Indulgent of the boy's specialness, a patient Lucas wasn't annoyed to explain. "Because both of them would say the same thing."

"That's right..." Suah's head leaned back as his eyes widened. "Wow. You just made near and far the same thing."

"Something like that..."

The revelation was flush on Suah's face. "I can't wait to tell Hawa."

"A friend of yours?" Lucas expected an elaborate description but only got a nod. He decided to move on to another topic, something that might amuse and divert the boy. "You like turtles?"

Suah's eyes brightened. "Sure."

"Well, all along this side of the island, turtles like to come in and feed along the reef. If you're lucky, you might be able to see some."

"From here?"

"Anywhere around the boat; just look down in the water." Worried about the boy leaning over the side and falling in, Lucas pointed to the bow. "The netting is a good place to get a straight-down look at things."

"OK, that sounds like a fun adventure." Suah scampered off.

Lucas called after him. "No running! Bad things happen when you run on a boat." Suah skidded to a halt then inched away. Lucas grinned and returned to his duties on autopilot.

Just going to the front of the catamaran was a new exploration for Suah. On all the snorkel trips he had been on before, never once had he left the back of the boat. Even if he didn't see a turtle, just being on the netting was going to be a great new experience.

Carefully, he navigated up the port side of the boat where it narrowed. His imagination was running wild with what the turtles would look like if he was lucky enough to see one. He had forgotten all about the fact that Hailey had carved out the front of the boat as her special space to luxuriate.

Emerging onto the bow, Suah froze at the sight of Hailey lying on her stomach with music earbuds in her ears. She had spread a towel out over the starboard half of the netting and had untied her bikini top to get an even tan on her back. Suah didn't want to disturb her since she looked asleep.

But he also didn't want to miss his chance to see the turtles.

Cautiously, he crept forward. With all the stealth in him, he concentrated on claiming the other side of the netting as a turtle-watching spot. Careful in the extreme, it took him nearly five minutes to progress a dozen steps to the net and then settle down in a prone position ready to see the live aquatic show. Hailey's head was pointed towards the cabin; his head was pointed out to sea. When he turned his head, he could see the bottoms of her feet.

Once in place, the excitement of being on the net and seeing the ocean rushing by below him was enough to put Hailey completely out of his mind. The view from the net was unlike anything he had ever imagined. The water was clear and the variety of colors flashing here and there was amazing.

For several minutes he tried not to blink, determined not to miss a thing. Outcrops of coral and rippling patterns in the sandy bottom were backdrops for an occasional fish wiggling by. Sometimes there were tall stalks of wavy seaweed to look at; other times the bottom dropped far away and the depths were swallowed up by blackness. The view, always the same but always different, eventually lulled him into a hopeful trance, one that expected to see a turtle any second.

"Oh my God! Geez!"

The shout from Hailey startled Suah with a stroke of fear. Not knowing what had happened, he recoiled onto his side and looked back.

"When did *you* get here?" With one earbud dangling, Hailey was up on her elbows, her shoulder twisted back so she could see him. "Don't you know better than to sneak up on people?"

Suah said nothing. He had learned from enough time with Blake that a workable survival skill when faced with aggressively angry people was to simply say and do nothing.

Suffering her own effects from being startled, Hailey took a moment to get her bearings and repositioned herself. She seemed not at all concerned that raising up and moving around had exposed her breasts. She had come from a progressive family who never cast aspersions on nudity.

Occasional family jaunts to a favorite off-shore nudist resort had embraced the idea of baring it all. Still, Jaxon and Claire tried to ingrain in her an understanding of the practical and cultural limits of its expression.

Those limits, when defined as such, could be yet another piece of the parental structure she needed to test by rebelling against.

Turning around and sitting up, she began to reapply sunscreen.

Certain social situations were never great for Suah. It was hard to know what people expected or what he should expect from them. Most times when he felt lost in how to act around people, he withdrew and became quiet and locked in place. This was one of those times. He didn't want to provoke Hailey any more than he had. But he also didn't want to miss the turtles.

Hailey suffered him in place until she could no longer ignore him. "What are you looking at? Haven't you ever seen breasts before?"

Suah nodded.

"Really, where?" Alternating the lift of her arms, she stroked lotion across the ribcage and over the side of each breast for effect.

Suah had to think; he had been to a lot of places either on tour with Gianna or on vacations with her. Certain beaches had been clothing optional.

He thought out loud, "France...Jamaica...Mexico."

"Oh yeah, I'm sure." After a mocking laugh, Hailey plugged her earbuds back in, turned over onto her stomach and settled back in place.

Suah breathed a sigh of relief. Not being believed was not so bad if the crisis was over and he could go back to his search for turtles. Shifting in place, he pressed his face against the netting. The watery world passed by.

It wasn't long before it became obvious that the boat was slowing. The slowing was gradual but steady. Suah raised up as Lucas dropped anchor.

From the back of the boat, Lucas called out a loud, singsong announcement. "Snorkel time!"

Suah sat up, as did Hailey. When he turned around, she began to laugh.

Not knowing what was so funny, Suah froze. He wasn't sure but, by the way she was acting, the source of the humor was him.

She spoke to his puzzled face. "You want to know what's so funny?"

He nodded.

"Too bad I don't have a mirror."

Suah's hand smoothed his left and right cheek. He felt fine. Whatever it was that had tickled Hailey into a good mood was fine with him.

The fact that she could finally get in the water also helped brighten her disposition. She grabbed a snorkel and mask out of her carry-on tote and bounded up and off the bow and into the ocean.

Suah was left to wonder what her reaction was all about. He looked down across the beach towel she had left behind. Only her bikini top remained as a clue but that was no clue at all.

Suah stood and made his way back to the front of the cabin. There he caught a glimpse of himself in the reflection of the cabin window. Right away, the secret was out and a smile burst onto his face. It was a face covered with small diamond-shaped impressions from where he had leaned against the netting. It was quite a different look for him. One that was fun while it lasted; he just hoped it wouldn't be permanent. Not like a tattoo.

With Hailey in the water, the voyage took on familiar overtones for Suah. He could now watch the snorkeler explore around the boat, just as he had done on every boat ride before. It'd be different having only one person in the water to watch but he was OK with that. Person-watching was still people-watching.

As Hailey swam out and then back towards the stern of the boat, Suah followed along. Working his way back down the side of the boat, he crossed the aft deck where Jaxon and Claire were sitting out enjoying themselves.

"Hey Suah," Jaxon called out. "Why aren't *you* in the water?"

Suah looked back from the side of the boat and just shook his head.

Standing nearby, Lucas drew Jaxon's attention, "He never goes in. He likes to watch."

"Watch what?" asked Jaxon. "What about watching the fish?"

Lucas shrugged as Claire got up and made her way over to Suah's side. Standing next to him, she looked out to find the whereabouts of Hailey. The teenager was quite a ways off, circling some underwater feature.

"Can you swim?" asked Claire. After Suah's nod, she prompted, "It might be fun to go in."

Suah gave her a glance but nothing more.

Gently, she pursued the topic. "You might even see a turtle."

That got a jerk of the head. Suah looked back at her and thought about it. The day was such a big adventure, perhaps he should try something new. One thought later, his burst of excitement deflated.

"I don't have a swimsuit."

"Oh, I see…," hesitated Claire.

Jaxon stepped up. "What are you two talking about?"

"He doesn't have a suit."

Jaxon thought a second then asked Suah, "Are you wearing underwear?"

Suah nodded.

"OK, there you go. That's like a suit," concluded Jaxon. He walked over and fetched a can of compressed air from his bag. Looking up at Lucas, he explained, "It's our signal to Hailey. It's the only way we can get her out of the water."

Jaxon sounded the horn. In the distance, Hailey popped up her head and started swimming back to the boat. Jaxon retreated to the cabin and sat back down. He spoke to Claire. "Just tell her to watch him out there. We don't know what kind of swimmer he is."

Claire turned back to Suah and helped him lift off his T-shirt. Stepping out of his pants, he stood in boxer shorts then stepped over to the seat where he had left his snorkel and mask. He stared at them awhile, a little nervous. After carrying them around for days, he was finally going to use them.

Claire turned to the water and called out to Hailey as she swam up to the boat. "Suah's coming in. Help him get started. Keep an eye on him."

Hailey frowned. Watching out for some stranger kid in the water was not her idea of a good time. "If he can't do it he'll have to get out," she warned.

Claire nodded and helped Suah down the access steps that led to the water. Hailey quickly told him what to do with the snorkel and mask. Suah hesitated on the bottom step. Holding his breath out of excitement much more than needing air, he leaned forward and settled into the water.

Claire watched as he followed instructions and began putting his face down and snorkel up. In no time at all he was swimming away at Hailey's side. As they went, a salient fact suddenly dawned on Claire. She turned, walked back to her seat next to Jaxon, and sat down.

"There's one thing we didn't notice…" she began.

Jaxon looked over at her, waiting for the other shoe to drop.

She heaved a sigh. "Hailey isn't wearing her top."

Jaxon could only smile and shake his head. He pushed up from the chair.

"Where are you going," asked Claire.

He shuffled to the beverage table. "You want some wine?"

Suah was no longer in between worlds. With only the sky above him, a whole new churning world with overpowering sights and sensations engulfed him. He was part of it and an alien all at once. He moved through a new kind of space but also in a new way. This was space he could float through and floating gave it a timeless sense of rapture.

If the wonder of feeling the tide lift and move him sideways wasn't enough—if the colorful spectacle of following fish as they glided through dazzling coral wasn't enough—then it was the angelic form who was his guide that electrified him with a sense of make-believe. It was as if a rare and wondrous sprite was flying him through a wishful daydream.

It didn't matter what Hailey thought of him tagging along. Her very form, moving through the water, appeared as a spirit of nature. Her lithe and agile body glided through the sunrays penetrating the water. Flowing forward, her smooth lines defined a vision of beauty, of life itself, let out to play. This was people-watching on a whole new level, an active level that came alive.

It didn't take long before both of them relaxed into the flow and let their explorations become spontaneous. With the fish showing the way, at times the adventure even became playful.

Suah found it interesting that Hailey's demeanor had changed once she was out by herself, exploring the water. There was a lightness, a glow to her essence that fostered a forgetfulness of self and everything that defined her world. It was as if a burden had been lifted. No longer was she caught between who she was and what was happening to her. The enjoyment of the moment was enough to transcend them both.

Suah lost track of time. So did Hailey. Discovering he was a good swimmer and not a chore had done wonders in putting to rest any dread and loathing she might have had.

Close to an hour passed before their burst of energy was spent. Treading water, Hailey called out, "Don't tell me you haven't done this before."

"I usually swim in the pool." He blew water out of his snorkel.

Hailey had a sly grin. "You're like a fish."

Suah caught his breath. "If I'm a fish, then you're a mermaid."

She laughed and swam back to the boat. Suah followed.

As Hailey stepped up on deck, Lucas tried not to stare. It wasn't every day that one of his passengers went topless. Even if they had, he'd never expect such nonchalance about it—especially with parents relaxing nearby.

At the steps, Jaxon helped Suah up. "So what'd you see down there?"

Suah was out of breath but managed to exclaim, "Lots and lots of joy!"

CHAPTER 14

Lucas took another look through the binoculars. "Mr. Muse, we may have a problem." It had been a long day, a full day, but even so, they were headed back into port a little early. By request.

Jaxon was well-versed in all the necessary precautions a celebrity should take. Announcing one schedule and keeping another was the easiest way to interject chaos into the plans of paparazzi and ardent fans who liked nothing better than to intercept, delay, or otherwise be a bother. Without having to ask, Jaxon suspected what Lucas had already found.

Jaxon walked up alongside him. "I thought coming back half an hour early would be enough. How many are there?"

"Twenty, maybe thirty. It's hard to tell."

"Can I see?" Lucas handed over the binoculars. "Well, it can't be helped," concluded Jaxon. "Unless you can launch a submarine with a team of Navy Seals, I don't see any way to sneak ashore."

"What about your town car?" asked Lucas.

"I called ahead. He'll be there."

"Maybe that's what attracted them," quipped Lucas.

Jaxon was inclined to agree with the sarcasm. "If so, I wonder how much the driver got for leaking the news."

Trying to be creative, Lucas offered a suggestion. "I'll go along if you want to pretend something's urgent and you've got to take off quick."

Jaxon pursed his lips and shook his head. "No, that would only start rumors that wouldn't be true. It's OK…" Jaxon smiled. "If this is the biggest problem I face today, I'm leading a charmed life."

Claire came to his side and snuggled against his arm. "What is it, honey?"

"The word has gotten out. We'll have company at the dock."

Gazing towards port, her eyes had a far away look. "I hope it's fans and not the media."

"Hard to tell. Either way, you and Hailey go to the car. I'll deal with it."

The mention of Hailey reminded her of another concern. "There's something you should know."

Jaxon waited, expecting Lucas to step away and give them privacy but it didn't happen. Claire glanced back, checking on Hailey and Suah. They were back in the cabin, out of earshot.

Claire continued, "Empty beer cans were found…"

"I found four cans in the trash, in the head." Lucas didn't like being in this position but felt he owed it to the Muses to let them know what was going on.

"I take it none of us put them in there." Jaxon was vexed and grasped at the last straw. "What about Suah?"

Claire shook her head. "It's on her breath."

Jaxon sucked in air and looked to the distant hills. "What next?"

"We don't want a scene," coaxed Claire.

"Agreed," snapped Jaxon. "We say nothing now. Heaven forbid we give her an excuse."

"What do you mean?"

"I think it's at the point where she may be willing to embarrass us."

Jaxon looked back into the cabin. Hailey and Suah were talking and laughing. Her level of amusement with such a boy was out of character. It didn't take a trained eye to suspect that inebriation was involved.

Claire was all about defusing the situation any way she could. "Once we're home, we can talk to her. *I'll* talk to her."

"Be my guest, but that's not the problem." Jaxon flipped a hand towards shore. "We can't predict what she'll say or do between the boat and the car."

Lucas felt empowered to give his opinion. "The way she's acted today, it wouldn't take much to set her off."

Jaxon handed the binoculars back to him. "Then we'll have to do something to upstage her, won't we."

"Like what?" asked Claire.

"I don't know. I'll be extra loud and happy with the fans…"

"What about the boy," suggested Lucas.

"What about him?" countered Jaxon.

"Playing up the fact that he's with you might draw people's attention."

"No," said Jaxon, flatly. "He's not a part of this. I won't make him one. I'll call ahead and have the driver meet us right at the boat. You and he can run interference while I do my best to make a scene." He looked to Claire. "Like you said, let's just hope it's fans…and not reporters."

Jaxon turned and watched Hailey and Suah interact. Another oddity occurred to him. "What's going on with Suah's pants?"

Claire looked back. "Oh, he didn't wait for his boxer shorts to dry. He put his pants right back on and they got wet. That's all."

Jaxon rubbed his forehead. "That's all we need. Something else to explain away."

Over the next ten minutes, the charter boat sailed closer to shore. Jaxon watched as the harbor and its docks loomed larger. He could only hope that the minor but nagging issues of the day weren't about to do the same.

Before anyone was prepared for it, the catamaran slid into slip number nine and came to rest. A small sea of faces on dock watched with excitement and anticipation. Weaving through them, the town car driver made his way to the plank. He had been instructed to go right to Claire and start a conversation that would last until she was safely in the car.

When the time came to disembark, Lucas busied himself talking to Suah and Hailey about the trip, not letting Hailey get a word in edgewise.

Purposely standing away from the others, Jaxon smiled and waved to the delight of everyone waiting onshore. As the group led by Lucas rushed through the clutch of fans, Jaxon brought up the rear in vociferous style. He concentrated on making eye contact with those waiting and conveyed nothing but eagerness to meet them.

Hustled to the far side of the town car, Suah found himself standing back behind the action. After a rushed walk onshore, he had become a reluctant spectator. Unlike the others crowding up to get their piece of Jaxon Muse, this spectator just so happened to be holding a snorkel and mask and had pants that were marked with the outline of wet shorts underneath.

If nothing else, he had memories of a matchless day.

The town car's windows were tinted; there was no way to see if Hailey or Claire were waving goodbye. Swamped by the questions and affections of fans, Jaxon Muse was nowhere in sight. Suah had no chance to have parting words with him. The journey for Suah had ended. Return to reality was abrupt. His fairytale freefall through a marvelous day had suddenly impacted back on the asphalt of the dock's parking lot.

On the other side of the town car, one of Jaxon's fans dropped a flyer in her hurry to jockey closer to Muse. Suah could see from a distance that the paper had Jaxon's face on it. He strolled over and picked it up. It had advertisements front and back. One side explained all about a conference Jaxon was hosting. The other side had a picture of a book and a blurb telling all about it and how it was a 'must read' for everyone 'who was on the path.'

Suah backed away to a less hectic place where he could watch the action dissipate. In time, Jaxon had shaken enough hands, graciously accepted enough compliments, poised for enough photo-ops to justify a dash to the back seat of the town car.

As soon as the back door closed, the car rolled away. The great Jaxon

Muse was gone. For his fans, the magic of the moment passed like a vision of an astral projection half-remembered during a past life regression. Their giddiness abated, even if the aura of meeting the source of their life's inspiration lingered. All that remained were the docks, the boats, the lineup of booths selling slices of paradise in handy adventure packs.

Suah had only one regret. He never saw a turtle.

Turning south, he sauntered back to the booth behind *Island Aquatics & Adventures* and put his snorkel and mask back on the shelf. Brody was still absent which was all right. Suah was buzzing from a full day of splendiferous fun and wasn't much in the mood for conversation. Besides, he had something on his mind he wanted to do. He checked Blake's wristwatch; there was plenty of time before four o'clock.

Setting off across the parking lot, he headed into town.

He had walked the sidewalks of the main street enough to know right where to go. Down beyond the seawall he found a small, independent bookstore on the *mauka* or mountain side of the street. It was open for business but Suah found it quiet and mostly deserted inside.

Walking the aisles, Suah looked up and marveled at all the words compacted in such a little space. Somebody had spent a long time gathering all of this together. He saw stacks of books with photos of surfers riding monster waves. On another table, a spread of island-themed calendars tempted an impulse purchase. Prominently labeled, a spin rack of tour guides for the islands sat right out in the middle where everyone could see it.

It was hard to know how the place was organized. It certainly wasn't by book size; there were books of every size on every shelf. Suah wandered on. Maybe books that were easy to read were kept close to the end of the aisles where they'd be easy to find. It seemed to make common sense and wasn't common sense always true?

But if that was so, the book by Jaxon Muse might be up and away, back in the stacks. Figuring out how all of life and the afterlife worked wasn't easy *or* light reading. Arcane knowledge like that probably was locked away in a case. A trained attendant might have to get a special key to access it.

"May I help you?"

The voice from behind was pleasant if terse. Suah turned to find a nice older lady who was curious why a little boy with wet pants was in her store.

Suah nodded and produced the flyer with the face of Jaxon Muse on it.

"I'm trying to find this…"

The woman took the flyer in hand and glanced down through the glasses riding low on her nose. "Is this for *you*?"

Suah's nod did little to convince the woman.

"Are you sure you have the right book?" she quizzed.

Suah looked around. "He has other books but this is the one I want."

The woman was willing to play along and trotted back down the aisle. "Very well. Would you like that in hardback, paperback, or audio book?"

Suah followed. "The easiest one to carry around."

"That would be paperback." She turned down a side aisle and halted in front of shelves filled with books by Jaxon Muse. "Here they are."

Suah looked them up and down as the woman pulled a paperback in hand. To confirm the selection, she read the title from the cover.

"...*Surviving The Near-Life Experience*...by Jaxon Muse." She handed the book to him and returned the flyer as well.

Suah compared the cover on the paperback with the cover shown on the flyer. "That's it."

"Will there be anything else?" She had patience for all of this if he was serious. So far, despite his appearance, there was nothing to say he wasn't.

Suah cocked his head far to one side and tried to read a vertical sign hanging at the end of the aisle. "What is that?"

"That sign identifies the section we're in."

Suah squinted. "*Helf...Selp...*"

"This is the *Self Help* section," she corrected.

"What's that?" asked Suah.

Suah's genuineness in the way he asked spoke volumes. The woman caught on that this was a boy with special needs. With reservations about him fading, she was more willing to engage him a little while longer.

"This section is all about helping people and how they can help themselves."

"Help them do what?"

"Live their best life, achieve dreams, have better relationships, any kind of help they need."

"Are all of Jaxon's books in here?"

"Yes, Mr. Muse is well known in this section."

Flipping the flyer over, he showed her. "He's having a big meeting."

The woman leaned forward to look. "Yes, I see...that's tomorrow."

Suah kept the flyer extended before her. "Where's it gonna be?"

She looked again. "Well, let's see...it says it'll be in the convention center at *The Manuia Resort*. That's just south of town, not far from here."

At the front of the store, a telephone rang. The woman reacted. "Go ahead and look around. When you're ready, bring your book to the register."

The woman scuttled off leaving Suah to amble into the section and sit down cross-legged on the floor. Gazing up at the shelves in front of him, he took in the sight of row after row of book bindings with the name Jaxon Muse highlighted on them in bold type.

Suah was in awe. It must be quite a feeling to be able to help so many people. Jaxon Muse must be some sort of shaman, like a marabout. Suah's grandfather had tried to teach him all about those mystical holy men.

Marabouts were the ones who could cast protection spells and even bestow invisibility when it was needed. Those were the people who had secret knowledge. That awareness, coupled with their ability to relate to everything unseen, gave them special powers.

The rushed exit from the catamaran replayed in Suah's mind. No wonder so many people flocked to the docks to get a glimpse of such a man. If somehow they could learn just a fraction of what he innately understood, their lives could be so much better.

Suah gazed down and opened the paperback. A fire burned within him to know what all those words were trying to say. His eyes raced across one page, then another. He flipped through the book, trying to focus all of his attention on gleaning just one secret from its pages. The effort went on for a while but it was frustrating. His concentration and focus just didn't line up. He saw symbols, even words, but none of them translated into anything that he could even say, let alone understand.

His heart and breathing raced. Looking up from the book, he got distracted by the timepiece on his wrist. It was ten minutes to four.

And it was a long way to the food truck.

Scampering to his feet, he ran to the front of the store where he found the old lady sorting bookmarks at the counter. He slapped the paperback down in front of her. "I'll be back for this when I have money!"

He was out of breath already and hadn't even begun to run.

Before the woman could react, he was out the door in a panic. He found the sidewalks of main street clogged with shoppers and looky-loos. Running into car traffic to get around them wasn't an option so he had to bob and weave among slowpokes as he dodged elbows and cross-traffic pedestrians.

If he didn't get back to the food truck before Blake arrived to pick him up, there'd be hell to pay. He'd be the one needing some *Helf Selp*.

CHAPTER 15

Suah tore up the sidewalk and turned up a side street. It was little comfort that side street pedestrian traffic was lighter than on the main street. Late would be late no matter how many breaks he got along the way.

Rounding the last corner in a dead run, Suah sped by the food truck and searched the area. With fingers crossed, he hoped that a beat-up old Datsun would not be in view. Sweating and panting, he stood in his own dust cloud and had his hopes rewarded.

Blake was not there, although it was five minutes after four.

The hefty woman working food prep in the truck poked her head out of the pass-through window to see what was going on. Content it was just Suah acting odd again, she returned to her fryers and hummed with the radio.

Suah settled in to his regular spot for waiting. Hopefully, he'd have time to catch his breath and wipe the sweat away before Blake arrived. Suah didn't need another interrogation about what he'd been up to.

Ten minutes later Blake pulled up.

He was coming from the opposite direction he usually drove in from. He hung an arm out the window and kept the engine running.

"I don't know why they don't give you a phone," Blake complained. "Make me drive all the way down here for nothing."

Suah got up from his cross-legged seat on the ground and started towards the car. Blake had other ideas and held out his hand. "Hold up. Not so fast."

Suah froze. Variations in the routine with Blake couldn't be good news.

"It's your lucky day," sneered Blake. "Diego and Paige are going to that show he had tickets for after all. That means both of us have more free time tonight. I don't need to pick you up 'til eight o'clock. Do you know where eight o'clock is on that watch?"

Suah glanced down at the wristwatch and nodded.

"Isn't that surprising." Blake gunned the engine. "Well, I guess I'll see you then…if I remember."

Suah stood in place. "Are we going to eat?"

"Not now," snapped Blake. "I've got things to do. I'm sure you can scrounge something up. Just be back here by eight…and don't be late."

Suah watched the Datsun drive away. A change of plans like this hardly seemed like an adventure; at least not one he could feel right away. But like Brody had warned, he shouldn't think about it too much. The best things happened when you didn't try to force them.

Thoughts of Brody gave Suah an idea of where to go. Maybe Brody was working later in the day back at the booth. At least going there to check was something Suah could do to kill time.

Eight o'clock was a terribly long way away. After having such a full day out with the Muse family and searching the bookstore, he wasn't sure he had much more energy for grand quests and thrilling explorations. Then again, he had precious little choice in the matter. But he was used to that.

Taking the news in stride, Suah turned on heel and ambled away.

The walk back into town was out of place and yet too familiar, as if every step retreated deeper into déjà vu. He had just been there. But now the sun was sinking lower in the west and shadows were longer than anything Suah was used to seeing while normal explorations were underway.

Even the mood of the town was changing. The tourists looked the same but now they moved with a different purpose and cadence. Everything was less hectic, more unwound. The day people were starting to drop out of sight and night people were beginning their sensuous prowl.

The disappointment of finding Brody still missing at the booth was not completely unexpected. When things were not going one's way, the course of events could take on a momentum of its own. To reverse the tide, Suah was willing to push himself into going where he had never gone before.

Ignoring all reluctance, he walked into *Island Aquatics & Adventures*.

The shop was loaded with too many things to see. All kinds of water sports gear and other things unrecognizable to Suah surrounded him.

Right away, Molly reacted to the bell on the door and looked up.

"Suah," she called out. "What brings you here at this time of day?"

Suah took a couple steps into the store. "I'm looking for Brody Mud."

"Brody who?" Her forehead was furrowed but her mouth showed a grin.

The question made Suah freeze. He never expected that Molly wouldn't know who her own employee was.

Molly let it go. "Brody is off today, one of his rare days off. He asked for it since the boat was going out as a charter."

"Do you know where he is?"

"Beats me." Molly stepped from the counter and over to Suah. "If I had to guess, I'd say you'll find him sitting on a stool down at *Sops & Wobbers*— it's a dive bar cattycorner from the park on the water side."

"Is that his favorite place?"

"It sure is. He wastes more time down there sitting on that stool than you can shake a stick at."

Molly's colorful expressions weren't helping. "He gets paid to sit there?"

"The way he goes at it, you'd think so. If I could get paid for wasting time like him, I'd have it made."

"He must be good at it," concluded Suah.

"Well, if you're going to be good at anything, I guess it might as well be the thing you like to do. Isn't that what it's all about?"

Suah nodded, not sure if she meant what he understood. He turned to go. "Thanks, Molly."

She straightened merchandise on a rack. "If you see him, tell him Molly says to take it easy—leave some firewater for all the little devils who have to watch over him."

Suah retreated outside. He wasn't convinced he should relay a message he didn't understand. Repeating things that adults said was risky business unless you comprehended them. The way adults were, you could never be sure what you heard is what they meant. Hannah had once warned him about reading between the lines but he had enough trouble just reading the lines.

Suah remembered one time when he repeated something within earshot of a reporter that Olivia Platt had said to Gianna in private. The result was awkward for everyone even if later Gianna and Olivia thought it was funny. Once again, Suah hadn't understood why.

He headed off to find *Sops & Wobbers*. But first he got distracted by the park with the big tree. He had never been in the park right before sunset but seeing it convinced him it was a time of magic. The last light of day was shining pink-golden, transforming a common place into an enchantment.

Suah wandered around, up and down the diagonal paths that led to and from the tree trunk. He was awed by sunlight shining from a low angle through the wide branches. Many birds were flying in to roost for the night. Their motion and excited chirping provided a steady chorus to his reverie.

Finally he meandered on, farther south, out of the park. When he got to the area where Molly had told him *Sops & Wobbers* should be, he halted and stood puzzled. The idea that anyone's favorite place could possibly be in the vicinity was hard to believe. The only structure with any activity around it was a shack that appeared ready for demolition. The entrance to it was across the street from a small 19th century cemetery bordered by a low rock wall.

The shack looked like it had been dropped into place and the only thing preventing it from falling over was an old camper parked against one side. Suah crossed the street, aiming for the shack, but first he had to pass the side yard. It was a plot of grass and dirt bordered by a chain link fence.

Suah's attention was drawn to motion as he passed the yard. In the fading light of day, it was easy to wonder if he was seeing right. The motion appeared to be a mongrel dog. The dog was mid-sized and stocky and wore a hat with slits that allowed his ears to point through. It was a casual dress hat with a narrow snap brim and was worn with the comfortable look of a regular accessory. Around the dog's neck hung a real flower lei, sized perfectly.

Incongruently, the dog was hunched in profile in a classic canine pose. He was preparing to defecate. In the sky above, the clouds were turning brilliant pink and crimson in the last burst of light after sunset. The chorus of birds chirping in the park's big tree reached a crescendo. Humor and beauty and practical reality overlapped. Such a crazy mix brought a grin to Suah's face.

He shuffled to a stop at the shack's entrance and peered into the darkness. He could see people gathered around a bar by their shape and movement. The bar was lit with Christmas lights and small neon logos for liquor brands. The mirror behind the bar was festooned with life preservers of every size and variety. Laughter and a low thump of old pop music mixed with loud and opinionated cross talk. The place reeked of food, booze, and tobacco but it was the smell of fatty meat frying that attracted Suah in.

Suah got three steps inside before the big man behind the bar pointed at him and called out, "Hey, where do you think you're going? Big boys only."

Three people sitting on stools looked back to size up the intruder. One of those people was Brody. Seeing Suah, he jumped up. "Hey…Suah!"

"You know this kid?" asked the bartender.

Brody didn't answer; he was already en route to the boy. "What are you doing here?" Enhanced by an afternoon of drinking, Brody was less laid back and more talkative than when perched behind his booth at *Island Aquatics & Adventures*.

"Molly said this was your favorite place," answered Suah.

"This place?" Brody took a quick look around. "Hell, no. My favorite place is up here?" Brody pointed to his own head. "You know why? Because I can keep it just the way I want it. Nobody screws with it but me."

A lanky old man at the bar laughed. "Ain't *that* the truth."

The big man bartender waddled to the near side of the bar to watch what was going on. Brody glanced back and took notice then turned to Suah.

"Did you come in here to get drunk?" The fake drama of Brody's question was loud enough for the bartender and several witnesses to hear.

Suah shook his head no.

Brody addressed the bartender. "You see? There's no way you're going to corrupt this boy. He came here to sit and talk so cut him some slack."

The bartender poured a refill for a regular. "All right, but you keep him up at the bar next to you where I can see him."

A young car mechanic sat at a nearby table with his girlfriend. He downed another shot of tequila and yelled out to the bartender. "Hey Roy, what's this place turning into? The PTA?" The comment was met with scattered laughter and follow-on humor.

Brody ignored it all and led Suah to a stool next to him at the other end of the bar. Pointing at his empty beer bottle, Brody wiggled his hand to get the bartender's attention. "I'll take another one and my friend will have a soda."

The bartender complied but was still reticent about allowing the boy in.

Brody motioned towards the glass of soda. "Hey, dress it up for him…"

The bartender reached down and came up with a wedge of lime that he stuck unceremoniously on the rim of the soda glass.

Brody pulled the glass closer to Suah. "That's better."

Suah took a long sip through the straw and then popped the wedge of lime into his mouth. In no time at all he had the wedge chewed and swallowed.

The lanky old man down the bar was watching. "Damn! That boy must be hungry. You see the way he took down that lime?"

"You want something to eat?" Brody leaned over to Suah and got a nod before calling out to Roy. "Order up a burger and fries for the young man."

As Roy wrote out the order for the kitchen, Suah gazed up at the sloping roof. "It looks like the ceiling is going to fall," noted Suah.

Brody took a swig of beer. "It's all part of the charm of being alive."

Suah looked around. "I saw a dog outside wearing a hat."

Mention of the dog startled Brody into looking down the bar. He called out to the lanky old man. "Hey Jack, what time is it?"

Jack was huddled in conversation with another man but turned to answer. "It's after sunset." He stared down the bar at Suah. "Hey boy, you wanna know how we tell time around this place?"

Suah looked around for the missing clock, nodding all the while.

Jack deferred to the bartender. "Tell him, Roy."

The bartender leaned back on the bar. There was a lilt, a wistful poetry about his delivery, "You know it's time for the sun to go over the hump when *Mad Dog Maui* walks out to take his dump."

The bar erupted in laughter.

"*Mad Dog Maui*?" asked Suah.

"That's his name. He's Roy's dog," answered Brody, pointing to the bartender. "Everyday at this time, *Mad Dog* goes out to relieve himself."

"Like clockwork," noted Jack.

"I wish I was a regular guy like him," another man added.

A man at the far end of the bar asked Roy, "What do you feed that dog?"

Roy kept a straight face as he patted his large belly. "He eats what I eat."

Jack, the lanky one, lowered his bottle. "Oh shit, now we're in trouble..."

More laughter and side comments added to the confusion as someone changed the music playing on the jukebox.

"Don't knock it," snapped Roy. "He's a good dog—and he snores a hell of a lot less than my ex-wife used to."

"You sleep with him?" asked Suah.

"He sleeps like a baby right next to me in that trailer next door."

"You live there?" Suah was surprised.

Roy nodded. Jack lit up a cigarette. "How old is that heap?"

"That *heap* is a classic. A '59 Fan Travel Trailer."

The mechanic called out, "You've modified that sucker quite a bit."

"Yeah, so what?" asked Roy. "That makes it a *custom* classic."

Roy walked away to attend to a new customer. Everyone else returned to their individual conversations. For Brody, it was a chance to talk to Suah.

"So what's going on with you," asked Brody.

Suah sipped at soda. "I've got some more time to explore."

"Why aren't you at home? Where's your dad?"

"I don't have one."

"Join the club." Brody gazed into the mirror behind the bar and took a swig of beer. "It's not the worst thing that can happen. You have a mother, don't you?"

Suah nodded.

"Well, where is she?"

"Working."

"It happens. I've gotta go to work too in a little while."

"You sit at the booth at night?" asked Suah.

"Naw, not there. I've got all sorts of jobs. They come and go. One night a week I help move and set up equipment for a house band. They play for tourists down the street."

"Oh, you're a roadie."

Brody chuckled. "You know about roadies?"

"I've met some..."

"Really, well, I don't think what I do qualifies. These guys play at the same crappy lounge two nights a week. The group is hardly a band and I wouldn't call that going on tour."

From experience, Suah shook his head no. "What other jobs do you do?"

"Oh, you know, like everyone else I do what I can find. On weekends, like tonight, I clean a bar after it closes. I have to wait until two in the morning to start that."

"You must be up all night. That doesn't sound like wasting time."

"Oh, but it is," assured Brody. "Believe me, there are lots of ways to waste time. And I'm the master of all of them."

Suah looked around. "What about now? Is coming here wasting time?"

Brody cocked his head towards Suah. "I come here to *forget* about wasting time. What would you call that? Another waste of time?"

Suah shrugged. From behind them, the car mechanic called out, "Hey Brody, is that the same kid that sits with you for hours at the *IAA* booth?"

Brody looked back and gave a nod. The two of them had a history and reasons not to like each other. But there was no reason to get into that now.

The mechanic grinned and whispered something to his girlfriend. She gave him a playful shove, tossed her curls to one side, and laughed.

Louder this time, the mechanic called out to Brody. "So what's up, Brody? What are you trying to do—reconnect with your tribal heritage?"

Anyone ignorant enough to make racial or bigoted innuendoes was testing Brody's patience. He glared back at the man in warning but turned away, content to let it go.

"I don't get it," the mechanic pressed on. "What's with it with you two?"

There was no response. Other patrons in the bar took notice and waited to see what might happen. To make sure nothing did, Roy the bartender stepped sideways to get a line of sight on the mechanic.

"Hey," started Roy, "We don't need that in here. If you're really good at fixing things, you'll fix that leak in your mouth."

"Can't a guy be curious?" the mechanic challenged.

"I'm curious why it matters to you," answered Roy.

The bartender's forceful challenge didn't sit well with the mechanic's hot headedness. All playfulness and fun dropped out of his reply, "I should think *everyone* would be curious. At first I thought Brody was planning to adopt. But now I think he's on a hot date. He likes them young and exotic."

"Shut your fucking mouth," shouted Brody. He lunged from his stool just as the mechanic pounced his way. In a flash they were into it, scrapping and throwing punches. The mechanic's girlfriend fell back with the powerful shifting of furniture. All at once, everyone in the bar was in motion. Many stood or jerked away from the action. Roy the bartender reached for a baseball bat and hurried around from behind the bar. He moved faster than one would expect a man of his size to hustle.

Brody and the mechanic rolled over and over across the floor. Their entangled anger became a wrestling match and the center of attention. No one noticed that an empty chair had fallen back on the mechanic's girlfriend.

When the two fighters collapsed back over the furniture, the force of their momentum had pushed the arm of a wooden chair down across the throat of the girlfriend. Her windpipe was crushed. She lay helpless on her back, pinned to the floor in shock and gagging for air. She couldn't cry out for help. As the fighters rolled farther away, chances weren't good that anyone would notice her and call for help in time.

Roy was determined to settle things down even if he had to break a couple heads. He hurried into the fray and jabbed at the fighters with the bat.

"That's enough!" he yelled and shoved the bat into the mechanic's ribs.

Back at the bar, Suah sat stunned and watched. Some of the other people at the bar ran off to take cover. Only Jack, the old lanky man, remained seated on his stool. He turned around and held onto his beer bottle, making sure none of the bruising action would cause a drop to spill.

Suah looked down and saw the girlfriend quivering and turning blue in the face. Before thinking anything else, he slid off his stool and scrambled over to her. He kneeled on the floor by her head then leaned forward and looked into her panicked eyes. Bending closer, his eyes locked on hers.

"*I know…I know…*" he repeated. He placed his hands over her ears and began swiping his fingers down along her head and across the sides of her neck. Rocking back and forth, he repeated the action while mumbling again and again, "*I know…I know…It's OK…It's OK…I know…*"

The rest of the world disappeared. For Suah, there was only the girl's face, the terror in her eyes, and the feeling of his hands moving over her. He could feel what she was going through. He could also feel the way it should be if everything was all right. His hands smoothed over her skin and paused at her throat. He did this again and again until all that remained was the feeling of the way everything should be.

The horror in her eyes abated only to be replaced with a startled fear of surviving a near-death experience. For the girl it was inconceivable that air was passing into her lungs once again. She was taking breaths that shouldn't be and she knew it. She had accepted the fact that this was death. She had felt her consciousness disconnect from her physical form and prepare for the end. Now to be back, to be whole again was just as unbelievable as ever being able to explain what had just happened to her.

Suah had no idea how long he was on the floor next to the girl. Time and space were minor conditions considering the silent passage of feeling and the enveloping connection he had with the girl. An energy of unknown origin vibrated away all other thoughts. When it subsided and his thoughts returned, he looked up to discover that the whole bar was silent. The fight had long since ended. Everyone was standing in silent wonder, looking his way, watching the girl's recovery.

Suah sat back on his legs and gathered his bearings. He was suddenly lightheaded as his hunger for food returned. Looking down on the girl, he watched as she lay on her back, taking in breaths that were deep and slow. She turned her head to look at him. It was a look of marvel and confusion, and in time, gratitude.

A bloodied and bruised pair of fighters stood nearby with Roy standing guard between them. The rest of the bar patrons had gathered around to watch the drama taking place away from the fight. Now that it was over, no one knew what to say. Not knowing what they had just witnessed, it was hard to know how to react.

One thing was certain. The whole bar had been startled sober by the wonder of events at hand. The jukebox had long since finished its last song which left the whole place quieter than it had ever been at that time of night.

The girl sat up renewed, as if nothing had happened. She was the one who felt the strangest. She had moved through a passage of panicked finality only to come out the other side like nothing had happened. She was too startled, too exposed to endure all the attention. She grabbed hold of her boyfriend's hand and pulled him towards the door.

"Let's get out of here," she gasped.

Bleeding from the lip and with an eye swollen, the mechanic held his sore ribs and followed her out the door and into the night.

Roy the bartender needed to get his place back to some state of normalcy no matter if anyone could fathom what had just transpired or not. It didn't matter if three-foot extraterrestrials appeared dressed as Elvis and sang *God Save The Queen* a cappella, that was enough deviation from the regular *Sops & Wobbers* routine for one night.

Roy marched his baseball bat back behind the bar and picked up the food order waiting in the window from the kitchen. Shaken but forceful, he set the plate of hamburger and fries on the bar. He spoke to Suah.

"Here you go. Your food's ready."

Brody couldn't move. Not only was he sore, he was stunned. He watched as Suah got up off the floor and returned to his stool. Reaching for the catsup, Suah stopped to look back at everyone still frozen in place. Not knowing what to say, he squirted catsup on his fries and started to eat.

With Suah back at the bar, everyone unfroze and made their way back to where they had been sitting. The overturned furniture was set right and one of the regulars grabbed a broom and swept broken glass off to one side.

Brody returned to the stool next to Suah but remained silent.

Roy exchanged a few thoughtful glances with Brody before stepping closer. He motioned to Brody's beer bottle. "You want another?"

Brody shook his head so Roy looked to Jack but the lanky man was still nursing the one bottle he had protected during the fight.

"This place is too goddamn quiet," snapped Roy. He marched over to the jukebox and punched some buttons.

Abruptly, a blast of music filled the bar. Given the mood of the place, the blare was discordant but at least it gave cover for a dozen conversations carrying on in murmuring huddles, all trying to decide what had happened.

Brody gazed over at the food disappearing from Suah's plate.

"You doing all right?" asked Brody.

Suah did more chewing than nodding but Brody got the idea.

Brody couldn't ignore the obvious any longer. "That girl on the floor was really in trouble…"

Suah kept eating. If Brody wanted answers, he was going to have to be more specific. "What were you doing to her?"

Once the question was out, Brody sensed it was too direct, even confrontational. He immediately soft-pedaled over it. "Whatever it was, it sure did the trick. Have you done that before?"

Suah sucked soda through a straw and nodded.

"How do you know what to do?" asked Brody. The line of questioning was fragile; the wrong approach might close the boy down.

"I have help," answered Suah.

"Help from where?"

Finished with his food, Suah concentrated on the soda. In between sips, he considered the question. "Some say help is far away, but when something needs to be the way it should be, Hawa comes close. I feel different when the far away comes near."

It was not the answer Brody expected or wanted. "What do you mean?"

Just then, Roy returned to their side of the bar. "Hey, Brody..." The bartender took a guarded, sideways glance at Suah and then leaned in to whisper. "Maybe it's time the two of you go. You're spookin' the place. It's bad for business, you know what I mean?"

Brody looked back over his shoulder at the subdued bar. Roy was right; the place had the energy of a transcendental encounter group who had all just been tasered. Worst yet, patrons were so preoccupied that bar sales had plummeted.

Brody nodded and slid off his stool. He rested his hand on Suah's back. "It's almost that time; I better get to work. Let's go."

Suah stood and started to follow. As they headed for the door, every eye in the place followed their progress. Noticing that they had captured everyone's undivided attention, Brody thought of something to make light of the situation. He rubbed Suah's head.

"Let's go see *Mad Dog Maui*. You know he's up to something good."

Roy called out, "See you later."

Brody gave a wave. Suah looked back but didn't wave. The bartender didn't look like he wanted one.

Once outside, Brody straightened up and stretched, then lit a cigarette. He stood in place and puffed his thoughts to the sky for a while. He looked undecided, stuck on something, between worlds.

Suah stepped over to the chain-link fence. Mad Dog Maui was harder to see as the darkness of night deepened but the dog's motion drew the eye. Suah watched as Mad Dog paced along the fence. His stylish hat and flower lei were still in place.

Back and forth the dog trotted on the other side of the yard. At regular intervals, Mad Dog would look up at something, anything in the darkness beyond the fence. Then it was back to the endless trot one way, then the other. It was the restlessness of a caged animal.

It appeared to be hyper, crazed, even mad. And yet, trapped behind the chain-link fence, Mad Dog's wild behavior might be the one appropriate response. Either way, there was something about nighttime that unsettled him. He was forever being lured to the one place where he couldn't go. As Suah watched, his thoughts drifted back to a grandfather he once knew.

"Well, I gotta go." Brody's voice came from behind.

Suah looked back to see him flicking a half-smoked cigarette into the street. "Maybe I'll catch you tomorrow. OK?"

Suah nodded and watched him stride across the street and then follow the rock wall of the cemetery until he was out of sight.

Being alone again made Suah want to check the time. But the thought of checking the time brought back thoughts of *Mad Dog Maui*. In the bar they had said, if you wanted to know what time it was, just watch Mad Dog.

Turning his gaze back across the yard, Suah had to stuff away sad feelings welling up; he knew not why. If Mad Dog was showing the way, then maybe everyone else in the bar needed to come out and see what time it was too.

There was more time in the day than just sunset time.

Suah ambled along the fence until it ended at the far street. Something that Brody had told him in the bar echoed back. "I come here to *forget* about wasting time…" Suah took one more look at Mad Dog's endless trot. Maybe that's why no one came out to watch the dog.

They wanted to forget what time it was.

Suah's energies were low despite being fortified with a hearty burger and fries. It had been a long day. Despite the lights of shops and cafés and the diverting antics of sidewalk performers and wood-carving artisans, there was nothing left he wanted to do other than go home.

Once through the park, he took the alleyway to avoid the busy sidewalks along the main street. He was halfway down the alley before finally checking Blake's wristwatch for the time. He had forty-five minutes to wait. By the time he sat down cross-legged at his customary spot where the food truck parked, the wait was down to half an hour.

The strangest part of waiting was the fact that the food truck had driven away for the night. Suah's familiar waiting corner looked nothing like what he was used to at four o'clock. For one thing, the cars and trucks whizzing by now had their lights on. Suah couldn't avoid watching their endless run this way and that. In his drowsiness, he got the same sad impression watching them as he had watching *Mad Dog Maui* trot back and forth.

If nothing else, the passing glare of headlights and the glow of red tail lights were enough to mesmerize the rest of the waiting time away.

When Blake arrived, Suah found him subdued, uninterested in the usual wisecracks. They drove along in silence, although Suah was surprised when they drove to Gianna's estate instead of heading back to Diego's place.

Suah rambled into the house and soon discovered that Paige had invited Diego to the estate after the show for a swim in the infinity pool.

Blake was not invited and drove off after dropping Suah off and letting

Paige know that Suah was in the house and going upstairs to bed. Since it was maid's night off, Paige and Diego had the place to themselves.

Suah trudged up to his bedroom, tired beyond belief and drawn to the promise of a good night's sleep. He sauntered into his closet to get pajamas on and opened his wardrobe door. To his dismay, he noticed that the drawing done by Brody was missing from where he had taped it in place.

A moment later, he was relieved to remember folding the drawing and putting it in his pocket when he got dressed that morning.

The drawing had brightened his mood after the nightmare about the ocean drying up. He had wanted it with him in case he needed a little pick-me-up during the day. Unfortunately, he had forgotten all about it and never took it out once to look at. Then again, the day's adventures had been enough of a pick-me-up. There was no need to look at it.

Pulling it out of his pants pocket, he noticed right away that something was different. Unfolding it, his heart sank to find that his wet pants from earlier in the day had smeared the drawing. The water damage had made a duplicate, ghost imprint all along the line of the fold.

Suah stared at it awhile, trying to make sense out of what the drawing had become. It didn't take long to see the possibilities.

Running out of the closet, he crossed the room to his desk and got out an ink pen. Carefully, slowly, he wrote his name above the original side of the image. Above the duplicate, ghost image he wrote another name—Hawa.

Satisfied with his work, he taped the drawing back in place behind the wardrobe door. There was only one thing left to do after such a day.

He climbed in bed and grabbed his little kaleidoscope toy. Resting back, he pointed it towards the light coming through his bedroom door and turned it with his hand. A familiar swirl of color and design appeared but before he could turn it anymore, he rested his cheek to pillow and fell fast asleep.

CHAPTER **16**

A tropical sun arose and Suah opened his eyes to find morning light streaming through his window's shutters. It was the fifth day since Gianna went on tour but their separation seemed longer.

The house around Suah was quiet. All he could hear was his breathing and his thoughts. He lay there, intent upon the rows of horizontal light patterns casted by the shutters that decorated the ceiling.

There had been so many adventures in the last four days. He felt changed by them but how could that be when he knew he was the same boy as before? When he wondered about things around him he felt one way. But when he wondered about himself it was all together different.

Tossing off the covers, he got out of bed yawning and shuffled into his closet to find something to wear. Draped on the dressing bench he found his clothes from yesterday. He had been too tired the night before to put them away. He snatched the shirt and pants in hand and headed for the hamper.

Halfway there, he felt something in the pants pocket. It was the flyer about Jaxon Muse he had picked up from the parking lot. One side advertised Muse's new book. The other side was all about the conference south of town.

With his memory jogged with sudden, renewed purpose for the day, Suah dressed in a rush and ran downstairs in search of Paige.

He found her on the sun porch with coffee and a magazine.

Looking up, her face brightened. "Good Morning, Suah. Ready for some breakfast?"

"When are we leaving for Diego's," asked Suah.

"We're not going there today."

The announcement left Suah stunned. "We're not?"

"No, it's probably best we give it a rest, do something else today."

Suah didn't know what to say. He never expected this—in so many ways.

He never expected Paige to pass up on a chance to spend another day with Diego when her scheme to offload Suah had worked so well on previous days. He never would have dreamed four days ago that he'd be disappointed to hear the news that he wasn't going to be paired up with Blake for the day only to be abandoned in town.

Then again, Paige *had* invited Diego over to swim in the infinity pool last night. Who knows how late their soiree had gone. And that was after they attended a show earlier in the evening. It had been a big day for them too.

Maybe they really needed to give it a rest.

Even so, this was terrible. This couldn't, shouldn't happen on the one day that Suah absolutely, positively needed to be into town. There had to be some way to get her to go. But what if Blake had already made other plans once he found out he'd be free of his Suah-chores today?

Worst yet, how could Suah ever convince Paige to go to Diego's and leave him with Blake if Suah couldn't explain why it was so necessary? He didn't feel comfortable lying about how he got the flyer on Jaxon Muse. How would he ever explain this sudden need to go to a grown-up conference south of town? Adults had a way of asking questions that tested such lies. Suah couldn't take a chance that she'd find how Blake was leaving him alone.

There was only one safe way to try to make her change her mind. Suah wasn't used to lying so he tried imagining what he was about to say was true.

"I really wanted to watch surfers today. It's all I've been thinking about."

"You've watched them all week. I thought you'd be tired of it by now."

"I don't want to do it tomorrow," admitted Suah. "But today is supposed to be one of the best days to watch them."

"Is that so..." Paige wasn't convinced and flipped a page in her magazine. Suah stepped up to the side of her chair. "Isn't there anyway I can go?"

Paige looked up, taken in by his enthusiasm. "Well...it's for sure I'm not going to Diego's place today." She paused to watch the hopeful anxiety in his expression. "...but I don't see any reason why Blake can't pick you up here."

Suah's face lit up. "That's perfect. I could see the surfers and you could give it a rest."

The turn of phrase brought a sheepish grin to Paige's face. Apparently, *give it a rest* meant something quite personal and humorous to her, especially when parroted back by Suah in such a direct way.

"All right," he smiled. "I'll give Diego a call. I can't promise anything. We'll have to see what Blake is doing."

Suah nodded as she reached for her phone. It only took a minute to confirm the arrangements. Of course Blake was going out and sure it would be no problem to have him swing by. Just like that, the crisis had passed. Suah had another day of exploring and adventure on tap. The only one left to convince it was a great idea was Blake. And that wasn't going to happen.

The Datsun appeared in front of Gianna's estate two hours later. The morning was half gone and Suah was getting nervous. He had a lot to do and dwindling time to do it. Already, the conference at *The Manuia Resort* was about to begin. Granted, there were morning and afternoon sessions, but Suah didn't want to take any chances that he'd miss it. Blake was only the first of complications Suah expected. So the sooner he got there, the better.

Blake didn't come into the house. He sat outside in the car with the engine running and waited for Suah to climb in the passenger seat. Suah steeled himself for whatever wrath he was about to receive from Blake. There was no way he wasn't going to be pissed.

"Look who it is…" On seeing Suah, Blake's animosity peaked.

Suah hesitated, fearing Blake's reprisal might be worse than expected.

"Close the door, butt-wipe," barked Blake.

With the door closed, Blake accelerated into their day.

"You think you're a wiseass, don't you?"

Neither yes nor no would be the correct answer. Suah remained mute.

Blake had already done a lot of thinking on the ride out to Gianna's place about what was going on. It wasn't enough to figure out what was in Suah's mind, why he had asked for this. Now Blake had to figure out the best way to get even.

"You must really like playing around in town. You're having fun, aren't you?"

Blake was going to make whatever assumptions he wanted. Suah had no control over the situation. He could only hope the trip to the food truck drop-off spot went quick and Blake's abuse was limited to a verbal barrage.

Strangely enough, Blake was rather cool, considering. Suah had expected a much more violent tirade. This was either a good sign or a harbinger of something worse to come.

"You told Paige this was a good day to watch surfers. Why is that?"

As was typical when Suah couldn't get out of answering, he shrugged.

"It can't be the surf," asserted Blake. "Surf's nothing special today…"

Suah held his silence; he dreaded any more conversation. Adults had their way of testing the lies of little boys but at least the adults Suah knew wouldn't hit him if the lie was uncovered. Blake was dangerous since he had many of the same testing skills as adults but none of their restraint. Above all, Suah hoped and prayed that Blake wouldn't search his pockets. If he did, he'd find the flyer that advertised the Muse conference.

The car pulled up to a stop sign. The cross street in front of them stretched south and north. To go into town, they always turned left but today Blake took pleasure in going right.

"You're going to get exactly what you asked for," snapped Blake. "We're going to see the surfers. From now on, any day I'm stuck with you, you're going to be stuck with me. No more playing around in town."

The car turned and Suah's heart sank. This was the worst possible scenario. Never in his wildest imagination did Suah expect Blake to actually do what he was told and take him to the beach with the surfers. In one stark moment, Suah's hopes for the day were crushed.

"How do you like that...Suah?" Blake spat Suah's name with a sneer.

Suah withdrew into himself and sat out the rest of the ride. Blake enjoyed Suah's quiet desperation and said nothing more. As much as Blake wanted to mess up Suah's plans, it still was an inconvenience to have him along. That fact alone took the brighter edge off Blake's enjoyment of Suah's misery. But for Blake, it was worth putting up with a little hassle if it meant ruining Suah's day.

The beach they drove to was one of the spots Blake frequented in rotation depending on surf conditions. It was a few miles north of town not far from the road. Pulling off into the dirt, Blake parked the Datsun by a row of windswept trees that bordered where the sand began.

Blake hopped out and went about his regular routine; first thing was getting his surfboard off the roof of the car. Suah got out and stepped near a tree to take a look around. A few other surfers were already there, a couple of them in the water. A jagged lineup of their cars and trucks stretched along the tree line. Suah looked at them wistfully, wishing one of them would take him away. Except for the rhythmic surf, the only other sound was the whoosh of cars passing by on the nearby road.

With surfboard under his arm, Blake headed for the beach. "Sit in the car or sit on the beach. I don't care."

Suah watched him go. Not sure what to do, Suah stood in place and looked around. The beach had no facilities; no restrooms, no tables, not even a trash can. It certainly wasn't an official park; it was barely a turnoff along the shoulder of the highway.

Sitting in the car would get too hot. Suah didn't see any other option than to sit on the beach. He picked a spot far away from the water, back under a tree. The thought of having to sit there all day weighed down on him. He was restless to find a way to resurrect his plans to get to Muse's conference.

If nothing else, the place where he was at was perfect for sitting and doing nothing else but thinking. It took a hour but eventually he hatched a plan. It would be the wildest thing he had ever done if he could pull it off but that didn't matter. He couldn't see any other way.

Blake spent all of his time in the water, on his board, either riding a wave or waiting for one far out beyond the break. He might have brought Suah to the beach but once they were there, Suah was on his own. That was perfect. Suah bided his time, hoping he'd get a chance to try out his plan.

Two and a half hours crawled by. Suah checked the clock in the Datsun; it was just past noon. If something didn't happen soon, the day would be shot.

He returned to his place under the tree. After another set of waves took its time coming ashore, two of the surfers swam in and walked up the beach. Suah could hear them talking but until they got closer, he couldn't make out what was being said. As they neared, Suah heard their plans for lunch. One guy named Duffy was heading into town to grab fast food for all of them.

Suah could only hope that this would be his chance at last.

Duffy walked up through the trees to the line of cars. The car at the end had parked parallel to the trees because it had an open trailer in tow and parking head-in would have left the trailer sticking out into the highway.

Suah stood up and watched his hopes be rewarded when Duffy headed for that last car. Suah glanced out to sea. Blake was still out with the rest of them. This was it. Suah had to grab this chance or give up on his plans.

Just as Duffy got in the car to leave, Suah dashed up behind the trailer in tow and hopped in. Right away, he laid flat and held on perfectly still. The other surfer on the beach was sitting on the sand, watching the waves, and thankfully didn't see Suah's dash. If the driver had missed him too, then everything should be all right. The car started and pulled away from the beach. Suah was on his way back into town.

He grinned; his face pressed to the floorboards.

The car with trailer in tow pulled into a service station that shared a parking lot with a fast food place. After Duffy got out and went in for food, Suah jumped out of the trailer, tore off down the side street, and headed for the alley. In a dead run, he veered around delivery trucks and parked cars until he got to the next side street. There he had to slow down and navigate through the comings and goings of people on the sidewalk.

It took nearly ten minutes at top speed, but he arrived at the park with the big tree. He was out of breath and full of desperate hope that he'd find Lolo still sitting on her favorite bench having her lunch.

Running past the trunk of the tree, he headed for the south side of the park but shuttered to a stop when an empty bench came into view. He didn't have Blake's wristwatch so he had no idea what time it was. The last time he checked in the Datsun it was right after twelve noon. Adding travel time in the car and his run through town, it couldn't be after one o'clock yet.

There was only one other place to check. Suah ran out of the park and up the street. Maybe Lolo had cut her lunch short and was already back at Lilyana's house. It was the only place left to try.

Halfway up the side street, Suah spotted Lolo and Gris-Gris in the distance. They were headed up the sidewalk that led to Lilyana's. When Suah tore up to them all excited and relieved, it took both of them by surprise.

"Suah!" gasped Lolo. "What's going on?"

Suah licked his dry lips and panted. "I've been looking for you."

Gris-Gris danced around and enjoyed Suah's pets and hugs.

"Why are you running?"

"I thought I missed you," explained Suah.

"Missed me for what? We weren't supposed to meet today…"

"I know…*I know*," stuttered Suah, catching his breath. "But I want you to go with me someplace."

"Go with you?" The suggestion was so out of place.

Suah produced the Muse flyer; he made sure the side advertising the conference was turned face up. "Here it is…"

"This?" Lolo scanned the page. "What about this?"

"Will you go with me? It's happening right now."

"This is at *The Manuia Resort*…"

"I don't want to go by myself. I want *you* to go."

"We'd have to go right away…"

"Yeah, we really have to go or we'll miss it."

"And how are you planning on getting down there?"

Suah hesitated. "I'm not sure."

"I don't know if I want to go to this thing." Lolo handed back the flyer.

"You really *need* to go with me. Jaxon Muse is going to be there."

"I can see that."

"Do you know who he is?"

"Sure, most people do. Lilyana talks about him sometimes…"

"Well, wouldn't you like to meet him?"

"No, not really. Why should I?"

"I want to see him," declared Suah. "I'd really like you to go with me."

Lolo sighed at the pleading innocence on Suah's face. If she said no, it wouldn't be on account of all the important things she had to do. If she went, it'd be over in a couple of hours. If nothing else, she'd get to see the heralded *Manuia Resort*. She had heard that *Manuia* was the way Polynesians said

Cheers! or *To Your Health!* Such a place sounded like fun to at least visit.

"OK," she said finally. "But we have to take the bus. We don't have a car and there's no way I'm going to walk that distance. It's hard enough for me to walk from here to the park."

Suah's face lit up. "That's fine! Let's go."

Lolo held her ground. "Do you have any money...for the bus?"

Suah halted and shook his head.

"That's all right," Lolo relented. "I'll take care of it."

"Thanks..." They started off down the sidewalk.

"I can't believe you're talking me into this," added Lolo. She maneuvered her walking stick with repeated twists of her body to assist her steps.

"I have a good feeling about it," remarked Suah.

The comment was strange. "What are you talking about?"

"I think it's something we're supposed to do."

"Oh really, and when did you get that crazy idea?"

"Yesterday, but I forgot about it until this morning."

"Do even know what Jaxon Muse is all about?"

"Oh sure, I went to the bookstore yesterday and found out."

"You did, huh. Let me see that flyer again."

Suah handed it over. Lolo checked out both sides this time.

"I still don't get it," Lolo concluded, handing the flyer back. "Why do you give a flip about *Surviving The Near-Life Experience*? You should be playing videogames or trying out for the football team."

"Why?" asked Suah.

"Because that's what you should be doing. I guarantee you, you'll be the only boy your age at this thing."

"Maybe, but other boys don't know you," Suah countered.

"What's that got to do with it?"

"Everything."

"It makes no sense," Lolo changed the subject. "How do you expect to get into the conference? Did you think of that? Did you buy tickets?"

Suah had to shake his head no to all of it.

"And you still want to go..." Lolo stopped and stared Suah down, hoping he'd think twice about the common sense of what he wanted to do.

Instead, Suah nodded. "It's the way it should be...things like that have a way of happening if you go with it."

Lolo looked puzzled. She sighed as they reached the bus stop. If nothing else, she'd get to see the resort. If nothing else, Suah was entertaining.

CHAPTER 17

The Manuia Resort was set back along a curving private parkway that skirted a championship golf course and a famous westside beach. The circle drive entrance was adorned by palm trees and flower-draped fountains and attended to by bustling valets and uniformed bellhops.

The architecture of the eight-story complex could only be described as chic French Polynesian. Its wide, open-air lobby put all who entered it on notice that even more elaborate luxuries awaited within for the lucky few who could afford the five-diamond room rate.

The main highway's bus stop was nowhere near the resort's entrance. It took Suah and Lolo ten minutes to walk along the parkway until they could say they had arrived on resort grounds. The time was nearly 2:30 p.m. Jaxon Muse's afternoon session was well underway.

After the bus ride and the long walk, Lolo was less than enthusiastic about her decision to let Suah talk her into coming. In fact, she hardly could believe she had gone along with the idea.

"This is funny," she laughed. "By the time we get in there—*if* we get in there, the thing will almost be over."

"That's all right..." Suah gazed up past sprays of orchids into the far reaches of the five-story high lobby. Across from the concierge desk, a pair of peacocks roamed free over mounds of manicured native plants. "...It looks like a place where the magic happens."

"Yeah," groaned Lolo. "The magic of $500 spa treatments and bottles of rare late-harvest wines imported from Europe."

As Suah wandered by parrots that watched him from their gilded perches, Lolo stopped to check directional signs.

"I think the conference center is that way. Let's see the flyer again."

Suah dug into his pocket and handed it over. Lolo searched for details.

"It doesn't say which room it's in."

"We could ask somebody."

"And get kicked out." She turned down a hallway. "Come on, this way."

Suah followed her down an ornately tropical hallway. At the far end, a wide conference center vestibule opened up on either side of them.

Off to the right, a directory board attracted Lolo's attention. "Here it is...She pointed to one of the listed events. "It's in the *Nuku Hiva Room*."

Suah had wandered off and already found it. A now-empty registration table sat off to one side. Guarding the doors, a resort employee watched Suah's approach. Beneath a brass plate on the nearby wall, a name card announced to all in fine calligraphy:

The Nuku Hiva Room
Surviving The Near-Life Experience

Lolo caught up. "So now what?"

Suah took a step forward, eliciting a check by the gatekeeper.

"May I see your registration card?"

Suah halted with Lolo hanging back. "I told you," grinned Lolo. "If you want to survive the near-life experience, first you have to survive getting by the guard."

Suah was not dissuaded. "I just want to see Mr. Muse."

The guard was polite but firm. "Maybe after the session."

Just then, one of the doors opened and a man hurried out and crossed the vestibule to the restroom. In the time it took for the door to swing closed, Suah and Lolo got a glimpse of what was going on inside.

They could see the room was large and full of circular tables with a dozen people sitting around each one. At the far end was a stage and a wall of video effects. For having so many people in one place, the room was quiet save for one voice. Suah recognized that voice. It was Jaxon Muse but speaking through a sound system that added depth and gravitas to each word.

The door slowly swung closed and the lush décor of the vestibule once again was the only thing to see. But Suah was not daunted; he had a mission and shrinking time to complete it. He turned back to the guard.

"Do you know what room Jaxon Muse is staying in?"

"I don't even know if Mr. Muse is staying at the resort."

"If we don't sit down but just stand at the back, would that be OK?"

Suah's questions were beginning to grate on the door guard and yet the uniformed man managed to stay in character as a refined and upscale service employee. He shook his head. "I'm sorry."

The man in the restroom appeared and made strides back across the vestibule. The guard dutifully opened the door for him. Once again as the door swung closed, Suah and Lolo savored their glimpse of what was going on inside. Something Muse said triggered a smattering of chuckles through the crowd. And then the door pressed closed again.

Lolo tried another approach. She worked her walking stick a couple steps closer to the guard. "OK, if we wait until the session is over, can you at least tell us what door Mr. Muse will leave from."

Suah chimed in, "It may be our only way to see him."

The guard had his fill of the annoying odd couple. He was ready to say anything to get them to wait somewhere else. With his professional composure intact, he pointed right and told a lie. "Mr. Muse will exit from the service door down that hallway. These doors are for conference goers."

"Thanks!" Suah toddled off with Lolo following after.

The hallway the guard had pointed to was anything but a service hallway. It was a connecting branch of curving arteries that linked wings of the resort towers with the central pool and spa areas.

Lolo worked her way up to where Suah was already taking in the view. From their vantage point in the open-air hallway, they could look down on massive pools and waterfalls and swim-up bars and grottos. Savage suntans and exotic cocktails stretched all the way to the beach.

"Wow," commented Lolo. "How would you like to play down there?"

Suah was noncommittal and said nothing. He had seen such places in various parts of the world. They hadn't impressed him when he was six years old and they didn't do much more for him now. He didn't get a tan and he didn't drink exotic concoctions. He could play in his pool at home.

"Come on," prompted Suah. "Let's find the service door."

Lolo didn't budge. "Wait a minute. I want to look around a little."

Suah halted and turned back. He was silent but his body language spoke volumes. Detours from the mission weren't in the plan.

"Give me a minute. I don't see this every day."

"We haven't found the door," Suah reminded.

"We don't need to—not yet. The session goes on for another hour. Jaxon Muse isn't going anywhere."

Suah couldn't force her to go with him and he didn't want to get separated. He needed her to be with him and had no choice but tag along.

Lolo made her way in the opposite direction that led to wide, marble steps that curved as they descended through the foliage into the pool area.

"It won't take long," coaxed Lolo. She had come a long way to get there. Why should it be for nothing? The conference was a bust. At least she wanted to tour the property. This was her one chance to see the resort.

A silent Suah followed a few steps in her wake. The service door was somewhere behind them. Now they were headed in the opposite direction.

Ten minutes later, they had meandered around the curve of the connecting hallway and arrived at the base of the opposite tower. It was obvious that Lolo wanted to explore the pool areas but the slope of the marble steps wouldn't work with her walking stick. If she wanted to see the amenities closer, she had to take the elevator.

She pressed the down button. "I want to see the grottos."

Suah wasn't enthused. "We're getting farther away from the conference."

The elevator doors opened and Lolo worked her way into the car. She chuckled sarcastically, "We'd be far away no matter what. We could be waiting outside the service door and *still* be far away."

Suah followed her into the elevator and felt the car drop with a sinking feeling. He knew they were supposed to be there but why it wasn't working out didn't make sense. He had no choice but to flow forward with whatever was going to happen and hope for the best.

The elevator lowered to a stop and the doors opened. Waiting to get in, a girl stood in a sheer cover-up that gave tantalizing hints of a bright green bikini underneath. Her sunglasses were dark but apparently, even in the elevator, she could see quite well. She called out.

"Suah! What are you doing here?"

The lilting feminine voice was familiar as much as it was out of place. Suah looked up to discover Hailey Muse standing before them.

"Hailey! Are you staying here?" Suah and Lolo stepped out of the elevator and Hailey stayed out with them to talk.

"No," she answered. "But that doesn't stop me from trying things out." She gave Lolo a glance. "You two together?"

"Yeah, we came to see the conference."

Hailey's grin was puzzled. "My dad's conference?"

Suah nodded. "We really need to see him."

Lolo chimed in with an apologetic grin, "For some reason, Suah thought we could get in without tickets."

"Oh my God," gasped Hailey, turning back to Suah. "On such a beautiful day, you want to sit in a stuffy old room without windows and listen to who knows what?"

Suah assured her, "We need to be here."

"If you say so." Hailey glanced down at Lolo's walking stick. "So what are you doing down here?"

"I wanted to look around, see the grottos," explained Lolo.

"Oh, those things are awesome," gushed Hailey. "But you don't really get the full effect from outside. There's a whole section you can't see unless you swim under the bar. On the other side, that's where they keep the dolphins."

"Dolphins!" Lolo's eyes lit up.

"For a price they let you pet them. You can see it from the other side of the grotto but like I said, the best way to see it is to swim under the bar."

Suah gazed at the pools. "That would be fun to see *after* the conference."

Hailey laughed. "Are you still thinking about that?"

Suah looked back and gave a nod.

"I can't believe you want to do *that* all afternoon..." Hailey watched Suah's face waver between hope and disappointment. "If it'll make you happy, I can get you in. But don't blame me if you're bored out of your mind. Come on, follow me."

Suah was renewed and invigorated. They all got back into the elevator and followed Hailey as she strutted down the main hallway to the other wing of the resort. Passing the turnoff for the conference vestibule, they made their way through a service hallway which led to a backstage area.

Punching in a number code on a keypad, Hailey gained access to a private set of rooms where performers and other talent appearing in the conference halls could relax and prep to go onstage.

Hailey pointed off to one side. "The door over there connects to the conference hall behind the stage. My dad's got this whole area to himself. Whatever you do, don't go through there." Hailey pointed to another door. "That's where all the video people are camped out."

Lolo held back a step. "TV people?"

"Yeah, they don't like anyone around their equipment."

Suah asked, "Is this on TV right now?"

"No, it's not the news or anything. My dad's putting together a new video he wants to sell. It's a private crew but they're *so* into themselves anyway. They came over from Hollywood and want everyone to know it." She headed for one of the dressing rooms. "I'm going to change. Wait here."

A moment after Hailey disappeared behind the dressing room door, a rumble of applause was heard coming from the conference hall. Before Lolo could comment, Suah hurried over to the door that connected backstage. Opening it a crack, he peeked through.

Behind the proscenium and projection screens crowded nearby, the backstage area was relatively dark. There wasn't much to see although the open door did let through all of the sounds from what was happening.

Jaxon Muse called out and had the audience answer him as one. Again he called out and they answered him as one. It was hard to tell what the audience was saying but it sounded like they were repeating him. When Muse spoke into the microphone, what he said came through loud and strong.

"All the energy I need is offered freely by the universe."

The audience responded in kind.

"I unite with everything by letting go of the feeling of being separate."

As one, the audience responded.

"What is meant to be is what is best for me."

The audience answered in unison.

"What is best for me is what I know in my heart to be true."

As the audience responded once again, Suah shut the door with motion coming up behind him. It was Hailey.

"Not that way." Hailey's whisper was brusque. "Come on, I'll show you."

Suah and Lolo followed her out of the private area, back into the service hallway. As they went, Hailey explained.

"There's a separate door for kitchen staff. They've cleaned up from lunch a while ago so everything should be out of the way by now."

Suah asked, "How do you know so much if you don't like any of this?"

"My dad thinks dragging me around the world to all of his meetings makes him a good father; you know, keeping close, expanding my horizons." Her sarcasm ran deep. "Everybody thinks he knows everything but I know more than he does about how these things work."

"Why would you want to?"

"Are you kidding? The more I know, the more I can get away with. It's paying off for you, isn't it?"

Hailey led them to a set of double doors in the service hallway. There she stopped the two of them for final instructions.

"These are the side doors where they brought the food in. I'll open one of them and you sneak in. There are chairs lined up against this wall to the right. Get your butt in a chair as soon as you can and don't move. With everything going on, just hope they don't see you."

Suah asked, "How can you get *this* door open?"

Hailey pressed buttons on the keypad. "All of the conference doors into the *Nuku Hiva Room* share the same code." The door lock disengaged. "OK, get ready…"

Hailey pulled the door open a crack and Suah then Lolo rushed through.

A moment later, the door closed behind them and the wide expanse of the entire room lay before them. Amplified sound and colored lights bathed hundreds of people grouped by the dozens around tables adorned with flower-arrangement centerpieces. Large video screens at either ends of the stage displayed what the primary camera at any moment was showing.

Suah quickly found a seat along the wall and sat down. Lolo worked her way right next to him. Suah held his breath, waiting to see if anyone had noticed them. A few of the patrons at a nearby table gave them a glance but not a second look.

More importantly, none of the official resort attendants had noticed. Most of them were lined up at the back of the room, near the main doors. A few steps away from Suah, a large video camera perched atop a tripod. A man wearing a headset kept a steady hand on the camera's focusing and panning controls.

Looking around the room, Suah could see three other cameras covering the action from various angles. An unmanned camera also hung at the back of the stage from a harness attached to the lighting grid. That camera had a sweeping view that looked out from the stage into the audience.

Jaxon Muse commanded the center of attention. Backed up by an electrified wall of inspirational photos and aphorisms, he stood in the spotlight and worked the crowd. His delivery into the wireless microphone was dramatic. He made eye contact with as many as he could. Everyone at the tables gathered in front of him sat spellbound. This was the man of their inspiration. This was the message they had come to hear.

Suah thought back to his time in the bookstore, sitting on the floor, unable to gather one thought from the jumble of words that filled the pages of Muse's book. Maybe now he could listen and discover what the secret to all this excitement really was.

Jaxon Muse worked his charismatic magic far downstage at the nearest point where he could stand and be close to his audience without joining them. His voice was strong yet comforting. It captured everyone's attention and imagination with a flowing and lyrical style:

"It's not enough to focus on potentials and possibilities. We must move towards them and have confidence in *the way things should be*.

Some say *the way things should be* is an ideal, unreachable. They say the meaning of life will always remain elusive. But what kind of meaning are they searching for? What kind of potential is worth going after if it excludes *the way things should be*? That's all the ideal really is—just the way things should be. Think about that—the ideal is nothing more than just *the way things should be*.

There's an ancient proverb; to paraphrase, it says, 'If the eye is unobstructed, we see; if the ear is unobstructed, we hear; if the nose is unobstructed, we smell; if the mouth is unobstructed, we taste; if the mind is unobstructed, we are wise; if the heart is unobstructed, we love.'

I would like to add to that—if *we* are unobstructed, we unite with one another. The quickest way to descend into the near-life experience is to rule out the ideal, rule out the way things should be. For if the ideal isn't possible, then neither are we. If the ideal isn't possible, there is no hope.

But each one of us knows intuitively that isn't true. It isn't true because at our core our spirits are already ideal. We feel it in the expansiveness of our longing to merge with the universe. We sense it in the yearning we have to find true love. We know it in those moments when we forget ourselves and care unselfishly for a friend or a child.

The fastest way to feel good about ourselves is simply to find one another. When we do that we share the goodness that *is* our nature. Then we experience *the way things should be*. And what do we call that feeling?

Idyllic.

If you truly believe that everything happens for a reason, then the only question left is—are they *good* reasons? What exactly is a good reason? Something that benefits us? Is that how we should define it? Could it be anything more than that? How can we be so sure that anything is for our greater benefit when so often such connections only appear when we connect the dots backwards? How do we keep our balance if we're always thinking of our next step or the step before? Where we are is all that matters.

It's the only place we have.

Some will choose to settle on good reasons only to find they aren't enough. There's no way of knowing if good reasons alone will satisfy us. In our heart we know they won't. The knower and the known are never one and the same. We need something else; and we *have* something else. We have the power to clear everything away. And when we clear all of it away, something magical happens, something that can't be denied.

We find that we are the magic we've been looking for.

When we clear away all that swirls around us, all that sticks to us, when we can do that—whatever is left is what is meant to be. Whatever is meant to be can then shine through us as naturally as was intended by creation.

Just remember, if less is more, then nothing is everything. As Rumi, the 13th century mystic once said, 'Yesterday I was clever, so I wanted to change the world. Today I am wise, so I am changing myself.'

Clearing away everything we are not—can only leave behind everything we are. And what are we? We are pure spirits joined together in loving celebration of an infinite creation. Love is the only energy that truly exists. Like light itself, love is neither particle nor wave, but both. It forms our spirits and creates the glorious projection of possibilities called the universe in which we get to play. And it is play in its purest form.

Lao Tzu once said, 'If you realize that all things change, there is nothing you will try to hold on to. If you are not afraid of dying, there is nothing you cannot achieve.'

Wise words, but we know they're not enough, not for those who are lost in that middle ground, that lonely place where they can't be themselves, not entirely—a place where they're not really living, not completely.

Those are the people trying to survive the *near-life* experience.

If Lao Tzu met those people, he might say to them, 'If you realize that all things are you, then there is nothing you need to avoid. If you are not afraid of living, there is everything to gain...'"

The cadence of Jaxon's speech was both invigorating and lulling. Suah had a hard time keeping pace with the flow of ideas. The overall feeling in the room was inspirational but there was little substance for Suah to take away and think about later. It all went by too fast.

Just as Suah swept his eyes across the room to gather the reactions of people in the audience, a small commotion distracted attention to three people suddenly in motion at one of the tables. Two people had jumped up as another person collapsed. People near the action reacted the most. Other tables farther away stayed focused on Jaxon Muse until he too reacted to what was going on.

It appeared that a woman had fainted and fallen out of her chair onto the floor. Jaxon stopped talking and waved for resort attendants to come to her aid. The abrupt interruption forced everyone's attention on what was happening.

The video camera and tripod blocked Suah's view. He and Lolo stood up to see if they could tell what was going on. Stepping forward, Suah could see two resort attendants down on one knee next to the collapsed woman. The nearer one ran off, leaving a clear view between tables of the woman on the floor. She was convulsing and having a hard time breathing. The remaining attendant obviously had no medical training and didn't know what to do.

Jaxon Muse could see from the stage that what was happening was not a simple case of someone fainting. This woman was having a seizure of some kind, possibly had swallowed her tongue, maybe was having an asthmatic attack to complicate matters. Jaxon wanted to know exactly what was being done to get her help. He jumped down from the stage, switched off his microphone, and hurried over to the scene.

"Is help coming?" Jaxon spoke to the remaining attendant.

"Brian went to get somebody."

Jaxon could see the woman's condition was worsening. He spoke to the crowd. "Is there a doctor or nurse here?"

No one in the crowd responded. Some stood up to see what was going on; most remained seated and carried on their concerned side conversations.

Jaxon turned back to the attendant. "What kind of help is coming?"

"The front desk will call 9-1-1."

"That could take half an hour. Don't you have anybody on staff?"

"Just a lifeguard down by the pool. You want me to go get him?"

Jaxon didn't know what else to do. "Do it! Hurry up."

The attendant dashed from the room. Jaxon took off his suit coat, wadded it up and put it behind the woman's head so her seizures wouldn't bash her head and neck against the floor. Soon after, she went perfectly still and limp.

A man who was her companion at the table knelt down. "What's happening? She's not moving." There was panic in his voice.

Jaxon leaned down and listened for respiration. There was none.

The companion cried out what Jaxon had already confirmed. "She's not breathing!"

Jaxon tried to keep things calm. "Help is on the way…"

"She needs help now!" The man jumped up and shouted his question to the crowd. "Does anybody know CPR? Please, she needs help."

A woman two tables away came rushing over. "I know some CPR."

Jaxon looked up. "What do you mean, *some*?"

"I took a class years ago. I'm not sure I remember it all."

The companion was desperate. "Go ahead, try!"

The woman dropped to the floor next to the stricken woman and started.

Jaxon and the woman's companion, along with everyone else, could do nothing more than stand by and wait. Other people gathered around to see.

After a minute, the woman doing CPR raised up and paused; she was shaking. "I don't know if I can do this. She's not responding."

The woman's companion was insistent. "You have to keep trying!"

Just then, an approaching form made Jaxon looked to his right. "Suah!"

Suah stepped closer to see what was happening.

"What are you doing here?" asked Jaxon. The question was the least of his worries but came out automatically.

Suah ignored the question and knelt down at the crown of the woman's head. His calm, trancelike manner commanded the space by being so unlike everyone around him. He reached out his hands slowly, carefully and placed them on the sides of her head.

"What's he doing?" demanded the woman's companion. "We don't have time for this." He turned to the other woman and urged her to continue. "Keep going with the CPR?"

But the other woman stood up and backed away. She had tried and failed. She no longer wanted to be the center of attention or responsible for a life that might be over.

"Who is this kid?" demanded the companion. "What does he think he's doing? We need paramedics in here, not this!"

Jaxon stepped up to the man. "Calm down. The lifeguard's coming. He'll be here any second. He'll know CPR."

"If he ever gets here," the man snapped. He turned his attention back to what Suah was doing and called out, "Watch what you're doing—she's had a seizure…"

"I know…*I know*," answered Suah. "*But it doesn't have her…*"

The man moved towards Suah. "What are you talking about?"

Jaxon blocked him. "He's not doing anything. Leave him alone."

At the back of the stage, the unmanned camera hanging from the lighting grid changed focus and zoomed in. Somewhere behind a locked door backstage, a technical director was recording the action from five angles.

Suah sat back on his legs. His focus was near but his concentration was far away, drifting closer to someone else even as they ebbed away together.

"*I-and-I can dance…the timing and the flow is all that we know…*"

"What the hell is he saying?" The companion was getting agitated again.

Jaxon was taken aback by the odd mumblings. He had no answer.

Suah closed his eyes. His hands slid alongside the head of the stricken woman as if coaxing vapors from whispers. Suah rocked back and forth, first towards the woman and then back. With each forward motion, the voice within him murmured in tones low and soft.

You are here, you are enough...

He rocked back...

Imamu, skudakumoochooowte...

He rocked back...

Bote, Alma Bote, Ananta Bath...

He rocked back...

Obarati Ochee Afikomen Banafrit...

He rocked back...

Sikera Bote, Alma Bote, Subito Fröhlich Kutamba...

He rocked back—and then came forward one last time.

Your flame is blue, your flame is green,
I-and-I...and all unseen... "

All of those close enough to hear were spellbound. More people crowded around to watch the boy; some lifted cell phone cameras to capture the action. Others watched the video monitors. The strange words, the rhythm of Suah's rocking caught everyone off guard. His delicate touch alongside the woman's head was so expressive.

There was no other way to describe it. It was confident, loving care, a compassionate concern that was all consuming. Suah was nowhere else, thinking no other thoughts, existing for no other reason. In that moment, he was a channel for everything inexplicable and necessary.

Just then, the lifeguard rushed into the conference room through one of the main doors. People in the back pointed the way for him to go.

By the time he arrived next to the stricken woman, everyone who witnessed what was happening knew without a doubt—the lifeguard's presence was superfluous. He stood by, awkward, out of place, not saying anything because he could tell he was not needed.

Why that was so, everyone could only wait and see.

Something else was happening, something beyond any of them.

Just as soon as the feeling of completeness rippled through everyone gathered around, the stricken woman fluttered her eyelids.

A moment later, she took a breath. It was deep and filling.

On her first exhale, she opened her eyes.

The nearby crowd gasped as one.

There were whispered cries of "Oh my God!"

Jaxon Muse and the woman's companion crouched at her side. Looking into her eyes was looking into everything that couldn't be and yet was the way it should be.

A man at the stricken woman's table called out, "It's a miracle!"

The woman turned her head and looked up at them. She was disoriented and bewildered. "Where am I?"

"How are you feeling?" asked Jaxon.

"I feel fine." Her answer belied everything the room had witnessed. She raised up to a sitting position. "What happened? Did I faint?"

Most of the people gathered around were still too stunned to answer her.

Jaxon and the companion helped her back onto her seat at the table.

Jaxon patted her hand. "It's all right now. I'm glad you're OK."

The woman took a few more breaths and held a hand to her forehead. "I feel a little lightheaded." She chuckled, "I'm not usually like this."

Jaxon stepped to one side, giving the woman a clear view ahead of Suah. He was still sitting on the floor. He gazed up at her with a slight smile.

The woman looked down at him and cocked her head. The corners of her mouth curled up. "I know him...who is he?"

Jaxon handed her a glass of water. "Maybe you need to rest for a while."

Her companion stepped in. "We should go outside, get some air."

"Yes," the woman agreed. "I'd like that. I want to see the sky."

The companion gave Jaxon Muse a glance. The glance told Jaxon that the woman was not yet acting like herself.

Jaxon helped her up. "You let me know if you need anything..."

The woman turned to leave. "All right, I will." Her mood was light and airy, as if awakening from a nap to daydream in a field of spring flowers.

Behind all of them, up on the stage, a production manager made an announcement into a microphone. "Your attention please...we're going to take a short recess and make sure everyone is OK. We'll reconvene in fifteen minutes." A moment later, the room erupted with excited conversation.

Jaxon helped the stricken woman stand up and go with her companion. The standing crowd parted and made a path for them as they walked out through the main doors and into the vestibule.

Jaxon turned back to find people mobbing around Suah. He was still in the same place on the floor, sitting back on his legs. But now he looked trapped and unsure of what to do. Jaxon rushed to his aid.

"All right, please! Stand back! Give the boy some room. Please..."

At the sound of Jaxon's voice, the mob gave way a little, at least enough to make room for Jaxon to approach and take Suah by the hand.

"Come with me..." Suah stood and followed Jaxon.

Halfway to the side of the stage, Suah broke free and ran into the crowd.

"Suah!" Jaxon yelled out. People began to crowd around Jaxon, asking him questions, imploring him to explain what had just happened.

Suah ran deeper into the mob. As he ran, people followed him. They snapped photos with their cameras and reached out to touch him. Suah pulled away from their clutches and fought his way to Lolo.

As he ran, five video cameras turned to follow the action. The closest camera's picture appeared on the video screens at either end of the stage.

Lolo stood back against the side wall, close to the kitchen access door where they had entered the room. She was shaken, nervous, stunned.

Suah ran up to her. "Come on. This is our chance!"

She said nothing as he took her by the hand and tried pulling her forward.

"Come with me," implored Suah. "We can see Jaxon Muse now!"

All she could do was shake her head. She wanted no part of being the center of attention and yet, Suah's movement toward her refocused the attention of the entire room in her direction. She froze.

Two resort guards muscled their way up to Jaxon. One of the guards took appraisal of the agitated crowd while the other one asked Jaxon, "What do you want to do?"

Jaxon pointed. "Get the boy out of here. We'll go backstage. Follow me."

With guards flanking him, Jaxon plowed through the crowd. On approaching Suah, they found him holding Lolo's hand.

A guard blasted open the kitchen access doors. "This way…"

Jaxon reached out. "Come on, Suah!"

"Not without Lolo."

The other guard opened his arms wide and herded both Lolo and Suah into the hallway with Jaxon. Once there, all of them hustled up the service hallway. A guard punched in the code on the keypad and within moments they were all backstage in the Jaxon's private area.

Outside the door, Suah could hear the muffled talk from conference goers who had followed them, desperate for answers for what they just witnessed.

Jaxon nodded to the guards. "All right, thanks. Now give us some privacy, please…" The guards retreated back into the service hallway.

The relative silence of the private room settled around them.

Jaxon turned back to face Suah. "What happened out there?"

In light of how improbable things were, the question sounded rhetorical.

Suah didn't know how to answer; the question covered so much.

Jaxon stepped closer. The rush of events and all it might mean had him rattled. The last thing he wanted to be was frantic but the situation made any other reaction seem useless.

"Why did you go up to that woman?" asked Jaxon.

Suah was calm but taciturn in the face of an interrogation. Jaxon waited until the boy's pensive expression formed into words. "She wasn't all right."

"That's right. She was very sick..." Jaxon was annoyed at his own reticence to just come out with it. "...she was *beyond* being sick...she wasn't *breathing*! What did you do?"

Jaxon's sudden terseness shut Suah down. He said nothing.

Regretting his outburst, Jaxon knew he'd have to work to get Suah back to the point where he'd feel comfortable talking. He'd have to ease up to the topic he was interested in.

"How did you get in the room? Did you have tickets?" The very idea of it was highly implausible. Jaxon sat down, thinking that a sitting position might appear less of a threat, less imposing.

Suah shook his head.

"Then how did you get in?"

Suah wouldn't talk so Lolo answered for him. She didn't want any trouble and thought Jaxon might go easy on her if she cooperated.

"Hailey let us in," she confessed.

Jaxon snapped back. "Hailey?"

"It's a long story," pleaded Lolo. "Can we go?"

"No!" called out Suah.

Jaxon turned to the boy, surprised that he spoke. "Why not?"

Suah gathered strength from knowing that his mission could still be accomplished. "You need to see Lolo..."

Lolo said "What?" and Jaxon said "Who?"

"This is Lolo," explained Suah. "I wanted her to come to see you."

"Why?" asked Jaxon, looking over at her. Apparently, from her expression, he was asking for both of them.

Suah took steps towards Jaxon. "You can help her..."

"What are you talking about?" asked Lolo.

Suah turned to Lolo. "Jaxon Muse knows everything about *Helf Selp*. The doctors can't make you all better, but Jaxon Muse knows all about *the way things should be*. He can help you walk the way you used to."

Lolo was peeved and embarrassed. "Is *that* what this is about? Is *that* why you dragged me all the way down here to this stupid thing?"

Not understanding her anger, Suah could only nod.

"Is this your idea of some sick joke?"

Suah persisted, "Jaxon helps people all over the world..."

"My God, you're such a freak. And why are you calling me *Lolo*? That's not my name!" Starting to cry, she headed for the door. "I can't believe you did this to me."

"Don't go," implored Suah. "Wait and see; he really can help you."

Jaxon was content to sit and watch the dynamic between the two of them. So much of their story was coming out without him having to ask a thing.

Lolo pushed through the door and disappeared into the hallway.

Suah started to run after her but Jaxon jumped up and stopped him.

"Whoa, hold up. That's not a good idea." The door closed behind Lolo and Jaxon spun Suah around.

"You need to help Lolo..." implored Suah.

"Do you know where she's going?"

"Maybe the park with the big tree..."

"All right. You can find her later. Right now, you've got a lot of people riled up and they're still out there."

"What do they want?" asked Suah.

"They want to know what you did to that woman and *how* you did it. They want to know who you are and anything else they can find out."

"Why are you so angry?"

"I'm not angry. I'm concerned, for you. You've started something you're not going to be able to stop."

"Why would I want to stop something I started?"

"Because you're not going to control it and probably won't like it."

"Then why would I start it?"

Jaxon dropped to one knee to get eye-level with the boy. He held Suah by the shoulders and spoke softly but firmly. "I was there, Suah. I saw everything. That woman was as close to being dead as anyone could be."

Suah felt his inner voice stir.

"What is seen and unseen is different...I know...I know it is..."

Jaxon recoiled. "What is that? What are you doing right now?" The day's events were making Jaxon consider the farthest reaches of what was possible. "...are you channeling something? Who is that talking?"

Suah came back. "That's Hawa."

"Who's Hawa?" Jaxon's energy was pumped up. Suah was beginning to talk more freely. Jaxon needed to take advantage of it before the boy shut down again. "Tell me...who's Hawa?"

"I-and-I. Hawa tasted the world first."

Jaxon racked his brain. He had heard that expression before, but where?

"What is I-and-I?" prompted Jaxon.

"Hawa and me," answered Suah. "Hawa wants to dance but only I-and-I can dance."

Just then, the door leading to the video production room opened. The production manager took a step through. "Mr. Muse, sorry to interrupt, but we told the crowd fifteen minutes. We need you backstage. He have to go over how you're going to handle this…"

Jaxon was torn between staying with Suah and finishing the conference. He really needed to talk more to Suah but ending the conference without wrapping it up would only make matters worse. He needed to go out before the people and try to calm things down.

"All right," answered Jaxon. "Give me a minute. Oh, and Jeff—I want all the video from today kept under tight security."

"What about all the cell phones…?"

"That can't be helped but we're not going to add to it."

"Sure thing." The production manager retreated and the door shut.

Jaxon turned back to Suah. "Listen, I need to finish the conference. It won't take long. Stay here until I get back. You'll be safe. Will you do that?"

Suah had his own question to ask. "Will you help her?"

Jaxon had no time to get into it or explain. "We can talk about that later. We'll go over everything, OK?"

Left with some hope, Suah nodded.

Jaxon confirmed, "All right, remember, we've got a deal—you stay here and we'll talk about anything you want when I get back."

Again a nod. Suah sat down.

Jaxon took a breath to compose himself. He stared at the floor for a few moments, gathered his thoughts, then slipped through the door that led back stage. The door shut, the room fell into silence, and Suah was left alone.

A couple minutes later, Suah heard muffled music and then applause coming from the conference hall. Soon after, Jaxon could be heard speaking through the sound system. Suah couldn't make out what he was saying, but once again it gave an impression of passion and being in command.

Suah looked around the backstage room and saw the vacant dressing rooms. He felt a little better knowing he and Jaxon Muse had a deal. Suah could talk to Jaxon after the conference and Jaxon would talk to Suah about anything. Anything included helping Lolo.

Thoughts of Lolo shot a shiver of alarm through Suah. How could Lolo be helped if she ran away? He had to tell her about the deal with Jaxon Muse. She had to know that help was not only possible but coming soon.

Suah jumped up and ran to the service hallway door. With any luck, all of the conference goers would be back in session. The hallway should be clear.

He opened the door a crack and had his suspicious verified. No one was hanging around out in the hallway. He could make his break for the outside. Naturally, Lolo would be headed back to the bus stop. Since she couldn't walk very well, it should be a snap catching up to her.

Suah ran outside and across the entrance driveway. Up the parkway he tore as fast as he could. It shouldn't be long before he saw Lolo.

He had to bring her back, now that Jaxon had made a deal.

Minutes later, Suah arrived at the main highway. He was drenched with sweat and out of breath from running. He made quick work of crossing the highway and couldn't wait to see the bus stop. It was a couple blocks north of where he stood. But the timing couldn't have been more unfortunate.

As he gazed, a bus with an open door accepted Lolo up its steps. Suah couldn't understand how she had made it all the way to the highway so quickly. She must have gotten a ride from somebody. He took off in a run to try catching the bus but it was too far away and he was already too winded. The run up the parkway had taken most of his energy. The little that was left would never get him there in time.

He stood and watched Lolo and the bus drive away, back to town. Not only had he missed her and the bus, he had no money to get on the next bus. Even if he had, the next bus was half an hour away.

There wasn't much sense going back to talk to Jaxon Muse if Lolo didn't come along. The whole point of coming to the conference was so he could set things right for her. Jaxon seemed agitated with him anyway. Suah didn't want to upset him anymore.

Standing by the side of the road, Suah was tired and disappointed. Nothing had worked out like he planned. Now he had the long walk back into town. That would take a couple of hours, at least.

He started to walk but as he walked something even worse occurred to him. In his excitement to see his mission be a success, he hadn't quite thought everything through.

There was no way he was getting back to the beach with Blake. It was bad enough that Blake would be really mad at him. But first things first.

Suah halted on the thought. How was he going to get home?

CHAPTER 18

A conga-beat ringtone interrupted the whisper of the trade winds.

Startled awake, Paige grabbed her phone and turned off the alarm. She squinted then donned sunglasses. On seeing the time, she sighed. 4:15 p.m. Suah would be on his way home from the beach. Where had the day gone?

It was time to get dressed and do the nanny thing again.

She sat up in the lounge chair. The drift of cotton-ball clouds reflected in glassy pool water. If nothing else, she had gotten some rest and deepened her tan. That was all the multitasking she had in mind for the day. Reaching to the back of her neck, she retied the string holding up her bikini top.

It was nice for once to enjoy some of the niceties of Gianna's estate instead of being onsite merely as hired help. Suah's change of plans in the morning had turned out to be just what Paige needed. It was *so* perfect, she wondered why she hadn't thought of it herself.

Then again, she had a good excuse for being a little out of it. Yesterday with Diego would have distracted and worn out anybody. Not only did he have stamina as a lover, he could certainly out-drink her.

She stood and gathered up her towel and lotion before taking a leisurely walk to the mud room off the kitchen. The maid's half-day was done so there was no one else in the house. Paige shed her bikini as soon as she got in the door. She reached for clothes on the counter just as her phone rang. Looking down, she saw it was Diego. Sighing with a smirk, she answered it.

"Miss me already?" Her nakedness only enhanced her coy grin.

"What do you think?"

"I think you should get a new hobby. The current one is making me sore."

"You'd send me into the arms of another woman?" He feigned surprise.

"I was thinking of something a little more domestic. Maybe adding on a room or digging a pool."

"That would definitely use up some energy…" He left it hanging.

"Let me guess," added Paige. "But it wouldn't be nearly as much fun."

"You know me so well."

"I know more about what you like than what you don't like…"

"So when are we going to have some more fun?"

Paige sat back against the low counter and smoothed a hand up and down along her leg. "I don't know…"

"You've had your day of rest. You've got the house to yourself."

"You're forgetting about Suah."

"No I'm not. He has his bedtime…and we'll have ours."

"That would never work. You know how I am; I make too much noise."

"You didn't in the pool last night…" Diego's reminder had mischief in it.

"That doesn't count. You took advantage of me when I was passed out."

"I did not! You were relaxed, that's all."

"Is that what you call it…"

Diego painted the scene in low, romantic tones. "You know better than that. You had *every* advantage. You floated in the spa with strong hands holding you up. You laid back and gazed at the stars. All you had to do was let go and have slow, passionate love made to you."

Taken with the thought, Paige had to grin. "Like I said, I passed out."

"So what about the guesthouse?"

"What about it?" Paige stepped to the door and let sunshine set her bare skin aglow with its warmth.

"I'll stop by later, after you tuck Suah in. He can have his special little dreams…and we'll have the guesthouse, where we won't disturb him."

Paige wavered. The warmth of sunshine on her skin converged with thoughts of what the night could be. Standing naked in the light was making the temptation harder to resist.

Diego went for the assumptive close. "I'll be there right after Gianna's webcam thing with Suah. OK?"

Scheduling details jolted Paige out of her reverie. "No…"

"Why not?"

"I mean…she's not calling at the regular time. Tonight it's earlier, at six o'clock."

"Why the change?"

"She's in Sydney. It's a concert day. She has to call before she goes to the stadium."

"All right," concluded Diego. "Even better. That gets it out of the way even earlier. So when should I get there?"

Paige weakened. To answer with a time was to commit herself to the plan. She raised a hand to her breast. "Eight o'clock…but we have to tone it down; we can't go all night like last night."

Diego enticed, "Whatever you want. You call the shots. I'll leave whenever you say."

Paige hesitated. "Promise?"

"Promise…" He spoke with the expectancy of adding more. "You know, we're spending so much time together, we might have to find a way to stay together on a more permanent basis."

Paige caught her breath. "You like to have fun, but don't play with me."

"I'm just sayin'...it's something we need to explore. Don't go getting all weirded out about it."

Paige chuckled. "Yeah, that would be so unlike me."

"Ah, anyway..." stammered Diego. "That kinda thing is better talked about in person." He laughed. "Forget I said anything."

She forced a businesslike mask over her smile. "Consider it done."

Diego needed another way to change the subject. "Hey, I just checked the time. It's twenty to five. Any sign of my kid?"

Startled back into the moment, Paige rushed back to the counter. "Oh, my God! I've got to get some clothes on!" She set the phone down. Through the speaker, she could hear Diego laugh.

"What the hell are you doing over there? Starting without me?"

"I was by the pool..." she explained. Hurrying on panties and Capris, she bent closer to the phone. "When was the last time you heard from Blake?"

"Oh, I don't know. This morning he said he was only going out for a little while. Then around noon, he called and said he might make it a full day."

"So, you're not sure when he's coming back?"

"Well, he never stays out past four, not on a day with such lousy surf."

Paige hurried on a bra. "That's almost an hour ago..."

"Yeah...OK."

"It's not OK if he thinks the webcam call is at nine o'clock tonight."

"I don't think he keeps track of that."

Paige buttoned her blouse. Her anxiety level was rising. "You know what happens if Suah isn't here at six to talk to his mother, don't you?"

"Don't jump ahead of things. That's over an hour away."

"But you don't know where he is or how long it's going to take him."

"I know he's on his way."

"How?"

"How did we know any other day?"

"Listen," snapped Paige. "At three o'clock Sydney time, that's six o'clock here, Gianna is going to sit down expecting to see Suah. Do you want to be the one who has to explain to her why her boy isn't available? Huh?"

"All right, already," snapped Diego. "I give Blake a call and tell him to get his butt over there. Don't worry; he knows there will be hell to pay if he screws this up. Believe me, he'll do anything to avoid that."

CHAPTER **19**

Blake cruised the old Datsun down the main street of town. Looking left and right, he scoured the sidewalks in front of the restaurants and shops for any sign of Suah. Light of day was fading and with it went any hope that the situation would have a good ending.

With one hand on the wheel, he grabbed his ringing cell phone off the seat next to him. After a glance to check the caller, he pressed phone to ear.

"Duff, any luck?"

"No, man. I've been all over the place. He's nowhere."

Duffy sounded defeated. He had been the one who had gone for food at lunchtime. His car pulled the open trailer, the place they figured out hours ago must have been Suah's getaway hiding spot.

As soon as Duffy had gotten back to the beach with food, Blake had come in from the surf and discovered Suah gone. It didn't take long to surmise what had happened.

Since then, Blake had been on the hunt to find the boy. Feeling partly responsible, Duffy had joined in the search. After nearly five hours of frustration, both of them were beyond aggravation. Blake wanted a miracle before he exacted his vengeance. Duffy just wanted it to be over.

"Where are you?" asked Blake.

"I'm at the park, on the north side."

"Did you go in the village shops?"

"Yeah, I checked around the seawall again and some of the shops but come on man, there's no way we can look everywhere. There's got to be a million places to hide. Did you cruise the alley?"

"I just came from there. I walked it this time."

"He must be with somebody," concluded Duffy. "Maybe he took off with them. Are you sure he doesn't know anybody down here?"

"How should I know?" snapped Blake. "The kid's a little freak. If he knows anybody, it's probably some whacked-out bum that sleeps on the beach." Blake turned off the main street and pulled up behind Duffy's trailer and parked. To his right was the big tree and the sound of birds chirping in anticipation of their sunset roost.

Seeing Blake's arrival, Duffy ended the phone call and ambled towards the Datsun. Blake got out and met him on the sidewalk.

"So what now?" asked Duffy. "I've got to take off pretty soon."

Blake knew that Duffy wouldn't search very much longer but hearing it confirmed only reinforced how late it was getting. Blake couldn't look him in the eye. Instead, he swept his gaze across the park. Before he could think of anything to say, his phone rang again.

He checked the caller and flushed red. Leaning back on the hood of his car, he let out a heavy sigh. "Shit! It's my dad."

Duffy folded his arms and shook his head to commiserate.

Blake answered the phone. "Yeah, what's up?"

"Where the hell are you?"

Blake hesitated. Telling the truth meant trouble but not telling it meant worst trouble. If nothing else, the fact that Suah had run away from him was on his side. Maybe it was lucky this hadn't happened on any of the other days when Suah had been dumped off at the food truck. The only way out of this might be to tell the truth and blame it all on the kid.

"I'm in town," answered Blake.

"Doing what?" snapped Diego. "Paige needs Suah home right now. Get on the stick and get him there."

"I want to…" admitted Blake. "First I have to find him."

Diego's tone ramped into high gear. "What do you mean *find him*? Where is he? What the hell have you been doing?"

"Nothing! We went to the beach, just like I said."

"Then what are you doing in town?"

"He got away from me…"

"Got away!"

"He snuck off in another car while I was surfing. Honest, I've been searching for him all over town!"

"Goddamn it! Can't you do one simple fucking thing? All you had to do was keep your eye on him."

"He was on the beach. I didn't think he could go anyplace."

"You don't think at all! How could he get in some car and drive away?"

"It wasn't a car; it was the back of a trailer."

"I don't give a shit what it was! Don't you have the sense to tell the guys you're with to watch out for such things?"

"They aren't going to watch him; they don't care…"

"Do you realize what's about to happen if you don't get him home? In less than an hour, his mother is going to call to talk to him."

"I didn't know that…"

"You know it now! You should have been there by now!"

The power of Diego's tone struck fear into Blake. He pushed up off the hood of his car and paced. "I'm trying to find him," pleaded Blake. "Me and Duffy have been looking for hours."

"For hours!" Diego went ballistic. "When did this happen?"

Blake wavered. It was too late to take it back. Impressing on Diego how long they'd searched was a lame attempt at scoring points for effort. It had slipped out. Only afterwards did Blake realize the way Diego would take it. A child missing for hours only pointed out the severity of what they faced.

Blake's voice quavered. "When Duffy went for lunch, around noon."

For a second, Diego was too livid and concerned to talk.

Blake stopped pacing but his hand shook as it held the phone to his ear.

When Diego spoke, he was controlled but forceful. "In forty-five minutes, Gianna Chase will make that call. Suah better be there. You hear me?"

Mad at the situation, Blake grasped at straws. "Maybe Paige could tell her he ran away or something…"

"Oh, yeah, that's really smart!" shouted Diego. "Don't try to think, dumb ass! Just find the kid and get him home!"

Diego hung up and left Blake standing with few options left.

Duffy shuffled around. "He's really pissed, huh?"

Blake nodded and searched the ground for a way out.

"Why did you have to mention me?" asked Duffy.

Blake looked up. "It's no big deal. I didn't say it's your fault or anything."

"Yeah, I guess so. Well, I don't know where else to look…"

Blake knew what was coming next so he cut to the chase. "I know, you've got to go."

Duffy stuffed a hand in pocket and fished out his car keys. "If you need anything else later on, give me a call."

"OK, thanks." Watching Duffy take off, Blake leaned back on his car. The Datsun wasn't much but even that he'd lose if things didn't work out.

Blake watched Duffy's car and trailer turn the corner and disappear. He stood, locked in place, and tried sorting out the shambles of the day. It was so crazy it didn't make sense. The one and only day that Blake actually did as he was told and took the little bastard to the beach, that's the day the kid snakes away and gets everyone in trouble. Go figure.

There was nothing left to do but continue the search until it was too late.

Blake resolved: if it got to that point, there'd be some serious payback. Guaranteed. If he was going to lose everything, he had nothing left to lose.

CHAPTER 20

There was a polite knock at the door. Gianna Chase ignored it and continued picking at her room service food while reading a magazine.

The knock came again. Not taking her eyes from the page, Gianna called out, "Ava, there's someone at the door."

From the next room, Gianna's personal tour assistant rushed in. Her petite frame belied what a powerhouse aide she was. "I'm sorry; I didn't hear it."

Gianna didn't answer; she was too engrossed in the article being read.

The door opened and the hallway guard let Olivia Platt pass. Ava smiled and nodded to her and she smiled back. Olivia was as calm as a business manager could be when their one and only client was on tour.

Olivia headed straight away for the picture window where Gianna sat. Sizing up Gianna's casual dress and gourmet late lunch, Olivia took note that Gianna didn't look up from the page.

"What's so engrossing?" Olivia only asked the question as a way to start the conversation. She could tell from the magazine's page layout what the topic was, even when, from her vantage point, it was upside down.

Gianna glanced up. "You know very well."

Olivia took a seat then gazed out the window. "Wouldn't you rather look at the *Royal Botanical Gardens*? They're quite beautiful this time of day…"

Finishing a section, Gianna lifted a napkin from her lap and tossed it onto her plate. "My God, it never stops…"

Olivia sighed. "We knew this was coming. If anything, it could be worse."

"Excuse me but it's not comforting to think so." Gianna sat back and crossed her legs. "Is there anybody in the press corps who *hasn't* had an interview with the oh-so debonair Jacob Ferrère?"

Olivia smirked, "*Guns & Ammo*?"

"Don't give me any ideas." Gianna's sideways glance told all.

"Let him talk," reasoned Olivia. "He's already overexposed. I give it another week and the tabloids will *have to* find something else."

"Rag sheets are one thing but this is calculated."

Olivia reached for a water glass. "Exactly. It's a campaign. His people are going to milk this until his picture opens next month. That's all it's about."

"Oh, so I shouldn't take it personally…"

"Of course it's personal but it's also good business."

"Making it about me is giving it legs—and you know it."

"Yes, you've got to hand him that; it's clever—and expected."

"He's put himself in the perfect position to use *my* celebrity status to promote his film…"

"And isn't *that* a piece of work," laughed Olivia. "You have to admit, it's going to need all the help it can get. If anything, take comfort in the fact that the timing of your breakup seems more about promoting his film than throwing you off balance right before the tour."

"Either he tried to sabotage my tour or he's using my pain to promote his latest ego-extravaganza. To me it's shitty either way. As far as I know, he had *both* in mind from the very start!"

"If nothing else, the more angry he makes you, the less time you have to be sad. You're not the kind of person to have two emotions at the same time." The observation by Olivia was more personal than professional and not one she intended to share so blatantly. As soon as she said it, she regretted it.

"And how does that work out on stage?" Gianna's reference recalled a rough opening night in Tokyo a few days back.

Olivia didn't want to go down that rabbit hole. In a few minutes, they were heading over to the *Sydney Entertainment Centre* for a sound check before the concert. There was no sense rehashing bad energy before a show.

"This town loves you," asserted Olivia. "That's all you need to know."

Gianna stood and paced to the next window. "You don't want to disappoint somebody you love."

"You're not going to disappoint anybody…"

"The Centre is sold out; how many seats is that?"

Olivia didn't skip a beat. "An end-stage layout with a reserved floor at the Centre—that's 11,546 seats."

Gianna kept her gaze on a ferry boat leaving Circular Quay down below. "You're the one who said I'm in the emotion business. Emotion is the way I connect. That's what you said."

"That's right." Olivia couldn't deny what they both knew was true.

"So what emotion will I have tonight?"

Just then, Ava entered the main suite from the bedroom. "Excuse me, Gianna. It's time for your webcam call."

Olivia and Gianna fixed their eyes on one another but Olivia left Gianna's question unanswered. Gianna said nothing more. She made strides into the bedroom and sat down at the dressing table.

Before her, a laptop waited; it's webcam window was open.

"I haven't connected yet," explained Ava. "…in case you were delayed."

"That's fine," answered Gianna. "Thank you."

Touching the screen, Gianna initiated the call. After a pause, the display window changed and Paige came into view.

"Gianna! Hello!" smiled Paige. "How's life down under?"

Gianna leaned back to get comfortable. "So far so good but I haven't done anything yet."

"Where are you staying?" asked Paige.

"*Sir Stamford*—at Circular Quay."

"Sounds nice."

"It has its diversions," bantered Gianna.

"I'll have to check it out online…"

"You're into antiques, aren't you?"

"Oh, you know it."

"Then you should stay here when you get down this way. They have some interesting Georgian pieces and Louis the 15th."

"Really?" Paige sounded eager.

"Yes…well, I have to leave in a few minutes. Is Suah nearby?"

Paige smiled as she stammered. "Well…no…"

"What's the matter?" prompted Gianna, suddenly serious.

"Oh nothing. It's stupid; my fault really. Diego and Blake stopped by to drop off some kind of game for Suah. They got talking about pizza and Suah decided he wanted one…"

"So what happened?" Gianna interrupted.

"Well…I let Suah go with them to pick up the pizza."

"You what?"

"I know," implored Paige. "It's totally wrong, against the rules. I shouldn't have. They should have been back by now."

"So why aren't they?"

"On the way back, Diego's car got a flat. Then he found out the spare wasn't much better."

Gianna leaned forward. "If I call back in an hour, will Suah be home?"

"Oh, no problem, Ms. Chase," gushed Paige, apologetically. "I'm so sorry."

Gianna was annoyed. "I don't like the idea of you letting Suah go with other people for any reason, even people you know."

"It'll never happen again. I don't know what I was thinking."

Gianna reached for the screen. Her index finger hovered over the button to disconnect. "I'll call back at seven o'clock your time."

Paige nodded. "We'll be here."

Gianna jabbed the button and strode out of room. Along the way, she passed her assistant. "Ava, I'll need the laptop set up in my dressing room at the Centre. I'm going to have to make another call—an hour from now."

Olivia heard the last half of the instructions to Ava as Gianna entered the main suite. Turning her head, Olivia watched Gianna's body language and read her mood. "Something going on?"

Gianna paced to the bed and back. "The last thing I needed."

"Did you talk to Suah?" asked Olivia.

Gianna approached the table where Olivia sat observing her restlessness. "No. He's out getting pizza with Diego and Blake and their car's had a flat."

Olivia's grin was tinged with puzzlement. "Don't you have a rule…"

"Yes!" snapped Gianna. "I'm not paying her to hand Suah over to somebody else, even for a few minutes—I don't care *who* it is. I can't believe she did this."

Olivia shrugged. "It's true, she completely ignored your rule. Then again, a ride to get pizza doesn't sound too threatening."

"That's not the point!" Gianna paced to the wet bar and snatched up her sunglasses. "I need to get to the Centre."

Olivia stood and followed. As she went, she shared a glance with Ava.

Olivia mumbled, "Nothing like a sound check to put things in perspective."

"That's right…" Opening the front door to the suite, Gianna took a step out and looked back at Olivia. "Maybe you should sit down front while we go through it."

Olivia knew what was coming and showed Gianna a grin in anticipation.

Gianna concluded, "You can tell me what kind of emotion I'm going to have tonight."

Five thousand miles away, another call was made.

"It's after six! Did you talk to Blake?"

"Yeah, I told him to get Suah there or else."

"Well, he isn't here! I just had to lie to Gianna, now where is he!"

"He's on the way."

"He better be! She's calling back at seven. If he doesn't get here, I have nothing to say. It's over! It's all over!"

CHAPTER 21

The headlights of passing traffic whizzed by leaving darkness behind. Suah kept a slow but steady pace on his walk back to town. Once or twice, he looked down at his wrist. It was a newfound habit, one that expected to see what time it was. But not today. He wasn't wearing Blake's wristwatch.

His legs ached and he was hungry. The farther he walked, the more he was sure he could put up with hunger and a little soreness if only he could get something to quench his thirst. He knew a spot in the alley in town where a garden hose was sometimes connected to a faucet. To keep his pace and motivation going, he aimed his steps in that direction.

He knew if he kept going along the same side of the road he'd end up at the food truck pick-up spot. But that was the last place he wanted to be. He didn't expect Blake to go there this late but he didn't want to take any chances. Who knew what Blake would do if he was mad enough.

A dozen daydreams later, Suah reached the southern city limits of the town. Grateful to finally be off the busy main highway, he took a side street that ended at the east side of the park with the big tree.

A scattering of dingy amber lights lit up the area underneath the big tree. A few people were walking about, talking a stroll, or sitting on a bench. At first glance, the park looked inviting. If he didn't find his way home, it might be a good place to sleep on a bench overnight.

Crossing the street, he approached the sidewalk that bordered the park. His pace slowed and the energy of the place was all encompassing. At night, the park had lazy energy that was a bit foreboding. Shadows under the sprawling tree limbs were deeper and the limbs appeared more jagged and menacing than during the day.

Judging by the way it looked, the park could easily be an enchanted forest where magic things went to hide. In other ways, it was a normal public place that just so happened to have an extraordinary tree growing in it. The odd mixture of impressions made it a typical place that left one feeling surreal.

Suah strolled along the border sidewalk and took in the sights inside the park. One of them was the bench where Lolo ate her lunch every day. The sight of it made him remember their last conversation at the resort.

She was so upset at him for bringing her there. It was hard to understand why. The only explanation Suah could come up with was all the commotion that had gone on before. None of that had he planned. The way all the people acted would have made anybody nervous. But once they were alone with Jaxon Muse, it should have been all right.

Suah wondered. The only other explanation for Lolo's reaction might be the last thing she said. She was mad at him for calling her Lolo; she said it wasn't her name. That was a surprise. She'd never told him any other name. But then, he never said her name much if at all; they had always just talked. Even if he got it wrong, was it such a bad thing that she had to run off?

Perhaps he should have told her why they were going to the conference right from the start. Maybe it wasn't such a good idea to make it a surprise but he didn't see why. It was hard to understand people sometimes. There didn't seem to be any steady way to guess how different people would react to the same thing. Weren't surprises saved for special occasions like birthdays and other parties where people celebrated things? Getting the help of Jaxon Muse certainly would have been special, something to celebrate.

Suah walked on. He knew the park's drinking fountain was broken so he trudged in the direction of the alleyway. After the distance he'd come, the little bit left he had to go to get to the alley wasn't much of a challenge in comparison. Besides, he was back on familiar ground. After the last few days, he knew these sidewalks like the floor plan of his house, and he knew that like the back of his hand.

The water faucet he remembered was one third of the way down the alley. By the time he got to the alleyway's entrance, the last glow of twilight had faded, the stars were out, and darkness had settled in. He stopped a minute and looked down the alley's gloomy expanse. It was hard to see anything.

It wasn't so much the darkness that was unsettling as the unknown that might be hiding in it that gave him pause. He had never been one who feared monsters under his bed or boogeyman in his closet, but there was something about the darkness outside in nature that was different—to be respected.

Faint memories of open fields and village life in Africa still filled him with a rush. It was a gut response, a vestige of a time when big animal noises in the dark, untamed fields, and his grandfather's captivating tales of magic in a world unseen had made the unknown a palpable thing.

Suah stepped on, into the darkness. His grandfather had filled him with enough instincts about the dark to know where to step and when to be still.

When he finally found the faucet, the garden hose was missing. He tilted his head and drank right from the spigot. In rhythmic gulps he took in large drafts of water and felt better. He breathed in and splashed his face. *There were good things to be found in the darkness—if you knew your way.*

CHAPTER 22

The tension in the town car came in waves. Isolated behind a soundproof partition, Jaxon Muse and his daughter endured the ride back to their vacation rental. Hailey slumped off to one side with thumbs working a smart phone. Jaxon tried to lecture her but found her practiced teenage snub nearly impenetrable.

"You can't just let people into the conference like that," Jaxon reiterated.

Hailey gave him a dagger glance. Even that was a concession.

Jaxon answered what she was thinking. "That includes people we know. You barely know Suah and you know nothing about the girl he brought with him, do you?"

Hailey said nothing. A lie was obvious and the truth did her no good.

"Maybe…" Jaxon suggested, "…maybe it's not so wise to include you in these trips after all."

Being punished was one thing, but for Hailey, being cut off from travel and all the mischief she was used to enjoying on the road was a threat that took it too far. That was a suggestion serious enough to quiet her thumbs. Letting the phone drop to her lap, she looked up.

"So what…" she huffed. "Every time you get a little upset you're going to pull out the nuclear option on me?"

"What other way is there to get through to you?" asked Jaxon.

Hailey pled her case. "All I wanted was to get a ride home with a friend I met at the pool. What's the big deal?"

"I'm not talking about that."

"I was. You ignored it."

"I didn't ignore it. I just didn't give you the answer you wanted. I asked you who this friend was and you really didn't know."

"I told you his name."

"Is that all you need to get in a guy's car?"

"Geez, nothing like being paranoid."

"Being cautious is not paranoia."

"I didn't think I was supposed to assume the worst in people; just the opposite." Conceding the point, she changed topics. "I don't see why we have to rent a fortress house behind a gate anyway. You know I wanted to stay at the resort all along."

"You know the drill," countered Jaxon. "I never stay at the same place where the conference is going to be. There are good reasons for that..."

"Yeah, yeah, but *The Manuia* isn't the only resort on the island."

"It doesn't matter. At any resort, we'd face the same issues."

"I don't get it," snapped Hailey. "You're supposed to have these zillions of people who like you so much but you go to so much trouble hiding away from them." She picked up her phone and bowed her head to it. "After today, I bet you're going to have to work a lot harder keeping them away."

Jaxon's mood shifted as his thoughts drifted back to the numinous. "What happened today is beyond any of this; it shouldn't be misconstrued."

Hailey worked her thumbs. "Yeah, well, everybody has their own ideas about that."

Jaxon shifted his gaze to look her way. "What do you mean?"

"I guess you were too busy schmoozing after the conference to check what's happening online."

"Like what?" Jaxon was suddenly interested.

"*Miraculous healing* is a big trending topic right now...along with *Near-Life Experience*."

Jaxon reached for her phone. "Let me see that."

Hailey reluctantly handed it over. She grinned, "It's wild what some people are saying about it..."

Scanning down the list of posts, Jaxon was dismayed to see so many people leaping to wild conclusions, not only about what had happened at the conference, but who the boy and woman involved truly were and what their relationship to Jaxon Muse might be.

Hailey snatched her phone back. "What does it mean to *talk in tongues*? Did Suah do that?"

Jaxon was pensive. "He said something; I don't know what it was."

Hailey flipped to another website. "Well, there's some guy in Sri Lanka who claims he can decipher it."

"How does he know what Suah said?"

Hailey read down the post. "He says he saw the video."

"Where?" Jaxon tensed.

"Right here; he's got a link to it."

"Give me that," ordered Jaxon.

He grabbed the phone and navigated the link. Right away, a cell phone video taken during the conference started to play. Jaxon's gaze intensified as he watched. Suah could be plainly seen rocking forward then back. The stricken woman was lifeless to all outward appearances. People were crowded around including Jaxon Muse in plain view.

> *"You are here, you are enough..."*
> Suah rocked back...
> *"Imamu, skudakumoochooowte..."*
> He rocked back...
> *"Bote, Alma Bote, Ananta Bath..."*
> He rocked back...
> *"Obarati Ochee Afikomen Banafrit..."*
> He rocked back...
> *"Sikera Bote, Alma Bote, Subito Fröhlich Kutamba..."*
> Suah rocked back—and then came forward one last time.
> *"Your flame is blue, your flame is green,*
> *I-and-I...and all unseen..."*

Hailey slumped back and rested her head on the leather seat. She could see the consternation in her father's face and she loved it. The more time he was occupied handling his own crises, the less time he'd have to make any for her.

To let him know she had stumbled on all the dirt she could while searching the topic online, she added one last observation. It was only what other people were saying so she couldn't be taken to task for it.

"A lot of people think they saw a miracle..." Her opening line was just the setup. "...but some think you staged the whole thing to sell books."

Jaxon's jaw was firm. He handed her phone back. "To be expected. No matter what you do, you're going to run into those types."

"Oh," observed Hailey. "So we shouldn't think the best of people—well, not *all* people."

Jaxon eased back. She thought she had caught him in another hypocritical deviation from his pure and straightforward philosophy. But the events of the day had changed his focus. For once, their endless contest to see who would gain the upper hand seemed pointless. His smile was slight.

"You know, Hailey," he started. "Being right for the wrong reasons is not really possible when you stop and think about it."

She absolutely couldn't let him have the last word. She stared into the lighted display of her phone. "Neither is being wise..."

She left the rest of the statement understood between them.

The town car drove on.

CHAPTER **23**

Gianna Chase stepped to a point downstage center and let her eyes sweep the auditorium. Thousands of empty seats pulled at her with their potential energy. Each numbered space represented the time of someone's life.

In less than an hour, strangers who appeared out there would join with her to make magic. Their combined magic would be conjured up out of incantations set to a beat and amplified as if thundered down from on high.

It was a modern interpretation of an ancient and hallowed ritual.

Tuning out all extraneous noise, Gianna listened to the silence and drew strength from it. These were the moments before a concert she cherished the most. Only here and now could she hear the wishes of everyone on their way to see her. Those wishes were the desires that prepared her to be kinetic.

Behind her, craft workers prepped the concert set and made final adjustments to spotlights in the lighting grid. Several sound checks were complete; one more was on tap for cameo backup musicians. In between section breaks, she had a few moments to contemplate the indescribable.

A voice crackled in her earbud. "Ms. Chase, just a reminder. Your seven o'clock appointment is in ten minutes."

Gianna switched on her wireless mike. "Thank you, Matthew. Could you tell Ava I'm on my way?"

"Right away."

Gianna turned on heel and left the stage via a short set of stairs that led to a corridor defined by blackout drapes. Along the way, one of the new backup singers dashed up to her.

"Hello, Ms. Chase." The young woman was more excited than nervous but her nervous energy alone could have lit the stadium. "I just wanted to thank you for this opportunity."

Gianna slowed but kept walking as the young woman tagged along. "You're Diana, our new singer," smiled Gianna.

The woman brightened even more at being recognized. "Yes, tonight I officially join the tour. It seems like I've been an understudy forever."

"You'll do great. You killed it on your audition tape."

"You saw that?" The girl had hoped but never expected that Gianna herself would get so involved in a quick replacement for someone taken ill.

"I not only saw it," grinned Gianna, "I recommended you." Gianna stepped into an elevator. "See you onstage."

The young girl beamed. The elevator doors closed. Gianna's spirits were buoyed by the encounter. Despite anything else going on, it was energizing to be in the position to nurture new talent and make someone's dream come true. The girl's joy was contagious and just what Gianna needed.

When the elevator doors opened again, Ava was standing in the hallway with her digital tablet, prescient as only a top assistant can be.

"The laptop's on your dressing table, ready to go."

Gianna made strides down the hallway with Ava marching right after.

"What about the second costume change?"

"Taken care of. You have twenty seconds more off the transition."

"And the house lights?"

"They'll come up at the end of *Make The World Well Again*."

"Did Elijah call?"

"No. You're due in hair and makeup in twenty minutes."

Gianna and Ava entered the dressing suite. Gianna went straightaway to her dressing table and sat down. Looking into the mirror, she locked gazes with Olivia sitting on a couch behind her.

"You still here?" asked Gianna. "I thought you had something you wanted to leak to the press corps."

Olivia remained seated comfortably. "It'll wait."

Gianna glanced at the webcam screen and then back into the mirror. "That'll be all for now, Ava."

Ava knew the signal that Gianna wanted time alone with her business manager and made a quick and graceful exit.

Gianna waited until the door was closed. "I know when you're concerned about something. What is it?"

They had no time to develop this conversation and be elegant about it. They'd known each other long enough that it shouldn't matter, but it did.

Olivia hesitated then answered. "Nothing much. We both know things have been a bit tenuous. Since the call at *Sir Stamford* didn't go as planned, I'm interested to see how things work out."

It was obvious to Gianna but she wanted to see if Olivia would admit it. Troubles at home might impact the tour; that was the crux of the matter. Olivia was standing by as friend but also as business manager just in case.

Gianna reached for the laptop screen. "That's what I thought."

After a touch of a button, the webcam call was placed. The gap of silence that followed held expectations and anxieties but couldn't hold them at bay.

The screen changed and Paige appeared in the webcam window. Her closed-lip smile looked forced. If there was one thing that Gianna had learned as a survival skill in the entertainment business, it was the facility to read the person behind the mask.

"Paige…" Gianna spoke out of surprise. Again, as back at the hotel, she expected to see Suah.

"Hello, Ms. Chase…" Paige tried to be relaxed and pleasant.

On tour time now, Gianna went right to the point.

"We seem to have a problem."

"I know…" admitted Paige. "I'm so sorry, but there's nothing I could do. Suah isn't back yet."

Gianna bristled. "There's nothing you can do. Do you have a phone?"

"Yes."

"Can you call Diego on that phone?"

"Yes."

"If you called Diego, could he tell you his location?"

Paige could tell where this was headed. This time she could only nod.

Gianna persisted. "If you knew his location, could you drive your car there and pick up Suah?"

Paige said nothing; she didn't even nod. She tensed and glanced down.

"I asked you a question," demanded Gianna.

"Yes…yes I could, if I knew where they were."

"Why don't you?"

Paige hung her head. "Diego doesn't have a flat."

"Then you lied to me," snapped Gianna.

"…they won't tell me where he is."

"What are you talking about? Where's Suah!"

Paige began to cry. "I don't know."

Gianna began to shout. "Is he with Diego and Blake?"

Paige shook her head and didn't stop shaking it. "…I don't know."

"What DO you know?"

"They told me he was on the way…"

"When was that?"

"An hour ago."

"And you've just been sitting there? Did you call and check?"

"I called…but he hasn't been answering."

"Oh my God…" Gianna shouted through her tears.

Olivia rushed to her side and spoke into the webcam. "Paige, this is Olivia. Drive over to Diego's place right now and find out what's going on."

Paige wavered. "I don't know if they're there…"

Gianna leapt up from her seat and brushed by Olivia. Flinging open her dressing room door, she marched into the hallway and shouted at the first person she saw. "Get Ava; I need Ava in here right now!"

When Gianna returned to the room, she found Olivia sitting before the laptop, trying to cajole any other facts she could get out of Paige.

"Step aside," ordered Gianna. She sat down and glared into the monitor. "You no longer work for me. If you want to avoid prosecution by the authorities, you will get your ass in the car and go find Suah."

Before Paige could answer, Gianna jammed a finger on the button to disconnect the call. From the hallway, Ava rushed in.

"Did you want to see me?"

Gianna jumped up and paced. "I need you to call the police right now!"

Ava froze, not knowing what was wrong.

Olivia explained. "…call the island police back at Gianna's estate."

"Is something wrong at the house?" asked Ava.

"Suah is missing!" Gianna's cry was labored with anguish.

"Missing!" Ava was stunned.

Helping Gianna collapse into a seated position on the couch, Olivia took over for her. "Just call the police. Tell them that Suah Chase is missing. He was last seen with Diego and Blake Fry. Tell them they also need to check with Paige Atwater; she was the nanny on duty when Suah went missing."

"Yes, ma'am." Ava took notes then rushed from the room.

Olivia closed the door behind her then hurried back to Gianna's side. Sitting next to her, she pressed their hands together. "It's going to be all right," promised Olivia. "I'm sure it's just a misunderstanding."

Gianna was inconsolable. "This can't be happening. I knew I shouldn't have gone without him. What was I thinking?"

"Don't go blaming yourself. Let's take this one step at a time."

"She doesn't know where he is! You heard her…"

"Ava will make the call. We'll find out what's going on."

"She hasn't been with him for hours! Who knows where he might be…"

"Getting ahead of ourselves isn't going to do anyone any good."

"The one time I leave him; I should have been there." Gianna faded back.

"Gianna, stay with me…we'll get through this…"

Olivia felt Gianna's weight slump into her; she had fainted.

Olivia rushed to the room phone and punched in a four-number extension. "We need portable oxygen and fruit juice in room 1408. Bring it right up and keep it to yourself."

Rushing back to the couch, Olivia positioned Gianna on her back and stuffed pillows under her legs to prop them higher. Unscrewing the top to a bottle of water, she turned with a knock at the door.

"Who is it?" asked Olivia.

"It's Ava."

"Come in." Olivia poured some water on a face towel and dabbed it on Gianna's forehead.

Ava shut the door behind her. "I've made the call. They had a bunch more questions I couldn't answer."

"That's OK. They have what they need to get started."

"What happened?" asked Ava.

"She fainted."

"She's due in hair and makeup in ten minutes."

"I'm well aware of that."

"Should I let the production staff know there might be a delay?"

"No!" snapped Olivia.

"I can ask if the opening act will extend their set, give us some time…"

"I said no changes…" With her conversation with Gianna not yet finished, Olivia knew she'd better qualify that statement. "…not yet."

Ava was well aware of Olivia's single focus on making the tour succeed. Ava only took issue when that focus excluded what was best for Gianna. It might be stepping out of her role as assistant, but Ava wouldn't stand by without raising the issue that Olivia made obvious by avoidance.

"If Suah is missing…do you really expect her to go on tonight?"

The question went to the heart of the matter. Olivia stood and faced Ava.

"There's nothing Gianna can do from here. You made the call. Everything that can be done is being done."

"But she may be too upset…"

Olivia stepped forward. If anything, she was thankful for Ava's impertinence. It served as needed rehearsal for a conversation she expected to be having with Gianna in a few minutes. She stared Ava down.

"The best thing for Gianna right now is to do what she loves—be with the people who love her. Are you one of those people?"

Ava didn't flinch but she also didn't answer. She wouldn't give Olivia the satisfaction. Besides, the question was insulting and condescending. Olivia might get her way but at least Ava could take some satisfaction in going on record that Gianna was much more than a singing machine.

Knowing that she'd have to work with Ava going forward, Olivia followed her punches with strokes meant as salve for Ava's ego.

"You're so close to her; she relies on you so much." Olivia relaxed and lightened her tone. "It's easy to be upset. But we all want the best for her. Even if we have differences, at least let's agree on that."

Time and opportunity would not let Ava take it any further. The best she could do was smooth the way for whatever was about to happen.

"I'll let hair and makeup know they'll have less time."

"Good idea."

At the door, a production assistant knocked. "Olivia?"

Opening the door, Olivia showed Ava the way out and took the juice and handheld oxygen canister from the production assistant.

"Any trouble getting up here?" she asked.

He shook his head. "No. Is she OK?"

"She's fine. She's resting a bit." Moving into his line of sight, she started closing him out.

"What's the oxygen for?"

"It's stuffy up here. We thought it might be a good energy boost."

She closed the door and hurried back to Gianna's side.

In a few minutes, she had Gianna sitting up.

"What happened?" asked Gianna.

"Nothing. You got a little lightheaded." She handed her the juice. "Here, drink this, you'll feel better."

Gianna held the juice but didn't drink. "Did you find out anything?"

"Ava made the call. Everything is being handled. They said there's nothing more we can do from here."

"What time is it?" Disorientation hadn't faded yet.

Deciding to take a chance, Olivia opened the door. "Hair and makeup are waiting. We can extend the warm-up act if you want…"

Gianna watched Olivia make her assumptions. It was crass on Olivia's part but Gianna could see how it was the cleanest way to have the kind of conversation they needed to have. No argument. No discussion. Olivia would assume one thing. Gianna would respond. That's all there was to it.

Gianna gazed over at her dressing table. The laptop screen was now dark but the lights around the mirror were bright. They reminded her of Diana, the understudy singer who had thanked her for a chance to fulfill a dream.

She stood and gathered strength. "It's time…to believe in magic."

CHAPTER 24

Scroto got up and moved to the far side of the patio. It didn't take a dog's instincts to know it was smarter to be positioned far out of the way when Diego acted like this—no matter what kind of animal you were.

Pacing in front of the TV football game, Diego pressed phone to ear and managed to be as loud as the commercials. "What do you want me to do?"

On the other side of the line, Paige yelled back. "Do something! What have you done so far?"

"I called Blake. I told him to get his ass over there."

"Call him again!"

"I did. He's not answering his goddamn phone."

"You told me he was on his way."

"I thought he was!"

"That little bastard just got me fired..."

"Now hold on—it was Gianna's kid that ran away."

"Ran away? What are you talking about? You never told me that."

"What difference does it make? It's not like you're going to call Gianna back and tell her, *oh, I made a mistake, Blake didn't lose him; he ran away.* You'd still be admitting he was with Blake and not you."

"When did all of this happen?"

"Blake said the kid took off around lunchtime."

"That's eight hours ago!"

"Tell me about it."

"Are you kidding me? I thought the two of them were just late."

"Yeah, well, it's not like that. Blake's been looking for him all afternoon. He says he's gone all over town and can't find him anywhere."

"Why didn't you tell me this earlier?"

"I thought he'd find him and have him back by now!"

"Even after he missed the first call?"

"Yeah, I thought it would work out."

"I can't believe this!"

"Don't worry; Blake is going to get his as soon as he gets home."

"I don't give a shit about Blake! You didn't have to face Gianna!"

"She'll calm down. It'll work out, just give it time. The kid will show up."

"Don't call me. Don't come by. I don't *ever* want to see you again!"

The call ended. Diego picked up his beer and threw it against the wall.

CHAPTER 25

The vacation house rented by Jaxon Muse for his month's stay on the island was part of a cluster of acre-sized parcels located on a southwest cove. The development was kept exclusive by a guard's booth and gated entry.

Behind manicured hedges and tall walls, a meandering street wound its way past long driveways and strategically-placed foliage. Each driveway was a hint that somewhere at its other end one would find a two-story, custom house lining the shore of a private beach.

The town car turned off the highway and headed up the street towards the guard's booth. Slowing on approach, the car attracted the attention of photographers lying in wait. Jumping out of parked cars, a trio of shadowy forms started running alongside the car.

Jaxon Muse shifted in his seat and lowered the soundproof partition separating the back seat area from the driver.

"Whatever you do, we don't want to stop here."

"Yes, sir," the driver responded.

Photoflashes aimed at the backseat windows.

Hailey jerked around. "Where did *they* come from?"

"Sit back," ordered Jaxon. "We don't know how well these windows are tinted."

"I don't care," snipped Hailey. "I'm ready for my fifteen minutes of fame."

"Haven't you heard? It's down to two minutes; hardly worth the trouble." Jaxon lifted a slim portfolio case and shielded his eyes.

One of the photographers stuck his face close to the window. "Mr. Muse…" he yelped. "Any comment about the boy who did the healing at your conference today?"

The driver slowed to a stop at the guard's booth and powered down his window an inch, just enough to offer an access card. Normally, a coded keypunch on a pad would be enough to open the gate. But with the photographers jockeying for position, the driver didn't want to take any chances by opening the window all the way.

The guard verified the card and activated the gate.

The photographer pressed his face to the window again. "Wait, Mr. Muse…do you confirm or deny that the boy at the conference is Suah Chase, the son of Gianna Chase?"

Hailey came out of her slump. "Gianna Chase? What are they talking about? I didn't know Gianna Chase had a son."

Jaxon pressed his portfolio against the window to block the view. "You don't but rest of the world does."

"I don't see why…"

"The rest of the world doesn't spend all its time shopping and partying."

Ignoring the comment, Hailey chuckled, "That's crazy; he was on the boat with us all day. You didn't know?"

"Gianna Chase has always been very private about the child she adopted."

Hailey sniped, "So which is it? Does the world know or doesn't it?"

The driver accelerated, tearing the window away from the photographers face. The trio in pursuit was left at the guard's booth empty-handed.

The town car made a quick getaway along the street and up one of the driveways. A minute later, they safely parked under the entrance portico. Stepping through their front door, Hailey headed one way, Jaxon another. Along the way, Jaxon encountered the maid.

"Good evening, Mr. Muse."

"Good evening. Where's Claire?"

"I believe she's lying down, resting."

"Thank you." Jaxon headed upstairs and into the bedroom. There he found Claire dozing with the light on. Next to her in bed was an e-Reader that had gone into hibernation.

Movement in the room was enough to wake her. "Ah, good, you're home." Her eyes were droopy but her mind was alert.

Jaxon sat on the bed next to her. "How are you feeling?"

"All right. Since we're having a late dinner I thought I'd take a little nap ahead of time."

"I'm not that hungry," admitted Jaxon. "But I'm happy to watch you eat."

"Before I forget, Perry called."

Jaxon stiffened at the name of his agent in London. "Did he say why?"

"No, but he wants you to call him back, no matter what time it is."

The suggestion set Jaxon's mind to wonder. While he wondered, he changed the subject. "Did anybody else call?"

"I got a call from the doctor."

"Were you expecting one?"

"Not really, but you know how those things go."

"What did he want?"

Claire paused. "He wants me to start the advanced protocol."

Jaxon took a moment to process and decide how to react. The methods to treat Claire's disease had repercussions from mild to severe. Up to now her chemo was somewhere in between. The advanced protocol meant moving beyond that, nearer the severe. Jaxon could only ask, "When?"

Claire was somber but realistic. "He said as soon as I can."

"You mean as soon as we get back to the mainland."

"I don't think so," countered Claire. "He said it's possible to start while we're here. He said it's up to us but he'd recommend it. What do you think?"

Jaxon couldn't tell her what he thought. How do you tell the one you love that the treatment of last resort was the only hope left?

Claire had never been told exactly what the advance protocol entailed. Certainly, it wasn't described as her last chance. That fact was something Jaxon had investigated for himself. He knew Claire hadn't looked into it. She didn't want to dwell on disease or treatment details; she thought it would only make the process of recovery complex and frightening. It was better not to know and simply concentrate on getting better. As she was apt to say, that's all she really had any power over anyway.

It was hard for Jaxon to keep worry and grief from bubbling to the surface. He didn't want to take a chance that she might see any of it. He gave her a smile and patted the blanket covering her legs.

"Let's talk about it in the morning. Rest a little more and I'll give Perry a quick call." Jaxon stood to go.

"All right," she sighed. "Oh, by the way, how did the conference go?"

Jaxon was left speechless as a flood of impressions and reactions coursed through him. There was so much to say and no time to say it in the moment. With so much to share, there was no reason to bother her with a swirl of things still in flux. Jaxon chose to be upbeat and not entirely evasive.

"It went well but it's always dynamic. As usual, there were surprises—and great energy."

"I'm glad," smiled Claire. "You worked so hard on this one. It was so big and you had all the video people to contend with. It's a marvel how you pulled it all together. But this one's recorded; we'll have it always."

Jaxon's smile faded fast. The implications of her last statement brought up so much, much more than she knew. He retreated to the door. "I'll be back to get you after the call. We'll have dinner."

She nodded, smiled then turned her head to the pillow and shut her eyes. Jaxon retreated from the room and headed straightaway for one of the guest bedrooms that had been transformed into his office away from home.

After encountering photographers outside and all he had seen on Hailey's phone, Jaxon needed to return his agent's call and see what he wanted. At least Perry could fill him in on what was going on. More critically, Perry would put a professional perspective on things. He could help Jaxon identify what to ignore and what he must pay attention to.

The curtains were open at the large picture window. The darkness of the bay would be backdrop for the call. Jaxon activated his computer by speaking to it. "Desktop open…make phone call…call Perry."

A black screen came to life and followed his instructions. A long distance number was dialed as Jaxon eased into his chair and crossed his legs.

The ringing went on awhile before a man answered. "Yes, yes, who is it?"

"Perry, it's Jaxon Muse."

"Oh yes, Jaxon…" The voice trailed off.

"Did I wake you? What time of the morning is it over there?"

"I'm not quite sure…five-thirty, I think."

"Sorry to disturb you but you said to call any time."

"Of course, no worries…quite all right. I need to get an early start today anyway. Lots to do. You really know how to stir the pot, don't you?"

Jaxon never had to pull punches or be reserved with Perry. "You mean what happened at the conference."

"Bloody right what happened at the conference!"

"How did you find out?"

"It wasn't hard; the whole thing started trending and then all the video posts went viral."

"I only saw one video…" remarked Jaxon.

"One! My God, no. What did you do—get 50 Nikon D700s and arrange them in a circle? There are so many videos out there from so many angles; I thought I was watching a fashion report from *The Oscars'* red carpet."

Thinking back on the crowd at the conference, Jaxon didn't answer.

Perry was nearly awake now but fully engaged. "As soon as people started saying they recognized the kid, the media got interested. The blogosphere just won't let it go. I had to call and find out directly from you—do you know this kid or not?"

"Yes and no…"

"Jesus and the Saints preserve us! Don't give me that kind of answer! You either know the boy or not? What about the woman? Tell me you didn't set this thing up…"

"Of course not! What do you take me for?"

"Good. It's bad enough a lot of people are going to think that anyway. We don't need Deep Throat coming out of the woodwork next week to prove them right."

"Don't worry. I don't know them—except, I gave the kid a boat ride yesterday, but that's all."

"You gave him what? A boat ride? What is this, *Pirates of Penzance* we're doing here? How did *that* come about?"

"Spur of the moment."

"I should think it would have to be. Who else went along?"

"Claire and Hailey."

"Now this seems odd. The Muse family decides to take a strange boy out for a boat ride, no other guardians necessary."

"You make it sound like it's a kidnapping."

"You have to think the way other people are going to connive. So, on this boat ride, did you happen to get the boy's name?"

"His name is Suah."

"Oh my God...the rumors *are* true!" The shock bordered on awe.

Jaxon inferred the reason behind it. "Let me guess. You're going to tell me Gianna Chase has a son named Suah."

"You didn't know?"

"I knew she adopted a child years ago but she kept it private."

"Even *more* reason why the name got out."

"At the time I didn't pay attention."

"Jaxon, please, this esoteric stuff you do is fine but you really must get more acquainted with more practical matters—*matters vegetable, animal, and mineral*, if you know what I mean."

Jaxon played with Perry's reference to the *Pirates of Penzance*. "I have no intention of being anyone's *model of a modern Major-General*."

"You may have to. Someone's going to have to take command of the comet you've latched onto."

"What are you talking about?"

"I'm talking about publicity you couldn't buy even with *your* money."

Jaxon shifted uncomfortably in his chair. "Hold up. I know you get paid to make me money but I'm not going to cheapen this. Something really happened in that room, something I can't explain..."

"All the better..."

"No, you don't get it. I want to understand this. I'm not going to capitalize on it."

"You have no choice. The public is going to decide what they want to do. Already, tickets for your next conference are trading high. Scalpers are getting $5000 a seat for your San Francisco gig next month. I'm positive we can get more if you promise the boy will be there with you…"

"Five thousand!"

"Do you know what this is going to do for book sales? Geez, could it be any more perfect? A woman dies while hearing about the *Near-Life Experience* and the son of Gianna Fucking Chase, of all people, steps in and does his Lazarus thing. It's golden! That's the *real* miracle going on here!"

"Perry, listen to me!" Jaxon leaned forward and gripped his desk. "I don't want you going overboard on this."

"All right already with the boat references!" gushed Perry. "I'm not out to demonize you; I just want to manage what's coming at you. You certainly don't want it to take its own course; no sense going three sheets to the wind."

"Why not? Why not just let it blow over?"

"Sure, it'll blow over. Everything does. But while it's here, somebody's going to spin it in their favor."

"I'm not going to take advantage of Suah or the woman he helped."

"You say you value the experience; you want to understand it. All right then, make sure everybody knows *your* version of what happened."

"That doesn't require a publicity campaign."

"Believe me, in a few weeks, the history on this will be written. You don't want to be the bad guy and you certainly don't want to be relegated to nothing more than a footnote with source material on the astral plane."

"The facts will speak for themselves."

"Don't be naïve. The impressions people get off this will influence your brand and what you'll be able to do with your career going forward. Impressions are manufactured and you know it. This is no time to let others paint your portrait. You have to listen to me."

"Listen to you suggest what?"

"First things first. You have to get to this boy and the woman he helped. You need them in your corner. They need to see your sincerity, your desire to understand what went on. They have to be on your side. It's the best way to insulate yourself from what others will dream up in the weeks to come."

Jaxon closed his eyes and let out a deep breath. "If what you say is true, if this boy is Suah Chase, then we'll always be late to the party. Gianna Chase is going to determine where this comet goes. She's A-List; everybody in world knows her and you know the media is going to make *that* the story.

There's no way I'm going to hold any sway over Suah."

"You have a window of opportunity. Gianna is in Australia on tour, half a world away from you. She's already being dogged everywhere she goes on account of her breakup with that horrid but lovely Jacob Ferrère. All of that has her busy enough. Now it appears, for some reason, she didn't take Suah on tour with her. It may not *seem* like a big deal but to insiders, it's significant. You can bet they're going to make hay out of that fact alone."

"So what's the opportunity?"

"Do you know where Suah is?"

"I imagine at home."

"But Gianna is not there. You need to see him, talk to him before Gianna locks him away and believe me, she will. I hear she's super overprotective. Once she gets back home, you'll never see him again. If you really want to understand what went on at your conference, you need to get to him *now*."

Jaxon eased back. For all the ways Perry was wrong, something in what he said was right. Jaxon had tried to ask Suah about the healing but didn't get to finish with him. Despite making a deal to talk with him about anything he wanted if he stayed backstage, Suah had run off.

Jaxon desperately wanted to know what Suah had done and how it was possible. It went to the core of everything he preached and believed but saw precious few examples in everyday life. He needed to talk to Suah.

"What do you suggest?" asked Jaxon.

Perry thought a second. "Well, I certainly wouldn't prance over to Gianna's estate and ring the doorbell. That wouldn't look good on so many levels. If you really didn't know who the kid was, being so presumptuous could appear awfully contrary."

There was a moment of silence on the phone. Jaxon waited.

Perry continued, "The boy can't simply be wandering around by himself. He has nannies, teachers, maids, people who watch him while Gianna's gone. The idea would be to somehow put out a general request to find him. Even offer a reward; that will lend it some weight. Someone's bound to see, tell a friend of a friend. For a price, someone will give him up."

"I hate this sort of thing," barked Jaxon. "Offering a reward? Why wouldn't *that* be misconstrued?"

"People who like twisting things will twist *anything* you say. You might as well put out there what you need to get what you want."

Perry might be right but Jaxon was tired of talking with him. Something about the business side of things was always anathema to Jaxon's higher sense of life purpose and spiritual quest. He had known Perry for years but Jaxon also knew that if business concerns were not a fact of life, Jaxon would have nothing to do with him.

"All right," concluded Jaxon. "I'll see what I can do."

"Don't forget," prompted Perry. "Be earnest. You want to *understand* the miracle, not mass-produce it."

On that, the call ended. Perry's last words struck a nerve in Jaxon.

What if such a thing *could* be mass-produced? What if people all over the world *could* learn to do what Suah did so effortlessly? Jaxon imagined all of the ways the world would be transformed. Beyond the initial epidemic of healings, what else might reverberate through the social order? Surely, energies of connection and care *that* deep and profound would have beneficial side effects running through every aspect of everyday living.

The result would be nothing less than transformative.

Excited by the prospect, Jaxon shifted forward. His hands hovered over the computer's keyboard with intent but no context. What was the right thing to do? If he offered a reward to get in contact with Suah, how much should it be and how would he get the word out?

At the corner of the screen, an icon showed he had unread email. On impulse, he opened a window to check his messages. Scanning down the list, his eyes fixed upon one name. It was the name of Claire's doctor.

Jaxon started to click it open to read it. But he paused. He knew what it contained. In that moment he didn't want to see it, couldn't bring himself to look on those fatalistic words: *advanced protocol.* Seeing them would give 3D weight to the realm of ideas and make the terrible news more real.

Wavering at his desk, Jaxon looked up at the picture window. Beyond the glass was the distant blackness of night but on the glass glowed his own near reflection. Looking into it, he couldn't lie to himself. Despite all of his enlightened philosophy and New Age spiritualism, he really did have a selfish reason for wanting to see Suah again—he wanted Claire well again.

Honestly, Claire had little time left if a higher power didn't intercede. If there was the slightest chance that Suah could heal her—or at least teach Jaxon how to do what he had done—Jaxon had no choice, he had to try.

Jaxon opened a browser and navigated to his personal blog. Normally, he or one of his aides would post a daily message of inspiration or aphorism. But not tonight. Jaxon set to work. The message would be short and elegant but to the point. He would offer a reward to be put in touch with the boy who had done wondrous things at *Surviving The Near-Life Experience.*

CHAPTER 26

The darkness of night had not only sealed Blake Fry's fate, it'd hardened his resolve. He had long since slipped into a zombie state, numb with anger and exhaustion. The only energy left in him was fight or flight. With his fate determined, he wavered between an explosion and a collapse.

He was determined to find Suah more than ever. It didn't matter that both web calls to Gianna had long since past. It didn't matter that bringing Suah back wouldn't mitigate Blake's punishment in the least. The only thing that mattered to Blake now was his doggedness for revenge.

After cruising all of the places where Suah should be, Blake had driven the Datsun across the main highway into areas he never expected Suah to go. The boy was strange enough to Blake that he decided he couldn't rule out the implausible. Besides, there was nowhere else to look.

But now that even the doubtful areas had been covered, Blake sat waiting at a red light and resigned himself to one more pass along the small side streets back in town. That's where Blake had always dropped Suah off. That's where others had told Blake they had seen Suah during days past. Everything reasonable said that's where Suah should be found.

By now, Blake held out little hope of finding the boy but at least the longer Blake searched, the longer he'd put off going home and facing Diego.

The fact that Suah hadn't turned up so far only made Blake entertain his own sarcasm as more credible. It was no longer such a wild idea that the kid could have simply left the planet that was so foreign to him.

The light changed and Blake stepped on the accelerator. He checked the gas gauge. It had dropped below one quarter full which only steamed him more. An entire tank of gas had been wasted on this detour to dead ends.

Maybe Duffy was right and the kid had gone home with someone he met in town. It was hard picturing Suah making friends with anybody, let alone convincing them to take him home with them. Blake figured the only way that could happen was if some stranger had recognized him as Gianna's kid. A lot of people would do anything to say they knew a celebrity.

The old Datsun rolled forward. Traffic was getting lighter now that the dinner time rush was abating. If nothing else, it might be easier to spot a kid alone on a sidewalk out this late.

Just then, Blake's phone played a short group of tones, signaling he was receiving a text message. Slowing down, he navigated the phone with one hand and checked for messages. The incoming text was from Diego.

Come home now or don't come home at all

Diego's words encapsulated the stark reality of what Blake was facing: uncertainty and dread. For Diego to tell Blake, in effect, to give up on the search and come home, it had to mean one of two things—someone else had found Suah or Diego didn't much care to find him any longer.

If Suah had been found, chances were Diego would have said so. That left the second alternative. Diego not caring would only happen if he and Paige had had a fight. Them splitting up would be major, far more major than the annoyance of losing the kid.

If Diego thought Blake was in anyway responsible for Paige not wanting to be with him anymore, Blake might as well not go home. He wasn't facing just punishment; this was deep shit.

Memories of past beatings by Diego flashed to mind.

Blake's mouth went dry. It felt like his skin began to crawl with a million anxious ants. He was hoping to stay out late, late enough to let Diego calm down a bit. But if Paige and he had split, there would be no calming him down no matter how late Blake stayed away.

The Datsun rolled down the side street and for the umpteenth time its bald tires approached the entrance to the alleyway. Blake's eyes darted in distraction. It was hard to find any mental space other than for the worry and rage that boiled as he mulled over his situation.

Never before had Diego and he reached a point where it might be better if he never went home. It was one thing to talk big about leaving home but quite another to have to run away out of fear of being there.

At the edge of vision, an apparition intercepted light. Blake shot a glance to his right and caught sight of movement, then a form. At first he couldn't believe his eyes, then he couldn't believe his luck.

There was Suah, nonchalant as you can be, strolling out of the alley and turning down the sidewalk in front of him. For Blake, the sight elicited both pleasure and pain. The excitement of success quickly decayed. In its place was the sting of everything he had been put through since noon.

Accelerating the Datsun to the curb, he jumped out and took off in a run after Suah. Briefly frozen in the Datsun's headlights, Suah shot away like a gazelle catching sight of a predator. Back into the alley they flew, one after the other as fast as their legs would carry them.

"Come back here, you little fucker!" shouted Blake.

Suah not only ignored him, he accelerated. The idea of retreating into the alley was smart because it was the darkest place around and hard to see in. But it wasn't so smart because it was long and narrow with only one way out.

Suah was fast but Blake was seven years older and buff from countless days riding the waves. Blake poured on the speed and lengthened his strides. What started as a contest between them was fated to be a rout.

Maybe if Suah had fled down the street instead of returning to the alley, maybe then he could have zigzagged and darted in ways that the larger, less agile predator didn't expect and couldn't respond to in time.

As it was, the gap between them closed rapidly. By the time Suah got back to the place where he had drunk water from the spigot, Blake's hands were on him. They grabbed him by the neck and shoulders with such force that it sent Suah flying headlong into the side of a dumpster.

"You think you're a wise ass, don't you!" shouted Blake.

Suah rolled over only to have Blake stomp his leg mid-thigh.

"You think you caused me trouble—you don't know trouble!"

Suah raised his arms to shield himself but Blake only used them to pull him up to his feet. As soon as Blake got Suah standing, he reared back and punched him in the face. The force of the impact blew Suah back onto the ground. Before he could roll with the punch, Blake was on him again.

"Now it's my time, shithead!" yelled Blake. Raging with the pent-up energy from hours of searching from behind the wheel of the Datsun, Blake was blinded by anger and couldn't hold back.

Jerking Suah back to his feet, he grabbed him by the arm and flung him like a ragdoll against a cinderblock wall. Helpless to direct the impact, Suah hit with a force that knocked him dizzy. As the momentum carried him down the wall, his face scraped the blocks and began to bleed.

Blake caught him before he could fall. Frantic to avoid pain, Suah tried twisting away but had his T-shirt ripped from his back in the process.

"Where do you think you're going? There's nowhere to go—you're mine!" Blake held him by the back of his neck and kicked the legs out from under him. Suah went down, hitting the back of his head on the pavement.

In the dark, Blake had no visual cues to tell him how much damage he was doing. As the blows continued, all he knew was his hand was getting wet and Suah was getting slippery.

Suah fell after being punched in the face again. He crumpled on the ground and lost a shoe. Blake kicked it out of the way and then started kicking Suah. Over and over he kicked him in the shoulder and pelvis.

Suah had nowhere else to go but cringe in a fetal position. That only made his rounded back an easy target. Jerking in response to each kick, Suah tensed and relaxed with painful shutters. Blake tried to stand him up again but Suah's legs wouldn't support him any longer.

"This is what you get for fucking around with me," roared Blake.

Suah coughed on blood and hugged himself to protect his stomach and ribcage. The sound of Blake's voice had gone into a tunnel and drifted farther away. Looking up through one swollen eye, Suah thought he saw a star but it wouldn't stay put. Round and round it orbited a point in space where nothing was happening and no one was there.

The beating had gone on for over fifteen minutes. The only thing that slowed Blake down was his own exhaustion. Out of breath and sweating from the work out of throwing Suah around, Blake finally paused and looked down on the crumpled form beneath him.

Suah was no longer moving. Kicking at his leg, Blake found him unresponsive. It made little sense beating him anymore if he wasn't conscious to feel it. Blake grabbed him by a shoeless foot and dragged him to the water spigot. Along the way, Suah's back and face slid along the alleyway's gravel.

Dropping his load by the spigot, Blake turned on the water and washed the blood from his hands. The runoff from the water blast rolled down and soaked around Suah on all sides.

Finally satisfied he was clean enough, Blake turned off the tap and straightened up. His work was done. He felt better. He had had his release. He stood for a minute and looked down on his prey.

It had been a successful hunt after all.

He started to walk away but then he turned around. In a moment of sheer power and dominance, he leaned back and roared a whoop and holler to the sky. Content, he ambled away in the direction of the Datsun.

The cool water flowing against Suah's bruised and bloodied face momentarily revived him. He faded in and out of consciousness. The alleyway mixed with dreams. Faint memories of open fields and village life in Africa filled him with a rush. It was a vestige of a time when big animal noises in the dark, untamed fields, and his grandfather's captivating tales of magic in a world unseen had made the unknown a palpable thing.

He tried opening his eyes but only had memories of the stars above. His grandfather came to him with whispers about the dark, where to step and when to be still. He breathed in and felt the cool water on his face. *There were dangerous things to be found in the darkness—if they knew your way.*

An ageless time endured a changeless space. Suah had no idea how long he had been unconscious. He only knew that returning to the world meant a painful and confusing reentry. The pain he could understand; the confusion he couldn't. Something else was in his space with him. Someone else was making him aware of the present moment.

He opened one eye and found darkness shrouded by a dark form. Sounds of breath and wet tongue touching flesh mixed with the periodic whoosh passing of traffic in the distance.

Shivers of shock started to set in. Suah wanted nothing more than to go back to sleep. He felt he needed to sleep a very long time. But the form hovering above him wouldn't leave him be.

Rolling his face off the pavement, Suah looked up. The darkness in the alley was pitch-black but his eyes had plenty of time to adjust. His awareness was informed more by instinct than by his senses. It was clear that the form lurking over him wouldn't be satisfied until Suah was fully awake.

Suah reached up and groped the air. The form was still there, somewhere. After several failed swipes, Suah made contact with fur. All at once, Suah knew. The form above him was Gris-Gris.

The dog had been licking his face for some time now.

Suah could only measure time by the movement of the star field overhead. The star that had spun in circles earlier was now gone. In its place was a patch of stars that only slightly shifted back and forth.

Gris-Gris stayed by his side for an hour after that. It took that long for Suah to sit up. Half an hour later, Suah managed to stand. He didn't know why he would even want to. He had no idea where to go. He decided to let Gris-Gris show the way.

Gris-Gris led him out of the alley and along the sidewalk to the main street. The hour was late and the shops were closed. Some of the restaurants were still open, especially the ones that had bars.

Suah followed on. Gris-Gris led him through the park with the big tree and then headed south out of town. A little ways beyond the city limits, they took a beach access trail. It seemed Gris-Gris wanted to be on the beach.

Suah could only walk so fast. Several times he had to stop and rest or sit down on a curb. He hurt in so many places; he throbbed in so many more. Just to walk caused him pain but he trusted Gris-Gris.

They headed out on the darkened beach and found a dry place to sit on the sand. Suah saw right away that Gris-Gris knew best. The sound of the surf was soothing. They could see the stars better. They would be left alone.

CHAPTER 27

Ava was in hyper mode backstage. She marched her petite frame along the access hallway with such force and direct intent that even the macho equipment grips took notice and got out of her way.

"I don't care what the plan was," she snapped at the phone. "There's a *new* plan. Just do it!"

Gripping her digital tablet, she pressed it to her chest. With cell phone stuck to one ear, she intermittently listened in as production crew chatter buzzed away in her other ear's earbud.

"Finale presets full up...ready encore roller...get those guys off now!"

Ava approached the intersection where the access hallway met one of the ramps, draped in blackout curtains, that led to the rear of the stage. Two dozen choral performers in red robes flooded back into the hallway after the rousing end to the concert's last song. On a collision course with Gianna's personal assistant, they were the immovable object to Ava's irresistible force.

Ava waved her digital tablet at them as if the motion alone would part the sea of red. Distracted by their own excited side conversations, few of them noticed at first. Ava lowered her phone in frustration as she plowed ahead.

Up behind Ava ran Gianna's security manager Raho running interference. He was buttoned down in a stretch black suit but had a streak of loose and wild in him as evidence by his Maori tattoos and diamond ear piercing.

"Coming through! Step aside...make way!" he barked.

Ava followed his lead. "Isn't there a rule about blocking hallways?"

"Where're you headed?" asked Raho, snubbing her question.

"*The Box.*" She didn't break stride. "Is everything in place?"

"Everything on my side."

Ava shot him a glance. "Your side needs to know about every other side."

The security man had enough swagger to ignore the comment. "What's the timing? One encore and out?"

"That part of the plan hasn't changed."

"Just checking."

The traffic in the hallway thinned as they reached the mid-section backstage. A single makeshift door was unmarked but everyone on the crew knew it as the portal to Gianna's private area. Located at the rear of the stage, it was an area where rapid costume changes and anything else Gianna needed during a performance had to happen. The area was nicknamed *The Box.*

Ava hurried inside. Raho pointed to another man to stand guard at the door and then took off the other way. On entering *The Box*, Ava's eye was attracted to the other side of the small room where a split in the curtains let through a shaft of white-hot colored light direct from the stage.

Thunderous applause matched the intensity of the light. Standing off to one side, Gianna's wardrobe assistant waited for the final costume change before the encore. Gianna would change into street clothes, enabling her to make a quick getaway right after her last appearance on stage.

The wardrobe assistant and Ava barely had time to glance at one another before Gianna rushed through the curtains. The sweep of her intensity matched the wider blast of sound and light.

On entering *The Box*, she lost her stage face. "Have you heard anything?"

The subject of Gianna's question was understood. "I've called the police station several times," answered Ava. "The situation hasn't changed but they're interviewing Paige Atwater and Diego Fry separately as we speak."

Gianna stepped behind a portable partition with wardrobe assistant in tow. "It's been over two hours! What have they been doing?"

Gianna's impatience was understandable but Ava was helpless to explain or relieve the situation. "They assured me their full attention is on this."

"What's *that* supposed to mean?" Stepping out of her formfitting gown, Gianna was handed a pair of designer jeans. She rushed them on and was given a tailored, bejeweled blouse to put on.

Ava checked her notes. "They've called in the FBI and issued a *MAILE AMBER Alert*. Police departments on the other islands have been notified. "

Lurching out from behind the partition, Gianna stepped back into her high heels and stared at Ava with sudden concern. "A *MAILE Alert*? Whatever for? Those are only activated when they believe a child has been abducted and is in danger."

Ava didn't realize that Gianna was so well-versed on island police procedures. She tried to stall, "I'm sure it's precautionary; they want maximum effort brought to bear…"

Beyond the widened curtains, the stage lights switched down in intensity. In reaction, the clapping crowd stepped up their efforts to force an encore.

Gianna took in a deep, calming breath through the mouth. "Look it up online. I want to see it when I get back."

Ava glanced at the light. "Is it still going to be one encore?"

Gianna stood a moment and shut her eyes. Ava could see she was fighting back tears. Gathering strength, Gianna looked at her. "What do you think?"

With that, Gianna hurried through the curtains and into the light.

The crowd erupted. Gianna could be heard speaking her parting words to her fans. A moment later the music began, then Gianna's singing.

Ava accessed the digital tablet to find the *Maile Amber Alert* webpage for the islands. As she navigated the page, her phone rang. It was Olivia Platt.

"Is everything ready on the inside?"

"I've switched everything..." Ava paced into a wedge of light and back again. "It's all coordinated with Raho. Half of his crew will be on diversion."

"Good," sighed Olivia. "Have you talked with Gianna?"

"A minute ago." Ava turned her back on the wardrobe assistant.

"Does she know?"

"No, she doesn't. I did what you said."

"You did the right thing. One word of this and there wouldn't have been an encore."

"Probably so..." Ava didn't disagree with the altered message; she just regretted having to be the messenger.

"Blame it on me if she blows up at you. You know very well she can't do anything about this, not right now."

"It's not that. She hates being kept in the dark about anything."

Olivia was firm. "Who's doing that? We're simply waiting until the appropriate time to let her know."

Ava chuckled out of nervousness. "That's great except she's the one who determines what's appropriate."

"Stop worrying. We're handling it. It was your follow-up that gave us the heads-up. You know what a bubble we're in during a concert. Can you imagine what would have happened if we walked into this blindsided? Believe me, she'll be thanking you."

Ava brushed past the buttering up and changed the subject. "How about you? Do you need anything to get in place?"

"I'm already there. See you in a bit; I've got to go."

The call ended. Ava stood, nursing her thoughts. On stage, the encore was winding down. A crescendo of music and voice ended with a sustained ovation. A minute later, Gianna came rushing back into *The Box*.

"Show me." Gianna reached for Ava's tablet and read the webpage.

The MAILE (Minor Abducted in Life-threatening Emergency) Alert is named in memory of 6-year-old Maile Gilbert, who was abducted from her home in 1985 by a family acquaintance and killed.

Activation Criteria: A MAILE AMBER Alert can be activated when police believe a child has been abducted and is in danger. This alert is not intended for runaways or custodial interference cases unless it is determined that the child may be harmed, and will be activated statewide when all of the following criteria have been met:

The child must be 17 years of age or younger

There must be sufficient information to indicate that the child has been abducted and is in immediate danger of serious bodily injury or death

Sufficient information is available about the child and the abductor and/or abductor's vehicle

Gianna stood silent a few moments. She wavered between fury and despair before handing the tablet back to Ava.

"Did you read this? Does this *sound* precautionary?"

"They might have made an exception because you're so well known."

"I need to talk to them," demanded Gianna.

"First, we have to get you out of here," Ava asserted with a step. She had to wait while Gianna hurried into her leather jacket.

Gianna sensed Ava's urgency. "Is there a problem?"

Reacting to the intensity in the room, the wardrobe assistant faded back to stay out of the fray. Ava fortified her resolve and stepped towards the exit.

She was direct but evasive. "There's a gang of media outside the *Entertainment Centre*."

Gianna was surprised. "Since when?"

"They started gathering mid-concert. Word's gotten out about recent events." Ava only implied what these *events* might be in hopes Gianna would think they were limited to what she knew before taking the stage.

Gianna joined her at *The Box*'s closed door. "It was bound to happen. It's just odd they should show up here. It's not like I'm going to talk to them."

Ava concurred. "We never expected they'd react this fast—or there'd be so many of them."

"Very well," sighed Gianna. "Lead the way."

Ava opened the door and engaged a phalanx of plainclothes bodyguards who provided escort. Along the way, uniform stadium guards were posted at key intersections and directed them. Down a freight elevator and through a maze of corridors they flew, stopping for nothing until progress halted as they entered a loading dock area. There stood security manager Raho by a lineup of three limousines. He motioned to the second limo.

"Ms. Chase, this one is yours."

With Raho holding open the door, Gianna stepped into the limo's rear seat only to be surprised to find Olivia Platt waiting for her.

"Olivia! Did you change your plans?"

Olivia was morose. "I did when everybody else did."

The three limos accelerated through large roll-up doors and peeled off in different directions into the night. Police stopped traffic to let them pass.

Gianna was about to comment on Olivia's demeanor but got distracted by what she saw out the window. She leaned forward and craned her neck around to check out the perimeter of the *Entertainment Centre*'s parking lot.

"Whoa! What's with all the satellite trucks?" Gianna gave Olivia a glance but got nothing in return. "Ava said the media was outside but she didn't tell me about the TV crews." As the three limos accelerated away, several motorcycles powered up and started their pursuit. If one of the escaping cars contained Gianna Chase, one of the photographers was bound to get lucky.

Olivia leaned forward. "There are a couple things we need to cover right away. We couldn't tell you before because you were onstage."

"Tell me what?" Gianna jerked around and tensed.

Olivia punched buttons on the media center. "There's something you need to see. It got posted on the internet about the same time you had the island police issue their *MAILE Alert*."

"Is it something about Suah?"

Olivia answered by pushing PLAY. Gianna waited for a video to start.

When it did, Gianna sat transfixed. Suah could be plainly seen, sitting on the floor, rocking forward and back. A stricken woman lie in front of him. People crowded around in silent amazement. Suah was speaking softly but with a caring passion that was trancelike.

"You are here, you are enough..."
Suah rocked back...
"Imamu, skudakumoochooowte..."
He rocked back...
Bote, Alma Bote, Ananta Bath..."
He rocked back...
"Obarati Ochee Afikomen Banafrit..."
He rocked back...
"Sikera Bote, Alma Bote, Subito Fröhlich Kutamba...
Suah rocked back—and then came forward one last time.

"Your flame is blue, your flame is green,
I-and-I...and all unseen..."

Gianna sat stunned. Had the world shifted into an alternate universe while she was onstage? How could this video be real?

"What is this?" The obvious display had to be something else but true.

"Cell phone video taken yesterday at *The Manuia Resort* by someone attending a conference called *Surviving The Near-Life Experience*. The conference was put on by Jaxon Muse. Do you know who he is?"

Gianna sat dazed. "I've heard of him..."

"He's that motivational guru; has a big following with New Age types. He preaches the standard empowerment fare: inspiration, enlightenment, personal fulfillment, universal transcendence, that sort of thing."

"Who cares?" snapped Gianna. "All I want to know is—why was Suah there and what was he doing on the floor by that woman?"

"If you watch the whole thing—and you can watch it from many different angles, it appears that Suah revived the woman after she collapsed."

"What was wrong with her?"

"People at the conference are saying she looked dead."

"That makes no sense..."

"Doesn't matter. The social buzz has taken off. When the videos first got posted, followers of Jaxon Muse started talking about it worldwide. Then the *MAILE Amber Alert* went public and the press ran with the story."

Gianna's breaths came quicker as she watched a replay. "What is Suah saying? I've never heard him talk like that before."

"Me neither," added Olivia.

Gianna thought it through. "You said this was taken yesterday. How long has he been missing?"

"Paige told us that Diego and Blake were with him this afternoon."

"Who knows if we can believe any of them."

"Other than that, no one else has seen Suah since he left this conference."

"He couldn't have gone there by himself. Who took him there?"

"According to blog chatter by conference goers and people studying the videos, Suah was there with a girl, someone he called *Lolo.*"

"That's a native word on the island..."

"Yes, it means *dumb, crazy, paralyzed*. The girl in the video is not native but she does appear to be crippled."

"How can that be her real name? Do we know her?"

"No way. We've checked out everyone."

Gianna pointed to the screen. "Look at this! Jaxon Muse is talking to Suah like he knows him!"

"We're just as surprised as you are."

For Gianna, the simplest answer aligned with common sense. "This has to be a setup."

"If it is, the woman on the floor played her part well."

"I want her found." Gianna wasn't sure what to do but wanted action.

"What do you want, her SAG card?"

"She should be checked out by a doctor. Get her background."

Olivia was not so quick to pass judgment. "Muse is already so successful. He doesn't need to stage miracles to get attention."

"Maybe he wants to take it to the next level."

"Why would he need to top himself? In his line of work?"

"How long can he preach the same wise-man routine?"

Olivia shrugged. "Apparently, he's made a good career out of it."

"Along with how many others? They all say the same thing—love yourself, be authentic, find the source of cosmic energy within."

"But Muse has credibility. He's spent years building his persona."

Gianna watched the crowd react. "What if he started believing his own press? Wise isn't good enough anymore; he wants to be a messiah."

Olivia laughed. "He certainly doesn't need *that* kind of publicity."

Gianna watched the video as Jaxon Muse had guards rescue Suah and Lolo from the encroaching crowd and hustle them out a side door. The pictures told the tale. "He knew this would get out."

"Whether he knew or not is irrelevant. We knew your split with Jacob would get out—that doesn't prove we planned it."

The topic of Jacob was still too raw with Gianna. Olivia immediately regretted using it, even if the example was dead-on.

Gianna pushed past it but used it. "You can't tell me that Muse isn't going to benefit from having spontaneous miracles happen at his events. You want to bring up Jacob? What were we saying earlier today about Jacob leveraging my celebrity to promote his new film?"

"What about it?"

Gianna thrust a finger at the video screen. "What is Muse doing with Suah? Do you believe for one second that Muse didn't know who that little boy was on the floor? Of all the people in the world he could get for his spontaneous miracle…"

Olivia interrupted, "I don't buy that. If this was staged, they planned it in advance. How would Muse even know that Suah would be available? If Hannah hadn't quit as tour nanny, Suah would be with us right now. And even if Muse got the idea last minute, how would he ever get Suah, of all people, to memorize that gibberish we heard him say and perform it on cue? It doesn't make sense!"

"The whole thing doesn't make sense but it happened!"

"We'll know more soon enough," assured Olivia. "The thing to do right now is stay on top of things."

"Yeah, that'll be easy," groaned Gianna. "The rumor mill always latches onto the worst conclusions anyone jumps to. Everyone has an opinion."

"You're right. Some are posting what they claim is follow-up evidence."

"Evidence of what?"

"You name it. Still photos taken from the video have already been altered to show ghostly apparitions hovering around Suah. It doesn't stop."

"I still need to know what people are saying," countered Gianna.

"You don't need to upset yourself with all of that..."

"The truth about this is out there. I don't care if everyone is shouting; one of those shouts might be the thing we need to help us find Suah."

Olivia eased back in her seat; this was as good a time as any. "There is one other thing we need to cover. It's about Jaxon Muse."

"What about him?" Gianna came on edge.

"A short while ago, Muse posted a message on his blog."

"About Suah?"

Olivia nodded. "He offered a reward...to find him."

The car accelerated to make a stoplight and matched Gianna's reaction.

She was upset and blunt. "I'm suspending the tour. I'll pick it up as soon as I can but first we need to find out what's going on. Nothing else happens until I find Suah! If we have to reschedule tour dates, so be it."

Olivia showed no emotion. "I suspected as much."

"Good. Then we have an understanding."

Olivia was reserved. "At this point, very little is understood."

"I didn't expect you to be so agreeable," noted Gianna.

"If anything, we have an arrangement borne out of necessity."

Gianna announced, "I want to go to the airport right now!"

Olivia relaxed back. "We're going there."

"You made arrangements while I was onstage?"

Olivia glanced at the video screen, now dark. "Once you saw this, I knew you'd be going home."

"What kind of flight did you get?"

"The last commercial flight already left at 8:40 p.m.—so I chartered one."

"What about my luggage?" asked Gianna.

"It's at the airport."

"And *Sir Stamford*?"

"We're keeping you checked in at the hotel for the night in case anybody inquires. I know it won't keep your plans secret for long but it might give you a head start."

"Are you on my flight?"

Olivia nodded. "We take off in thirty minutes."

The limo took a turn. "What about Ava? Is she flying with us?"

"No. She's going ahead to the next tour stop to prep—just in case."

Gianna eased back. "In case what?"

Olivia hesitated; a kneejerk answer would be misconstrued. The situation called for more compassion and finesse than stating brutally honest options.

"Let's just say I'm a positive thinker. I believe things will work out."

Gianna held back tears and looked out the window at the night rushing by. "How can I do anything else?"

CHAPTER 28

Traffic outside of town was sparse after midnight. An unmarked police car raced along the main highway with its siren off. Red and blue wig-wag lights front and back alternated flashes in warning to other cars. Behind the wheel, Detective Mason Gaines split his concentration between making a turn and wrapping up a Bluetooth connection to an EMS driver.

"What's his condition?" asked Mason.

"Give me a minute. We're in the middle of things here."

"What end of the strand are you at?"

"North end. I gotta go."

The call ended. Mason slowed the car into a residential area as a shortcut down to the beach. A right and left turn later, he pulled up behind the open box of an ambulance parked at an angle and facing a beach access path.

Mason held down a button on the steering column. "Dispatch. Roller-2 going 10-9 at north side of strand. Over."

"10-4, Roller-2."

Mason stepped out of the vehicle and left the wig-wags flashing. After a long day, his suit was a bit crumpled but his necktie was still pulled up tight. He hurried along the access path. In the distance, jerking beams of flashlights marked his destination. Behind them stretched the blackness of open ocean.

Reaching the beach, Mason found two EMTs securing a body to a stretcher. Beneath the stretcher's broad straps, a dark blanket wrapped over the patient for warmth. One EMT stood up, acknowledging the detective.

"We found him over there..." the EMT pointed. "...next to the dog."

Mason lifted his thin flashlight and clicked it on. Its bright beam landed on a mongrel dog that sat and watched. Mason glanced back at the stretcher.

"How is he?"

The EMT closed the lid of a portable supply case. "He's stable but he's messed up. Looks like somebody beat the shit out of him."

Mason moved his flashlight beam across a wide area of smooth sand. "The tide's gone out. Doesn't look like any sign of a struggle here..."

The EMT turned around. "Maybe, but the kid is really scraped up."

"I guess being dragged across the sand wouldn't have done that."

"Hell no," snapped the EMT.

The dog ambled over to Mason and licked his hand. Mason scratched behind the dog's ear. "What happened to the couple who found him?"

"The patrol guys took a report and let them go, then the squad car got a call and they shot off somewhere else." The EMT grinned, "Maybe they heard you were coming." The grin disappeared as he looked down on the stretcher and shook his head. "It doesn't make sense."

Mason was beyond being philosophic but willing to humor the younger man. He looked at the stars. "No moon tonight. There's your answer."

"No moon?" the EMT quizzed.

"Yeah, things that don't make sense usually happen on nights with a full moon or a new moon. Tonight's a new moon."

"Maybe so," grunted the EMT, lifting his end of the stretcher. "It has to be some kind of voodoo like that. We're headed for Memorial. Are you going to follow us?"

Mason studied the beach. "I'll do better than that. I'll give you an escort."

It was a dreamless place between wakefulness and sleep. Jaxon Muse held his breath so he could listen to Claire breathing beside him in bed. An hour before, they had made love. It was unplanned and explosively brief, but also bittersweet and tender. Claire needed to feel him close, despite her flagging energies. Jaxon needed to be one with her, to hold onto her.

No one could say how much longer they'd be able to share their passion for one another. Any joys to be found had to be now. A raw urgency had made the love more intense, and yet its afterglow fell desperately incomplete. In many ways their moments as one that night had been a banquet. In other ways, neither one of them could escape the intimation of a last meal.

Jaxon hadn't gotten fully asleep since they rolled apart after spooning.

If he could only get his mind to settle down, maybe there'd be a chance at dozing off. But everything kept replaying from the last couple of days. The boat ride and the conference, disagreements with Hailey and the phone call with Perry, questions from paparazzi outside the car window and the video of Suah sitting next to the woman lying helpless on the ground.

Through webs of associations, memories spawned thoughts and questions unanswered. Jaxon tried to focus and find one clear thing, something that needed the kind of attention he was able to give in the moment.

He heard himself ask a question once again. *"Tell me…who is Hawa?"*

Suah's voice answered back, *"I-and-I. Hawa tasted the world first."*

Jaxon opened his eyes and stared up at the ceiling, intent upon *I-and-I.*

He knew what that expression meant. Up from a quieter space in mind came an answer. It was Jamaican; more specifically, Rastafarian.

I-and-I was the Rastafarian way of saying "you and me" or "we." It was one of the ways Rastafarians highlighted the equality of all people. Using the expression in common conversation demonstrated that we are all essentially one and the same in spirit. The meaning lifted out of Jaxon's mental fog.

He sat up in bed. What about *Hawa*? That wasn't Jamaican or was it?

Careful not to disturb Claire, he pulled on boxer shorts. The night air was warm as he hurried along the hallway into his office. With a touch, his computer awoke from hibernation. Quickly, he typed a search expression for *Hawa* into a web browser. It only took a minute to narrow down the results.

Hawa was a village development committee in the Janakpur zone of northeastern Nepal. Hardly a match for anything going on with Suah.

In India, Hawa meant *atmosphere, breeze, air*. Jaxon paused. Such a reference was interesting, given the metaphor for anything immaterial or wholly spirit. Jaxon noted the sameness but difference implied by *wholly spirit* versus *Holy Spirit* but searched on.

One particular search result link caught his eye and he clicked on it. The browser redirected to a website on comparative religions.

Scanning down the page, three items popped out at him.

Hawa (Hawaa) is a traditional Arabic name for the Qur'anic figure Eve.

The Hebrew word for Eve is hawwah, derived from the word for "life" or "living" or "full of life," the mother of all living things.

Awa (or Hawa) is an African feminine given name derived from Eve.

Jaxon let it wash over him. Suah was identifying with Eve for some bizarre reason. The boy had even said that Hawa "had tasted the world first." As the mother of all living things, Eve would certainly fit the bill.

Curious, Jaxon typed Suah's name into the search engine. Many references to people named Suah were returned. Among them was a link to a site that gave the meaning of names. Jaxon read the synopsis for *Suah*.

A boy's name deriving from the Gio region of Liberia, Africa.
Literally it means "new era" or "new beginnings."

Jaxon settled back. As trivia, it was all interesting but it left him no closer to understanding anything that had gone on in the past two days. It didn't explain Suah's fascination with identifying with Hawa. If anything, it only made the reasons for Suah's actions and mumblings more baffling.

Jaxon flashed back on what Hailey had mentioned. She said that someone in Sri Lanka had translated the gibberish spoken by Suah at the conference. Jaxon began a search for it. A minute later, he found the reference.

The man in Sri Lanka was a retired scholar from England who also found inspiration at times in books by Jaxon Muse. Although he was a man used to a rigorous exegesis of a topic, his take on what Suah had said was not all that involved. Nevertheless, Jaxon was interested to find his explanation wasn't entirely trivial either.

Jaxon scanned the man's summary. He had taken what he called *"Suah's Prayer"* and researched each word individually. He said it was actually quite easy to break it down once you realized that instead of one language, Suah had spoken by drawing words from many languages, seemingly at random.

<u>Suah's Prayer</u>
Imamu, Skudakumoochooowte,
Bote, Alma Bote, Ananta Bath,
Obarati Ochee Afikomen Banafrit,
Sikera Bote, Alma Bote, Subito Fröhlich Kutamba.

Jaxon read on. *"...the intrinsic problem with trying to speak when one draws individual words from random languages stems from the fact that each language has its own grammar rules. Therefore, any connections between words must be derived from our own implication of context. It's quite like reading a custom license plate on a car when all one has to work with is seven gibberish letters. Thus, L8ASUSL becomes Late As Usual. In the same way, Suah's Prayer has implied sense but only after interpretation."*

Next, the man in Sri Lanka defined each word from its native source.

Imamu - African Swahili name meaning "spiritual guide."
Skudakumoochooowte - Micmac Indian word for "Milky Way, the spirits' road."
Bote - Middle English for "remedy"
Alma—Latin for "nourishing" or Spanish for "soul"
Ananta - Sanskrit word for "infinity" "without end"
Bath—Hebrew for "full measure" "largest liquid measure"

Obarati - Croatian word meaning "bring down" "pull down"
Ochee - Muskogee Indian: "bubbling up water from a spring"
  "living waters"
Afikomen - Greek for "that which comes after"
  - Hebrew for "last eaten" "dessert"
Banafrit - Egyptian name meaning "beautiful soul"
Sikera - Greek for strong intoxicating drink, not made from grapes
Subito - music composition notation for "suddenly"
Fröhlich - music composition notation for "lively, joyfully"
Kutamba - in Shona, an African Bantu language, "to dance or play"

The prayer was then given its literal translation:

Imamu, Skudakumoochooowte
Spirit Guide, the milky way/spirit's road,

Bote, Alma Bote, Ananta Bath...
Remedy, nourishing soul remedy, without end, largest liquid measure

Obarati Ochee Afikomen Banafrit...
Pull down, living waters, that which comes after/the dessert, beautiful soul

Sikera Bote, Alma Bote, Subito Fröhlich Kutamba...
Strong intoxicating drink, nourishing remedy, suddenly lively/joyfully,
dance/play

Smoothing out word connections from implied context, the retired scholar concluded that the final prayer could then be recited in its translated form.

Suah's Prayer
Spirit Guide from the Milky Way, the spirit's road,
You who have infinite nourishing remedies of full measure for the soul,
Let us pull down that sweet living water to give to this beautiful soul,
Let this soul become intoxicated with your nourishing remedy
So they may spring lively and joyfully into dance and play.

Jaxon sat awhile, reading and reading the final prayer and the explanation of how the scholar deciphered it. Who knew if the man's interpretation was an idealistic stretch or not. If nothing else, for Jaxon, it was amazing enough that Suah had strung such random words together on the spot. Was this patchwork incantation something he had memorized from someone else?

Jaxon knew what many of his own followers would conclude. The fertile fringes of New Agers would take this for some kind of psychic channeling. They would claim someone or something was speaking through Suah.

It wouldn't take long for them to find out that Suah liked to identify with the name *Hawa*. People would then go nuts finding all sorts of mystical connections with an archetype for Eve, the mother of all life. Jaxon had seen and heard enough in his career not to dismiss out of hand everything the fringe might say. But he wasn't going to endorse such wild speculation.

If nothing else, this explanation by a man in Sri Lanka would only give weight to some of the more airy-fairy notions Jaxon would have to contend with at future workshop sessions and conferences. At worse, it would stir up a storm of interest. In such a storm, Jaxon would have to choose which side to take to find safe ground. He could only imagine the TV interviews he'd be facing. In such a late hour, it wasn't a thought he wanted to dwell on.

Left with little else to do, Jaxon opened his email.

His private email inbox was no surprise but the inbox for his public address was jammed with unopened mail. Scanning the list only deepened his despair. Apparently, his blog post about finding Suah had netted hundreds of people from all over who now claimed to have seen Suah or knew where he was. With subject lines like "Suah Found!" or "I Have Suah," the prospect of finding the boy had disintegrated into a needle in a haystack on-fire.

Jaxon resigned himself to a night of fitful sleep and reached to switch off the computer. But as he moved forward, his eye caught one variation in an email's "From" field. Every other email was from someone's personal address but one email had recently come in from an organization.

Jaxon checked closer. It was from a hospital. He clicked on it to open.

Subject: Suah in ER
Sent by: "Jackie Kemper" <jackiek@mmc.org>
To: "Jaxon Muse" jmuse@jaxonmuse.com
Mr. Muse—I'm an ER nurse at Memorial Medical Center here on the island. Suah Chase was admitted twenty minutes ago under guard by a detective. He's being treated for multiple injuries. Please don't contact me at the hospital about the reward. My private number is (808) 205-555-7354. Thank you. – Jackie

Jaxon checked the time. The email was about half an hour old. If it was true, that meant Suah Chase was admitted to the hospital almost an hour ago. Chances were, major media hadn't had time to respond yet. If Jaxon got down there quickly, maybe he'd have a chance to find out something before hospital administrators locked everything down in the morning.

Jaxon scribbled off a note to leave for Claire to explain where he had gone. Then he hurriedly dressed. He drove the spare, rental car instead of the town car. It would be less conspicuous. Within a half hour, he parked at the hospital and walked into the emergency room's reception area.

Before he could reach the counter, a man stepped up to intercept him.

"Can I help you?" the man asked with some suspicion.

Jaxon looked the man up and down to give himself a moment to think. The man looked civil but more than capable of not being so civil if need be.

"No, I'm fine," answered Muse. "Just came to see a friend."

"Who is he?" pressed the man. "Maybe I know him."

Jaxon took a step back. "Have we met?"

The man produced a detective's badge. "It looks like we have, Mr. Muse. I'm Detective Gaines, Mason Gaines. Would you mind stepping this way?" Polite to a fault, Mason offered a sweep of the arm as a guide.

"What is this about?" asked Jaxon.

"You've hit upon the question of the hour." Detective Gaines led Jaxon into a hallway. "Everyone's been asking that. It might be time for some answers, don't you think?"

Jaxon halted. "Where are we going? I didn't come here to be interrogated."

"Of course not," scoffed Detective Gaines. "I don't do that sort of thing. I like to have conversations; just people sitting down and talking."

"I'll be glad to talk with you any other time," explained Jaxon. "Right now, I'd like to see my friend."

"You mean our mutual friend—Suah Chase."

Jaxon stopped cold.

Mason Gaines studied Jaxon's demeanor. "I know why you're here, Mr. Muse. We might as well talk. Visiting hours are over."

"He was just admitted," countered Jaxon.

"And how would you know that?"

Jaxon wavered. "You think you're going to contain news like this?"

"You really shouldn't answer a question with a question. It might make some people think you're being evasive."

Jaxon said nothing, avoiding a response.

"Come on," prompted Mason with a grin. "Let's have some coffee. We may be up for a while."

Jaxon held firm. "All right, I'll make you a deal…"

Mason looked back, unimpressed. "How generous of you."

"Let me see Suah for one minute and I'll talk to you as long as you want."

"What will that prove?"

Jaxon stepped closer to Mason. "It will prove that Suah is really here."

"You think I lured you down here on false pretenses, just to talk? I could have you brought down to the station first thing in the morning. If fact, I would have preferred that. We'd both get more sleep."

"Not if you wanted to get a head start on something, something you're having problems with."

Mason checked the time on his wristwatch. "All right, why not. One minute. Follow me."

Detective Gaines led Jaxon to an elevator. They rode it to the fourth floor where a uniformed guard patrolled the hallway. After exchanging glances with the guard, Mason led Jaxon to a private room at the end of the hall.

"See for yourself." The detective ushered Jaxon into the room.

Jaxon walked in first but the detective stayed right on his heels. The light in the room was subdued but strong enough around the head of the bed to see a bandaged boy surrounded by monitoring instruments and a drip stand feeding him IV-fluids.

"Don't try to talk to him," warned Mason. "He's sedated."

"What happened to him?" asked Jaxon. A wave of sorrow sunk in.

"You don't know?" asked Mason, fishing for any subtle reaction.

Jaxon turned his head and glared at Mason. The two of them had a moment to see what they wanted. Then Jaxon repeated, "What happened?"

Mason relaxed. "Someone beat the hell out of him—broke his nose, fractured a couple ribs, knocked out a couple teeth. People in the ER said it looked like somebody took a cheese-grater to his back. He's lost blood and he's dehydrated."

A pang of grief struck Jaxon. All he could say was, "Why?"

Mason Gaines stood off to one side, silent. His gaze shifted between Jaxon and the stark white bandages covering parts of Suah's face.

Mason let the moments run out. "OK, Mr. Muse. Time's up. Let's go back and get that coffee."

Jaxon retreated to the hallway. "What's going to happen to him?"

Mason Gaines shoved hands in pockets. "Oh, he'll recoup here for a couple days, then it's up to Child Welfare Services."

"Welfare Services?" Jaxon never expected Suah to wind up in state care.

"He was theirs as soon as he got admitted."

"But why? He has family."

"At the moment, he has no viable guardian on the island. The one he did have is now under arrest for child abandonment and endangering a minor. As everyone knows, his mother is out of state, on tour. Unless she comes back before Suah gets released from here, CWS decides who gets him."

On the spur on the moment, Jaxon checked options. "What if his mother authorized someone else to care for him?"

Mason Gaines threw up his hands and began the hallway walk to the elevator. "That gets into all sorts of legal bullshit, power of attorney stuff. Don't even ask me about that."

"But it's possible," prompted Jaxon.

"Anything's possible," sneered Mason. "...unless you're asking a government bureaucracy. In other words, I wouldn't count on it."

Jaxon followed him past the hallway guard. "How long are you going to talk to me tonight?"

Mason held the elevator open as Jaxon stayed out, waiting for an answer.

"That depends," answered Mason. "How long does it take you to get to the point?"

CHAPTER 29

"Perfect timing. We're thirty minutes from landing." Olivia sipped her orange juice and watched Gianna Chase sway her way up the airplane aisle. The singing star looked weary from worry and restless sleep.

Gianna held a hand to her forehead. "What time is it?"

"The time where we're going or where we've come from?"

"Does it matter?" Gianna set her juice down.

"Only to people like me who have to keep track of such things. Now, let's see…" She calculated in her head as Gianna took a seat opposite her across the aisle. "…island time is 21 hours behind Sydney. We left there about 11 p.m. and it's a 9 hour and 45 minute flight…"

Gianna squinted out the porthole window at ocean and sky. "Don't tell me we've flown into yesterday."

"I'm afraid we have," confirmed Olivia. "Local time when we land should be 11:45 a.m.—but Friday, not Saturday like it is now in Sydney."

Gianna stretched her legs. "You've been sitting here all this time figuring that out?"

Olivia ended her forced levity. "Honestly? No. I asked the pilot a little while ago."

"I figured as much," confessed Gianna.

"I'm glad to see the sedative worked."

"Is that what you call it." Gianna rubbed her eyes and accepted her own glass of juice from a steward.

"You needed the rest," asserted Olivia. "There was no point being up all night."

"What you mean to say," Gianna corrected, "…is that I'm going to need all the energy I can get for what we're flying into. I suppose you've checked on things. Is there any word about Suah?"

"The best word possible," smiled Olivia. "He's been found."

Gianna lit up and came out of her seat. "He has! Where is he?"

"Now, don't get alarmed," Olivia forewarned. "They have him at the hospital…"

"Hospital!" Gianna dropped into the seat next to Olivia. "What's wrong?"

"It's nothing serious. He got a little scraped up on his adventure but he's going to be fine."

"What happened to him?"

"I didn't get the whole story. A couple walking on the beach found him last night. The main thing is—he's been found and he's being taken care of by people who know exactly what he needs."

Gianna eased back. "My God, what did he go through?"

"Don't worry yourself trying to figure out all of that now."

"So where is he?"

"*Memorial Medical Center.*"

"That's not far from home," noted Gianna with some relief.

"They say in a couple of days he should be released…"

"Couple of days? Why so long if he's all right?"

"They wouldn't go into details over the phone. I'm sure they just want to be on the safe side and be sure everything's OK."

"Do they know we're coming?"

"Oh yes." Olivia rolled her eyes. "Along with the rest of the world."

"It doesn't matter. We have to go there. I need to see him."

"I know. I've called ahead for a security team to meet us when we land."

The unsteady weight of Gianna's vigil arriving at some closure was too much for her to bear. She broke down in tears and doubled over.

Olivia leaned forward and hugged her. "It'll be all right. We've gotten the best news possible. Whatever is left we can deal with."

Gianna raised up. "Whatever is left? Is there something else?"

Olivia and Gianna held each other by the arms. Olivia relented, "You know there's always going to be something else. It's the nature of the game."

"What are you saying?" Gianna pulled back.

Olivia sighed and leaned back. "It's fallout. That's all it is, really. No matter what happens, people are going to wonder and guess."

"About what?"

Olivia ruminated. "We live in an age where reality and crass publicity stunts are one in the same. Appearances pass as verdicts. Any connection that can be made is going to be exploited. Our job is to use it without owning it."

Gianna fumed, "Damn it! Will you tell me what's going on?"

Olivia snatched a remote control off the seat next to her and pointed it at a video display. Cued up to play was a recorded news report from one of the popular "good morning" programs. Next to the seated news anchor was two inset photos. One of them was Jaxon Muse. The other was Suah Chase.

The news anchor was glib. "*…in other news, the strange case of Suah Chase continues to unwind. The adopted nine-year-old son of singing sensation Gianna Chase is reportedly recovering in a hospital after being* *found alone on a beach last night some distance from his island home. His exact condition is being closely guarded by hospital administrators who will not say why he needs treatment. Unofficial sources claim the blackout on information is due to an ongoing police investigation.*

　　This follows the extraordinary events at a motivational conference put on by Jaxon Muse in which the young Suah is said to have either healed a woman or rescued her from near death. Fragments of cell phone video, taken at the conference, have caused quite a stir around the world as people of all beliefs decide for themselves what they are witnessing…"

Gianna and Olivia watched as the photos next to the news anchor were replaced by a stylized logo for a video production company.

　　"…Rumors have been flying regarding what will happen to the professional video that was shot at the conference. Mad Cookie Productions was hired by Jaxon Muse to package the conference as a new video to be available for purchase this fall. Mr. Muse has made no public comment so far. But the search for a clearer picture of exactly what happened at the conference took an interesting turn overnight as raw footage from the professional video showed up in the mail slot for Bon Panache, a boutique modeling agency in Paris, France. Bon Panche's parent company just so happens to be media conglomerate EAC, Earth Artist Collective.

　　…This morning in Los Angeles, Mad Cookie Productions called a news conference. A spokesperson said it was a 'preemptive' action to set the record straight and help head off possible legal action arising from the theft of the video shot at the conference. The spokesperson stressed that the theft of Mad Cookie digital material was discovered only recently after a security breach was detected at their main offices in Culver City, California.

　　Meanwhile, in Paris, those at Bon Panache who have seen the raw footage are claiming it clearly shows Jaxon Muse calling Suah Chase out by name more than once and asking him, 'What are you doing here?' At another time, they say Jaxon appears to be running interference for Suah by keeping the stricken woman's companion at bay when the man demands that Suah stop what he was doing and allow another woman to continue CPR.

　　Any suggestion that Jaxon Muse and Suah Chase didn't know each other before the conference was put to rest this morning when the tabloid site Mazing announced that a fan of Jaxon Muse had sold them a photo she took of Jaxon Muse and Suah Chase on a boat together a day before the conference. Since the announcement, subscriptions to the Mazing site have posted an unprecedented increase…"

The photo on screen changed again. Now it was Gianna Chase.

"...*One is left to wonder what may come next. The gossip can't be avoided: if Jaxon Muse and Suah Chase knew each other so well, does that mean there's a connection between Jaxon Muse and Gianna Chase? Why was Suah Chase left behind this time while Gianna went on tour? Sources close to Gianna claim it was nanny troubles, but is that all there is to it? So far, no one has gone on record about any of this. Meanwhile, new questions aren't hard to find. Stay tuned for the latest developments as they break...*"

Olivia switched off the television. "That's a couple of minutes from one of the more responsible programs. Imagine what all the others are saying."

Gianna sat stunned. "Where did this come from? Who's behind it?"

"At this point, we don't know if *any* of it is planned."

"It can't be chance," declared Gianna. "They've got photos and video and witnesses. Suah was at these places. People saw and heard him and Jaxon Muse doing these things."

Olivia stewed. "How much you want to bet Bad Cookie sold that video under the table to EAC?"

"Well, that's obvious." Gianna shook her head and looked away. "Why get a hundred thousand from Muse when they can get that plus a million on the side. It doesn't matter. You know Muse will put out his video anyway."

"He'd be stupid not to."

"I'm not interested in Muse or miracles," snapped Gianna. "I only get interested when they start dragging my name into it."

"I've been thinking about that," Olivia chuckled. "It may work out fine for us; just the thing we need to drown out the Jacob Ferrère parade."

"Oh please," spat Gianna. "Don't get me started on that circus."

"No, really. Think about it. The publicity from this is already blowing the roof off anything he's doing. *Fatima Part Two* is one thing, but backdoor intrigue between you and Jaxon Muse? There's no end to what the press will do with that."

"You call that good?"

"Why not? It means there's no end to what *we* can do with it."

"You're forgetting about Suah. I'm not using him that way or any other way. Besides, even if Suah was out of the picture, I don't want to be associated with grand larceny frauds and Sim Sala Bim mystics who trade in New Age snake oil. As far as we know, Jaxon Muse is the one who sold that video to EAC with Bad Cookie giving cover. If he did, it's bound to come out. When it does, I don't want any of his stink on me."

"Suit yourself," shrugged Olivia. "There's nothing that says we have to be aggressive with it. A little bit of passive PR wouldn't hurt us in advance of the summer tour. You concentrate on singing and let me worry about it."

"Just leave Suah out of it," ordered Gianna.

"That's going to be hard to do."

"For you or me?" asked Gianna

"For both of us. I imagine after what's happened with Paige, you intend on taking Suah with you when you resume your tour. I can't see you trusting a new nanny in your home alone with Suah right now."

Gianna had been too busy worrying and singing to consider that far ahead. Now that Olivia brought it up, Gianna had no choice but concede some ground. "That's right. I want him with me."

Olivia shifted in her seat and crossed her legs. "And how is that going to work? If you take him on tour now, you'll find he has his own fan base. How are you going to insulate him from all of that? Lock him away in a hotel room the whole day with the a new nanny? That should be fun."

"It's something we'll have to manage," concluded Gianna.

"It's one thing to have fans and reporters coming after you; its quite another to think what it would be like if all that was going on with both of you at the same time. It's something we seriously have to think about."

"What's there to think about? I'll continue to do interviews and engage my fans. Suah will not."

Olivia reached for the last half of her orange juice. "I know you've been too busy to check your correspondence. When you get home, you really need to look at it."

"Why? Just tell me." Gianna's impatience with the situation was rising.

Olivia leaned forward. "Your fans want to hear songs. Suah's fans expect miracles. There's a world of difference between those two."

"What are you saying?"

"I'm saying that we're being contacted by people all over the world. They want Suah to heal their sick child, a crippled veteran, their injured mother. Some believe that just being in the same room with him will grant them access to some kind of celestial power source."

Gianna's grin discounted the gravity of what Olivia suggested. "How is that any different than some sex-starved stalker who hears one of my songs and believes he and I are reincarnated lovers meant to be together?"

"I still think this kind of fan base is nothing like what we've experienced. Don't assume that we're prepared for the situations that might come up."

"If they don't have access to Suah, what does it matter?"

Olivia took a moment. "I told you last night; I'm a positive thinker. I always want to believe that things work out…"

"That's right. There's no point believing any other way."

"There's also no point throwing caution aside. We have to know when we're over our heads."

"What are you getting at? What do you think is going to happen?"

Olivia settled back. "Maybe I'm thinking too far ahead."

"No, tell me," implored Gianna.

Olivia glanced at the open sky outside the window and then looked back.

"Promising that miracles are real is strong medicine. I can see how it would give people an enormous amount of hope. And hope is a powerful force, maybe one of the strongest."

"What's wrong with that?"

"Nothing—unless those hopes are dashed."

The two women looked to each other for answers but found none.

Gianna's brow furrowed. "I'm confused. A minute ago you were all fired up about smothering Jacob Ferrère's parade with a passive-aggressive PR campaign based on everything that's going on."

"We might as well…" confirmed Olivia.

"Now you're telling me you're worried that all this hype about miracles might make people mad when the miracles don't happen."

"If they get their hopes dashed, they might feel betrayed. It's a possibility we have to consider," admitted Olivia.

Gianna was bewildered. "You can't have it both ways. Encouraging any kind of PR is the same as engaging these people. So which is it?"

Olivia sighed, "Even if we do nothing, what's out there already is going to be encouragement enough…"

Gianna raised her voice. "So? Do you think it's a good or bad thing that's happening?"

Olivia sat a long while. Tormented by her thoughts, when it came to it at last, she had nothing else to say. "It all comes down to one thing."

"What?"

Olivia's grin was beleaguered. "Can Suah do miracles?"

Before Gianna could react, the pilot's voice came over the speaker.

"Please fasten your seat belts. We're starting our landing approach."

Gianna and Olivia buckled up as the jet banked.

An unseen runway, fated to be theirs, waited in the distance.

CHAPTER 30

Hailey Muse entered the sun porch with attitude to spare. With one hip thrown out to the side, she planted herself in a patch of golden morning light.

"I thought we were going out today?"

Jaxon and Claire looked up from their late breakfast and halted their conversation mid-sentence. Jaxon took note of Hailey's jersey shorts and tube top and remembered the family's planned trip to the North Shore.

"We were…" confessed Jaxon. "…but not today."

"Why not?" demanded Hailey.

"Things have come up." Jaxon was already on edge before Hailey arrived. After a late night and spotty sleep, he was in no mood for one of his daughter's entitled tantrums.

Hailey flicked her hands in frustration. "What are we, prisoners here?"

Jaxon hated the way recent events had affected everything but still felt driven to make something good come out of it. "I'm sorry," he offered. "We'll have to reschedule. Maybe tomorrow."

Hailey was crushed by the idea of being trapped in the house and had to vent. "We can't hide from everybody forever. If you didn't do anything, why don't you just go out and talk to them?"

"You don't understand." Jaxon held his temper.

"As if anybody does…" murmured Hailey.

"No one needs your sarcasm." Jaxon had his own frustrations peak. "There are more important things to think about than your need to amuse yourself."

Hailey folded her arms. "If there is, then explain it to me."

Jaxon started to get up but Claire's hand settled on top of his and held him back. Claire was always the peacemaker, even at times when Jaxon's instincts were inclined towards exacting some discipline.

Sensing that her father wouldn't erupt in front of Claire, Hailey was emboldened to say whatever was on her mind. "I watched the conference video. No wonder we can't go anywhere."

Jaxon was firm. "There's nothing wrong about what happened."

"Yeah, like I really believe Suah brings people back from the dead."

"I didn't know he was going to be there—if that's what you're getting at. You were the one who snuck him in. Should I have *you* investigated?"

Hailey shook her head and laughed it off.

"No, really," pushed Jaxon. He stood up. "You spent a lot of time with Suah the other day at the front of the boat, then the two of you went out snorkeling. What did you talk about all that time?"

Hailey balked as her smile faded. "Get serious."

"I *am* serious!" roared Jaxon. "Maybe you knew all along that Gianna Chase was his mother. You read fan magazines. You follow that sort of thing. So what did he promise you for getting him in? Tickets to a concert? Or maybe a backstage party."

"Like…I'm sure!" gasped Hailey. "What are you talking about."

"Maybe you thought it'd be a prank, something to embarrass me."

"Really!" Hailey was baffled.

Jaxon motioned towards the front door. "Hey, if you didn't do anything, then why don't *you* go out and explain it to the reporters waiting outside?"

"They're not waiting for me."

"How do you know? Have you talked to them? You don't think they'd be satisfied getting a hold of you? There's plenty of people at the conference who knew you were at the resort. You made yourself strikingly obvious. I'm sure people down at the pool would recognize you."

"I put on a swimsuit. So what?"

"How about the guy who wanted to give you a ride home? Isn't he the one who was slipping you drinks in the grotto?"

Hailey turned red-faced. How had her father discovered that? Caught by surprise, she screwed up her face in disbelief. "What?"

"Don't lie to me," snapped Jaxon. He had asked staff to keep an eye on Hailey and had no reason to mistrust what they had reported back to him.

He had her; she had to say something. "It wasn't like that."

"The bartender thinks different."

"What does he know? He couldn't see what we were doing?"

Jaxon took a step closer. "He didn't make any virgin drinks."

"There was more than one guy working the bar."

"OK. If you don't want to come clean about that, then at least tell me what you and Suah talked about on the boat."

"You're paranoid," concluded Hailey.

"And you're deluded. You don't think people can use you without you knowing it?"

Hailey shrugged. "Suah and I hardly talked. I was sunbathing. He looked for turtles. Big deal."

Claire spoke up. "Jaxon, please, what is this all about?"

Jaxon eased back from Hailey and sat back down. "Something isn't right."

Claire remembered the note from Jaxon. She had found it by her bedside even though when she awoke he was home beside her. "Does this have anything to do with you going to the hospital last night?"

"Hospital?" repeated Hailey.

Jaxon pushed his breakfast plate away. "I guess you haven't checked the news this morning. Suah got beat up."

"Whoa! Who did it?" asked Hailey.

"They have someone in custody. Get this—he's the son of some guy who's the boyfriend of Suah's nanny. How much more tabloid can you get?"

Claire persisted. "So what did you mean, *something isn't right*?"

"I don't know," admitted Jaxon, rubbing his forehead. "What I saw Suah do at the conference was real. I felt it. But…other things don't make sense."

"Like what?"

Jaxon glanced at Hailey. He wasn't going to go into everything in front of her but now that all three of them had gotten into it, there was no reason not to include her. Being forewarned might turn out to be forearmed.

"I didn't get to tell you about last night."

"You said you went to find out about Suah," added Claire.

"Yes, but most of the time was spent talking to a detective."

"The police? They questioned you?"

"He said it was a conversation. You know how that goes."

"What did he ask about?"

Jaxon took a breath. "Anything and everything about the conference or Suah. He wanted to know when I first met Suah and the last time I saw him."

"What is all that for?" asked Claire. "What's he implying?"

"He's a detective. He was fishing. That's not what bothered me."

"Then what?"

Jaxon looked up and caught her gaze. "He has Suah's nanny in custody. She's charged with child endangerment and who knows what else."

"Where was she when all of this was happening at the conference?"

"That's the problem. She claims she only did what Gianna Chase wanted her to do?"

"The police can't believe that?" chuckled Claire.

"That's not the whole story. According to this nanny, Gianna wanted her to drop off Suah someplace in town so he could be picked up by someone else. But Gianna wouldn't tell her who that was."

Claire tried reasoning it through. "What's the point of that?"

"According to the nanny, it's obvious to her to now—now that she's heard the news about the conference. To her, it makes perfect sense. Suah was to be dropped off so somebody from my organization could pick him up on the sly and rehearse him for his role at the conference."

"That's ridiculous!" Claire straightened up and shook her head.

"Not if Gianna Chase and I made some secret agreement."

"Oh, I can't believe this. You mean to tell me the police actually give credence to such nonsense?"

"They run up against the worst of human nature all the time. When they look around, what do they see? Millions of dollars of publicity over something that can't be proved or disproved. It's all about faith."

Claire's breaths came deeper but quicker. "Then why is Suah in the hospital? What explanation do they have for that?"

"I never said they're sure of any of this. You know how they are—they're just asking."

"So what about Suah?" Claire persisted.

"Plans can go wrong. He thought he was in big trouble for messing up the plan's timeframe. Everything had to be kept according to schedule to keep things looking copasetic."

"You're talking about the boyfriend's kid..."

Jaxon nodded. "He'd been beat up by his father before. When Suah made him late, he decided they should both have a beating."

"That part of it may be true but the rest doesn't make sense."

"As far as I know, Detective Mason Gaines already knows that. But he has to follow it down. It's the nanny's alibi. It doesn't completely excuse what she did, but it lessens her intent to abandon Suah while spreading some of the guilt around for good measure."

A silent Hailey spoke up. "What kind of guilt?"

Jaxon leaned back. "Certainly some kind of fraud. Maybe child endangerment if they want to stretch it that far."

"Sounds like a disgruntled employee trying to save her own neck," concluded Claire.

Jaxon turned towards Hailey. "Unless there's more to it we haven't heard. You swear Suah never made any deal with you on the boat—no exchange for getting him into the conference."

Hailey was stone-serious. "No! I already told you. We hardly talked."

Jaxon thought. "Then the only other person to check with is the girl Suah was with, the one he called Lolo."

"The girl all crippled and stuff?" asked Hailey.

Jaxon was dismayed. "Is that the only way you remember her?"

"Well, no." Hailey was flippant. "She was also crazy about dolphins. She didn't seem like any big conspiracy type to me."

"I never said that," declared Jaxon.

"Then why was she there?" asked Claire.

"Suah said something about wanting me to help her."

"Help her do what?"

"I'm not sure. Walk better, I think."

"That's whacked," chuckled Hailey. "If he wanted her healed, why didn't he do it himself? Isn't he supposed to be the big miracle worker?"

Jaxon stood. "I don't know. But she's the missing piece in all of this. I'd like to talk to her and see what she has to say."

"Only two problems," laughed Hailey. "You won't leave the house and you don't know where she is."

Jaxon stared at the table in thought. "Suah said something about finding her at the park with the big tree."

"Does he mean the park in town?" asked Claire.

"It has to be," concluded Jaxon. He looked up at Hailey. "You want to get out of the house? How about driving me there?"

Hailey was taken by surprise. "You never let me drive anywhere."

"Well here's your chance."

Claire interrupted, "Is that a good idea?"

Jaxon turned back to Claire. "They're waiting for me outside. If I stay down in the back seat and take the rental car, we should get through."

Claire held her thoughts. She was curious what might come from such a meeting but wasn't convinced it was worth seeing photos of it on TV and reporters questioning Jaxon's motives for being there.

Jaxon finished off his coffee and looked Hailey up and down. "You going like that?" Hailey nodded. "All right. Let's go."

After a kiss for Claire, Jaxon headed out the door with Hailey in tow.

Through the gate and onto the highway, Hailey found the ride through the gauntlet of photographers lying in wait smooth and uneventful. No doubt many of the more aggressive types had been attracted away by rumors of more interesting things unfolding at *Memorial Medical Center*. After a quiet drive, Hailey slowed the rental car to the curb and parked at the park.

Jaxon surveyed the people nearby. He spoke out loud but mostly to himself. "This is really hit or miss. There's no way of knowing when she comes here or even if she does."

Hailey sat, already impatient behind the steering wheel. "If she's here, at least she'll be easy to spot."

The reference to Lolo's condition was off-putting to Jaxon even if it was true. He didn't honor it with a response.

"Can I get out of the car?" asked Hailey.

Jaxon knew they were bound to get into an argument the longer they sat there. "All right, but keep the car in sight. I don't want to go running around looking for you when it's time to go."

Hailey got out. Jaxon watched as she headed into the park and over to the massive trunk of the big tree. From there, she toured around under the expansive limbs. All the while, time passed and Jaxon grew restless. Maybe this wasn't such a good idea after all. Chances of running into Lolo were marginal at best. More time passed and Hailey sat down on a bench.

Jaxon considered his options. He should make some statement to the press, possibly go on one of the many talk shows that had requested an interview with them. But he didn't want to commit until he knew what he was dealing with. He turned on the radio. A song played and then the news came on. It was an island station with island news. The DJ reported that Gianna Chase had just landed back on the island to visit her son in the hospital. Everyone was speculating if this meant the end of her concert tour.

Jaxon sank in his seat. With Gianna back, hopes of getting in to see Suah were all but gone. There was no way Gianna would let Jaxon near her boy, not with wild conspiracy stories swirling about. If she had plotted something, the last thing she'd want was to be seen together with Jaxon Muse.

Jaxon checked the time on the dashboard. 11:53 a.m. He switched off the radio and looked out the window towards Hailey. He might as well motion her back to the car. Nothing was going to happen. He waved his hand out the window. He had to repeat it several times before Hailey took notice. When she did, she started the long walk out of the park.

Hailey was halfway to the car when Jaxon spotted the slow distinctive walk of Lolo. She crossed the street in a crosswalk and headed down one of the diagonal pathways that led under the tree.

Jaxon motioned for Hailey to hurry. When she got in the car, he pointed at Lolo. "She's here. Stay with the car. I'll be right back."

Jaxon got out and made strides across the park. By the time he caught up with Lolo, she had reached a bench and sat down to have her lunch.

Calming his pace, Jaxon concentrated on being relaxed and friendly. "Excuse me…Lolo?"

She looked up with eyes that pinned Jaxon to the tree trunk behind him. "That's not my name."

"I'm sorry," offered Jaxon. "What is it again?"

"Leah, my name is Leah. You're the man from the conference, aren't you?"

"That's right."

She looked away from him. "What are you doing here? I don't want to talk to anybody about that."

"I'm not a reporter," offered Jaxon.

"Doesn't matter." Leah tensed into a hunch.

"I don't want to bother you," Jaxon assured her. He held his distance. "I just want to know why you were at my conference."

"Just leave me alone."

"I've been saying the same thing ever since that day," confessed Jaxon. "I didn't plan any of that but now I've been put in the position of having to explain it, be responsible for it."

"That's not my problem." Leah closed her lunch bag.

"No, it isn't," agreed Jaxon. "I don't expect you to know anything about it—but if you do, if you know anything, it might help sort it out."

"I shouldn't have gone there," declared Leah. "I don't want to think about it."

Jaxon took a moment to compose himself then announced, "I'm not going to come see you again. I promise."

He waited a moment but Leah didn't respond. He continued, "I guess I already know why you were there. We were there with Suah; we both heard what he said…" Jaxon let the inference float to its conclusion.

Leah's hurt and anger returned, just as strong as it had been that day. "He shouldn't have taken me there! Not for that."

Jaxon could see and feel her sincerity. "He's a kid. In his way, he thought he could help—he thought *I* could help."

Leah began to silently weep.

Jaxon held his distance but softened his voice. "When I was a kid, my mother had a thing about angels. She thought everyone had their own angel. She told us kids whenever we did something bad, it made our angel sad…"

Jaxon paused and let Leah dry her eyes with a paper napkin from her lunch bag. He could tell he had her attention even if he hadn't won her trust.

He continued. "My mother had all kinds of rules about getting along with angels. Not only would something bad make *my* angel sad, she said it would make *her* angel sad too because she had failed to guide me to do the good thing. So one time I did something really bad. Afterwards, I wasn't concerned so much about my angel; I thought he could take care of himself. The thing that really got to me was the idea I made my mother's angel sad."

Leah looked up. If nothing else, she was interested in hearing the rest of the story. Jaxon thought back. The little kid in him remembered it as if it was yesterday. He lowered his eyes, not wanting to show the emotion he had started in himself.

"So I wanted to do something, something good to make up for it. If nothing else, I wanted to do something to make my mother happy again. So I drew her a picture. I drew what I thought her angel probably looked like. I made it so sweet and soft, full of loving fluff. Only problem was, I drew the picture during one of my classes at school and the teacher caught me. He said I wasn't paying attention. He took my picture and hung it on the blackboard for all to see. I still remember the laughter. I never heard the end of it. I thought the humiliation wouldn't stop..."

Jaxon thrust hands in pockets. "...but you know, later that week, at the parent-teacher conference, my teacher showed that picture to my mother as an example of my lack of discipline. I would have liked to have seen his face when she looked at it and smiled and began to cry. When I heard about that, all the humiliation was worth it. I didn't care—because I realized that nothing good is ever wasted. Yes, it might have been wrong for Suah to trick you into coming that day—but the good in what he was trying to do isn't wasted. We may not know now, but something good will come of it. You know how I know?"

Jaxon waited until Leah shook her head no, then he answered.

"...because my mother's rules about angels say so."

Jaxon smiled at Leah then turned and walked away.

After a dozen steps, he heard Leah calling out. "Mr. Muse..."

Jaxon halted and looked back.

Leah was standing. "Why did Suah come to you? Why didn't he try to do it himself?"

Jaxon thought a moment. "Maybe he did. Maybe he wasn't ready for something like that. That's why he came to me. He thought I was."

"But you're not a healer."

The words hung in the breeze. Jaxon thought about them a long while then smiled. "Maybe Suah sees something in us that we don't yet see in ourselves. Who knows?"

Jaxon turned and walked one diagonal path back towards the car.

On another path, Leah slowly made her way out of the park. Upset and unsettled, she wanted to finish her lunch back at home.

Jaxon got in the car, only to face Hailey's inquisitive stare.

"So what did she say?"

Jaxon stared straight ahead. "She told me what I already knew."

"Then what are we doing here?"

Lost on the answer, Jaxon hung his arm out the window. "Let's go home and get Mom. There's still time to make the North Shore today."

Hailey's mood brightened at the suggestion. She started the car and drove away. As they turned the corner, Jaxon watched Leah make her way along the sidewalk. Watching her only affirmed his desire to talk with Suah again.

Cattycorner across the street behind them, another car started. It was driven by the man who had followed them to the park. But now he didn't follow their car. Now he was more interested in following the woman Jaxon Muse had met at the park bench.

As Leah made her way up the side street back to Lilyana's place, the man in the car rolled up behind but not too close. Sometimes he would pull over and idle at the curb to let Leah advance. Other times he would close the gap in order to keep her in sight.

As Leah climbed the steps to Lilyana's front door, the man parked the car. A minute after Leah disappeared inside, the man stepped up and rang the doorbell. Expecting a Reiki client, Lilyana answered by opening the door with a welcoming hello.

The man had read the business sign out front. "Are you Lilyana Gorst?"

"Yes, yes I am."

He presented his business card. "Good afternoon, my name is Nathan Mackey..."

Lilyana accepted the card, her eyes dropping to the most interesting part. After the man's name was listed his profession: investigative journalist.

CHAPTER 31

"There's no way we're sneaking in," groused Olivia.

Gianna adjusted her sunglasses and watched island scenery whiz by outside the car window. "I don't care. No one's keeping me away." She leaned forward. "Driver, change of plans; take us to the front entrance."

Olivia did a double take. "Is that wise?"

Gianna turned her sunglasses only briefly towards her business manager. "I have nothing to hide. I'm not going to act like I do."

Olivia turned towards the driver. "You better let the police know we've changed our entry point."

Gianna's attention dropped back to her phone. She scanned through the latest news stories then turned the phone's display towards Olivia. "Here it is; the photo of Suah and Jaxon Muse on the boat. What does that look like?"

"It looks like Suah took a boat ride with Muse."

"And no one else? Since when does Suah get invited on private excursions alone with the Muse family?"

Olivia smirked, "Especially a day before they perform miracles together."

"Exactly!"

Olivia had read the story earlier. "Reporters talked to the boat captain. He claims that Muse was only doing the kid a favor. The boy was used to going out on snorkel trips on that boat so Muse invited him on the day's charter."

Gianna fumed. "Well, you know *that's* a lie. He was *used to* going on that boat? Since when? Who is this guy?"

"Lucas somebody," answered Olivia.

"Well, I've never heard of him and I'm positive that Suah is not used to going on snorkel trips, with him or anybody else."

"Meanwhile," added Olivia, "Muse is hidden away on the island someplace. No one's been able to get a statement out of him."

"Maybe he didn't expect Suah to go missing." Gianna continued scanning stories on her phone. "When that happened, something blew up in his face."

Olivia nodded. "He has to get his story straight before he faces anybody."

The car took the final turn and entered hospital property. Along with TV news crews set up to do live-remote broadcasts, a bevy of other reporters, photographers, Gianna Chase fans, and curiosity seekers waited in the parking lot or were camped out at the various doors leading into the hospital.

Gianna's car and her bodyguard's car snaked along the main lane leading to the front entrance. They had to go slow to avoid pedestrians running across their path or jockeying into position to take a photo. As soon as it became obvious that the two cars were headed for the hospital's front door, others who were betting on side or rear entrances came running.

The cars stopped and the doors opened. Flanked by guards and escorted by uniformed police, Gianna parted the crush of paparazzi and faithful fans.

"Gianna!" The cry came from a dozen places left and right. Keeping her sunglasses on and her head aimed at the front door, Gianna made strides forward. As the press of people moved with her, the sound of cameras and insistent reporters assaulted the senses. "Gianna…!"

"…do you know Jaxon Muse?"

"…what do you think of Bad Cookie's video?"

"…why did you leave Suah behind on this trip?"

"…what happened to Suah?"

"…are you canceling the rest of the tour?"

"…is this all about promoting *Make The World Well Again*?"

"…do you believe Suah saved the woman at the conference?"

Gianna answered no one. After a fifteen-second dash, the explosion of photoflashes and shouts died down as she disappeared inside.

In the lobby, she was met by a hospital administrator, a nurse, and a uniformed policeman.

"How do you do, Ms. Chase." The administrator gave a slight bow of the head in greeting. "I'm Andrea Bay, one of the hospital managers. This is Naomi Treggor, Suah's daytime nurse."

Gianna acknowledged them but said nothing.

Andrea led them to the elevators. "The attending physician who treated Suah late last night is not here right now but I assure you Naomi is fully aware of everything and can answer any questions you might have. We appreciate the advance warning you gave us about your visit. It's obvious such visits can be quite disruptive to normal operations."

"I'm sorry but I can't help the disruption," Gianna interrupted. "I want to see my boy."

"Of course," deferred Andrea. "All I meant was, in the future, anything we can do together to lessen the impact of such visits…"

Gianna cut her off. "The best thing we can do is to release Suah healthy and well into my care. I agree; the sooner you can do that, the better."

"I understand," relented Andrea. "Naomi will be your guide. If you need anything else, just let me know."

"Thank you," answered Gianna with a smile.

Olivia and Gianna's bodyguard joined Naomi and the uniformed policeman for the ride to the fourth floor. On the way, Gianna turned her attention to the nurse.

"Is Suah awake?"

"Yes," answered Naomi. "He's been awake for a while. We may be catching him right before a nap."

"What time was he brought in?"

"I believe it was a little after midnight."

The elevator stopped and the doors opened. Naomi directed them towards an enclosed nurses' station. Suddenly more serious, she turned to Gianna.

"Before we go in, I wanted to brief you on some things." She led Gianna into the nurses' station. "We can go into here for some privacy."

Gianna waved Olivia to join them while explaining to the nurse. "I'd like my business manager to listen in too."

Naomi seemed hesitant but immediately deferential. "Why, sure…"

The three of them moved into the private space. Naomi was a short woman, a bit pudgy, but warm and caring like a mother hen. When she spoke, it was obvious that along with ample maternal instincts, she had deft command of her role as a medical professional.

It only took a few moments to get situated, but it was more than enough time for Gianna to become suspicious. "Why can't we just go in?" she asked.

Naomi was congenial but businesslike. "I wasn't sure how much you were told about everything that's gone on up to this point. I thought it might be best to make sure everyone was up to speed before Suah saw us."

"We weren't told very much," added Olivia. "I was told he was treated and was going to be all right."

"That's correct," Naomi confirmed.

Gianna added, "It wasn't clear when he could come home. I heard a day or two but if he's all right, why shouldn't I be able to take him now?"

"Well," started Naomi, "A two-day stay was recommended by his doctor. We just want to be sure that everything settles down from the injuries."

"What exactly are his injuries?"

Gianna's question went to the heart of the matter. Naomi could tell that neither Gianna nor Olivia had been adequately briefed.

There was no easy way to say it. "Suah was in some sort of fight…"

"A fight?" Gianna became rigid; her glance flashed to Olivia and back.

"The injuries are what you'd expect: cuts and contusions, some swelling."

Gianna teared up. "What else?"

"He has two fractured ribs…and he'll need some dental work."

Gianna raised a hand to her mouth, closed her eyes, and shook her head.

Naomi continued, "The doctor would like to watch Suah's progress for a couple of days to make sure there isn't anything else internally going on that we might have missed. Also, a regular schedule of changing his bandages would be advised, especially on his back."

Olivia spoke up when Gianna couldn't. "What happened to his back?"

"It was scraped up and took a while to clean out thoroughly."

Olivia had to ask, "Are the ribs his most serious injury?"

"Yes," confirmed Naomi. "That and his back. I say his back because of the chance of infection."

Gianna sat without saying anything. She stared into a point on the floor several feet away. Naomi could do nothing else than finish her briefing.

"The good news is that X-rays show that the rib fractures were a clean break. There are no bone fragments that could damage blood vessels or internal organs."

"How long of a recovery will he have?" asked Olivia.

"Most things should heal rather quickly. The ribs will take a month or two. During that time, it'll be important to manage the pain. He'll need to continue to breath deeply to avoid lung complications like pneumonia."

Gianna buttressed her resolve. "Can we see him now?"

Naomi stood and led the way. "Certainly." She quickly checked out Suah's room and then stood aside and let Gianna pass. Olivia, in respect for Gianna's private time, stayed out in the hallway.

Once Gianna entered the room, she was thankful that Naomi had taken the time to brief them. The sight of the bandages and monitoring equipment would have shocked her even more if she hadn't been forewarned. Stepping closer to the bed, it became horrifyingly apparent that Suah had suffered much more than a few bruises and scrapes. This was a little boy who had been beat up savagely.

Gianna doubled over with silent tears. She was grateful that Suah's one uncovered eye was closed and did not see her reaction. The thought of the pain he must have gone through blasted away the resolve to hold her emotions in check, to be strong for him. As soon as she caved in to her sorrow, she recoiled back and stood up straight. She didn't want him to see her so upset. What he needed was the hope implied by seeing a loving, compassionate face, someone who would be his strength through whatever recovery he would need.

She took halting steps toward the bed again. This time, she went all the way to the bed railing. She told herself not to look at the bandages. She forced herself to concentrate on the way Suah looked on the day she left for Tokyo. She remembered him smiling and eating his breakfast in the kitchen.

"Suah..." She called out in a voice too soft to be heard. She called again, "Suah...Mommy's here."

Suah's head rocked a bit from side to side and then his uncovered eye opened, drooped back closed, then opened again. For a moment, he searched the ceiling then he looked over at her and the corner of his mouth curled up.

His voice was softened by tiredness and medication but the essence of his excitement came through anyway. "Are you really here?"

"I'm really here," answered Gianna with smile. "I'm here for you." She took his hand and held it.

"Is Gris-Gris here too?"

"Gris-Gris? Who's Gris-Gris?"

Suah shifted, winced in pain, then settled back down. "We go exploring together."

From his drowsy state, Gianna could tell she might not have that much time with him today. "Suah, I need to know who hit you."

"Now I know what a *nutzo-crazy* adventure is really like."

"What happened?" Gianna persisted.

Suah rambled. "I tried to put it out of my mind but it happened anyway. That was backwards. I should have thought *more* about it. Brody Mud said if you think too hard about wanting an adventure, that's a sure way of making it not happen. I didn't want that adventure. I should have thought about it a lot more."

Gianna was lost. "Who is Brody Mud?"

"He gets paid for wasting time...but watching the life preservers on the wall, that's not wasting time. Lolo thought I wasted her time."

Finally, something Gianna recognized. The news reports about the conference video made mention of Suah being with someone called Lolo.

"Lolo. She was with you at the conference. Did she take you there?"

"No, I took *her* there."

"You!" Gianna was confused. How could that be? Suah must be partly delirious from his pain medication. "What happened at the conference?

Suah drifted in and out. He shifted his head so he could look more directly at Gianna. She could tell he was struggling to form an answer.

She bent closer and asked him again. "Suah, tell me, what happened at the conference?"

He took at breath and released it in frustration. He took another and then answered. "...*Helf Selp* is a pair-of-socks."

With that, Gianna gave up trying to get answers from him, not this time. She took his hand in both of his. "You rest now. Mommy loves you." She bent down and kissed him on the cheek.

"I'll rest now," repeated Suah. "Then we'll finish our adventure."

She watched him close his eyes. She stood by for several minutes more, just looking at him and turning over everything he had said. Was it all delirium or, like a dream, had he spun a drowsy web out of things both made-up and real? He would get better. There would be other days to ask him.

Satisfied that she had seen him, she was far from content. She backed out of the room then turned into the hallway. There she had to stand and let the waves of emotion crash through her.

Olivia stepped close and put her arm about Gianna's shoulder. "He's going to be all right," she reminded Gianna. "In a couple of days, we'll bring him home."

Gianna nodded to let Olivia know she heard her. Gazing over at Naomi, Gianna asked, "When would be the best time to visit him?"

Naomi was put on the spot. There were best times for nurses and best times for the hospital administrators. Gianna would take what she said as a commitment from the hospital but, given the unusual circumstances, Naomi wasn't sure she had the authority to say. She decided to be frank.

"Normally, for patients and nurses, regular visiting hours is best."

Gianna picked up on the way she said normally. "But this is far from normal, isn't it?"

"I know what Andrea would prefer...and what you would prefer. There has to be something in the middle."

"If I come once a day, about this time, would that work?"

"Maybe a little earlier, before he starts getting sleepy."

"Good idea." Gianna stepped forward and took Naomi's hand in hers. "Thank you for all you're doing for him."

"One last thing." Naomi was embarrassed to even bring it up. "Suah's been receiving a ton of flowers. We've had a hard time dealing with them..."

Gianna shook Naomi's hand. "What if I request people make a donation to the hospital instead?"

Naomi smiled and nodded but both of them were distracted by footfalls approaching from down the hallway. They looked over to see a rugged, middle-aged man in a suit heading their way. He carried an air of having permission, as if he needed no invitation to join their discussion.

"Ms. Chase..." he began. From his suit coat pocket he produced a badge. "Mason Gaines. I'm the detective assigned to Suah's case. I was wondering, if you're finished here of course, if you had a few minutes to talk with me."

"Yes," snapped Gianna. "I'd like some answers."

Mason shot a sideways glance at Olivia. "Then we have something in common already." He led the way. "There's an office this way we can use."

The room was barely an office. It was more like a wedge of extra space between the janitor's closet and a bend in the hallway. Olivia and Gianna's bodyguard waited outside. Gianna took the seat by the window and forced the detective to squint at the sunlight flooding through the window.

"This won't take long," Mason promised. "I just thought, while you're here, we could get this done and I wouldn't have to bother you at home."

Gianna was stone-faced. "Tell me you have in prison the monster who did that to my boy."

"Yes we do."

"Who is he?"

"His name is Blake Fry."

"The son of Diego Fry?" Gianna was even more upset to find out it was someone she knew.

"I can sum it up for you pretty quick. As requested, we interviewed Paige Atwater and Diego Fry about the disappearance of your son. That alerted us to go looking for Blake. As soon as we picked him up, Blake confessed. More than that, he was eager to talk. He thought his father was going to kill him anyway so he had nothing to lose."

"What's the motive?" asked Gianna.

"For the beating?"

"What else?"

Mason deferred answering that. "Payback for getting Blake in trouble with Diego. Blake was going to lose his car, might get kicked out of the house—after he got an ass-kicking, who knows what else."

"I hired Paige Atwater to take care of Suah. She lived with us four years; she was his nanny. What was she doing with him the last few days?"

"According to her, she was doing what you told her to do."

"And what exactly is that?" Gianna shot up out of her chair.

Mason was unfazed. "She says you gave her instructions to have Suah dropped off in town but you said don't worry because someone else would pick him up."

"Who?"

"You wouldn't tell her."

"And why, may I ask, would I do that?"

"She had no idea but as a loyal employee, she did as she was told."

"That makes no sense at all."

Mason watched Gianna pace. "She agrees."

"Really."

"It made no sense to her until just the other day."

Gianna halted and turned towards Mason. "The conference."

Mason nodded. "She now thinks you wanted Suah dropped off so someone from the conference could pick him up."

"And do what?" Gianna could see the pieces falling into place.

"Rehearse him for his performance at the conference."

Gianna was livid. "His performance?"

"Yes, she imagines that's why you found excuses to leave him behind this time. This *is* the only time since he was five that you've done that, isn't it?"

"This also happens to be the first time that Hannah, his on-tour nanny decided to quit. She managed to tell me that the night before I left!"

A nurse knocked at the door, then spoke through the closed door. "Please, not so loud; we have patients on this floor!"

Mason eased back in his chair. "I'm just saying what Paige told us. I'm not saying if I believe it or not."

Gianna tried to calm herself. "Who else was at this rehearsal? I guess the woman on the floor, she must have been there, along with Lolo, the girl seen with Suah and then there's the woman who faked the CPR. And, of course, Jaxon Muse must have been there, along with the video crew deciding which angle would best catch the action. This is turning into quite a production!"

Mason was noncommittal. "I'm not sure how one would orchestrate such a thing or how many people would have to be in on it. As far as Paige Atwater is concerned, whether she's guilty of child endangerment or simply blind allegiance to an employer is all she's concerned about."

"You're damned right. Her alibi defines very well her motive for lying."

"It's hard to deny the logic of certain things, don't you think?"

"What kind of logic is there in me sending Suah to do such a thing?"

Mason tilted his head in fake wonder. "Oh, I don't know. Paige mentioned something about one of your songs."

Gianna sat down and smiled. "That's so ridiculous. Do you really think I'm going to put Suah in the middle of such lame hocus-pocus to get publicity for a song that has more than enough popularity already?"

"I'm not really a show-biz type," confessed Mason. "I'm not sure how much publicity or money or attention celebrities really need. One thing I can tell you though, I've never seen one with a limit."

"I'm a singer, Mr. Gaines. I don't need to join the circus to get people to listen to my music."

"Point taken," offered Gaines.

"If anything," added Gianna, "it would seem more likely that the circus might want to use one of my songs to promote the big top."

"You think Jaxon Muse arranged it behind your back for the same reason: publicity."

Gianna stared him down. "How much is it worth to convince people you can do miracles?"

Mason relaxed into devil's advocate. "That hasn't been proven."

"People of faith don't need proof."

Mason said nothing and let the statement fill the silence.

Gianna stood. "If you don't mind, I have other things to do."

Mason paused before standing. "One last thing, Ms. Chase. Did you ever have any plans of releasing Suah into the care of Jaxon Muse?"

"Of course not. Why do you ask?"

Mason scratched his sideburn. "Well, I talked with Jaxon late last night, right here in the hospital."

"He was here? Why?"

"He said he wanted to see Suah."

"What time did you talk to him?"

"Oh, around one o'clock."

"How did he know so quickly to get over here?"

"He's got a good reason for that…"

Gianna remembered what Olivia had told her. "The reward. He posted a reward for information."

"That's correct; someone, probably here at the hospital, came through for him. But that's not the point. He seemed very interested in getting permission from you to have the hospital release Suah into his care—that is, if you didn't return in time for Suah's discharge."

"That's just strange."

Mason nodded. "That's what I thought."

Gianna started for the door but once again Mason stopped her.

"Off the record," murmured Mason. "I want you to know I think Paige is grasping at straws. It doesn't matter what she says; I've seen the way she says it. There's not a chance in hell she's telling the truth."

Gianna took in his poker face. "For a guy who isn't much into showbiz, Mr. Gaines, you really do improv well." She brushed by him and gathered up her bodyguard and Olivia and exited down the elevator.

Back in the narrow room, Mason was on the phone with his partner at police headquarters. "…it went pretty much as we expected."

"I don't know about this," the partner dithered. "Are you sure this is the way to shake it all out? You gave Jaxon the impression you believed Paige; now you're telling Gianna you don't."

"Yeah," countered Mason. "Let's see what they do with that."

"I don't know. You got both of them thinking the other one plotted it."

"And Paige says they're in it together."

"So, what do you think?" asked the partner.

"At this point…" Mason stepped to the window and looked down on the chaos below as Gianna struggled through the crowd of reporters and fans before ducking into her car. "…I don't believe anybody."

"If you ask me, it's a waste of time," concluded the partner.

"How so?" asked Mason.

"If we arrested everybody in show business that faked it, what the hell would we do for entertainment?"

There was very little talking in the car between Gianna and Olivia during the ride to Gianna's estate. Olivia asked a couple of questions and got the type of abbreviated answers that put her on notice to ask no more.

Gianna was tired. She had flown into yesterday only to find an uncertain future. All she wanted now was some calm to collect her thoughts and let her emotions settle down. Seeing Suah in such a condition had taken enough of a toll on her energy without having to deal with inscrutable detectives and a business manager who was primed to leverage anything for profit.

As much as Gianna wanted to be on tour, arriving at her island estate was the perfect oasis in which to relax and recover from the day's ordeal.

The driver negotiated her street slowly. Both sides were lined with the same type of crowd that had swamped her at the hospital. Luckily, her estate's long driveway and hilltop setting had plenty of natural foliage. It would provide all the buffer she needed to escape public life for a while and be alone with her thoughts.

Gianna invited Olivia in and went to the kitchen for a glass of wine. Olivia checked cable news for anything new. When Gianna entered the entertainment room, Olivia was standing with the remote control in hand.

"Something's coming up right after the commercial."

"About what?" asked Gianna.

"The woman who got saved at the conference."

Gianna took a sip of wine and watched the commercial end.

The news anchor read from the teleprompter.

"*...this just in. The Protoprime Society, a spirituality group based in Florida, has announced that they've hired an investigative reporter to discover the truth behind the alleged miraculous healing captured on videotape at a conference by Jaxon Muse.*

The reporter, Nathan Mackey, is well respected in both Europe and the United States for work he did as a war correspondent and then at several top news organizations before deciding to go independent.

When asked how they could afford such a resource, a representative of The Protoprime Society would only say they were honored to have generous benefactors. Although it's never been publicized, it's no secret that one of their chief patrons has been billionaire media mogul Wyatt Dumashe.

Mr. Dumashe is known for his philanthropic work, especially when it involves groups that seek to foster human enlightenment, global harmony, and guided planetary evolution.

A press release from Mr. Mackey today claims that he has not only interviewed the woman who was healed at the Jaxon Muse conference, he also convinced her to undergo a thorough and impartial medical exam.

In the interview, it is said the woman staunchly denies ever having seen Suah Chase before the moment she woke up on the floor at the conference.

Results of her medical exam show she is in perfect health with no signs of having gone through any recent medical trauma. As Nathan Mackey points out, this would be true if the healing was a fake but just as true if the event was a miracle. As a result, he has concluded that medical tests alone are inconclusive in determining what exactly happened...

Gianna was overwhelmed. "I'm going to change clothes."

Olivia switched off the TV. "I hope there's more of that wine."

"Help yourself." Gianna went upstairs and into her bedroom. After a quick change into something more comfortable, she wandered through her sitting room en route to the patio. On the sitting room floor, she discovered a lyric sheet spread out next to an open CD case. Next to the case was the album's cover, featuring Gianna in a gloriously fanciful pose.

Olivia called from the hallway. "Are you up here?"

"I'm in here," answered Gianna.

Olivia strolled into the sitting room and saw the arrangement of album items on the floor. "What's this?"

Gianna snapped out of her reverie. "Oh, on the Tokyo web call, Suah said he had been singing with me. This must be where he was doing it." Curious, Gianna pressed play and the cued up song started where it had left off.

"If we only mend our hearts, love will make the world well again...make the world well again...make the world well again."

Olivia watched Gianna listen for a while. "Didn't he want you to sing this to him on the call?"

Gianna nodded. To her own recording, she silently mouthed the lyric, *"...make the world well again...make the world well again."*

Olivia listened to the lyric and laughed. "Imagine what true believers would say if they knew Suah liked this song so much."

Gianna considered it and wondered back, "Why? What would they say?"

"They might think Suah is trying to do what the song says."

"Now there's a stretch." Gianna shut off the music.

"For true believers or for Suah?"

It took a moment for Gianna to sort it out both ways. "People will believe what they want but how could anyone think that listening to a song bestows supernatural powers? That's too outrageous, even for the Suah story."

"Maybe not *give* it to him," countered Olivia. "They'd say it directed him, inspired him to use what he already had."

Gianna strolled by Olivia in the direction of the patio. "Please..."

Olivia followed, having fun with how true believers might think. "Why not? You told Suah both of you were starting an adventure together."

"He also told me that morning he wouldn't do anything I wouldn't do."

"That could be interpreted as saying he'd *do* what you *would do*. And what would you do? You put it right there in the lyrics."

Gianna forced a laugh and stepped onto the patio, "If songs are that powerful, I'd better get started on some new ones right away."

Olivia sipped her wine with a comeback on the tip of her tongue. But then she looked up and saw Gianna standing in pain at the railing. Olivia held up and said nothing. She realized what Gianna meant by the last thing she said.

It had been a week since they stood together on this patio. A week ago, Gianna had gotten the final message from Jacob Ferrère. This was the first time Gianna had occupied that same space. Olivia glanced into the bedroom.

The busted glass picture frame was still facedown on the dresser.

For once, Olivia couldn't see any benefit in trying logic or tough love with Gianna. Maybe it was enough just to talk to her heart-to-heart. Olivia stepped up alongside and looked out at the gleaming ocean.

"It's crazy, isn't it? Millions of people would give anything to be in your shoes. You go all over the world and everywhere you go, people love you. You've scored the golden gig; but it's not a personal kind of love, is it?"

Olivia glanced over to see Gianna give a slight shake of her head.

"It's odd," added Gianna, then she paused.

"What?" prompted Olivia.

"It reminds me of something Suah said." Gianna's voice quavered and sometimes got caught in her throat.

"At the hospital…just now?"

Gianna nodded. "He mentioned somebody; Brody Mud was the name. Suah said he gets paid for wasting time…"

"Who's Brody Mud?"

"That's not the point."

"He gets paid for wasting time and what—you think you get paid to be loved? Is that it?"

"Getting paid to be loved *is* the same as wasting time. That's the way love makes it feel."

"There's no reason why you can't have both. Having fans and having a love life are not mutually exclusive."

"I sell more songs, more people like me. But it's always a love shared with the world. It's always been like that. Whenever I try for more, something always pulls it back."

"And Jacob would have made all of that different?"

"Not different, just completely personal, something for me."

"There'll be someone else. Give it time."

Gianna took a drink of wine in a huff and repeated, "Give it time. Meanwhile, I'm wasting time." Gianna turned and paced away.

"No you're not. You have Suah. You love him. He's personal. He's family. What do you say to him? What would he say to you?"

Gianna stopped and turned back. "What would he say? He just told me about watching life preservers on the wall—he said *that's* not wasting time!"

"What?" puzzled Olivia.

"He also said he'd been on a *nutzo-crazy* adventure! If nothing else, I think he nailed it with that last one, don't you think?"

Olivia was somber. "What do you want me to do, Gianna? Tell me."

Gianna turned to the ocean. "Get me a meeting with Jaxon Muse. Make it private; we can have it here at the estate. I have to get to the bottom of this."

Olivia was taken aback. "Are you sure you want to do that? Think how it would look?"

Gianna flailed an arm. "How does it look now?"

"But it's all speculation. We don't want to support any nonsense after the fact. You'd only be lending credibility…"

"I don't care. I need to know what Suah's been doing, what this is all about."

"And you expect Jaxon Muse to be open about that?"

"I don't know what to expect from him. That's the point. All I know is, I told my son to go exploring and have an adventure, and he did…"

"Come on, Gianna, don't blame yourself for this."

"…and now he's lying in a hospital and people are making him out to be a savior or a joke. I'm either incompetent as a mother or a ruthless bitch who'd use her own special-needs child in a shitty little publicity stunt."

"It's not necessary…"

"Don't tell me they're not saying it. I've read it just like you."

Olivia relented. "All right, I'll try to set up a meeting but I can't guarantee anything. How do we know Jaxon Muse will want to talk with you?"

"I bet he does."

"Why?"

"The detective at the hospital told me Jaxon was there last night; he wanted to see Suah. But more than that, Jaxon asked if they'd release Suah into his care if I didn't show up before they discharged him."

"Isn't that rich. What else did the detective say?"

"He said Paige told him I conspired with Jaxon to have Suah at the conference. I know what you're going to say so don't say it."

Olivia paused. "OK. So what exactly do you want me to tell Jaxon?"

Gianna stepped in close. "Tell him if he ever wants to talk to Suah again, he has to talk with me first." Gianna started to turn away but turned back. "Oh, and one more thing. Get Nathan Mackey on the phone…"

Olivia lowered the wine glass from her lips without taking a sip.

Gianna finished, "…tell him I want to be a part of his investigation."

CHAPTER 32

Hailey Muse steered the rental car up a dirt path and then slowed by a wooden sign made familiar by past visits. On the sign was handwritten script emblazoned in rainbow colors: *NANI AHI PUA* YOGIC RETREAT. Underneath, in vibrant green, was a translation—(*beautiful fire flower*).

Below the original sign a new sign of dark wood bore a carefully written message. "*A refuge for the practice of mind/body disciplines aimed at training the consciousness for a state of perfect spiritual insight and tranquility. All are welcome.*"

The Muse family had arrived at their North Shore destination.

Claire sat next to Hailey in the front; Jaxon sat behind her in the back with one arm spread out across the rear seat. He checked out the back window once again to see if they'd been followed. Up ahead, a few cars were parked in a level dirt area that comprised the retreat's parking lot.

Jaxon pointed. "Park over there, away from these cars."

Pleased with herself for driving so much in one day, Hailey was on her best behavior and decided to pocket the crass comment that came to mind.

"I hope Tristan has the fountains working," said Claire.

Jaxon's phone buzzed once and he reached for it. "You two go ahead."

Hailey helped Claire out of the car and up a path bordered by lava rocks. Jaxon sat back and retrieved a text message. Claire directed Hailey towards the nearest of several yurts scattered across the property.

Jaxon read the message: *can't make it onsite - call me.*

He got out of the car and shut the door harder than need be.

Claire looked down the path and saw his frustration.

Upon reaching the yurt's doorway, Hailey brightened up. "I'm going to go check out Puka Paia, OK?"

Claire knew what Jaxon would think but didn't have the energy to disagree. She nodded and Hailey happily ran off.

Jaxon came up the path. "Where's she going?"

"It's OK. She just wants to do a little exploring."

Jaxon stood with hands on hips and watched Hailey disappear along a path that led downhill towards the beach. He turned back to Claire.

"You know there's more than one reason why Puka Paia means *hole in the wall.*"

Claire didn't want to discuss it. The bohemian village that had cropped up near an ocean inlet's blowhole had a reputation for casual living that would challenge most parent's better judgment. But every parent had to pick their battles and as far as Claire was concerned, today was not the day to go to war. "She'll be all right." She changed the subject, "What was the message?"

It was time to confess. Jaxon paced out of the shade of the yurt and into the sunlight. "I didn't tell you. That woman from the conference was supposed to meet me here?"

"The one who got healed?"

"Yeah…"

Claire was disillusioned. "I thought this was a family outing."

Jaxon swept an arm in the direction Hailey had run. "I thought so too."

"Don't blame it on Hailey."

"It wasn't going to take the whole time."

"That's not the point. This isn't about getting away with Hailey and me; it's about seclusion for your meeting."

"Half of that is right," asserted Jaxon. "It's about both."

Claire puzzled, "You weren't even going to go out this morning."

"This morning I wasn't sure what to do. It wasn't final."

"So what now?"

Jaxon clutched his phone. "She wants me to call her instead."

"Will you at least come with me first to see Tristan and Faith?"

"Of course."

Claire stepped out of the shade and headed for a larger yurt across the grass. Jaxon kept close to her side, supporting her by the arm.

Before they got there, a slender woman in shorts and a flowing blouse stepped out of the yurt and, facing the sun, ran both hands through her long blonde hair. Seeing them, she smiled and directed quickened steps their way.

Claire and Jaxon knew her as Faith-Anchala, which meant *faith unshaken.* She was a yoga instructor and partner of Tristan in both marriage and ownership of *NANI AHI PUA.* On seeing her, Claire opened arms wide and beamed. Faith had been a dear friend for many years, although way back when Claire had known her fiery nomad spirit as Kimberly.

"Well, hello there! Namaste!" Faith hugged them both. "I'm so glad you could make it up this way."

"It's been too long," said Claire.

"The place looks great," noted Jaxon. "You've added on…"

Faith glanced back at a lineup of small cottages in the distance. "Tristan's idea—and it was a good one. Visitors stay as long as they like now. We can offer more comprehensive packages, deep immersion."

"Is Tristan around?" asked Jaxon.

"No, he's Upcountry with a group on a nature quest. It's just me and a few of the yoga regulars today." She turned towards the largest yurt. "We're doing our thing in Center Space, so the rest of the place is yours to explore."

"Well, you know the place I like..." smiled Claire.

Faith turned around and faced the oldest yurt on a far bluff. "Ah, yes. Pule Point. It's all yours. I'll come see you as soon as I'm done." She kissed and hugged Claire and then Jaxon before strutting barefoot back to Center Space.

Jaxon gripped his phone. "This won't take long. I'll meet you there."

Claire nodded and started a leisurely stroll past the plumeria.

Jaxon dialed as he stepped away to find privacy in the nearer trees.

The ringing stopped. "Hello, is this Helen?"

"Yes." The voice was slight and hesitant.

"It's Jaxon Muse."

"Oh, hello. I'm sorry about missing the meeting but my husband convinced me that going out to see you wouldn't be such a good idea."

Jaxon held back comment. Her husband must be the same man who was so obstinate at the conference, the one who complained about Suah and demanded that the woman who tried CPR continue it despite her reluctance.

"Don't worry, it's all right," answered Jaxon. "I just wanted to hear directly from you about your experience at the conference."

"I already talked with that reporter..."

"Nathan Mackey."

"Yes, I told him everything. You can listen to his interview. I really don't feel like going into it all again."

"I don't want you to," Jaxon assured her. "There are just a couple of things, key points I was wondering about."

In an effort to cut the call short, Helen went right to it. "You want to know if I think I was saved by a miracle. You want to know how it felt and if I've had medical problems like that before. You want to know if I knew the boy. Is that about right?"

Jaxon thought it best to let her state what she wanted to say. "Well, yeah, that's a start."

"Like I told Mr. Mackey, I don't know what happened that day."

"What did your doctor say? Did he see the video?"

"Yeah, he saw it. He said it looked like something called *Status Epilepticus*; it's a special kind of seizure that lasts over five minutes."

"Do you have epilepsy?"

"No. He said it didn't matter. He said ten to twenty percent of these things are first-time seizures."

"But most seizures aren't life-threatening."

"They are if they last over five minutes. He said about 200,000 people get this *Status*-thing in the U.S. each year; over 40,000 die like that."

"But you weren't in seizure for five minutes. I saw you. After a couple of minutes, you were lying there not moving, not even breathing."

"The doctor saw that too. He said there's a non-convulsive type of seizure but it's unlikely that I went from one kind to the other kind."

"So what happened?" asked Jaxon.

"He wasn't sure; it could have been cardiac arrest. We both think there was something in that room that made my asthma flare up. That on top of the seizure might have done me in."

"You have asthma?"

"Yeah, well, I have what they call allergic asthma. I don't get it unless I'm exposed to whatever I'm allergic too. For me, it's certain kinds of dust or food and plant molds. I think it was something in the carpet, I don't know. I guess when I fell on the floor, I put my nose right in it, whatever it was."

"So when they checked you out, what did they find?"

"They didn't find anything. I'm fine."

"What about the seizure and the asthma?"

"They're both the kind of thing that comes and goes. I have no history of seizures, so there was nothing to track it by. Like I said, I show no signs of asthma unless you put me in a room with something my nose doesn't like."

"Did they check your heart?"

"They checked everything. It got me annoyed, poking into things. Those people can be more thorough than anybody wants them to be."

Jaxon paced through the trees. "So medical tests are inconclusive."

"I can't say one way or the other but I'm here, aren't I? I'm alive."

"But I was right there. I saw you. You weren't breathing for a long while. Several minutes of CPR had no effect on you."

"Listen, Mr. Muse, I can't say what happened. I *can* tell you for sure I never saw that boy before and I sure as heck don't know what he was trying to do to me."

"After you came to, you looked at him. You said you knew him."

"I did? I don't recall."

"Then right away you asked who he was. What was that all about?"

"Don't ask me. I was out of it."

"You also said you wanted to see the sky."

"I remember that. I think I just wanted some fresh air. I don't know what it was but I had this feeling like I needed to be out under open skies. I needed to see that deep blue that goes on forever; you know what I mean?"

"I think I do." Jaxon lifted his gaze to the sky. "Helen, are you a very religious woman?"

"I'm spiritual; I wouldn't call myself religious. I'm a big fan of your books."

"What about them do you like?"

"My husband thinks it's silly, but some things I read give me hope."

"What kind of hope?"

"Oh, you know, hope that it all makes sense, that it means something."

Jaxon lowered his gaze to where sky met ocean. "That's what we all want, isn't it?"

"Some more than others, I guess. Some think they already know. From what I've read, it seems like you do. That must be a great place to be but I haven't been able to join you there yet." She laughed.

"You've seen the video, haven't you?"

"Oh, sure. I watched it with my sister. She was there that day too. She was sitting at the table with me."

"So what do you feel when you watch it?"

"Me? It's kinda strange to see myself on TV. I look at it and it doesn't seem like me down there on the floor. It's like I was never there."

"What about your sister; what does she think?"

"Oh, don't get me started on her. She's all into it; plays it over and over. She even went online and printed out that prayer. What'd they call it? *Suah's Prayer.*"

"So she thinks it was a genuine healing."

"To be honest, I can't make heads or tails out of what she says half the time. She thinks it's either a miracle or some kind of paranormal jump in consciousness. She definitely thinks the boy has a gift. What it is, who knows? If we knew that, it wouldn't be so mysterious, now would it?"

"I guess not." Jaxon's stroll through the trees led him to a spot overlooking the village of Puka Paia. "One last question. Do you know a girl named Leah? Sometimes people use the nickname Lolo in referring to her."

"You mean the girl on the video, the one with Suah?"

"That's the one."

"Naw, never saw her before. They sure are the odd couple, the two of them, aren't they?"

Jaxon held comment. "Thank you Helen for taking the time to talk with me. I appreciate it."

"No problem. You're the only one I *would* talk to about this anymore. I really don't want to be bothered. There's nothing I can say that's going to convince anyone of anything they don't already know or want to believe. Let everyone decide for themselves, that's what I say."

"Thanks again, Helen. Goodbye."

The call ended. Jaxon lowered the phone with rising thoughts. He had talked with Suah at the conference. He had talked with Leah in the park. And now he had spoken with Helen. Despite all the inferences given by Detective Gaines, Jaxon couldn't find any hint of conspiracy among the three of them. If Gianna Chase was up to something, she had hid it masterfully.

An icon on Jaxon's phone caught his peripheral vision. He looked down and realized he had missed a call. Checking, he could tell right away that the number belonged to Claire's doctor. Jaxon pressed redial and it rang.

"Vincent, it's Jaxon. Sorry I missed your call."

"Thanks for getting back to me," the doctor rushed. "I was just heading out and wanted to touch base."

"What's up?"

"That's *my* question. Claire hasn't started the advanced protocol."

"Not yet."

"Why not? We really shouldn't wait on this."

"I know…"

"You shouldn't have any trouble with the prescription across state lines. I made sure of that."

"No…no problem there."

"Then what is it? I pulled some strings to get it released for home use. Usually, that isn't allowed with trials like this."

"I got the prescription. There's no problem there."

"Then what's going on?"

Jaxon paused on a doubt never expressed, especially to Claire's doctor. "Last time we talked, you said something about the side effects."

"What about them?"

Jaxon ambled out from the trees and along the bluff. "That new opiate analgesic that's in the medication—you said it's designed to work on the central nervous system in a new way."

"It has to. It needs to counteract the pain reaction to the targeted chemo."

Jaxon couldn't hold back any longer. "But you said she might not be there, she might not even know me."

"Jaxon, it can't be helped. To block out that kind of pain, there's no other way. If it works, she can come off it and she'll be back. Don't worry."

"But if it doesn't work, then the last days I have with her will be lost—she won't even know me; I won't be able to get through to her."

"I'm sorry, Jaxon, but it's all about saving her now. We have to make some compromises to make a go of this."

"But what *is* this! What chance does she have either way?"

After a moment of silence, the doctor answered. "You told me to be honest with you, so I will. We know what chance she has if we don't try. That's all I can say about it."

Jaxon cried as he yelled. "Well, that isn't good enough—not for Claire! I can't see giving up the last days I have with her to try something that's one in a billion. Can you honestly tell me that makes sense?"

The doctor was businesslike. "At this point, treatment options are up to you. I can only recommend the best of what's left. If you're undecided, please make a decision soon. If the advanced protocol is going to have a chance to work, it has to be administered now. You understand?"

Jaxon stopped his wild pacing and looked out to sea. "Yes."

"I'm available if you need me. I think it best to leave it in your hands."

The call ended and with it went Jaxon's energy to stand. He sat down at the edge of the bluff and stared down at the village. Below, life went on as usual. The bohemian enclave looked small and the occasional person walking along seemed tiny and remote from a larger reality. It was as if Jaxon's awareness hovered above humanity going about its day but oblivious to the inner workings and outer design of the wider world.

Jaxon let his gaze wander. A stoic silence dried his eyes. The last thing he wanted to do was talk with anyone. That's when his phone rang. Numb with the habit of life, he checked the caller then lifted the phone to his ear.

"Perry, this isn't a good time."

"Why so glum? You have something against being popular?"

"From what I hear, you're too popular. How's that working out for you?"

The reference to Perry's failed love triangle with two sisters who hadn't known about the other one for some time, hit home. "Now you're getting nasty. I just thought you might like to know what's going on."

"You really think you know, huh?"

"If you don't want me to tell you, that's fine with me."

Jaxon could hear the ruffled tail feathers. This was no time to turn business associates into enemies. "I want to know; just make it quick."

"It's about your publisher."

"Which one?"

"The one that has *Surviving The Near-Life Experience*, of course."

"You're going to tell me they're happy with book sales…"

"Happy?" laughed Perry. "They're orgasmic. They haven't sold this many books since what's-her-name decided to tell all on who's-his-face."

"You said you had news. That can't be it."

"Of course not. From what I hear, good old Diamond Dawg, your editor-at-large, is concerned that all the conspiracy theories buzzing around you might gain traction. If they do, it could take some of the squeak out of your squeaky-clean image. That, in turn, might prove disastrous for future books."

"What can *he* do about it?"

"A little fire to fight fire. From what I'm told, he's ready to leak a new spin on Suah and you."

"I told you, I don't want to capitalize on Suah."

"I'm just an agent; he runs his own shop."

"So what is he going to say?"

"Oh, he's not going to say it. It's going to come out in a way that leaves the publishing house high and dry. They don't know how any of this is going to shake out; they want their plausible deniability."

"It's that bad, huh?"

"Not really. They're just going to say the conspiracies are right but for the wrong reason. You and Gianna *have* been working together with Suah, but it wasn't about any publicity stunt."

"What am I supposed to be, his mentor?"

Perry gasped. "How did you know?"

"This is so obvious, it's ridiculous. How can they think this will help?"

"No, wait, there's more."

"It doesn't matter. I know there's more and it's going to be equally ridiculous. Just tell them to cease and desist. I don't want them to float any stories about what went on."

"What makes you think they'll listen to you?"

"What!"

"It's your book but it's their business. They've got to run it for their shareholders, not to appease your conscience."

Jaxon gripped the phone tighter. "Just tell me the rest of it."

"Everyone knows that Suah Chase has some 'special needs' although that's never been defined. From what your editor dug up, Suah's doctors have never been pinned down exactly how or why he's different; he just is. It's not autism, although he sure doesn't relate socially like normal people."

Jaxon fumed, "I don't need to hear your bigotry about what's normal..."

"Relax, he's a great kid. All I'm saying is, it's a fact that years ago there were lots of news stories that came out about Gianna Chase adopting this African boy and then finding out that he was the *special* one in the bunch, if you know what I mean. The public knows this—or they can be reminded of it quick enough."

"So what?"

"Well, Diamond Dawg wants to spin it this way: after a chance meeting with Suah, you recognized that he was what they call a 'prodigious savant.' There are basically three types of savants. A prodigious savant is the very rare kind; there's been like 100 cases in 100 years."

"Why would this fit Suah?'

"It may be the *only* thing that fits. Prodigious savants aren't obvious by their behavior, they don't flap their hands or sit in a corner staring off or anything. It's possible they can go completely unnoticed."

"Then what makes them a savant?"

"Well, they're quirky, that's for sure, but they also have one spot of brilliance, some gift that goes off the charts. Their gift, whatever it is, is spectacular not only in contrast to any disability they might have, it would be spectacular measured against anybody else on the whole bloody planet."

"They expect this story to get traction?"

"Well, here's the best part. They're going to say you realized that sooner or later, a prodigious savant might come along whose gift opened up some channel in the mind or spirit to allow him to do miracles. In Suah's case, to heal people. Suah's gift isn't counting up all the prime numbers between one and a googolplex before breakfast. It's something better. You saw a way to mentor him so he could develop and channel his savant specialness."

"What about the conference? How do they explain that?"

"That was spontaneous. Dumb chance. You had Suah there to listen to your all-important message while he practice his gift on this Lolo girl he brought with him. Nobody knew that other woman was going to drop dead. And now you're off-balance because you never wanted Suah's gift to be known, not yet—not until it was ready to be introduced to the world. So, what do you think?"

"Why did you really call me?"

"I just told you."

Jaxon stood up and began to pace again. "If I didn't know better, I'd say you and Diamond Dawg are plotting this together. The purpose of this call is to sell it to me. Diamond Dawg is no good at that but you are."

Perry laughed. "So how did I do?"

Jaxon was humorless. "What I said I meant. I don't want to capitalize on Suah. Don't lecture me about shareholders. I suspect my publisher will listen to its parent company before me but I'm going on record with you—I don't like it and I don't want it done. Is that understood?"

"It's understood. But *you* have to understand, some things are bigger than any one person. Honey, one fly might not like the rubbish but you're not going to keep the rest of the flies off it."

"At least we agree on what we're dealing with."

Jaxon ended the call abruptly, letting disconnection be his exclamation.

In contrast, the trade winds buffeted his back with their warm softness. In the distance, Faith exited Center Space with her yoga class heading for the parking lot. Seeing him, Faith changed direction and headed his way.

"Well, that was a nice warmup. I'm all ready for Claire."

"Great," smiled Jaxon.

Faith led the way towards Pule Point. "Do you remember what I told you Pule means?"

Distracted with a hundred other thoughts, Jaxon shook his head. "You got me. I should know but I don't."

Faith walked at his side. "Pule means prayer. It's no accident that it's Claire's favorite place."

"It always has been."

Faith took his hand in hers as they walked. "I want you to know, I'm honored you came to me."

Jaxon held on tight. "I'm thankful you're here. I know Claire needs this—and I need it for Claire."

The two of them entered the small Pule Point yurt to find Claire sitting in a lounge chair, looking out to sea. The ocean side of the yurt opened up to a small, covered patio. On hearing them enter, Claire looked back at them.

"Come share the serenity," she said. "There's plenty of it to go around."

Faith stepped up alongside Claire and then dropped down into a lotus position next to her. "We have a little surprise for you."

Claire's eyes widened. "Surprise?"

"Your husband has arranged for a private energy and meditation session, just between you and me."

Claire's mouth dropped open as she looked to Jaxon for confirmation. His smile was all the evidence she needed. "A private session…?"

Faith held Claire's hand. "It's a perfect day. For the next hour or two, whatever you feel you have the strength for, we'll focus our energies at Pule Point together. Let's meditate on the possible, on *the way things should be*."

Claire began to tear up. Looking back at Jaxon, she made fun of her earlier statement to him with mock anger. "This trip wasn't about getting away with Hailey and me, was it?"

Jaxon played his part. "No, it's about seclusion for *your* meeting."

From a sitting position, Claire reached out for him. Jaxon bent down and gave her a hug. He whispered in her ear, "Contemplate the possible. All the great teachers have told us—everything is possible. Let Faith-Anchala lead the way. I love you."

They kissed and Jaxon stood up. He glanced at Faith. "I'll leave her in your energetic hands." Jaxon turned away and left the yurt.

Faith pulled up a lounge chair and placed it alongside Claire's. "Nani Ahi Pua means beautiful fire flower. The old woman who once lived here used to say it was the only way she could think of to describe the human soul. She believed our beautiful fire could overcome any pain."

"Right now," whispered Claire. "I'd settle for just some relief."

Faith smiled. "What if we don't have to settle? Let's meditate on the *what-if* within us…"

Outside, walking the bluff, Jaxon reflected on all he faced. After so many years of making a living by telling everyone that he had the answers, it was humbling to stand under an open sky and be stumped by his own life.

Unable to escape the reach of the outside world, he frowned when his phone rang again. He grabbed it from his pocket with one driving thought; if this was Perry calling back, he'd better be ready to be shouted at.

Jaxon was curt. "Hello?"

A woman's voice answered. She was brief, sophisticated, and savvy.

"Mr. Muse. Gianna Chase would like to meet with you. If you'd ever like speak with Suah again, I suggest you clear your calendar this evening."

CHAPTER 33

After visiting hours, the sun went down and a routine calm descended upon the fourth floor of *Memorial Medical Center*. Ever so often along the hallway, the soft steps of a nurse punctuated the silence and then were gone. Lingering smells from the dinner service an hour before diverged from the light but all-pervasive scent of disinfectant. A gurney and wheelchair waited along the wall. Fluorescent lights reflected in the polish on the floor.

Nurse Naomi Treggor left Suah's room after finishing the latest of her periodic checks. Earlier, Suah had eaten well, despite having to avoid the sore side of his mouth where he was missing bicuspids. Now he was resting; he even wanted the television turned off. To Naomi, it seemed a bit early for a child his age to be so sedate but she assumed it was the aftereffects of a heavy meal mixed with his latest, albeit mild, dose of pain medication.

Inside Suah's room, the lights were low, so low that it would have been hard to distinguish the pale green color of the walls. That is, if anyone was looking at them. But Suah wasn't. He was gazing at the ceiling with his one uncovered eye. His mom had come to see him. She had been at his side and had kissed him. She really had come back to the island and now he wanted nothing more than to go home and be with her and finish their adventure.

On the palette of gray above him, he imagined a swirl of colors. He saw them blend and morph, springing out around and through themselves over and over again. He made them amazing, with no hard edge but still distinct, with no one light source but still dimensional. He saw them and imagined they weren't just colors—they were alive and they were dancing just for him.

He felt drowsy and his eyelids drooped. As he blinked, the colors became a memory, then his eyes opened again. He was surprised to see how different the patterns were while in many ways they stayed the same. At times they seemed very close to him; at times they appeared incredibly far away.

The sameness of the slight sounds around him became an insistent meditation. The steady whoosh of air through air-conditioning vents was an impossible voice holding a hypnotizing note with infinite breath. He marveled at it and concentrated on his own breath. When he did, he heard a voice within him, a familiar voice—one he always knew would return.

I know...I know...It's time to charm...I-and-I can dance...I know...
It's only me but you're enough out here...there's nothing to do but play...
Be inside far and outside near...follow yourself to find the way...

CHAPTER 34

Night had settled in but the pop of photoflashes lit up Olivia's car as if it were noon. There was no earthly reason why anyone should be interested in seeing a picture of Olivia Platt driving a car, but if that were so, then why were so many professional adults tripping over themselves to possess such a thing? Olivia had no explanation for it except as the lowest common denominator of what she expected when human nature went on parade.

Having braved the gauntlet, Olivia drove up the hill and parked. She got out of the car and stood a moment to take everything in.

An uneasy calm pervaded the Gianna Chase estate. Of course, Gianna would have given the maid the night off. Gianna was always very private about her most sensitive times. On such a warm evening with no one else at home, Olivia expected to find her basking in the quiet of the rear-yard lanai.

Ignoring the front door, Olivia followed the wraparound porch and strolled to the rear of the house. There were no lights on. There she found Gianna in the lounge chair of choice with earbuds in, listening to music.

Catching her attention, Olivia stepped near her but stayed standing.

Gianna plucked out one earbud. "You're back? I expected you to call."

"I thought I'd check in on you, see how you were doing."

Gianna crossed her legs at the ankles. "I'm OK. I just had an urge to listen to some music. How about you? Have any luck?"

"I have a meeting scheduled within the hour."

Gianna was surprised. "Tonight?"

"Why not? He's on the island interviewing people."

"So where're you going to meet?"

"*The Manuia Resort.*"

Gianna had to laugh. "Of all places."

"He's staying there. From what I hear, the resort comped him quite a few perks. They think he and his entourage will draw them attention."

"His entourage?" sighed Gianna. "Another reporter celebrity."

"He was given money so he can move fast. He's hired minions to be his eyes and his ears."

"Why the major operation?" wondered Gianna.

"I think somebody believes this story will fade fast. If so, the first one out of the gate with something comprehensive will win the public's attention and get to capitalize on it. The also-rans won't make a dime."

"Did he ask why he's meeting with you and not me?"

"He wondered about it but in an offhand way."

"What did you tell him?"

"I said you were willing to meet with him after establishing a few things."

"If he's moving fast, I don't know if this is the right way to approach it. I still think I should get on with it, just set up a meeting with him tomorrow…"

Olivia was resolute. "We already went over this. It won't take long. I'll meet with him, feel him out. Remember, he's not just a curious guy; he represents the media. You have to trust me on this."

Gianna thought a moment then relented. "Did he make any conditions?"

"No." Olivia leaned back on one of the support pillars. "Nathan Mackey knows what he's doing. He won't close any doors when he's waiting for something or someone to walk through."

"All right. Take your time with him. See what you can find out."

"We already know he's in the pocket of Wyatt Dumashe."

"But we don't know what Wyatt wants." Gianna plucked the other earbud from her ear. "I know Wyatt. He's always been friendly to me but he's an inquisitive man. I can see why he'd be interested in something like this."

"But he's also a businessman," Olivia reminded. "In that role, it's wise never to assume or underestimate what he might do."

"He's doing it through *The Protoprime Society*…"

"They may be harmless but that's why they're valuable. They can be used as a coating of good intentions over something else." Olivia braved the first question she had come to ask. "What about Jaxon Muse? Are you ready for him?"

"More than ready." Gianna's answer sounded overly confident, even dismissive of Olivia having to ask such a thing.

Olivia persisted, "I'm still not convinced you should have the meeting here. It'll draw a lot of attention to the one spot that's your refuge."

"You know my reasons. I don't want to go over it anymore." Gianna was more exhausted by the topic than angry. "I trust my space. I need to be confident the meeting's private. Let him come to me."

"I wish I could be here…"

Gianna interrupted. "You have your own meeting to get to. Did you do the press release?"

"It went out a hour ago. It said you had come back to the island to be with Suah and you were cooperating with the police investigation."

"Did you mention something about sending donations to the hospital instead of flowers?"

"Yes." Olivia hesitated on the final point. "I also said that the tour was on hold; it hadn't been canceled."

For a moment, Gianna said nothing and gave Olivia all the time she needed to ask the second question she had come to ask.

"When are you starting back on tour?"

Gianna got up from the lounge and stepped out on the decking by the infinity pool. "That hasn't been decided. Why did you say anything?"

"Because it's high time we put out something. It's not the kind of thing we should leave hanging."

"It's only been a day."

"It only takes a day to throw the schedule off. Once that happens, everything down the line gets displaced. You know that."

Gianna tensed. "You act like I expected all of this to happen."

"No, I just expect we can work around it."

"What do you suggest?"

Olivia stepped out to the edge of the pool to be near to Gianna. "The hospital said Suah should be released in a couple of days. It'll take three or four days to finalize the new on-tour nanny and make road arrangements. We should announce the rescheduling of the next tour date but keep all the other dates as they are; that will minimize confusion for everybody and any losses we have to absorb. As soon as we have everything set up for him, Suah can join us on tour."

Gianna was unconvinced. "The timing of that may not dovetail."

"We work around it. But we keep the tour going. The best thing to diffuse all the nonsense going on back here is to be out there singing to the world." Olivia pointed at the far horizon.

Gianna tugged at the straps of her silk slip dress and let the delicate drape of Tuscan rose fabric fall to the ground. Standing naked, she glanced at Olivia. "I'll think about it."

A moment later, Gianna dove into the pool and swam away. The conversation had ended, leaving Olivia with much unsaid.

Gianna swam to a place where the infinity view merged with the dark ocean. She stared into it and treaded water before relaxing and floating on her back. Opening her eyes, the stars came into focus.

All around her, near to her, the water was satin against her bare skin. Up above, so far away, pinpoints of endless wonder teased her to reset her perspective.

With ears under water, she couldn't hear Olivia walking away but she knew she was gone. She could feel it. She knew when her house was empty. It had a feeling all its own. So did the sky. She stared into it and enjoyed the feeling of floating.

Floating left her in between worlds, neither fully of the earth nor part of the sky. In such a state, the world might be her oyster but she was the pearl locked inside. The sky might be her inspiration but she was the one held by gravity from ever fully reaching it. Somehow in between them both, she'd have to be enough. Somehow despite both, she would find that one thing she could hold onto and call her own.

She swam to the stairs and got out of the pool. Lifting a towel from one of the lounge chairs, she dried herself then flung the towel over her shoulder. She didn't usually walk through her house naked, not with maids and nannies around and certainly not if Suah was at home. But tonight was different. The house was empty and the thought of facing Jaxon Muse had emboldened her. It felt freeing to assert herself and do as she pleased.

She went upstairs to get dressed but detoured for a glance in Suah's room. She turned on the light and stepped to his nightstand. The little things he valued were all around. She reached down and picked up the small kaleidoscope toy, the one he liked to play with before going asleep.

Pulling it up before her eyes, she pointed it at the lamp and turned the end. A swirl of colors spun patterns that overlapped and merged in ways that managed to look different but always in the same way.

As beautiful as it was, most children would have gotten bored with such a thing. But Suah never did. Many would call that part of his *specialness* and silently congratulate themselves for being too sophisticated and socially enlightened for such a toy. But that was just their latest euphemism for a segregating distinction that could only be taken in a condescending way.

Gianna lowered the toy and looked at it. She hated the way the word *special* had been said to her face in describing Suah. It was so obvious that the primary intent was to make the speaker feel good about themselves.

The fact that Suah didn't get bored with things like a toy kaleidoscope made him *special* in all the best connotations of the word. He never lost his wonder for simple joys because he always brought himself to them in a full and open way that was ever-revealing and new.

How could that be called a developmental disability?

If anything, it was the culture around him that was crippled by its own narcissist illusions of grandeur. It saw itself as the final arbiter of truth, taste, and meaning, even if it had made those things mass-produced and disposable.

Yes, it was true that most children would have gotten bored with such a toy. But then, most of those children watched 40,000 commercials a year and their appetites and expectations had been programmed for obsolescence. They couldn't even enjoy a simple pleasure until they checked the latest affectation disguised as a meme to see if it was deemed cool enough to do so.

Why wasn't *their* condition listed in the DSM-IV as a special need?

Gianna's frustrations surged and became tears.

No one had been able to categorize Suah. There was no page in the hallowed DSM-IV to describe him. No one was going to construct a box to put him in for the DSM-5. With the events of the past few days flashing to mind, Gianna faced a terrifying thought.

Everyone, including herself, had tried to find a shape to put Suah in.

In the moment, the realization struck Gianna—what people saw when they looked at Suah, for the most part, wasn't Suah. What they saw was only the shape they had put around them. They weren't reacting to him at all. They were reacting to their own preconceptions of the way things should be.

The way things should be.

Where had she heard that? The video from the Jaxon Muse conference.

Gianna chilled at the thought. Had she done the same thing by trying to protect Suah from the outside world? A specter of guilt and shame in what that implied was too much to handle in the moment.

She set the kaleidoscope back in place and walked around the bed to check out the top of Suah's dresser. Everything was as she remembered it, either by happenstance or because it was planned. Even if Suah had moved something out of place, the maid would have set it right.

There was an order, a predictable comfort about the sameness of things. Continuity and security made children feel safe. It was supposed to make everyone feel safe. And yet, Gianna suddenly felt confined.

There was something lifeless about trying to keep anything so secure and controlled. The unexpected could always happen. Hiding away from the thought that it could, wouldn't make the uncertainty go away.

Maybe the adventure that she and Suah had been on would turn out to be the best thing for both of them. Given all that had happened, she only hoped so. As she had told Olivia on the airplane, how could she do anything else?

She ambled into his closet and looked around. Again, everything was in place. At random, she opened up a wardrobe door to inspect inside. Suah's clothes were folded just as she expected to find them.

That wasn't what surprised her. She turned and was struck by something on the back of the wardrobe door. It was a piece of paper taped in place. The paper had a most peculiar drawing on it.

Gianna pulled the drawing off the door and held it in hand. The drawing was water-damaged but still recognizable. At the top, in Suah's uniquely unpredictable handwriting, a scrawl of letters labeled the drawing's two sides. On one side was the name SUAH. On the other side, HAWA.

Arrows were drawn from the names and pointed to the images sketched below. The image of Suah had been done in a fine charcoal pencil. The image of Hawa looked to be a smudge made off the original drawing.

Gianna turned the page over and was surprised to discover that the front was a color photocopied flyer advertizing a snorkel cruise. The directions said it set sail from slip number nine. Below that was the name of the business.

Island Aquatics & Adventures.

CHAPTER 35

At the concierge desk, a hostess in a Polynesian print dress greeted Olivia with a smile and a pleasant, "May I help you?"

"My name is Olivia Platt. I have an appointment. I was told the contact name is Protoprime."

The hostess checked a touch screen embedded in the counter before her. "Ah, yes, here it is. May I see some identification?"

Olivia wavered, a bit annoyed, then produced a driver's license.

The hostess took a glance. "Very well. Your party is waiting in beach cabana number five...

"Beach cabana?"

"Yes. Do you know the way or would you like an escort?"

"An escort, please."

The hostess quickly scanned the vast lobby but no one caught her eye. "I can take you. Right this way."

Olivia followed the young woman through the wide, open-air lobby of *The Manuia Resort* and into an elevator. After a short ride down, they headed out along a meandering path that skirted the pool area. On either side of them, twin eight-story towers jutted up and were dotted with the lit-up windows of individual suites.

Reaching the beach, the hostess turned and headed for the one beach cabana that was enclosed by draperies on three sides and lit by candlelight inside. The hostess came to within several paces of the spot and stopped.

Olivia asked, "Is it customary for the guests to be able to use the beach cabanas at night?"

The hostess smiled, "We always try to accommodate the wishes of our guests." She motioned towards the drapes warm with the glow. "Here is the Protoprime party. Please enjoy your stay." She bowed from the shoulders and strutted away.

Olivia watched her go then turned back to the cabana. She hadn't noticed before but two brawny men in tan pants and casual shirts looked to be standing guard nearby. She approached one of the men.

"I'm Olivia Platt..."

"Right this way."

The man led her to the open end of the cabana, the end that faced the water. There she could finally see her host and the seating arrangements.

Storm candles were positioned at the rear corners of the three walls formed by the drapery. Two lounge chairs faced the water but were turned slightly inward towards each other. A small table divided them. Chilled wine and tall glasses were at the ready.

In one of the chairs sat a man in his late thirties with a shock of hair left wild presumably to distract from his receding hairline. He wore sandals and light long pants topped by a black cashmere T-shirt. It was a copy of Armani but Olivia thought it looked reasonably good for being a knockoff.

The man stood and extended a hand in welcome. "Nathan Mackey…"

Olivia shook the hand with half of hers. "Olivia Platt."

They sat down and Nathan poured the wine. With his smooth attitude and attention to detail working in tandem, he promptly set about establishing the comfort and rapport necessary to ease completion of matters before them. This in spite of any frostiness they had exchanged on their earlier phone call.

"In such a lovely place, I saw no reason not to conduct our business in a lovely way. I hope the setting is all right with you."

"Fine," remarked Olivia. "I like an ambiance that elevates business to the level of a seduction. It seems a bit more honest, now doesn't it?"

Nathan grinned with one side of his face. "I heard you were a shrewd negotiator. Gianna Chase is very lucky to have you in her corner."

Olivia was not about to waste time. "As I'm sure Wyatt Dumashe is to have you in his."

The first blow was landed. Nathan took it with a bob and weave. "We all have our proxies. Some are known, others are more personal and strategic. It's hard to imagine that this is all about Gianna Chase for you."

"And why is that?"

The wine was poured but Nathan ignored it. "How complicated can the ground rules be for what we need to do? If Gianna wants to be part of my investigation, as well she should be, she'll set the conditions as we go along. Nothing we decide tonight can't be modified tomorrow if she changes her mind. And that's the way it should be. Trying to pretend that it's more complicated than that is odd to me. It seems like nothing more than a pretext for you to insert yourself in the process. For what reason, I can only guess."

Olivia laughed. "My my, are all investigators as stuck on themselves and obsessed by their own dismal view of people as you?"

Nathan eased back and finally enjoyed some wine. "I could tell you didn't like me that much when we spoke on the phone."

"Why would you say that? Dear Mr. Mackey, never think for a minute that just because I see through your amateurish tactics that it means I dislike you personally. I simply understand what you're after and what you are willing to do to get it."

"Really. And what am I after?"

Olivia's grin was coy. "A bigger you. You'll do anything to elevate yourself, however you define that."

"Is that so…"

"Maybe this year it means the Pulitzer Prize. Who knows? Whatever it is, it means dragging anything and everything out in the open and rearranging it the way you see fit so you can get the biggest bang for the buck."

"I don't think so. The way you describe it, that would put us in the same line of work."

Olivia forged ahead. "And, of course, I expected you to want to know what I'm after. But that's simple. I came here tonight to let you know that my job is to make sure that people like you don't warp the public's perception of who Gianna Chase really is. Telling the truth is one thing; fabricating a truth to get a bigger story or do the bidding of your rich patrons is something I'll not stand for. Try that and I'll expose you…"

Nathan smiled, "And *you'll* get the Pulitzer Prize."

"You want to dig up secrets? I've got one for you. Gianna is very good at what she does. In fact, millions around the world think she's the best at it. But being brilliant at one thing doesn't mean you are good at handling everything. In many respects, Gianna is a babe in the woods. She doesn't think the way people like you think; her mind doesn't even go there…"

"So you watch out for her," Nathan interrupted. "You like playing the role of the mother, don't you?"

"I like protecting her so she can do what she loves to do."

"And Suah, you like protecting him too?"

Olivia was disgusted with his attitude. "What do you think?"

"I think you can never tell what will unravel when you start pulling threads. Take Suah, for instance. Something extraordinary seems to happen and naturally, people want to know more about it. I get involved and start looking into it. Suah leads me to Gianna and Gianna leads me to you."

Nathan waited for a comeback but there was none. Olivia was content to let him speak and see where this was leading. He eased back; his posture shifted to a place more settled and assured.

"Having benefactors is very nice. It gives people like me resources to go deeper into things than otherwise would be possible. The results are surprising sometimes. They really show how the closer one goes, more is revealed. Everybody has a story. The interesting part is, all our stories are intertwined. That's what the public likes to see. Not just the shiny surface, but layers underneath."

Olivia had heard enough. She suspected where he was headed and wanted to undercut its validity right away. She relaxed back.

"Going after me is a waste of your time."

"If it is," countered Nathan, "then I guess I get paid for wasting time."

Nathan leaned in closer to her across the small table. "Anybody can do a story on the obvious. You know as well as I do: no one's going to find out if Suah Chase can do miracles. That's a matter of faith."

"Gianna wants to know what happened."

With a flick of his hand and a puff of air, Nathan blew that off. "Listen, you're close enough to the media to know that facts don't prove anything. The proof of anything you want is in the editing. There isn't going to be any single bullet theory to explain or explain away the things that happened around Suah."

Olivia was content for the moment to let him talk in hopes that by speaking his mind he'd reveal more of himself. "And why is that?"

"Truth is relative. It's the figure-ground perception thing—you know, the vase, Rubin's vase, the faces-or-vases illusion. One person sees a vase. Someone else sees two faces looking at each other. I'm not in the fact business; I'm in the perception business. Facts are just the raw materials used to make perceptions."

"So what perception does Wyatt Dumashe want you to make?"

Nathan settled back, his grin submissive to his caution. "It's never a portrait. It has to be a montage."

"Well, I must say, that's nebulous enough to make me want to recommend that Gianna not meet with you after all."

"You want facts," snapped Nathan. "You can watch them tonight. The first of my reports broadcasts in primetime. It's all there—Suah saving a drowning victim on a boat, Suah saving a girl injured in a bar fight, Suah healing a dog's injured leg. With the team I have, it didn't take long to interview people and get their stories. But that's just it; it's only their stories, their figure-ground perceptions of what happened."

Olivia stiffened in surprise. "You have people saying that Suah did other healings, other miracles?"

"Crazy, isn't it," laughed Nathan. "Who would ever think *that* would happen. I even have a woman who never met Suah but she told me she had a spontaneous remission of her fibromyalgia after she started using *Suah's Prayer* as her meditation mantra."

"*Suah's Prayer*?"

"Yeah, all that twaddle Suah mumbled over the woman at the conference. The guy who translated it called it *Suah's Prayer*. You know the faithful is going to eat that up like a fire sale on Eucharist."

Olivia paused to process the new facts. "If you're looking for manufactured perceptions, I should think you'd be all over Jaxon Muse."

"So far, he won't talk, but that's his problem because there are enough of his words out there in print to nail him any which way circumstantially." Nathan lifted his phone and navigated with a thumb. "I can quote him all day; he doesn't have to talk to me. Here's what he said in a book that came out two years ago—'*We all have the capacity within us to do miracles even though we rarely express it. The first step in fulfilling our potential is believing in the fullness of who we are.*'" Nathan dropped the phone to the chair. "You want motive for a hoax, start there."

Olivia sat in awe of the chameleon behind Nathan's conscience. She decided to challenge it. "So what's *my* story, *my* figure-ground perception?"

Nathan looked her up and down. "You're interesting."

"How is that?"

He grinned at his invisible muse. "Everyone likes to believe they're complicated. I've never met a person who didn't think it would be hard for anyone outside of their inner soul to really understand their true essence."

"Even you?"

"Even me. But I looked at that in myself. I discovered there is a complicated layer around us. We put it there either as protection or bluster."

"That's usually the same thing."

"Yes, but underneath it all is a simple need. Everybody's got one and everyone is different. If someone like me can get through all the fake complicated stuff, we uncover that one thing. That's when we have something everyone wants to look at. People are endlessly fascinated in that, can't take their eyes off it. Because it's the very thing, exposed in others, that they themselves would never admit to. In my line of work, that's the diamond pit in the rotten fruit."

Olivia recognized Nathan to be a man who liked to hear himself talk. She sipped her wine and pushed him back on topic. "You still haven't answered my question."

"What is your story? Oh, well, that's the oldest archetype in the world." Nathan stared into her eyes. "You need to be the perfect mother."

The words, his delivery made Olivia uncomfortable but she maintained her poise and showed him a practiced public face.

"Only problem is," continued Nathan. "You never had a child. After four failed marriages, your greatest need wasn't met and your lifestyle and history made adoption difficult if not impossible. But you had a career. That you were good at even though it didn't fill your need. Or did it? Maybe it could. Maybe by mothering one gifted babe-in-the-woods to pop stardom, you could have a career and be a mother too."

Olivia was losing control. "Top reporter isn't big enough for your ego, I see. You also fancy yourself a psychologist."

"If you ask a man on the corner what he believes and he tells you, does that make him a philosopher? I guess so; I guess we all are. The point is, Ms. Platt, it's easy to see patterns in the facts that swirl around you. You pushed Gianna on the idea of adopting Suah, then you backed away from that when he didn't turn out as planned. You not only needed to be the perfect mother, you had to be the perfect grandmother—and Suah was far from perfect."

"How dare you!" Olivia's whisper might as well been a shout.

"Years ago, you tried to convince Gianna that taking care of Suah wouldn't be possible in her kind of world with all the touring and the demands on her time."

"Things were out of control…"

"Funny how you came to this conclusion not long after something unusual was discovered about Suah. You had to know for sure. You were relentless investigating his birth. Then you did everything but ask Gianna flat-out to send him back to Africa."

Olivia shot up from her chair. "I won't sit here and be insulted like this!"

"I spoke with Hannah," added Nathan. "Among others…"

The mention of Hannah, Suah's original touring nanny, caused Olivia to halt her march from the cabana. She looked back.

"Yes, Hannah was very helpful. She was also very sad to have to watch all those years as you manipulated your surrogate child. Nothing could threaten the family you put together. You defended the nest admirably, even if that meant sabotaging Gianna's love life."

"What!" Olivia stood tall in a cold sweat, her nerves on fire.

"You couldn't let another adult in Gianna's life. She might start listening to them instead of you. And mother always knows best."

"Are you done?" Olivia demanded.

"I have one last question." Nathan leaned back in his lounge chair but his body was ready to jump. "Now that Suah can do miracles, has he earned his place as your grandchild? Is walking on water perfect enough for you? Will you keep him around?"

Olivia struggled but regained her composure. She stared at him until she thought she could speak without breaking down. "Under all the complicated bullshit, you said everyone has a need. So, I'm curious; what did you discover about yourself? What is *your* need?"

It wasn't what Nathan expected. He reached for his wine and took a long sip before answering. "I need to be worthy." He hesitated and watched her reaction. "I'm ashamed of who I am and I don't want anyone to see it."

Olivia was taken aback by his bluntness. To win, he was willing at times to be honest. The clarity of that was telling. He had his priorities but leading them all was an insect-like desire simply to win.

Then he added to it. "I think it comes down to this: if I manage to rip the complicated shells off everyone else, maybe then no one will pay attention to what I'm hiding under mine."

Olivia was seething. "In other words, you're an asshole."

Nathan smiled. "If you think I'm worthy of it, I guess so."

Olivia stepped to the cabana's opening then turned back. "Go ahead and peddle whatever story you like. You think you're so insightful. You're not the only one who manages perceptions. I'll put out my own versions of your deepest insights. They'll be right up there on all the tabloids, right next to the story of the dog-faced boy and Martians that ate my babysitter."

"What will that prove?"

"Prove? Don't you remember, there is no proof, there is no truth. Sing your sweet song, I don't care. I'll drown it out with a hundred others singing off-tune."

Olivia marched away. She glared at the two men guarding the cabana. Her strut never wavered until she had passed the pool and entered the resort's lobby. She knew the place well from past visits.

It took only a second to hesitate before turning a certain way. At the end of one particular hallway she'd find the cocktail lounge. Maybe nothing else was certain, but she knew they made a fine vodka martini.

CHAPTER 36

Gianna Chase hurried downstairs in an empty house, undecided on how best to quell her nerves. Jaxon Muse would arrive any minute and the waiting had become unbearable. She started for the kitchen then changed direction towards the entertainment room. Along the way, her knee-length silk poncho flowed like wings around her.

She turned on the TV and stood near the large screen. Using the remote control, she scanned the onscreen guide. A friend had called earlier to alert her that a documentary by Nathan Mackey would be on. Gianna had set it to record but thought it best to watch later, after Jaxon Muse left.

Now her nerves needed distraction. On impulse, she decided to watch some of it. Instead of starting the recording from the beginning, she opted to watch the show live, even though it was halfway through.

When the channel came on, Nathan Mackey was the voice-over narrator. The video being shown was shot on the streets south of town not far from Gianna's estate. After establishing the area, the editing quickly took the viewer closer, then inside a drab little bar called Sops & Wobbers.

"...*it was here, at a run-down watering hole called Sops & Wobbers where witnesses say the next miracle happened...*"

Nathan's style or narration had classic journalistic flair and confidence. He described places and events as a means to get to the people involved. Once he got to them, he reveled in showing them warts and all.

As the camera panned the bar, Roy the bartender was shown at work serving his regulars. Gianna was struck by a peculiar feature that distinguished the place. Covering the walls all around the bar area were dozens of life preservers of every shape and kind.

The image immediately took Gianna back to Suah's hospital room and to Suah mumbling in what she thought was delirium. She could still hear him.

"...*watching the life preservers on the wall, that's not wasting time.*"

The doorbell rang and split her concentration.

Why hadn't she considered that some of the things Suah had mumbled in the hospital might have meaning? If what she saw on TV had a connection, then how had Suah ever gotten into that bar? There was no other way to see the life preservers on the wall unless one went inside.

The doorbell rang again. Jaxon Muse had arrived. Either that or she was in for another surprise. She switched off the TV and tossed the remote onto the couch cushions. Stepping to the wall, she punched a button on the security monitor and brought up a closed-circuit image of the front porch. It was all the verification she needed. With a determination usually reserved for show-time moments right before stepping on stage, she made strides for the front door and opened it.

Jaxon Muse looked up from the wide porch and caught her eye. His relaxed manner was disarming. "It's not every day I get to meet a star."

In the spirit of cooperation, she returned the favor. "It's not every night I get to contemplate the universe with one so wise."

He smiled, as if to say: *touché.*

Gianna looked past him at the long black town car in her circle driveway. "Did you drive yourself?"

"No, but I told David to stay put. I didn't think you'd want any more company while we talked. He'll be all right; he's got HBO and satellite radio in that thing."

Gianna grinned. "He'll probably call for pizza delivery. Maybe I should make an exception and tell the security people to let them drive up the hill."

"That won't be necessary…"

She stepped back and opened the door wider. "Come on in."

Jaxon accepted the invitation and crossed the threshold.

Gianna turned and walked away, letting him close the door. As she padded off in bare feet, her voice led him across the marble floor tiles and into the formal living room.

He paused at its arched entrance to take in its magnificence. It was a space adorned with a Steinway grand piano and an open-air terrace. The view overlooked the lights of the town and the reaches of dark ocean beyond.

More than that, it was adorned with Gianna's presence; that alone would have filled the room with splendor. He couldn't help but be a bit starstruck. He had long enjoyed her music as a fan. To meet under such circumstances was not only surreal, it was discomfiting.

Gianna headed for the wet bar. "Driving around here in a car like that is a good way to get followed."

"True, but if I'm going to be followed leaving here, what's the point of sneaking in?" Jaxon ambled into the room. "Any car coming through your gates becomes fair game."

"I suppose you're right." Gianna sat on one of the bar stools and crossed her legs. "No matter how we do this, news is bound to get out. There's no sense trying to hide in a spotlight."

Jaxon added, "Your light is too bright for that."

Gianna ignored the compliment and gazed at the red polish on the tips of her painted toes. She bounced her free foot a little and deferred to Jaxon's sense of chivalry. "Care to pour me a drink?"

"Sure, if you'd like." Jaxon stepped forward. Letting him command the space behind the bar was either a power play to put him in a subservient role or a considerate gesture to let him feel comfortable. Usually inclined to think the best of people, Jaxon assumed it was a signal that he should feel at ease sharing her space.

"I have to warn you; I'm not the greatest mixologist."

"Then muddle me up some Chenin Blanc." Gianna turned towards the bar and watched him work. While he was occupied, she could get to the point. "You haven't been on any talk shows lately."

He pulled a cork. "Neither have you."

"I've been on tour. Some say you've been in hiding."

Jaxon looked up at her. "Hiding away would be the worst thing to do if I was trying to perpetrate a hoax."

"You mean it looks suspicious, like high-definition video that just so happens to leak out at the perfect time."

Jaxon stopped pouring. "Or children who want to ride on a particular boat charter a day before they show up at a conference without a ticket."

Gianna held back a nervous grin. "We're dastardly people, aren't we?"

The pouring of wine resumed. "The worst."

"It looks bad if you start believing the worst of what you hear."

"Some enjoy believing the worst; it's their entertainment." Jaxon set her a glass of wine in front of her. "Others just get rich peddling it."

Gianna ignored the wine. "It would be colossally stupid of me to risk everything I have on a hair-brained stunt. Being called a fraud, an opportunist, a bad mother, and worse is hardly the kind of publicity I need."

"I came to the same conclusion about you earlier today." With his own wine poured, Jaxon set the bottle down and watched her reaction.

Surprised, Gianna said nothing as he stepped around to her side of the bar.

He remained standing. "I didn't come here to accuse you of anything, Gianna. I know you didn't do anything wrong. I came here to see if you thought the same of me."

Gianna considered his overt gesture of openness against everything she had seen and heard in the past twenty-four hours. Compared to her side of the story, reasons for his possible culpability were harder to dispense with. She stood and took a stroll with her wine towards the open-air terrace.

"Let's continue this outside."

Jaxon had his answer. An easy absolution was not to be forthcoming.

Gianna settled into a comfortable lounge and waited with her thoughts until he had eased back in a companion chair across the way.

"As I see it," she began, "There are three possibilities, if you discount an outsider. Either we plotted something together or one of us did it alone."

"We both know we didn't collaborate."

"That leaves one of us as the culprit," asserted Gianna.

"If what we're talking about is fraud—yes."

"What else would it be?"

Jaxon was enthused by the challenge. "What else *could* it be?"

"Realistically speaking?"

"I include the possible in the real," asserted Jaxon.

"You can say anything is possible."

"What's wrong with that? I believe everything is possible, don't you?"

"Even if the simplest answer is usually true? We don't have to invent wonders to explain simple misunderstandings."

"I was there, at the conference. I felt the energy in the room. What happened to that woman was not a simple misunderstanding."

"If you tell me you believe it was a miracle, then it seems to me more likely a hoax because that would be the payoff for staging such a thing."

"If you want to get real, then get real. How could I stage such a thing using Suah? How would I even know he'd be available? And if, by magic, I did get access to him, how would I get him to memorize all that he said and do it right on cue? You talk about risk; one little flub would have given the whole thing away. And it doesn't end at the conference. Nathan Mackey is on TV right now saying there were at least three other healings done by Suah over a four-day period. Are telling me I arranged them too?"

"What other healings?" asked Gianna.

"I saw a headline. I only read part of it; something about a drowned boy, a woman in a bar, and a dog."

Gianna glanced back towards the entertainment room. The mention of *Sops & Wobbers* on the TV came to mind.

Jaxon continued. "The woman who saw him heal the dog said afterwards that he recited something. When she asked him about it, he gave her the name Maadoops."

"Maadoops?" Gianna thought a minute.

Jaxon scooted to the edge of his seat. "This woman, Lilyana, she remembered what Suah said and told Mackey."

"I'm listening." Gianna was interested but didn't show it.

Jaxon recited, "*A part of I-and-I is near. A part is far. Only fingers and heart touch them both.*"

The mention of *I-and-I* jogged Gianna's memory. She smiled, "Oh sure, I know Maadoops. That isn't his real name, of course; that's a nickname."

"What does it mean?"

"It's Jamaican slang. *Maad* means awesome and *Doops* means friend. He's all about being an awesome friend; it's what he sings about, it's how he plays his music and lives his life."

"Who is he?"

"A steel pan player, you know, the steel drums. He's local to the island and I asked him to sit in on a couple of songs I recorded a couple years ago."

"The *Love and Sunshine* album..."

"That's the one. You know it?"

"Are you kidding? It's a favorite of mine."

"I'm glad you enjoy it."

"Is that the only way Suah knows Maadoops?" asked Jaxon.

"Yes. Suah went with me to Jamaica for the recording session. I recorded the whole album down at GeeJam, near Port Antonio."

"GeeJam?"

"It's a small resort and recording studio on the northeast side of the island, along the coast. In between recording sets, Suah and Maadoops would hang out sometimes. Suah was fascinated with the general voodoo vibe that Maadoops kept going on about. Suah said it reminded him of the kinds of things his grandfather used to whisper to him."

"His grandfather was into voodoo?"

"No, not exactly. The native religious traditions in West Africa are rich and like everywhere else, there are fringe elements. I was told that Suah's grandfather became quite obsessed with a lot of mystical things."

Jaxon's curiosity was piqued. "Like what?"

"No one I spoke with was really sure. Sometimes he'd get all wide-eyed and serious and scare Suah with talk about *the unseen world*. Other times, he would point at something they saw every day and laugh and make Suah think he was missing something in plain sight. It got to the point where the villagers didn't think it was safe for Suah to stay with him any longer. That's when they took him to a boarding school for orphans."

"Suah had no other family?" asked Jaxon.

"No. His mother died when he was born and his father fell victim to tuberculosis not long after that. His grandfather was all he had until the age of five."

"But he did have family; his grandfather was family."

"Maybe so, but he wasn't stable enough to keep Suah. The village women all along had taken care of Suah. The grandfather knew nothing about raising babies. For five years they tried to make it work and keep them together but eventually it got out of hand. But you're chasing down phantoms, Mr. Muse. Nothing in Suah's background is going to prove he can do miracles."

"It's not about proof. It's not even about persuading you that I'm not a fraud. You've convinced me of that. "

"I have?" asked Gianna.

"A lot of people think Jesus Christ rose from the dead after three days. Many other people think *that's* a fraud. After two thousand years, neither side has been able to prove to the other side what really happened."

"Then why are you here? What do you really want?"

"I want to understand the best I can. The only way I think I'm going to do that is by talking with Suah."

"I won't let you or anybody else use Suah."

"Aren't you the least bit curious? Consider for a minute that I'm telling you the truth and it wasn't a hoax? Wouldn't you like to know what force, what power was healing those people?"

"Suah is a little boy with a big imagination and a bigger heart. I can see how people are taken with him but don't start seeing something that isn't there. That's the kind of thing I'd expect from Suah's grandfather."

"Maybe so. Maybe Suah is just a boy who was in the right place at the right time to witness improbable events. Maybe he isn't doing the healing at all. Maybe he's a channel for something else. Either way, the potential of what could be done with such a thing if it ever was understood and harnessed is immeasurable. Can't you see that?"

Gianna set her wine glass down. "All afternoon I anticipated the questions I was going to use to pin you down. Why did you take Suah on that boat ride? Why did you clear a path for him to do what he did at your conference? How did he ever get into that conference without a ticket?"

"I can explain that," Jaxon interrupted. "My daughter Hailey…"

Gianna held up a hand. "It doesn't matter. You've convinced me. I can't waste my time trying to prove this one way or the other. I'll leave it up to the police. If there's anything to find, I'm sure Detective Mason Gaines will uncover it soon enough. If he can't, then Nathan Mackey will expose something. Regardless, there's no way I'm going to do an investigation any better than they can. So, I guess that's it."

Gianna got up as if the meeting was drawing to a close.

Jaxon remained seated, startled at how abrupt she wanted to end the conversation. "How can you leave it like that?"

"Like what?"

"This is your son. Aren't you the slightest bit curious about what's going on with him?"

"He told me what went on. He said he'd been on a *nutzo-crazy* adventure. I think that was rather perceptive of him, don't you?"

"If it's *not so* crazy – I don't get it."

"No," corrected Gianna. "*Nutzo*-crazy…you know, like *nuts*."

"He told you that?"

"At the hospital, a little while ago."

"What about the other things people have heard him say? If nothing else, shouldn't we at least find out where he's coming up with this stuff?"

"I'm sure they're things he's picked up along the way, either from his grandfather or from other people like Maadoops." Gianna turned towards the living room.

Desperate to stop Gianna from marching him out the front door, Jaxon stayed seated and racked his brain for something else that might change her mind. He thought back to the brief conversation he'd had with Suah back stage at the conference after the healing of Helen.

"What about Suah's fascination with Eve, the mother of all things."

Gianna turned back. "Eve? You mean *Adam and Eve*?"

"Yes, he identifies with her, talks to her; a lot of what he recites comes out of these dialogues he has with Eve. Where does that come from?"

"I don't know what you're talking about."

"Backstage at the conference, after the healing, he said something. He seemed to be in trance half of the time. When I asked him who had said it, he told me Hawa had said it. I looked up the meaning of Hawa—it's Eve."

Recognition came over Gianna's face. "Another example of a simple misunderstanding. Once again, there's no big mystery. Hawa is the name of Suah's twin sister."

"He has a sister?" Jaxon's interest perked up.

"She was delivered first, before Suah—but she was stillborn."

Jaxon deflated. "Oh, no…"

"She was dead long before the birth. She had *Turner Syndrome*; it's a genetic condition where a girl doesn't get a normal pair of X chromosomes."

"How do you know that?"

"Years ago, when I was thinking of adopting a child, my friend Olivia did a lot of the groundwork for me. When I got infatuated with Suah, she looked into his background. His boarding school had his medical records."

"But he was from a poor village, wasn't he?"

"Yes."

"Then how did they know all this about a stillborn child?"

Gianna began to wave it off. "It's a long story…"

"That's all right," Jaxon insisted. "Sum it up."

Gianna took a moment to gather her thoughts. "That part of Africa has one of the highest number of twin births in all the world. At the time Suah was born, there happened to be outside researchers near his village; they were studying twin births in the area. They gathered the data. A copy of their report was added to Suah's medical records."

Jaxon stood. "Did they find anything else special about the birth?"

"You want miracles?" asked Gianna. She paused and thought back. "One of the school administrators thought Suah was a miracle baby. She said if you read the report, you'd think it was a miracle he was alive."

"Because of the stillborn twin?"

"Lots of reasons. The twins shared the same amniotic fluid, the same placenta."

"That's rare, isn't it?"

"It's rare for identical twins—only one or two percent…"

"Identical twins?"

Gianna nodded.

"You can't have boy-girl identical twins," Jaxon asserted.

"You're right—99.9% of the time. There's only been about ten recorded cases of it happening. Suah and Hawa are one of them."

"How is that possible?"

"The same way that Hawa got *Turner Syndrome*, the chromosome thing."

"Is *Turner Syndrome* always fatal?"

"No, there were other complications. The umbilical cord was tangled. Hawa got starved of oxygen. The researchers said even if she had survived, she would have suffered cerebral palsy."

Jaxon watched Gianna's eyes. "You thought Suah was special right from the start, didn't you?"

"Of course, I did but I didn't need to read medical records to know that. All I had to do was look at his face. I went to meet him because I saw his picture, not because I read his medical records. That came later."

"Did the records predict he might have developmental challenges?"

"No, they saw no evidence of that. If anything, that was the most improbable thing about the birth. Researchers predicted Suah would be fine."

"And you think they were right."

"Everyone is different in their own way, Mr. Muse. We only start labeling people when their differences vary beyond what we'll tolerate. What are the labels really measuring anyway—acceptable differences or our ability to be tolerant? That's the real question people should ask themselves."

"You're not surprised that Suah talks with Hawa, even recites things he believes she's saying?"

"I've known about Hawa as his invisible friend from the beginning."

"Some people who do things like that are called schizophrenic."

"And yet we happily teach children about Santa Claus, the Tooth Fairy, and the Easter Bunny. To me, it wasn't a red flag. He had talked to Hawa in his village before I adopted him. His teachers knew all about it and let him have his fantasy. They told me they saw no harm in it."

"These were the same people who wouldn't tolerate his grandfather's mysticism but they accepted this?"

"It didn't compare. For a shy and retiring boy, Hawa gave Suah an outlet, a friend he could always count on, someone to be there for him no matter what. After losing his family, they saw no reason to take that away from him too. I agreed with them."

Jaxon was more excited. "You don't find it interesting that every time Suah is around one of these healings, he has a conversation with Hawa?"

"I couldn't say. Some people claim they talk to the spirit world, other people pray to saints. A friend of mine believes her high-school sweetheart watches over her like a guardian angel. He died in a river boat accident many years ago. I don't see the difference."

"There might not be a difference. We don't know; not yet. But if you let me talk to Suah…"

Gianna pulled a piece of paper from her pocket and unfolded it. It was the drawing from Suah's closet. She showed it to Jaxon. "There's no mystery about a boy who feels a connection to a sister that he lost."

Jaxon gazed at the charcoal pencil drawing and the companion smudge.

"But he never knew her."

"He knows *of* her. He knows she existed. People in his village have a lot of folklore about being a twin. He knows the possibility of them being together once was there. She isn't a complete figment of his imagination. He did share a womb with her for nine months."

"And that's enough? That explains all of it for you?"

"You said you believe that anything is possible. Well, that's all Suah's doing. He simply believes it with the innocence of a child. Did Suah ever tell you why he came to your conference that day?"

"He said he did it for Lolo, the girl that came with him. I found out just today her real name is Leah."

"And how exactly was your conference supposed to help Leah?"

"Not the conference; Suah wanted *me* to help her. She's disabled. He wanted me to fix the way her arms and legs work."

Gianna was surprised. "He wanted *you* to heal her."

Jaxon nodded, distracted by his own memories of that day.

"Now, how could you ever think I put him up to that?"

"No, no—I never thought that," insisted Jaxon.

"If Suah has this gift, why didn't he heal her?"

"I know, it doesn't make sense," Jaxon cried out. "He's the one who can do things. It's around him that inexplicable things happen. But there he was, asking me to heal her. And this was right after he had brought Helen back. I watched her lay on the floor lifeless. I didn't understand it. I wanted to talk to him about it but he ran away."

"Apparently, he thought *you* were the healer. Now where would he have gotten that idea?"

"Who knows. He was on the boat when we came back to shore and all the people were there waiting for us."

"What people?" asked Gianna.

"People wanting to see me, wanting autographs. Some of them had my new book they wanted me to sign. Maybe he got the idea from that."

"*Surviving The Near-Life Experience*. Is that the name of it?"

"That's right, same as the conference."

"You're drawing a distinction, a play-on-words with the near-death experience. Why?"

"The near-life experience is about people not living up to their full potential, not fully engaged with life. Their lives sputter along at the lowest common denominator; they're alive but they're not really living. Ironically, many people say they were revitalized by their near-death experience; afterwards, they feel a purpose for being here and have an enthusiasm for not wasting a minute of time. There are a whole lot of people that need to be saved from the near-life experience."

"There's nothing in that about healing," noted Gianna.

"You're asking me to get inside Suah's head. I don't know why he thought I could heal her. If you let me ask him, maybe he'll tell me."

"I don't think that's possible, not with the media swirling around both of us. As long as I keep him close, I can keep him in the eye of the storm, away from the worst of it. It's the only way I can try to prevent people taking advantage of him for their own gain."

Jaxon thought back to the earlier call with Perry. "You're right, there are a lot of rumors are out there but they're not all bad. We might be able to use some of it to deflect and diminish whatever negative press might come up."

"You mean if I let you talk with him?"

"Yes."

"I have no intention of getting involved in a PR battle to see which lie trends better with the public."

"It's not about lying; it's about raising the right questions. What if the rumor says that Suah is a prodigious savant whose unique gift is being able to heal people? Think about it—if such a savant was actually discovered, wouldn't people want to study, nurture, and develop such a person?"

"That's just as ridiculous as any other story I've heard." Gianna stepped back into the living room.

Jaxon followed her. "It doesn't matter how ridiculous it is if people are interested in it; you know that."

"And we never have to say whether we believe it or not, no matter how much the spin leads people to a conclusion. How transparent."

"If we give enough people the slightest bit of wonder, let them start questioning whether or not it could be true, that's all we need."

"For what? To conjure up another hoax?"

"No!" shouted Muse. "To give us plausible room to work together, to work with Suah to uncover the truth."

"I think we're done with this conversation," announced Gianna.

"Please, Gianna! All I want to do is talk to him. Nobody has to know!"

Gianna froze, taken aback by his sudden passion. "Why do you need to talk to Suah so badly? It can't be about him. What is this really about?"

Jaxon sat down on one side of the piano bench. He leaned forward, his forearms resting on his knees. His words were choked with emotion. "My wife Claire...she doesn't have much time."

"She's sick?"

"It's inoperable. We've hid it so far but we won't be able to hide it much longer. She won't be here much longer."

"There must be something else to try besides surgery."

"There's only one thing left. I can tell the doctors don't have much hope it'll do any good." Jaxon let the silence, from all he meant to say but couldn't, fill the void that engulfed the room.

Gianna formed words around the obvious. "You think Suah can save her."

Her words were seminal to Jaxon's hopes. "It's possible. It's not unreasonable to think so given all that's happened. What would you do in my position?"

"That's hard to say. I haven't spent twenty years studying the universe and our place in it. I can't imagine the perspective you have."

"It's really very simple," confessed Jaxon with tears in his eyes. "I'm afraid of losing my wife. I don't want to lose her. I'll try anything to set things back the way they should be, to keep her here with me."

Gianna said nothing; she watched him for a while, until he looked up at her. "Sorry," she said, "It's not what I expected."

Jaxon sank deeper into his despair. "Yeah, I guess not. How could I be a man with regular feelings? I should have all the answers, is that it? Go ahead, say it. I've made a career out of telling people how to live and what is meaningful in life. There's no way anything should throw me off-balance."

"That's not what I meant."

"But it's what you're thinking," snapped Jaxon.

Gianna paced away from him and turned back. "It may surprise you to find that what I'm thinking is more about Suah than you. Olivia warned me; Suah would have a different kind of fan base."

"What do you mean?"

"Promising the public miracles is nothing like promising them a new song. I didn't want to see this coming. I didn't understand how it could pervade everything."

Jaxon stood and walked over to her. "This isn't about being Suah's fan."

"If not, it's still about what he can do for you."

"Why are you so cold about this?"

"Cold?" Gianna was amazed.

"I'm talking about losing the life of the one I love."

"I know that…"

"You don't have to believe it but I think Suah has a gift. I've seen him use it. Nobody else I know has things happen around him like that."

"Mr. Muse, please…"

"There's nothing wrong with having hope is there? That's all I'm asking for. It's not wrong to believe after you've seen all the signs!"

Gianna paced to the wet bar to vent nervous energy. "This is not what I thought you were coming here for."

Jaxon persisted. "If Suah could be with Claire for just a few minutes, that's all I'm asking for—who knows what might be possible?"

"First you wanted to talk with him. Now you want him to visit your wife."

"Is that so bad? It's such an easy thing to do. It doesn't hurt anybody to try. I don't understand your resistance. It's a simple thing to give a person hope. You have it in your power. It costs you nothing!"

"That's not true," countered Gianna. "The risk involved in something like that is open-ended. How do I know a video won't be leaked on the Internet the next day? What if the wrong reporter gets a hold of the story?"

Jaxon stepped closer to her. "How long will you deny what Suah can do? If he really has a gift, you're going to have to lock him away forever. There's no other way you can contain a story like this and I don't think even that will do it. The longer you deny it, the worse it's going to be for both of you."

"The whole thing is too easily manipulated."

"Yeah, so, it's just like everything else. You might as well come out and tell the truth; go ahead and admit it's a mystery to you. What others say after that is on their own heads. If anybody asks, you can tell them that everyone has a right to their own opinion. As far as you're concerned, you don't know; it's a mystery."

Gianna sat back on a bar stool. "I don't know. I'll have to think about it."

In her willingness to consider it, Jaxon found reason for optimism. "You can set the terms. I'll make whatever arrangements you want. I promise, no audio or video recording. I'll tell no one. All I want is to give my wife a chance she otherwise wouldn't have. It's so little but it means so much!"

Gianna thought back to what Olivia had warned her about on the plane. "And what if nothing happens? What if you don't get the miracle you're expecting? How will you treat Suah then?"

"Do you even have to ask? This isn't about sure things; it's about hope."

"And what happens when hopes are dashed?" asked Gianna.

"If hope was a guarantee, it would have another name."

"That sounds nice but it doesn't answer my question. You're talking about putting Suah in the position of being the last resort. The higher the expectations, the greater the fall. Believing in magic in shooting very high."

"All I'm asking for is a chance."

"But it's a chance without realistic odds. People are blind to realistic odds when they start believing in magic. To me, it sounds like a setup for a rude awakening. Why should I risk Suah as collateral damage?"

"All I can do is ask you to trust me—trust in the kind of person I am, the kind of life I've lived. Read my books, ask anyone who knows me. I'm not the kind of person who'd be vengeful or ungrateful. If nothing happens, it's no one's fault."

After a pause, Gianna relented. "I'll think about it. I'll call you with my answer."

"When?"

"I don't know. I can't promise a time. But it won't be long."

Jaxon searched her face for an early indication but found none. "All right. Thank you for considering it. I'll let myself out. Good evening."

As he walked from the room, Gianna called out to him. "Mr. Muse, have you ever heard the name Gris-Gris?"

Jaxon paused. "Gris-Gris?"

"You've done so much research into things over the years, I thought you might know."

"Ah, yeah, I've heard of Gris-Gris. I believe in parts of Africa, it's a generic name for any magical charm or amulet. Why do you ask?"

"Oh, nothing." Gianna avoided his eyes. "Just wondering."

Jaxon continued across the marble tiles and out the front door.

Gianna was left sitting with thoughts that fought rising emotions. It would be so easy and compassionate to let Jaxon have his way, to let Suah pay a visit to his wife. But Gianna knew what Olivia would say.

How could they be sure that this wasn't simply part two in an elaborate miracle hoax? What better way to pump up the publicity than to involve his stricken wife in the saga, if indeed she was really sick. Jaxon said they had kept her illness a secret and the doctors had little hope.

Who were these doctors? Could they be bought? Was Jaxon Muse that devious? Had he become so scheming that he'd even find a way to use his wife's final hours as a publicity stunt? Was that even possible?

Gianna slid off the bar stool and marched outside and around the wrap-around porch to the back yard in search of her phone. She found it right where she left it, next to her music player and earbuds. Olivia should be finished with Nathan Mackey by now. It would be good to get a report.

Gianna lifted her phone only to find she had voicemail from the hospital.

"…Ms. Chase, this is Andrea Bay, one of the managers here at the hospital. We met earlier today. Would you please give me a call at your earliest convenience. It's about Suah. Thank you."

Gianna quickly dialed *Memorial Medical Center*. "This is Gianna Chase, returning your call…"

"Oh, thank you for getting back to me so soon, Ms. Chase."

"You said it was about Suah. What's going on?"

Andrea Bay stammered, "Ah, to tell the truth, we're not sure. Suah is up and about. He walked up to the nurses' station and told the nurse on duty that he feels fine and wants to go home now."

"I don't understand. Nurse Treggor said he wouldn't be released for a couple of days. He had to be monitored for his back and his ribs."

"Yes, that's right, but he appears to be all right now."

"All right? What do you mean?"

"I know it's confusing; we're trying to sort it out…"

"Sort what out? What about his injuries?" asked Gianna.

"His back is tender but for all intents and purposes, it's healed."

"What about the fractured ribs? Are you telling me those are OK too?"

"Apparently…"

"How could you make a mistake like this? Don't you have X-ray machines?"

"Of course we do, Ms. Chase…"

"Have you checked him tonight?"

"Yes…"

"What did you find?"

"We took new X-rays a half an hour ago. His ribs are fine. I don't know how we could have misdiagnosed this. I don't think we did. We have his X-rays from last night; the fractures are clearly visible."

"It's obvious you've gotten his files mixed up with someone else's."

"There's no one else in the hospital right now being treated for broken ribs. I don't see how that could have happened. It's not possible."

Gianna gazed out at the infinity pool and the dark ocean beyond. Stepping out on the deck, she looked up at the stars. In the pocket of her dress, her hand clutched the charcoal pencil drawing. "I guess anything is possible, Ms. Bay. If nothing else, we all should know that by now."

CHAPTER 37

"All right, David. Let's go." Jaxon Muse settled back in the rear seat of the town car but was unable to pull his gaze from Gianna's front door.

"I thought you were going to be longer," commented David, the driver.

"So did I," answered Jaxon, unwilling to say more.

David read his reticence and started the car. Slow and easy, they drove down the hill from Gianna's estate and waited for security to let them out on the street. Photoflashes popped from behind the wrought-iron gate.

David gaped left and right. "Geez, look at this. They're all over the place." He shot a glance back at Jaxon. "You said there'd be more when we came out but did you expect all this?"

Jaxon was at a loss to explain it. "I don't know. I guess the Nathan Mackey thing on TV was a bigger hit than anyone expected."

"They know about that already?"

"Sure they do."

The gate opened and David eased the car out through the mob of cameras and people crowding the car.

A man yelled at the car's side window. "...Are you going to have a statement for the media, Mr. Muse?"

A woman on the other side of the car shouted next. "...Did you know this would happen? Is that why you came over here tonight?"

David steered a path through it all. "What is she talking about?"

"Beats me."

Another voice was heard. "...Mr. Muse, have you spoken with Jackie Kemper since she was let go?"

Jaxon turned on hearing the name and had a photoflash burst in his face.

"Who's Jackie Kemper," asked the driver.

"She's a nurse," answered Jaxon. "I paid her a reward for telling me where I could find Suah Chase."

"They say she was let go. Do they mean she got fired?"

"Maybe..."

David punched up headlines on the dashboard display. He tried reading while navigating the car forward in a crawl. "Yeah, here it is. ER nurse Jackie Kemper fired from *Memorial Medical Center* for gross negligence. They say she disobeyed hospital policy on patient confidentiality."

"Watch out!" shouted Jaxon.

David startled alert just in time to avoid running into a pair of photo-graphers running in front of the car.

"Forget the damn news, just get us out of here," ordered Jaxon.

"Yes, sir." David took the wheel with both hands and drove an aggressive zigzag up the street. Along the way, the mob thinned until David could punch up some speed.

David checked the rear-view mirror. Headlights behind them turned when they did. "We've got three or four tails on us. Where you want to go?"

"Take me home. If they want to wait at that gate, let them."

They rode the rest of the way in an uneasy silence. David was curious but knew his place and didn't want to risk censure by intruding. Jaxon was full of things to say but most of them were things he needed to tell himself.

By the time the town car pulled up and parked at the entrance portico, Jaxon wanted nothing more than to see Claire and leave the rest of the world outside. As soon as he opened the front door and heard the TV news on, he knew it wasn't meant to be—the world always had a way in.

Jaxon found Claire on a couch in the living room. Her eyes were glazed and unblinking as she watched a news report. He looked at the TV and then at her. "Did you watch Mackey tonight?" he asked.

She nodded. "Did you pay a reward to find Suah Chase?"

Jaxon sighed. In the flow of things, he had neglected to tell her about everything. He knew better than to let her find out about things like this in the press. "I know, I should have told you. It happened so fast…"

"The woman was fired from her job."

"I know. I heard."

"What were you thinking?" Claire looked disappointed in him.

"It was a quick thing, something Perry suggested…"

"Perry! Since when do you take orders from Perry?"

"Suah was missing. I didn't know what else to do."

"Why was it up to you? He's not your child. The police were looking for him. Everything was being done. Why did you have to go and do a stupid thing like that? You know how that looks?"

After the emotionally draining session with Gianna, Jaxon was at his wit's end. "Does it matter? Really?" He flung a hand towards the TV. "No matter what we do, that thing will make of it whatever they want."

"So you just give up and start acting like them, huh?"

"I don't see the big sin in offering a reward. People do it every day. They even do it to find their pets!"

"He didn't need to be found. He was already at the hospital."

"I didn't know that."

"It's not just about the reward. It's why you did it. You had to get down there before anybody else, wasn't that it?"

"So?"

"It looks suspicious. With all the conspiracy stories flying around, why do something that just feeds into it? Sneaking around, paying rewards, trying to get in to see Suah before anybody else; how does that look?"

"I wasn't sneaking around. I put a post on my public blog. If paying a reward got me to Suah faster, if it saved him any pain or helped him in any way, I thought it was worth it."

Claire held a hand to her forehead. "This is all so unnecessary."

Jaxon stepped closer to the TV. "What about the nurse, Jackie Kemper? She could have avoided all of this. She didn't have to send the information about Suah using her work's email address. She knew hospital policy. Why didn't she get a family member or friend to contact me? If you ask me, it sounds like she *wants* the attention."

Claire settled back. "Well, she's sure getting it tonight. She called a news conference a little while ago."

"A news conference! For what?"

"Haven't you heard?"

"I heard she was fired."

"That's just the half of it. Now that she doesn't have to worry about losing her job, she's decided to go public with all she knows."

"About what?"

"About all the hospital is trying to hide. Especially about what happened tonight while you were over at Gianna's place."

"Something with Suah?" asked Jaxon.

"Suah's been healed."

"Healed?" Jaxon froze.

"There's nothing wrong with him. He wants to go home. His fractured ribs aren't fractured anymore. His back has healed up—just like that."

Jaxon sat down. "You're kidding…"

"The hospital can't explain it. The nurse says they're scrambling around trying to come up with some story that fits. They don't want to admit they screwed up on such a simple diagnosis…"

Jaxon finished her thought, "…but they also don't want to go on record saying it's an unexplainable but genuine healing."

"That's about it," confirmed Claire.

"How did they find out?"

"Nurse Jackie said that after Gianna visited Suah today, Suah started acting strange. Next thing they knew, he was walking the halls, talking to the nurses at the nurses' station, telling them he was fine and wanted to go home. He told them his mom was home and he wanted to go home too. Jackie said they took X-rays and confirmed it. They can't figure it out."

"I'll be damned..." Jaxon's frustration melted away.

Claire muted the TV so their lower tones could be heard. "If this nurse wanted attention, she picked the right night to go public. News of this came on right after Nathan Mackey's program finished up."

"What was your impression of him?"

"I thought the program was fairly balanced, considering how sensational one can make the topic. Honestly, I don't see how anyone can watch that program and not think there's some mystery about what's going on."

Claire was distracted by the images on the TV. She unmuted the set. "There she is..."

Jaxon turned to find live video from an airport concourse. Jackie Kemper was rushing along towards a departure gate with several reporters and camera crews clustered around her. She was answering one of their questions.

"...I'm going to stay with my sister for a while. I'm not sure about future plans." Jumpy with excitement, she kept her eyes on the path in front of her.

A reporter shoved his mike over others vying for space. "What do you *really* think happened in that hospital?"

Jackie kept stride but flashed him a glance. "There are only two choices: either the hospital is woefully incompetent or a real miracle happened there tonight. I've worked with those people for several years now. I know for a fact; they're not incompetent. That's all I have to say."

Arriving at her gate, Jackie presented her boarding pass while airport guards kept the press at bay. Claire muted the set again.

"She said a lot more at the news conference."

"She said enough," commented Jaxon.

"How did the meeting go with Gianna? Did things get straightened out?"

"I don't know..." Jaxon watched as the TV showed a replay from Nurse Jackie's earlier news conference. "...we'll have to wait and see."

"Are you hungry?" asked Claire.

"No, I'm fine. Where's Hailey?"

"In her room."

"Is she OK?" asked Jaxon.

"Yeah." Claire tempered her concern knowing all had ended well.

"Did she ever tell you what happened with her clothes?"

"She says she swapped them for another girl's clothes at the ashram."

"There's an ashram in Puka Paia? Aren't ashrams secluded."

"It's secluded enough. I know the place."

"So what happened?"

"She says she went skinny-dipping with some others in one of the natural pools they have there. When she and this other girl got out, they decided to swap clothes. She said it was their way of expressing the unimportance of material things."

"Since when has Hailey ever been into that?"

Claire shrugged.

"And she wants us to believe that's all there was to it?"

"That's all she said."

Jaxon stood and started to leave the room. Claire didn't want the evening to end with a blowup between father and daughter. Claire also needed an answer from Jaxon about something far more important.

"Vincent called while you were gone."

Jaxon stopped in his tracks. "What for? I talked with him earlier today."

"I know, he told me. But he said he wanted to talk to me, see how I was doing. He is my doctor, you know."

"So what did he say?" Jaxon couldn't hide his upset.

Claire was direct. "He said you picked up the prescription days ago."

"That's right," confessed Jaxon.

"He wanted to know if it was my decision not to take the pills."

Jaxon said nothing.

Claire couldn't mask her hurt. "Why didn't you tell me?"

"We went over this…"

"And nothing was decided—unless you decided for yourself."

Jaxon stepped back and sat down next to her. "You know I'm worried about the side effects."

"So am I but what can we do?"

He took her hands in his. "We can hold out until it becomes absolutely necessary."

"Vincent believes that time is now. Do you know something different?"

"No, but…" Jaxon fought to find the words.

"He went to a lot of trouble to get the advanced protocol for us. It'll only be worthwhile if we use it as planned."

"So what are you saying?" asked Jaxon.

"I'm saying I need my pills. I want to take the chance."

Jaxon lowered his head. "You don't understand…"

"What don't I understand?"

"They call it advanced with good reason."

"I know that."

"I don't think you do." Jaxon fought to hold onto his composure.

"Why? What else should I know?"

Jaxon looked up into her eyes. He knew then it was wrong to keep the truth from her. If she was to make the decision with him, she had to know what he knew.

"These pills…" he began. "They're something new. They're…a last resort. Once you start taking them, there's no telling the effect they might have. You might be out of it, unable to relate to the world around you."

"But they'll be working on the sickness, won't they?" asked Claire.

"Yes, yes, of course, but if it doesn't work…our last days together will be lost; you won't even know I'm around. You might not recognize Hailey."

Claire took the news in silence. She was strong in spirit but the intensity of what Jaxon was describing took its toll. She never knew the advance protocol might be such a debilitating and final attempt at a solution. Either way, what choice did she have?

"You said this is something new, a trial. They aren't sure either way what might happen, are they?"

"No," admitted Jaxon. "But it's what they expect."

"So let's not worry about what we don't know. Let's have faith in what we do know. From what you've said, these pills are my last chance. There's no way I want to miss my last chance—to stay here with you and Hailey."

Jaxon looked down and squeezed her hands.

Claire's voice was soft and reassuring. "It's all right. We've done everything we can. Let's not stop now. Let me have my pills."

Jaxon wiped tears from his cheek and nodded agreement. "All right."

He looked up. On the TV, another replay of Jackie Kemper's news conference played without sound. At the bottom of the muted screen, a news crawl rolled letters across Jaxon's field of vision.

"…*Gavin Brice, boat assistant with Island Aquatics & Adventures, confirms story of woman who claims her drowned son was saved by Suah Chase*…"

Jaxon hesitated. He turned back to Claire. "Why don't we start the pills in the morning. Let's have tonight together without any of that."

Claire knew she had to be firm. "No, we've waited long enough. You've had the pills for days. I should have been taking them already."

Jaxon nodded and stood. After making his case with Gianna to see Suah, the idea that the evening should end this way was unthinkable. And yet, what was the chance Gianna would change her mind? She was far more practical than he; always had been. She saw what was going on as a mystery with a rational explanation yet to be found; he believed it was Suah's gift in action.

Heading upstairs, Jaxon fought contrary impulses. If the experimental medicine was ever going to have a chance to work, Claire needed to start taking it right away. Then again, a meeting with Suah might only be a phone call away. That call could come at any time.

Gianna hadn't say when she would call, which only made matters worse. How long could he wait for something so good if in reality it never came? He felt helpless. There was nothing in any of his philosophy to tell him the easy answer. It didn't even have to be the easy answer. He'd accept tackling the hard road if only he could be certain it was the right thing to do.

He walked into his upstairs office and unlocked a side drawer in his desk. Reaching in, he found the small package that contained the individually wrapped prescription pills. He opened the lid and looked at them. They were small and round and white, innocuous to behold as an aspirin would be. It was hard to believe that packed within each 500mg dose might be the power to save or take away a life.

Jaxon placed the package on his desk and sat there a long while. There was nothing to look at out the window but the blackness of ocean and sky stretching over an invisible horizon. He couldn't really see either one of them, but he knew they were there. He tossed it over in his mind. The unseen and the knowable; was it a paradox to place so much trust on a core belief in strongly felt but unseen improbabilities? Was it faith or folly? How could the truth of the situation seem so very near and yet the answer be so far off?

He took out his phone and checked it. No calls. Not yet. But that didn't mean he wouldn't get one. How would it feel if he gave Claire the pill and *then* got permission from Gianna to see Suah?

He closed the package up and locked it back in the drawer. Stepping into the bathroom, he opened a bottle and shook one pill into his hand.

Some said faith was foolish. But this wasn't about faith. It was about hope. For the time being, the advanced protocol would have to be aspirin.

CHAPTER 38

Gianna sat slumped on a couch in the entertainment room. Her full attention was on a replay of Nathan Mackey's investigative report.

The maid entered the room. "Ms. Chase, you have an incoming video call on the house line."

"Who is it?" asked Gianna.

"Your tour assistant, Ava."

"Very well. You can route it in here."

Gianna paused the TV and activated the picture-in-picture display. Within an inset screen, Ava's face appeared.

"Ava, what's going on?"

Ava was rushed but apologetic. "Sorry, Gianna, I usually would never bother you at home…"

"It's all right."

"I just wanted to be sure you were OK with the arrangements for coming back on tour."

"Why shouldn't I be?"

"Have you seen them?" asked Ava.

"I know in general what I asked for. I haven't had time to check every detail. What's your concern?"

"I've never seen things locked down like this before."

"We have to take into consideration everything that's going on."

"But most of your personal appearances have been cancelled. Except for concerts, the rest of your itinerary has been wiped clean."

"Everything?" Gianna was surprised.

"Just about. And another thing, except for travel days, these arrangements have you and Suah hardly ever together. I know the new au pair is going to be in place but that's never been a replacement for the two of you spending time together. I wasn't sure how you were going to like that."

"Send me a copy of what you have," ordered Gianna.

Ava explained. "I realize things are different with all the media attention Suah is getting but some of this seems excessive. I know you don't like distractions once you get onsite so I thought it best to double-check now."

"You were right to do so. When you send that over, include the names of anyone who was part of the planning process."

"There's only one name. It was drawn up by Olivia."

"Everything?"

"Yes. I checked around. That's what everyone says."

"All right, send it over. I'll have a look."

"Right away," answered Ava. "Have a good night."

"You too." The call ended and the picture-in-picture box disappeared, leaving only the frozen report by Nathan Mackey on the screen.

Gianna reached for her cell phone and pressed a speed-dial number. The phone rang a few times before being answered.

"Olivia?" asked Gianna. "Where are you?"

"I'm trying to get up the hill. Have you seen your street?"

Gianna stood and paced. "Only on TV."

"They're doing live-remotes from down here. It looks like we've entered the perfect storm."

"What do you expect? Mackey is on TV, Jaxon Muse was over here in his town car, and the hospital can't figure out why Suah is suddenly all right to come home."

"I heard about that," Olivia confirmed. "Nurse Jackie sure picked the perfect time to go public and make a spectacle of herself…"

While Olivia talked, Gianna stepped over to her computer and retrieved the incoming email attachment from Ava.

Stuck in traffic, Olivia droned on. "…just when you think it couldn't get any weirder, it does. I thought my meeting with Mackey was enough strangeness for one night…"

Gianna opened Ava's attachment and started scanning the proposed tour itineraries. As she scrolled through the itemized flowchart, she kept the side conversation with Olivia going.

"So I take it you wouldn't recommend me working with him…"

"How did you know? You must have seen his show."

"Actually, I did. I found it interesting."

Olivia chuckled. "Oh, he *is* interesting, I'll give him that. He's interesting like a Black Mamba or a tarantula. He and Wyatt Dumashe are up to something. I don't know what it is but I don't trust it."

Gianna had seen all she needed to see. The itinerary was as Ava described. Olivia had taken Gianna's concerns for security on tour and turned them into an excuse to isolate her and Suah from the world and each other. It was such an overreaction, it was hard for Gianna to fathom whatever was in her mind to do such a thing. But this wasn't the time to ask her directly.

"Don't worry about Mackey," added Gianna. "I have no intention of having anything to do with him."

Olivia was surprised. "You changed your mind?"

"I'm letting it go," announced Gianna. "Reporters and detectives will find what they want to find. They're better at it; let them do it. I'm going to concentrate on my own priorities."

The news buoyed Olivia's spirits. "Then we can get back on tour."

Gianna closed the email attachment and strolled away from the computer.

"I'm going to get back to being a mother to Suah—and yes, I'm going to be singing."

Olivia reminded her, "We need to leave tomorrow morning to make the next tour date."

"I know that."

"But when is Suah coming home?"

"Tonight. I got a call from Detective Gaines. Because of all the media circus going on outside, the police suggested I stay home and they would bring Suah to me. I'm waiting for him now."

"He's on the way?" Olivia was stunned.

"As we speak," smiled Gianna. "As a matter of fact, it would be better if you didn't come up to the house tonight. I'd like tonight just to be about Suah and me. You understand…"

Olivia pulled the car to the curb and let it idle. Outside, all around, people milled or ran with equipment. Flashes from cameras hit her in the face.

"Of course. But what about the tour? We're not ready for Suah on the tour. The new nanny doesn't start for two days. We tried to get her earlier, you know that."

Gianna made her way through the living room and out onto the open-air terrace. "I know that. It's a problem. I haven't figured it out yet."

Olivia thought out loud. "We expected Suah to be released from the hospital in two days. Everything was planned around that."

"We'll have to find a way to take him tomorrow."

Olivia was stressed. "I don't see how that's possible. The security isn't in place. Who will take care of him? After tonight, can you imagine what kind of frenzy will be after him?"

Gianna paced to the end of the terrace and looked down on the lights of the town. "Well, we have to do something because he's definitely coming home tonight. In the morning, I'm not leaving him alone again and that's final! Call me with a plan. I have to go." Gianna hung up.

She hated being so abrupt with Olivia but she had to. A moment longer and she might have said something she would have regretted. She had known Olivia for so many years, it wouldn't be right to react to the tour itinerary too harshly until they had a chance to talk it over.

Problem was, it should have been talked over before now. The night before leaving was not the time to have these discussions. Olivia obviously didn't want a discussion. She wanted it her way.

But why? It was almost as if Olivia didn't want her plan questioned. For some reason, it was too important to risk having it changed. But why would she be so overprotective?

Overprotective. The idea of it flooded Gianna with her own excuses for the way she mothered Suah. She thought back to her stroll through Suah's bedroom; the kaleidoscope toy, the dresser with nothing out of place, the closet with clothes neatly folded.

Gianna walked back into the house and climbed the stairs.

Maybe Olivia was only trying to do for them what Gianna had tried to do for Suah. If so, then Gianna for the first time in her life suddenly could feel the suffocating presence that could only see itself as loving care.

What was Gianna protecting Suah from all these years? Being harmed by the world? Or was she simply protecting herself from losing him? For if he changed, if the world had a chance to interact with him too much, he wouldn't be the same boy and she'd lose the one person she could call family; someone personal just for her.

If Gianna hadn't seen the overprotectiveness in herself, she wouldn't have recognized it in Olivia—not in a way that let her hold back the instinct to lash out. Gianna was never about accumulating regrets. Why start now?

Stepping into Suah's room, Gianna stopped at his desk for a piece of tape before heading into his closet. There she opened the wardrobe door and pulled the charcoal drawing from her pocket.

Looking down on it, she wondered who had drawn it. Suah certainly hadn't done it. The lines were too fine and sophisticated to be the work of a child. Maybe a savant child could do it, but only if the child's extraordinary ability rested in art. Gianna had seen Suah's drawings and this was nothing like them. His crude lettering of the names *Suah* and *Hawa* above the drawing drew enough contrast to give it away that someone else's hand had made the image come to life. Who that was, for now, would be a mystery.

There was so much mystery to the day.

Gianna taped the picture in place, right where Suah had placed it. She wanted him to find it there when he got home. She was protective that way.

CHAPTER **39**

The automatic glass doors slid open and a frazzled Naomi Treggor rushed into the hospital lobby. Manager Andrea Bay was there to meet her.

"I warned you it wouldn't be easy," scoffed Andrea.

Naomi heaved a sigh of relief and turned around to look outside. Past the uniformed police guarding the doors, a mosaic of faces and lights and recording equipment was in constant flux. The TV lights in particular were especially bright. Naomi averted her eyes.

"It feels like I fought my way into a fishbowl," she quipped.

"It's at its worst now but maybe it's for the best."

"Why is that?" asked Naomi.

"If it all works out, we'll be done with this tonight instead of having to wait two more days."

"The questions aren't going to end tonight."

Andrea tilted her head towards the outside crowd. "No, but all of this will. They'll all move on someplace else and that's fine with me."

"Is Suah ready to go?" asked Naomi.

Andrea led them to the elevator. "He's *been* ready; it's all he talks about. He wants to get home and find out how to continue his adventure."

"His adventure?" The doors closed and the elevator started up.

"Yes. Did he ever talk to you about that?"

"I don't know, maybe. He talked about exploring."

"Most of the time he doesn't talk at all. Other times, he comes out with the strangest things."

Naomi turned to Andrea. "Thank you for letting me say goodbye to him."

Andrea noted her sincerity but was too jaded to feel it herself. "You were his primary nurse. I understand." She shook her head. "It's about all I *do* understand."

"Have any idea how it happened?" From the context of the situation, Naomi needn't say more.

"I have no explanation for it," admitted Andrea. "There have been documented cases of spontaneous remission…"

Naomi interrupted, "But those were things like T-cell leukemia or lung and liver cancers, not broken bones and torn flesh."

"Cancers are far more serious…" noted Andrea.

"I changed his bandages. I saw the way the boy came in here. When has an open skin wound ever healed at this rate before, especially gashes like that? You still have the X-rays; I know they show a clean break. Any orthopedic surgeon would tell you the same thing."

Andrea closed her eyes a moment and let the wave of Naomi's enthusiasm pass her by. "You're telling me what I already know. Repeating it isn't explaining it."

"First we have to recognize it deserves our attention."

"If you're asking me, I don't think it can be explained, the same way those cases of cancer remission can't be explained. To tell you the truth, I'm not concerned about explaining it. I simply want to get this hospital back to normal operations."

"Does that include locking away all record of this so it can't be studied?"

The elevator doors opened but Andrea didn't move. "One nurse this evening already lost her job over a matter of patient confidentiality. I'd hate to lose any more valuable people."

"Are you ordering me not to talk about what I saw?" fumed Naomi.

"*Memorial Medical* has a reputation as a state-of-the-art health care facility. It is not *The Protoprime Society* nor do we want our health care providers running around, concerned more about miracles than medicine."

Naomi wouldn't let it go. "Since when did open-minded scientific inquiry become something in conflict with the medical profession?"

Andrea kept her voice low, her emotions in check. "It says *Medical Center* on the sign outside, not *Research Center*. If you want to do pure research into energy fields, astral projection, or faith healing, more power to you. You're free to go and do that; but not here."

Andrea marched out of the elevator and left Naomi standing. The elevator buzzed, having been forced open for so long. Naomi stepped out into the fourth floor hallway. The doors closed behind her. She didn't see them close but she knew they were the perfect visual metaphor for what was happening.

The hospital was a business with a reputation to preserve. There was no way hospital administrators would do anything that might be perceived as endorsing a miracle, even if they held the evidence in their hands. Science had become a business and profits would always trump progress.

Andrea had walked one way. Naomi walked the other way, towards the nurses' station but she found no one there. At the end of the hallway, a cluster of uniformed nurses and patients in hospital gowns jabbered back and forth.

Naomi approached one of the nurses. "What's going on?"

The nurse was flustered. "Oh, Naomi, I'm glad you're here. Maybe you can help get these people back in their rooms."

"Why are they out here?"

The nurse leaned closer to whisper. "They heard on the TV about Suah. They know he's about to leave. They claim they want to say goodbye but that's not it."

Naomi overheard side conversations. "They want to be healed…"

"You've got it. The poor kid got swamped."

"Weren't you guys watching?"

"It happened so fast. What are you going to do if they won't go back to their rooms? Call the guards?"

"Well, this is ridiculous…" Naomi waded into the group. "Excuse me, coming through, watch out…" She muscled her way to the doorway of Suah's room for a look inside. Two nurses were inside, trying to persuade a lanky man with his bare butt showing through the hospital gown to leave the room. Behind them, on the bed, Suah sat wide-eyed and dressed, ready to go.

Naomi pushed her way through. She spun around and closed the door to Suah's room, shutting everyone in the hallway out and the lanky man and three nurses in.

"Excuse me," Naomi raised her voice. "Mr. Tanner, is this your room?"

The lanky man jerked around to see one more nurse. "Another one…"

One of the nurses stood between the man and Suah. "He says he won't leave until he gets a chance to talk to Suah."

"Is that so," snapped Naomi. "Well, the hypodermic needle in my pocket says something else." She stared the man down. "You want me to put you asleep for forty-eight hours? Isn't your son supposed to be coming tomorrow to visit you? I'll tell you all about it after you wake up two days from now."

The man's face dropped into a frown. "You wouldn't do that."

"If you don't get out of this room right now, I will. Don't test me."

The man wavered as he held out a hand towards Suah. "I just want to talk with him a minute…"

Naomi was firm. "If I let you do that, everybody else in this hospital will want their minute. That's a hell of a lot of time that we don't have. Now, back to your room."

The other nurses pushed him. "Come on, let's go."

Naomi opened the door and the three of them exited. Naomi quickly shut the door, leaving her alone with Suah. She turned her back to the door and leaned against it. She looked at Suah's surprised face and smiled.

"You sure know how to get into adventures."

Mention of adventures brought a mischievous smile to Suah's face. He relaxed a bit on the bed. "I didn't know hospitals were this exciting."

Naomi rolled her eyes. "Only when you're in them." She pushed off from the door and stepped closer to him. "You're an exciting kind of guy."

His smile waffled into a sly grin. "I'm glad you came to see me."

"Me too. It's an exciting night. You get to go home and see your mom."

"She's supposed to be in Madrid," Suah announced.

"Well, I'm sure she'd rather be here with you. That's why she's here."

Naomi noticed the comfortable way Suah moved and breathed. The bandages were gone and he was wearing brand new clothes. She remembered that terrible night when in the ER she had to cut his old ones off him while he lay bleeding on the gurney.

"Where did you get the clothes?"

"I don't know," answered Suah. "But I like 'em."

"You're a spiffy dude," smiled Naomi. She stepped closer. "Do you mind if I see your back?"

He shook his head and raised his T-shirt. Naomi bent close and couldn't believe her eyes. The scrapes and gashes were gone. In their place was a mottled surface where pristine skin showed a pinkish-brown glow and gave off the warmth of a healthy circulation.

Tenderly, she moved her hand around to his side to feel his ribs. "Does this feel OK?" Suah nodded and she looked him in the eye. "You know it's very special to heal like this."

He looked doe-eyed. "People are supposed to heal in hospitals."

Naomi pulled his shirt back down. "But usually not this quickly."

He smiled. "The tortoise and the hare both got to the finish line."

Naomi couldn't help but notice his mouth. She hadn't noticed it before but his mouth was the one thing that hadn't healed; he still was missing two teeth. She couldn't pass up the chance to ask about the incongruity.

She pointed at her own teeth. "What about your teeth? They didn't heal."

"They're gone," noted Suah.

"You couldn't make them come back?"

Suah thought about it, looked up and all around as if looking for a place to hide the truth. Finally, he confessed, "Hawa thinks I look funny. She likes to laugh."

Just then, the door opened and another nurse stuck her head in. "Naomi, we just got word they're coming up for him. It's time to go."

Naomi nodded. The nurse left the door open and other nurses and a doctor from the ER gathered round. Naomi took Suah by the hand to help him hop off the bed.

"You come visit me sometime, OK?"

Suah nodded as she led him to the door. "If I come, can I have some more butterscotch pudding?"

Naomi smiled, "If the cafeteria doesn't have it, I'll make some myself."

"You know how to make that?" Suah was surprised.

"Sure, anything is possible if you put your mind to it, isn't that right?"

Suah looked up to her. "You sound like Jaxon Muse. Do you write _Helf Selp_ books too?"

"What kind of books?"

Another nurse murmured to Naomi, "I think he means _Self Help_."

Down the hall, the elevator doors opened. Andrea Bay was there to escort Detective Mason Gaines to the room. The other nurses and doctor stepped aside as the detective made strides closer to the group.

"There he is," called out Mason. He spoke to Suah, "Are you all set? Wanna go home?" Suah nodded. "Well, say goodbye and we'll be off."

Suah turned to Naomi but glanced at the others. "Thanks for helping me."

Naomi gave him a hug. "You take care. We'll all miss you."

Others in the group said goodbye and hugged him.

Mason Gaines gave them a minute then stepped in. "You ready to ride in a police car?"

That got Suah's attention. "A real one?"

"Of course a real one. If you want, I'll even let you turn on the siren."

Suah giggled, "Oh, wow."

Mason waved at all. "Goodbye everybody. Thanks again."

Suah was led into the elevator and down to the basement floor. When the elevator doors opened again, Mason Gaines led the way across the loading dock to a rear entrance where the hospital received supplies.

"This doesn't look like a hospital," commented Suah.

Mason grinned. "Not everything is as it seems. You'll learn that if you become a detective."

Suah stepped up to the police car. "Where do I sit?"

Mason opened the front passenger door. "Up front with me."

"Oh good," sighed Suah. "The bad guys always sit in back."

"Very good," noted Mason. "You watch TV very well."

They got in the car and closed the doors. Suah belted in then sat nervously looking over everything inside. The center console was a nest of radios, dispatch displays, GPS equipment and a video camera pointed out the front window. Off to one side was a shotgun pointed at the roof. Mason leaned closer to Suah before starting the car.

"Have you ever been on Mr. Toad's Wild Ride at Disneyland?"

Suah nodded.

"Well, this may be like that so you hold on, OK?"

Another nod.

"You're going to see a lot of lights and people rushing around. Don't pay any attention to them. I gotcha. Everything is going to be OK. Before you know it, you'll be safe at home with your mom. Are you with me?"

A final nod. Suah watched as a hospital employee raised the big roll-up door to the outside. Mason started the car and revved its engine into a growl. Up the ramp they rolled. Once outside, they were flanked by two other escort police cars with lights flashing. The escort cars and uniform police on foot cleared a trail through people and cameras and into the street.

Once they hit the street, all three police cars accelerated. Mason was on the radio with the escort cars, coordinating their run through surface streets down to the main highway. Suah couldn't help but look around. There were so many lights and people going every which way, it looked like a carnival had come to town.

Mason pointed, "See that button on that box right there. Push it once."

Suah obeyed and got rewarded with a blast of siren. His face erupted with a smile. Mason saw the smile and the gaps where two teeth used to be. Suah wasn't self-conscious about it in the least. The joy and purity of that made Mason smile back. "Go ahead, push it again."

Delighted, Suah leaned forward and reached for the button. The blast of siren split the air around the car again.

Mason gripped the wheel. "Now that's how you let them know you're coming." Once they reached the main highway, Mason relaxed a bit. "It's smooth sailing from here. Before you know it, you'll be home."

With one police escort in front of them and another behind, they cruised down the highway with the darkness of night all around. For Mason Gaines, it was the first chance he had to talk with Suah alone. He had planned it that way but he'd only have a few minutes. That's all he needed.

"Do you know what a miracle is?" Mason's question was direct and went to the heart of the matter. How Suah answered something coming at him out of the blue could be telling.

Suah looked over at Mason and answered without a pause. "My grandfather says life is a miracle."

"Are you sure?" asked Mason. "Because if that's true, then everything we do is a miracle. That can't be right."

Suah looked confused. "Why not?"

Mason chuckled. "Well, if everything is a miracle, then what do you call it when something extra special happens, something that's so exciting that you can't explain it?"

"I don't have to explain it."

"Why not? Aren't you curious why special things happen?"

Suah thought a moment. "I saw a double rainbow once. That was special. I can't explain it but it's still exciting."

Mason decided to draw the conversation more direct. "You were there with Jaxon Muse when the woman fell on the floor. She was very sick. Did you do something special to make her all better?"

"No...nothing special," answered Suah.

"Did Jaxon Muse tell you to go over to that woman and say things over her to pretend to help her?"

Again, Suah answered, "No."

"So how did that woman get better? People call that a miracle."

Suah gave his head a shake. "It was just the way it should have been."

"But things are not always the way they should be. If they were, we'd have a perfect world."

"That's right." Suah gazed out the side window. "*Half of I-and-I is near. Half is far. It takes fingers and heart to touch them both.*"

"What does that mean?" asked Mason.

Suah looked up at him in surprise. "You don't know?"

"Who told you that?"

"Hawa."

"Who's Hawa."

"She's part of me. She's always been there." Suah tapped his chest. "My grandfather told me she's as close as right here..." He looked through the window and up at the sky, "...but I always find her far away, playing and dancing with my stars."

"Your stars?" Mason wrinkled his brow in confusion.

Suah's thoughts were elsewhere. "I like looking at them before I go to sleep. Sometimes I dream about them. Hannah says that I shouldn't day-dream so much. But why not if you can the stars during the day."

They turned up the street leading to Gianna's estate. It didn't matter; Mason had heard enough. He couldn't see how anyone could use Suah Chase in any elaborate hoax. How could they ever rely on him to follow a script when the boy obviously had a tenuous grip on reality?

It was highly unlikely that Jaxon Muse or anyone else would have been able to rehearse Suah to perform miracle tricks. Whatever had happened was simply a mystery. More importantly for Mason, it now appeared well beyond the purview of police powers to sort it out.

The three police cars had no trouble navigating through the throng of people lining the street, waiting to get a glimpse of the celebrity boy. Security at Gianna's estate let the first escort car through and the other two police cars followed the lead car up the hill. One by one, they slowed into the curve of the circle driveway and parked.

Seeing home at last was the ultimate excitement for Suah. He remembered his long walk back from *The Manuia Resort* into town. He had been so thirsty and hungry that night. He remembered how marooned he felt, walking along alone. He couldn't imagine then how he'd ever get home.

And now here he was, arriving home in a police car of all things. His imagination wouldn't have ever dreamt such a thing. But it couldn't be denied. It came to be just as sure as if it were always meant to be. It only confirmed what someone had whispered in his ear so long ago.

What is possible is not only greater than what we imagine;
It's greater than anything we can imagine.

Suah jumped out of the car and ran to the front door. It opened before he got there and Gianna came running out with arms open wide and a smile that cried tears to joy.

"Mom!" he shouted.

She knelt down and hugged him. "Oh, Suah…"

Mason Gaines exited the car and waved the other two cars off. They started up and slowly made their way back down the hill.

Mason stepped closer. "You have quite a boy."

Standing up, Gianna hugged Suah to her side. "Thank you for bringing him home."

"He sure was excited to get here."

Suah hugged his mom but turned his face to Mason. "Thanks for letting me push the button."

Gianna looked to Mason. "What is he talking about?"

Mason grinned then struck a pose. "Oh, it's a secret between Suah and me. You know, detective stuff."

Gianna felt all the emotions of the day flow through her. She wanted the day to end the best way possible in every way. That included whatever unfinished business she had with the police.

"Whatever else you need from me, just let me know."

"Don't worry about that. You two just enjoy being back together."

"I'm scheduled to leave tomorrow; starting back on my concert tour. I hope that isn't going to be a problem. You weren't planning on confining me to the island or anything, were you?"

Mason waved it off. "No, no, nothing like that. You go ahead, do what you need to do."

"I should let you know; I talked with Jaxon Muse tonight. He was here."

Mason nodded. "I know…"

"You do?"

Mason smiled. "Of course I do—the whole world knows. I don't need detectives to find out what you're doing; I just turn on the TV."

Gianna smiled but the smile faded quickly. "You're all right with that—I mean, meeting with Jaxon Muse? We just needed to sort things out."

"Fine with me. After today, I'm not looking into you or Jaxon or any of that anymore. I'm done with it."

"What about your investigation?"

"I think I wrapped that up the other day when I interviewed Paige Atwater and Diego and Blake Fry. Anything else is a sideshow passing as an alibi."

Gianna had to ask. "You don't care if the sideshow was rigged?"

"I'm a police investigator, not a psychic investigator."

Gianna relaxed. "Thank you."

Mason gave a nod then took a step back. He pointed at Suah. "You have fun now, but watch out on those adventures."

Gianna and Suah stood and watched Mason get in his car and drive away.

Gianna turned them back towards the open front door. "Come on, let's go inside." She stopped him in the entrance hallway. "Let me look at you."

She stared into his eyes and he gazed back, then broke into a grin.

Tears welled up in her eyes as she smiled. "We certainly have some *nutzo-crazy* adventures, don't we?"

He smiled and let the gap in his teeth show. "The best!"

She held him by the shoulders. "What would you like to do?"

He thought a second then got excited. "We can do anything?"

She knew it was going out on a limb, but what the heck. "Anything."

"Could we make butterscotch pudding?"

She laughed. "Of all the things in the world I thought you were going to say, that wasn't it. But yes, we certainly can do that. Come on."

They headed into the kitchen. Suah climbed up on a stool.

"Jaxon Muse was here today?"

Gianna turned back from the refrigerator with milk in her hand. "That's right. I asked him to come over so we could talk."

"Talk about what?"

"Oh, about everything that's been going on."

"Did he say anything about Lolo?"

Gianna worked away on the pudding. "He said her real name is Leah; it's not Lolo."

"So he did talk about her!" Suah was excited.

Gianna stopped mixing the pudding. She was more serious and made eye contact with Suah. "Would you like to talk with Jaxon Muse again?"

Suah answered with vigorous nodding of the head.

Gianna developed the line of thought. "You'd like to talk to him about Leah, about fixing how her arms and legs work, is that it?"

"He can help her," asserted Suah.

"Why, because he writes books, because he has those big conferences? Is that why you think he can help her?"

"His books are in that section. The lady told me all about it."

"The lady?"

"At the bookstore."

Gianna thought it through. "How would you like to visit with Jaxon Muse before joining me on tour?"

Suah reached over and stuck his finger in the loose pudding mixture to taste it. "I'd like that."

"You're sure? You two could visit and talk together all you want. That would be OK with you?"

With fingers returning to the pudding, Suah nodded again.

"Wait here a second. I want to check on something…"

Gianna hurried from the room and made her way into the entertainment room to retrieve her cell phone. She quickly navigated a search to find a number in a long list of contacts then dialed the number.

As she paced, she talked out loud to herself. "…what time is it over there?" The line connected and a man's voice answered. Gianna stopped her pacing and started the conversation with, "…Wyatt? Is that you?"

CHAPTER 40

The lights were low in Hailey's bedroom. Swiping fingers across her tablet computer, she watched as colors and motions of Internet game play advanced to the next level. Propped up on elbows, she stretched out across the bed on her stomach and amused herself with a flurry of comments popping in on her chat window.

She enjoyed playing the games that the boys liked to play. What better way to tease and interact with them. There were always newbies wanting a challenge but it was the regulars she had the most fun with.

Playing by private rules was the most fun. If they lost, they had to make a donation to her PayPal account. If she lost, she had to take and send a private picture of her that they'd like. It was fun getting some extra spending cash but even more fun winning the game and denying them what they liked.

One of her regulars made a challenge to a higher level and she accepted. She knew him by the nickname Phantom and by his avatar picture, a stylized version of the letter "P" as a lightning bolt. She hadn't been on this game level before but she was warmed up from playing for a while, was up for the competition, and felt confident she could take him or at least have fun trying.

Her fingers danced across the touchscreen and tried to keep up but it soon became obvious that she wasn't ready for what this game level had in store. After a flurry of action, the Phantom zoomed past her and secured the win.

Right away, the chat window erupted. The Phantom, whoever he was, was due his prize. Others who had sat out the advanced level and only watched the two of them play were understandably jealous. She didn't lose often but those few she *had* lost to had more than bragged about their prizes.

As was her custom, Hailey signaled she accepted his win and was preparing his prize by posting an animated icon in the chat window. Her icon was a heart with wings fluttering away from the bonds of Earth.

Standing up from the bed, she posed before her mirror with tablet computer in hand. She wondered just how generous she was feeling tonight. The way he had won *was* impressive for that level of play; it deserved a proportional reward. Especially since the Phantom was one of her long-time regulars going way back. She had teased him unmercifully many times before but he'd never gotten rude or nasty like some of the others. After her day of play at the ashram, she was feeling charitable.

Loosening the knot on her short silk robe, she let the fabric fall open until it exposed one breast. Stepping a bit closer to the mirror, she framed the shot so her face couldn't be seen but her torso from navel to neck could. She snapped the photo and checked it. Half of her was covered, the other half was bare. Perfect. With a couple swipes of her fingers, the picture was saved and sent to the Phantom. As was her custom, she signed off the game site before any other interaction could take place.

She liked that game. It was just as much fun winning as it was losing. Each had their thrill. She dropped the tablet computer on the bed and listened at her door. The house was quiet; it was long past her parents' bedtime.

She headed for the kitchen and checked the refrigerator but saw nothing appetizing. She wasn't really hungry. She was more restless than anything. Staying cooped up in her room the whole night, avoiding her parents, was a major downer. She needed to get outside but it was late. There was always the pool in the back yard...

It was nearing midnight but Gianna had never called. Jaxon Muse sat slumped in a chair alone with his thoughts. He wondered what the new day would bring. Did he have the strength to let go of the hope that something unexpected and glorious could happen?

It was crazy to think that one would have to be strong to let go of hope. The act of letting go and being strong should be polar opposites but this one night, waiting for a phone call, had proved to him how strength and letting go also could be fused together with the fires of passion. Everything had its flip-side, even the most positive, cherished ways of looking at oneself and one's life. He knew that intellectually; it was far different having to feel it.

The night was quiet and a half moon bathed the yard in its silver blue hue. On the far side of the patio, on the other side of the yard from where Jaxon sat, a sliding glass door opened and drew his attention.

Out stepped Hailey in a short robe. They hadn't talked since their brief dust-up on the ride home from the North Shore earlier in the day. Jaxon wasn't in the mood to get back into it with her now. No doubt, she would rather not be bothered with anything her father had to say.

He felt heavy, sunken in, paralyzed by the inertia of darker thoughts that came and went but mostly lingered. And so he sat and watched as she stepped out, squatted down, and tested the pool water with a brush of her fingers. Finding the water temperature acceptable, she walked to the steps at the shallow end and let her robe drop to the deck.

Her body was blissfully bare; most of it in shadow but the finer lines of it were edged in radiant moon blue. She moved slowly, not wanting to make a splash. The beauty of her descent into the water shot through Jaxon with a rush of everything he could no longer hold back. From a distance, he couldn't see her face; she was simply a vision of the perfected female form. Seeing that form was an instant sense memory that took him back nearly twenty years, back when he and Claire were dating.

He and Claire had skinny-dipped on a night quite like this so long ago. Claire had looked just as radiant and perfected, but even more so Jaxon remembered the way he loved her back then. It was a love all-encompassing and shiny-new, a love with a desire and ache that had redefined the man he was and the person he would become. It was a love that still burned in his heart as if he and Claire were the ones swimming in the moonlight now.

Hailey turned over and did a backstroke lap to the deep end of the pool then glided back with more sweeping reaches of her arms and gentle kicks of her legs. More laps followed, each repeating the fluid motions and glimpses of body shapes that mesmerized for the way they took Jaxon back in time.

Jaxon felt hollowed out by the beauty he was seeing, by the unequaled beauty he remembered so well embodied in his one and only Claire. How could being witness to such beauty be such a fountainhead of loss, even bitterness? Why was he being teased or tested with a vision of what Claire and him once had together in their best of times—now that they were on the verge of losing it all?

He wanted to look away but couldn't. If he didn't have the strength to let go of hope, he wouldn't have the power of will to take his eyes from a fortuitous vision that brought the best of times with Claire back to him, if only as a bittersweet daydream.

Hailey finished her swim and climbed the steps of the shallow end. She reached for a nearby towel and stood and dried off with her back to Jaxon. As she tussled the towel against her wet hair, the illusion that she was Claire on a summer's night so long ago was complete. Jaxon was rendered a captive of his sight. As hopeless as it was to yearn for the past, he had no choice but imagine he was eighteen again and his Claire was just as healthy and aglow with all her youthful charms. Life and living were simpler then.

Hailey donned her short robe and stepped back into the house and closed the sliding glass door. She never knew that Jaxon was in the yard. Jaxon lowered his eyes, knowing it was better that way. She could keep the illusion that her swim was a private moment. Jaxon could keep the illusion that no one knew about his. Hailey's illusion would stay real to her if he didn't tell.

His illusion would always be an illusion for it was the present hoping the past could be a resurrected future for him and Claire.

Overcome with feeling, Jaxon rested his head back and closed his eyes. If nothing else could, maybe a little sleep would grant him relief from the uproar of all the memories that Hailey's swim had evoked. There was no point torturing himself with all the good times he and Claire had had. Every breath he took would be in the future, not the past. He needed to meditate on that and let all the rest of it fade back into its proper place.

Jaxon dozed, he didn't know how long, before his phone began to vibrate on his lap. At first he discounted it as a fragment of hope, wrapped in a wish, displayed in his dream. The vibration returned and he awoke.

"Yes?" he said groggily. "This is Jaxon. Who is this?"

The voice was soft-spoken in the late hour. "This is Gianna...Gianna Chase. I'm sorry it's so late..."

Hearing the name, Jaxon jerked alert. "Gianna! What time is it?"

"Almost one, I think. I'm really sorry about calling so late but I leave in the morning and it took longer than I thought to really think things through."

"That's OK, the time doesn't matter. I was hoping you'd call."

"This isn't easy for me. You have to know this takes a lot of trust—in you, but even more so, trust in myself."

"How do you mean?" asked Jaxon, still waking up.

"I only want the best for Suah. Deciding what that is—I always thought that part was easy."

"It's never easy being a parent."

"I was told once that the things that take the most effort give the greatest reward. I don't mind doing whatever it takes; I just want to know I'm doing the right thing."

"All the wisdom in the world can't compare to a mother's instincts," offered Jaxon.

"My father had good instincts too," countered Gianna. "It was a shame I lost him when I did. Maybe that's why sometimes I go overboard trying to be there for Suah. Some call Suah *special*. I prefer to call him *exceptional*."

"That he certainly is..."

"I went back and forth tonight," confessed Gianna. "Trying to decide what was best for him. Not for me—for him. It's not easy changing up something that has always seemed so clear before."

Jaxon followed along the best he could considering how vague she was being. "That's the balancing act of parenting, I guess. We have to grow as they grow. It can get hard to manage things when *everyone's* changing."

"I called Suah *exceptional*," added Gianna. "I'm beginning to believe I'm not even aware of all the ways he really *is* exceptional. Too much has happened for me to ignore what could be. The last thing I ever want to do is stifle Suah and the talents he brings to the world, whatever they may be."

"Having that validation from you is so important to him."

Gianna paused. "I asked him tonight if he wanted to talk with you. I was surprised how eager he is to get back together with you..."

"I'm happy to hear that." With a burst of optimism, Jaxon teared up.

"I think he mainly wants to talk about Leah."

"He still thinks I can heal her?"

"It's funny; nothing shakes him of that one idea. But it's not up to me to decide what he should care about. If he wants to talk to you about that, then I should let him. While he visits you, if you want him to meet with Claire, I can't see the harm in that."

Jaxon wept. "Thank you...thank you!"

Gianna could hear Jaxon's emotion. "I know the hour is late. I shouldn't keep you too long..."

Jaxon recovered. "...you have an early morning too."

"That's right, I'm flying out to rejoin my concert tour. There are a couple of details we need to work out."

"Anything...what do you have in mind?"

"You want Suah to visit you. My staff tells me I won't be ready for him on tour for a couple of days. We were expecting he'd be released from the hospital and fly right away to join me. With all the publicity around the Mackey show and the circumstances of Suah's early discharge, I don't see how I can take him with me tomorrow—but I won't leave him here alone."

Jaxon picked up on where she was going. "You want me to keep him for a couple of days until he can join you on tour?"

"Would you? It'd be the best thing, I think, for everyone concerned. Suah would get to talk to you like he's been wanting. You'd have a chance to be with him and introduce him to Claire. And I wouldn't have to worry about who knows what happening on tour because security and logistics weren't in place to protect him."

"I'd be honored to watch him," answered Jaxon.

"There would be a few conditions," added Gianna. "I've thought this through and think it's only right considering what might happen."

Jaxon tensed. "What do you think is going to happen?"

"There's no need going into that now. It's one person's opinion and most often it's wise to keep opinions to oneself."

"So what are the conditions?"

Gianna started down the list. "You can pick up Suah before eight o'clock tomorrow. You'll have him tomorrow and the next day—two days. On the morning of the third day, he must board a plane for Rome, the next stop on my tour. That's firm; I don't want him away from me any longer than that."

"That's fine," agreed Jaxon.

"Also, during those two days—tomorrow and the next day, I'd like any proceeds from the sale of your current book and conference ticket sales given as a charitable donation to the non-profit group that runs the school and community center in the village in Africa where Suah was born. I think it's only right that a small portion of the money you're making from the publicity around Suah should go to help a place I know is close to his heart."

Jaxon absorbed the news. "All right, I can do that."

"You promise me it will be done."

"Yes," affirmed Jaxon. "What else?"

"I'm concerned about where all of this is going to happen. I'm not convinced that staying on this island will insulate what you're doing with Suah enough to protect him."

"I'm staying at a gated property," explained Jaxon.

"Even so, I'd like to select the place. There's another reason. Whatever you might discover by working with Suah should be shared with the world. I don't want to leave new knowledge in one person's hands. I'm sorry, I don't mean to offend you, but I think it'd be better if you shared whatever you discover right from the beginning. Multiple perspectives, free exchange of thoughts is what we need, not one person's analysis released over several years in a stream of profitable books and lectures."

Jaxon was skeptical. "How are you going to ensure that will happen?"

"I'm hardly in the business of providing insurance. All I can do is arrange the best framework in the time given. A friend of mine has a ranch on a Caribbean island. From here, his place is half way to Rome, which works out nicely for getting Suah to me on tour. What I suggest is that you take Suah for the next two days to his ranch and have whatever conversations you need to have. All I ask is that whatever you find, you share with my friend."

"And the name of your friend?"

"Wyatt Dumashe."

Jaxon was floored. This was the last thing he expected. "But isn't he behind *The Protoprime Society*?"

"Yes, I know, and *The Protoprime Society* is financing Nathan Mackey. Don't worry about that. Wyatt and I had a nice long talk and he shared with me some information that didn't make it into Nathan's television show."

"About what?"

"I'd rather not go into that right now. The thing is, I called him because I know he has the ranch and has offered in the past to let me stay there whenever I liked. I also know he is intensely interested in all things mystical and new-earth aware. I told him that I would guarantee that you'd share with him directly anything you discovered at his ranch—if and only if he kept Nathan Mackey on a proper leash when it concerns either one of us."

"Did he go for it?" asked Jaxon.

"You're welcome at the ranch tomorrow as soon as you can get there."

"What makes you think Wyatt would honor such a deal?"

"Because he only hired Mackey because of his interest in all things mystical. The fact that Nathan is the aggressive type who likes to dig deeper than he's asked to is only a problem if his handlers don't edit him properly. Wyatt assures me that it's in everyone's interest to do the right thing."

"How long have you known Wyatt?"

"As long as I've known Olivia Platt, my business manager. She used to work for him."

"What happened with that?" asked Jaxon.

In the late hour, trading confidences seemed appropriate given the circumstances. "She decided he was too old to have a child with. She broke off their affair."

"Their affair?"

"The business side of things was never the same once they split."

"You took her on as your business manager after that?"

"I knew nothing of it until years later. By then, she and I were a team and she seemed happy enough with her third husband. But none of that matters now. All I need to know is if you'll accept the conditions."

Jaxon took a moment to review them before answering, "Yes."

"Oh, just one more thing," added Gianna. "I was surprised to hear that Suah has his own conditions. He wants Leah, a man named Brody Mud, and a dog called Gris-Gris to join you and him at the ranch."

"How is that going to be possible?" asked Jaxon. "Even if we find all of them, they might not be available or want to go."

"I know, I told him that. He still wants us to try. He said Leah would

know where to find Gris-Gris and Brody Mud works at *Island Aquatics &
Adventures*."

"Where do we find Leah?"

"Didn't you see Nathan Mackey's program tonight?"

"Not all of it…"

"It was on there. Leah lives with Lilyana Gorst in town. She runs a
business out of her home."

Jaxon was reeling. "Anything else?"

Gianna paused for her own review. "No, that's it. That's enough, don't
you think?"

Jaxon chuckled. "It's going to be a different two days."

"Take good care of my boy."

"I will."

"And remember, on the third day, he has to be on that plane to Rome."

"He will be."

The call ended and a stark, after-midnight silence returned to the dark
patio where Jaxon Muse sat. He lowered his phone, dazed with all that had
been discussed and decided. He had what he had hoped for. Now that he had
it, it didn't seem real. Before, when he didn't have it, nothing else mattered.

After going through all the conditions, he had to admit it was going to be
a wild, circuitous route. Keeping a steady focus convinced him he was ready
no matter what. They were headed for the one possibility that only someone
whispering their dying wish could dream with utmost sincerity. That was
because it was the one wish made by a heart prepared to believe it.

Jaxon felt certain that Suah's gift would come through for Claire. It had to
and he knew why. There was no other way Claire was going to stay on this
Earth—and Jaxon wasn't going to let her go. The opportunity was now theirs
to seize. It was no longer about making peace with what had to be. It was
now all about following through on the way things should be.

Jaxon gazed out across the yard. The moon had moved quite a bit since
Hailey first appeared and sparked such fond remembrances. A full reflection
of the half moon was now on the surface of the water. The water was calm
like glass. Just looking at it, you'd assume you could walk right across it.

If you didn't know better, you might even try.

Jaxon stood and walked to the edge of the decking. He looked down at the
water. He couldn't help but wonder about taking that next step.

CHAPTER 41

It was early at the estate, so early that the rising sun had yet to breach the verdant ridgeline in the east. But Gianna was dressed and her limo was waiting. She stepped up to the town car as Jaxon got out from the driver seat.

"Where's David, your driver?" asked Gianna.

"We spoke so late last night, I wasn't sure I could get him." Jaxon spied Suah behind her pulling a suitcase across the entryway's marble tiles and out the estate's front door. He added, "It's better this way. Good morning, Suah."

"Good morning," came the answer. Suah stopped next to his mother.

Gianna turned to the boy and squatted down to be face-to-face with him. "Our adventure continues, my love. In two days, you'll be with me in Rome and you'll get to meet Sandy, your new au pair."

Suah qualified, "She'll be with me when we go to concerts…"

"Yes, but that's not all," Gianna corrected. "She's your new nanny for concerts and for home. She'll come home with us after the tour."

"Something new?" asked Jaxon.

"Yes. Paige didn't want to travel and Hannah didn't want to relocate to an island. I think it's going to be better this way."

"Much better," added Suah, rolling his eyes. "Only one set of rules."

Gianna smiled. "More like you only have to train one nanny instead of two." She glanced at Jaxon. "Until you get to Rome, you two can talk about whatever you want. OK?" Suah nodded.

Jaxon grabbed Suah's suitcase and put it in the trunk. "We've got a lot to do before we can get going."

"That's right," agreed Gianna, turning back to Suah. "You've got to go exploring and find Leah, Brody, and Gris-Gris."

"That's not exploring," Suah corrected. "That'll be easy."

"OK, give me a hug." Gianna hugged and kissed Suah and held him tight. He hugged her back and then she opened the town car's rear door for him. He climbed in the wide back seat. "See you soon!"

She blew him a kiss and closed the door.

Jaxon stepped up to her, his eyes on the skies. "What happened to all the news choppers?"

Gianna didn't even glance at the sky. "I called Mason Gaines and told him I thought they were a nuisance and a hazard. He agreed."

Jaxon grinned. "Better not let that get around; the press will say you've gotten special treatment from the authorities. They might even say you're fraternizing in a scandalous way."

"Who cares? At least they aren't around to see what car Suah got into."

Jaxon looked back at his town car and her waiting limo. "A lot of people are going to have to flip a coin."

"The only problem is—half of them will be right."

Jaxon took a step closer. The grin faded from his face. "Thank you, Gianna. Thanks for giving Claire and me this chance."

Gianna noted the change in tone with some awkwardness. "You don't have to thank me. I just hope some good comes from it."

Jaxon paused on the thought. "Me too."

Sensing his pain and fear of loss, Gianna leaned forward and gave him a hug. Needing a hug more than she ever would know, he held onto her longer than a friendly goodbye would warrant. He didn't care and she didn't complain. They parted ways with a wave of the hand. He got into the town car's driver seat and her driver held the limo's rear door open for her.

A minute later they were both headed down the hill to the security gate. In the early morning hour, only a dozen or so paparazzi and fans had survived the vigil of the night before. Activity at the gate rousted them into action as the two cars rolled out onto the street and headed for the main highway. As they did, three cars made U-turns and followed them.

At the highway, the town car turned one way, back towards town, the limo turned the other, headed out. None of the following cars turned and followed the town car; all of them turned and followed the limo.

The sun was up and the day had begun.

Jaxon drove along with Suah enjoying the sights from the back seat. The impulse was there for Jaxon to start asking Suah right away about all he had done and how it had come about. But Jaxon restrained himself. He had two days with Suah. He didn't want to scare the boy off or pressure him. First things first. It was best to round up whoever would go with them and get on the plane. It was going to be a long flight. There would be plenty of time to talk to Suah about miracles later.

"So where to first?" asked Jaxon.

Suah thought a minute before an impish grin creased his face. "When we get to town, can we pull over after the first light."

Jaxon checked Suah out in the rear-view mirror. "Why there?"

Suah hugged his knees. "The food truck. I'd really like to get some cunnel fake."

CHAPTER 42

Gianna's limo pulled into the hangar and rolled up alongside her private tour jet. The three cars that followed her had been left far behind, stranded at the gate. The news helicopters they had called in were blinded by the roof of the hangar. No one would see who was getting on the tour plane with her.

Taking brisk steps, Gianna left the limo and climbed the stairs where she was met by her regular flight attendant. "Welcome aboard, Ms. Chase."

Gianna smiled and gave the attendant a brief hug; they had been on many flights together. "It's going to be a long flight. Bear with me; I'm on an adventure."

"Sounds exciting," offered the attendant.

Gianna's dubious look waned as she passed by. "Oh yes, and whoever said uncertainty and expectation are the joys of life must have had a shitty little life. When can we be on our way?"

"We're ready to push off," the attendant assured her.

Gianna walked down the aisle. "Fantastic. That must mean Olivia is back here somewhere."

Olivia looked up over glasses low on her nose and leaned her head into the aisle briefly from one of the leather seats. She didn't answer.

Gianna took a seat and noted Olivia's sulk. The reason for it needed to be dealt with head on. "I'm expecting a call from Wyatt," announced Gianna. "I thought I'd better warn you in case you didn't want to participate."

Olivia didn't flinch. "That's considerate of you but I think I'll stay."

Gianna busied herself by noticing Olivia's cranberry juice and pressing the attendant call light. The flight attendant was right there. "I'll have one of those, please."

"Yes, ma'am." The attendant dashed away.

Gianna took a breath and stared at Olivia. "It's going to be a god-awful long flight. I don't intend on spending it in bitchy silence with you. All right; you dislike my plan. Your objections are noted. You hate it when I don't include you in decisions but this time, considering the circumstances..."

Olivia interrupted, "After all these years, you don't think I can maintain objective composure around Wyatt?"

"I didn't say that."

"Then what are these circumstances you're talking about?"

"After the way you reacted to meeting Nathan Mackey, I thought the last

thing you'd want to be bothered with was handling anything directly with
Wyatt. I needed a secluded place where Jaxon Muse and Suah could get
away."

"So the only place you could think of was Wyatt's ranch? And how will
that look to the rest of the world?"

Gianna accepted the cranberry juice from the attendant then turned back
to Olivia. "Oh, I don't know. It might look like I'm not hiding from his
investigation into what's going on with Suah."

The cabin door closed and the jet began to move but not under its own
power. A small utility vehicle was pulling the plane out of the hangar.

Olivia looked out the window. "I wish you had consulted with me."

"I didn't have time," countered Gianna. "With everything going on last
night, it was the best way to handle it. I couldn't leave Suah here and Muse
and Suah wanted to talk. Wyatt's place is halfway to Rome and it's secluded.
As I remember it, the last time we spoke you didn't have a plan."

Olivia was unconvinced. "There are so many other ways to go about it."

"But this is the way we're doing it. Accept it and move on. We can't work
together if you're going to be pissy about it. If you don't want to deal with
Wyatt, fine; I'll deal with him directly. You stay out of it."

Olivia bit her lip. Complaining wasn't going to reverse the damage done.
All she could do was to try to direct things along a proper path from here.

"You said he's supposed to call. What is that about?" asked Olivia.

Sensing that Olivia was moving on, Gianna settled back. "He mentioned
something to me last night but didn't have all the details in front of him. As
you might expect, not everything dug up by *Protoprime* investigators was put
into Mackey's documentary."

Olivia shot Gianna a glance; memories of a stormy encounter with Nathan
Mackey in the beach cabana flooded back. Nathan had threatened to expose
all he had found about Olivia's past with Gianna. Even though Olivia knew
she had only ever acted in Gianna's best interests, some of it might not
appear so noble out of context when presented by a muckraking journalist.

Olivia grew defensive. "What kind of crusade has this become? I thought
they were interested in miracles and Suah. What does everyone else have to
do with this?"

Gianna took notice of Olivia's riled presumptions. "It *is* about Suah. Why,
do you know something different?"

Olivia backtracked. "No, it just seems every time we turn around, Wyatt
has his goons investigating something else. What is he really after?"

With a look of surprise, Gianna challenged her. "Don't tell me he's investigating you. Is that what this is about?"

Olivia assumed it was written on her face. Nathan was bound to come out with it anyway; there was no point denying it. "Nathan warned me that he had uncovered things that might be embarrassing to us, one way or another."

"Embarrassing to us or to you?"

Olivia looked Gianna in the eye. "I assumed he expected one to mean the other."

Gianna waved it off. "I don't have time for that. It's just more crap on the pile. There's enough rumor and innuendo out there already. The only thing I'm concerned about it Suah. You may not like me talking to Wyatt, but if he uncovers anything that can help my son, I'll support him any way I can."

"And you believe his reasons for doing all of this."

"He could have gone public with this already. Instead, he wants to talk it over with me, present the facts, see what I think. To me, that says a lot."

"So when are we supposed to hear from him?"

Gianna pressed the call light again. "He's waiting for my call." The flight attendant stepped up. "You can make the call now. I'll take it here."

Olivia said nothing, only watched as the screen for the video call silently powered down from a recess in the ceiling.

Gianna swiveled the screen so Olivia would be out of frame. "You can participate if you want. Otherwise, he'll never know you're here. Fair enough?"

Olivia nodded and kept her seat. It wasn't until after take-off that the call finally came through. The jet accelerated towards their cruising altitude then banked to the southwest as Wyatt Dumashe appeared onscreen.

"Gianna, good day to you!" he bellowed. A tall and strong man with broad shoulders and a broader personality to match, he sported a close-cropped beard and a wavy salt-and-pepper mane pulled back into a ponytail.

Gianna avoided a glance at Olivia to check on her reaction. "It's nice to see you again."

Wyatt got right into it. "You caught me at a busy time but we really need to go over this."

"From what you told me before, I didn't think it was time sensitive."

"It's not so much time sensitive but it could be critical to what's going on with Suah. Something like that shouldn't wait and I didn't want to go public with it until I had a chance to talk to you."

"Thank you, Wyatt. I know you didn't have to do this."

"Nonsense. By the way, how are Muse and Suah doing?"

"They're rounding up the others and heading over to your jet as we speak. That was generous of you."

"It made sense. Nathan and his crew can fly back to the mainland on commercial carrier. It won't kill them. They'll be flying first class."

"When I said generous, I also meant the use of your ranch."

"Again, it makes sense. It's just sitting there. If Muse can find out anything and share it with *The Society*, all the better. It's about time we worked together to explore the mysteries around us."

"You said you're busy; I won't keep you," offered Gianna. "Why don't you tell me about what you found out?"

Wyatt shifted in his seat on a high-rise patio. Beyond him through a clear divider was a cityscape seen from dozens of stories up. "Well, from what I can tell, it all came about quite unexpectedly. *The Society* sent a researcher to Africa to gather biographical information on Suah, you know, facts about his village, his family, what his life was like before the adoption."

In deference to Olivia, Gianna asked, "Why bother with such a full-blown investigation if you're really interested in the mystery of the healings?"

Wyatt chuckled, "It's no secret people are intensely interested in Suah. But many of them don't know much about his background. It's the human interest angle, nothing more sinister than that."

Unable to restrain herself, Gianna glanced at Olivia to catch her reaction but found none. Gianna looked back at Wyatt. "I see. Go on…"

"Well, you know all the details on Suah's birth. You had access to reports about that from long ago; we talked about that."

"Yes…" Gianna remembered how Olivia had done her own research before the adoption.

"Those were medical reports," noted Wyatt. "They took the perspective of outside researchers collecting data on twin births throughout the indigenous population. It was accurate but very clinical. When the bio-researcher from *The Society* got to Africa recently, she started asking the native people what they thought about all the Suah news. They had an interesting take on the whole matter that was quite surprising."

Gianna clarified, "The researcher asked the village people about the news that Suah could heal people?"

"That's right," confirmed Wyatt. "She asked them about that but also what they remembered about his birth and family."

Gianna's jet started to level off at its initial cruise altitude. As the angle of the jet settled down, she leaned forward with interest. "So what do you think is so critical?"

"It has to do with Suah being a twin." Wyatt looked concerned. "More to the point, it has to do with the death of his sister."

"Hawa…"

"Yes, Hawa. Not only was she stillborn; as we know, she died in utero. The villagers have longstanding traditions and beliefs about such things."

"Superstitions," Gianna commented.

"We have to be careful with these labels," warned Wyatt. "People in our own culture believe in 'soul mates' and 'guardian angels' and all sorts of things that are just as superstitious, if you want to go there."

"It wasn't meant to demean their culture," Gianna explained.

"Of course, I didn't think so. My point being, for whatever reason, these people have developed their own world view. Included in that is a folklore about twins that I must say is not that far afield from what many in the Western world also whisper or worry about in private company."

"What kind of view?" asked Gianna.

"It's quite simple, but crucial. You see, for them, twins share a connected soul. They believe that when one twin dies, it throws the other twin out of balance. Worse yet, the closer to the birth you get when a twin dies, the more the other twin is unbalanced by the death."

Gianna added, "But Hawa died before the birth…"

"Exactly, even worse. To help set the balance back, usually the family creates a wooden effigy of the missing twin as a surrogate host for the dead twin's soul. In Suah's case, since his mother died in childbirth and his father died soon after, Suah was left in the care of his grandfather."

"The grandfather never had the effigy made," Gianna deduced.

"Not only did he lack the money to commission one, he was vehemently against having one made by anyone else."

"Why?"

"You'll have to ask him. Villagers say he got it in his head that somehow an effigy would mess up the mystic nature of something unique that was going on. Little of what he said made much sense to them."

"I don't understand," prompted Gianna. "Why would any of this be crucial to Suah now?"

"Many in Suah's village blame the oversight of this twin-effigy thing for why Suah is different. They think his soul is unbalanced."

"How does that make sense?" asked Gianna. "From everything I heard, the villagers, even his school encouraged him to keep Hawa as an invisible friend. They did nothing to put her to rest."

"Since the grandfather wouldn't allow the effigy to be made, it was the only thing they could do to try to keep her bonded with him."

"It didn't put the matter to rest if they still think his soul's unbalanced."

"The plan has never been to put her to rest—it's to anchor her to the Earth with Suah. Remember, they share a connected soul. Until that connection happens, they say Suah will be different, even disturbed."

Gianna took it in. "All of this just because an effigy wasn't made?"

"That's how powerful it is for them. When one of these twin effigies is made, the mother or family member carries it around, takes it on trips, keeps a place for it in their house just like it was a real child."

Gianna leaned back. "So this is why they think Suah is different from other children."

"Yes, and that's why they gave him latitude at the school where he was at. They think this whole frenzy now about him healing people is ironic."

"Ironic? How?"

"Because they seriously believe *he's* the one who needs to be healed."

It might be superstition, but something about the purity and clarity of the idea resonated with Gianna. She looked down to hide her pained reaction.

"The doctors never could tell me why Suah was special. They never found a label that fit him."

"Who knows," added Wyatt. "Maybe this is why."

Gianna hid the depths of her emotion. "I suppose the villagers think an effigy still needs to be made."

"It's the only thing they know that patches things enough to let a normal life proceed."

"What are these effigies like?"

"Oh, they're pretty basic: carved out of wood, about ten to twelve inches high, the figure is usually shown standing with hands on hips for some reason, I'm not sure."

"If one of these were made, where would it be kept?"

"I imagine with you. You're Hawa's stepmother. Then again, if the whole idea is to heal Suah, that would lead me to believe that wherever Suah is, the effigy should be somewhere around him. Keeping the two in close proximity is part of reconnecting the souls and restoring the balance."

Gianna was running inside in a dozen different directions. "So what do you think I should do?"

Wyatt leaned back. "I'm just presenting the facts. I'm staying out of it. I thought the whole subject was compelling and *The Protoprime Society* would like to include it in the bio they're going to air on Suah. I simply wanted to run it by you. I thought you should know, plus I wanted your approval to leave it in the bio."

Gianna thought a minute. "Would it be possible to hold off on the bio until I make my decision?"

"Will it be a while?"

"No," Gianna assured him. "I just need a little time, that's all."

"I see no problem there," agreed Wyatt.

"If you find out anything else…"

"I'll pass it along. You can count on it."

"Thank you," Gianna concluded.

Wyatt reached for the button to disconnect. "Very well. We'll be in touch. Take care."

The screen went blank. Gianna filled up with everything it might mean for Suah and her. She looked to Olivia for guidance.

"So what did you make of that?"

Olivia was reserved, pensive. "You mean Wyatt or the effigy thing?"

"Both…" Then Gianna reconsidered, "But let's not talk about Wyatt."

"I never heard of it before but I never went looking for it either."

For Gianna, fear and wonder and hope swirled together in the pit of her stomach. "Could it be possible that this might help Suah?"

"Do you think he needs help?" Olivia looked confused.

"I don't know," confessed Gianna. "I want him to have a happy life…"

Olivia was terse. "You always jump on others for calling him *special* and yet you protect him like he is. They say this may be your one chance to give him balance, to make him normal. Now why would you ever want to do that? Wouldn't that be admitting that he's *special*? How could you ever say that?"

Gianna recoiled. "I know you like being blunt but I see no reason to be malicious."

Olivia relaxed to diffuse the tension between them. "It's just a reality check, that's all, Gianna."

"Who's reality—yours or mine?"

Olivia started to say something but held back. "I'm sorry. I meant to be concise, not careless. If you really want to pursue this, I'm not the one to ask. Why don't you contact Jaxon Muse? He's made a career out of equally ethereal things. If anyone has a perspective on superstition, he will."

CHAPTER 43

Rapid changes could make the world feel surreal. That's the only way Jaxon Muse could explain it. Just twelve hours before, he was sitting in the dark out by the pool watching Hailey swim. With fading hopes, his world had become a passing charade; his life had all but contracted into a hollowed-out space too small for his heart's desires to fit into.

Now he looked around. A half day later, the incredible was happening. He was soaring through the sky at nearly the speed of sound in a private jet Jaxon knew had a sixty-five million dollar price tag, and that was before Wyatt Dumashe made improvements. The destination was a 750-acre ranch on a Caribbean island over 6300 miles away. And Suah was with him.

The G650 jet had a forward galley and room for sixteen passengers and six sleeping berths. Claire rested in the aft sleeping berth across the aisle from him. Sitting silently, Jaxon had kept her company until she dozed off. It had been an eventful morning. But now, the porthole shades were pulled down, hiding the early afternoon sun. The sliding door into the main cabin was closed and the only sound to be heard was the calming rush of flight.

On the other side of the door, the surreal nature of the day found its most visible expression. It was time to rejoin the motley group that had been assembled over the last six hours. Jaxon was careful to be quiet as he stood and exited the rear compartment. Sliding the door closed behind him, he took quick appraisal of where everyone had settled in throughout the cabin.

Suah was sitting on his legs in a leather seat nearby with his nose pressed to one of the portholes. The dog he called Gris-Gris was curled up on the floor next to him. Cattycorner from them, farther forward, Brody and Hailey sat across from one another on opposite ends of facing couches. A flatscreen television was on but they were talking over it. A little ways farther on, Leah sat in a swivel rocker facing the couches, an interested but ignored observer.

Jaxon couldn't get over the oddness of how everything had happened. How Suah managed to convince Brody and Leah to come along on a spontaneous vacation was nothing short of a miracle by itself. How both had agreed with no notice to drop everything and be whisked away to the Caribbean was either a testament to Suah's mystical powers of persuasion or Brody's and Leah's need to get away from lives where nothing much happened that otherwise wouldn't be the same when they got back.

Jaxon took a seat across the aisle from Suah. "What's so interesting out there?" asked Jaxon.

Suah swung his head around, taking notice of Jaxon for the first time since he returned from the aft compartment. Suah glanced farther forward. "I can't believe no one's looking out the windows. There's lots to see."

Jaxon relaxed with the incongruity. "We're flying over ocean, aren't we?"

"Now we are," Suah admitted. "But we did go over an island."

"So what now? Are you waiting for another island?" smiled Jaxon.

Suah excitedly stuck his nose back against the porthole. "You think there'll be more?"

Jaxon had to tell the truth. "No, we won't see land again for hours."

Suah kept his gaze on the view. "It was so cool looking at the island. Everything was so small." He turned back to Jaxon. "I saw cars on the road. They looked like little pieces of pepper moving on a plate."

Jaxon chuckled, "They didn't look like ants?"

Suah was certain. "No, they were too tiny. Just like the trees. The trees were small smudges of green crayon. They looked flat on the ground."

Jaxon couldn't help but broaden the perspective. "If we were up in outer space, in orbit, you wouldn't even see the trees or the cars. They'd be so far away, they'd disappear."

"But they'd still be there," added Suah.

"That's right; they'd still be there."

Suah gazed across the aisle, enraptured by the thought. "Wow...we can look at things and not even see what's there."

"How true." Jaxon wondered if Suah realized all the ways that statement could be taken. Before Jaxon could ask, Suah added more.

"You want to know what's really goofy?" asked Suah.

"What?"

"I found out if you get too close to things, the same thing can happen."

"How is that?" asked Jaxon.

"It's like this airplane. If I cover my eyes and put my nose up against it..." Suah put his open palm flat against his nose, "...I wouldn't see an airplane when I opened my eyes. It'd be too close. All I'd see is a color."

"You're right. When things get too close or too distant, we don't see them for what they really are anymore."

Suah looked back out the porthole. "Hawa and I argued about that."

At the mention of Hawa, Jaxon perked up. "You did?"

"I told her what grandfather said. She said he was only half right."

"What did your grandfather say?"

Suah stared into the clouds floating by below the plane's altitude. "He said 'the closer you go, the more is revealed.' Hawa said that's right most of the time but not all of the time."

Jaxon's curiosity was piqued. "How did she prove it to you?"

Suah grew more serious. "Well, when she's far away, I can't see her. But when she comes too close, the same thing happens."

"Why do you think that is?" prompted Jaxon.

Suah cocked his head. "I don't know. Maybe she isn't here or there. Maybe she's somewhere else. Maybe I only see her when she's in between."

Just then, Jaxon's phone buzzed with an incoming email. He let Suah contemplate the sky and opened the message to find it came from Gianna. He read it quickly but had to read it again more slowly. The synchronicity was uncanny. She needed Jaxon's advice about what to do concerning something that Wyatt's researchers had uncovered about Suah and his twin sister Hawa.

Jaxon read the brief description of the issue: Hawa's death in utero, Suah's unbalanced soul, the wooden effigy that was never made, the need for Suah to be healed. What did Jaxon think?

Jaxon took a minute to let it sink in. He stared up across the aisle at Suah and then reread the message. Jaxon couldn't answer Gianna right away; he hoped she didn't expect a rapid response. He'd have to think it through.

He vacillated and found it ironic, given the conversation they'd just had. Maybe he was too close to the situation to decide the proper thing to do. Maybe he was too far from village life in Africa to fully comprehend the true import of a token piece of wood that many, with their enlightened academic viewpoints, would either discount as little more than superstition or elevate as a cherished but apocryphal element of another native culture.

Jaxon needed another perspective. The first person that came to mind was Perry's sister. Perry was shrewd and puckish as Jaxon's agent, quite unlike the studied and intense nature of his accomplished sister. She was a respected clinical psychologist in London who had worked with troubled children before. It would be interesting to get her take on what to do.

Should Gianna give any credence to the notion that Suah needed to be healed from an unbalance in his soul? Was it wise to go through such a ritual to appease the native spirit at the core of Suah's psyche? Would it do any good? More importantly, did any of this shed the slightest light on why Suah was not like other children? Jaxon quickly composed a forwarding message and sent it to Perry. As he pressed send, he was reminded: *we can look at things and not even see what's there.*

CHAPTER 44

Night fell abruptly and deepened swiftly for everyone enclosed in the pressurized tube shooting through the sky. Flying east was flying over a world that was always moving, ever spinning in the opposite direction. For Jaxon Muse, the flight and the spin added together to give an unsettling impression of the hurried passage of time. Of time running out.

More than halfway through their ten-hour flight, excitement and restlessness had given way to boredom and finally sleep. Everyone had found a berth or sleeping place scattered throughout the cabin that suited them. Jaxon stayed in the aft section with Claire. The sliding door was open; the cabin lights were low. The sound of steady flight was lulling white noise.

Jaxon was brought nearly awake by shuffling steps near him. He half-opened his eyes to find Suah drowsily making his way to the aft bathroom. The jet had two restrooms, one forward and one aft. The rear one was nearest to where Suah slept but to get there he had to shuffle by Claire and Jaxon.

Suah disappeared into the aft darkness. After keeping close quarters with the whole group for hours, Jaxon found the moment promising. Being the only other one awake with Suah was an opportunity Jaxon couldn't pass up. He pulled back the blanket over him and sat up, then slid the compartment door closed. A closed door would block Suah's escape back to the main cabin, but more importantly, the privacy would allow the two of them to talk without disturbing the others.

Returning from the bathroom, Suah startled to find Jaxon sitting up.

"I didn't mean to frighten you," whispered Jaxon.

"That's OK," mumbled Suah.

Jaxon cleared a space for him. "Here, why don't you sit down."

"You can't sleep?" asked Suah.

"I can't decide if I want to sleep or not," explained Jaxon. "Sometimes when I sleep, I have bad dreams. But when I stay awake, it still seems like a bad dream."

Suah sat down. "How does that happen?"

"Sometimes in life there are things so different, so intense that they don't seem real; they seem like a bad dream."

Suah wondered, "How do you wake up from that?"

"You don't," answered Jaxon. "You have to live with it—or you find a way to overcome it."

"What are you going to do?"

Jaxon looked across the aisle, through the darkness, at Claire's sleeping form. "I need to find a way to overcome it—and I'd like you to help me."

"You want me to help you out of your bad dream?"

Jaxon nodded in the dark. "Yes...I believe you can do it. I've seen you do it with others."

"I don't know anything about bad dreams, not about making them go away. I don't like talking about them; they might come back."

"Have you had a bad dream recently?" asked Jaxon.

"I had a dream I didn't like..."

"What about?"

"I don't like to talk about it."

"It's OK. Getting it out is good. It helps us understand. Our dreams are there to tell us things."

"Even the bad ones?"

"Yes, especially the bad ones. So, what was it?"

Suah shrugged. "It wasn't much. It was about a boat. The captain didn't care that his boat was filling up with water. Then the ocean started to shrink. It shrank so much that the captain told all the people to start bailing water out of the boat."

"Why start bailing water then?"

"He wanted to try to fill the ocean back up. But it didn't work. The ocean dried up and the boat and all the people had nowhere to go. It was sad."

"Why do you think it was so sad? What did it tell you?"

"When some things are lost, they're gone forever."

Jaxon was thankful that the darkness hid his tears. "That's right. Some things are gone forever. To stop them from going away, it takes something very special. That's what people call a miracle."

"My teacher told me there's all kinds of miracles. She said sharing a smile with someone when you're sad is a kind of miracle. Is that the kind of miracle you want?"

"I would like that...but it's not the miracle I think you can do."

"I can't even stop my own bad dreams; how can I stop yours?"

"I don't know how you do it; I wish I did. But I know you can."

"What do you want me do to?"

"I need you to help Claire; she's very sick."

Suah looked up. "She might go away forever?"

Jaxon had to wait to speak. "Yes, that's right."

"My teacher says when we go away forever, we go to a better place. Don't you want that for her?"

"Of course, some day, but I'd like to spend as much time together as we can. We love each other and want to be together." The passion to explain welled up in Jaxon. "It's like you and Hawa. You like to be together; you don't want to be far away from each other."

"Hawa says we're always near even when we're far apart. But Hawa can't go away forever. She's never been here."

The jumble of talk frustrated Jaxon. He tried driving home the point. "Hawa talks to you when you help people, doesn't she? What would Hawa say to help Claire?"

Suah sat, saying nothing. He looked across at Claire sleeping.

Jaxon slid off the berth onto his knees and pulled Suah to a standing position. They moved closer to Claire's side.

Jaxon was insistent. "If Hawa was here, what would she say over Claire? What would she have you do? Can you ask her now…do it for me?"

Slowly, a change came over Suah. His gaze didn't blink as he considered Claire sleeping before him. He was dozy but intent upon the moment. He reached out and lifted Jaxon's hand. He moved it forward and joined it ever so softly with Claire's hand. All the while, he murmured low.

"…*Jamais vu*…*passing through*…
…*out of the blue*…*Presque vu*…
…*seeing through*…*Déjà vu*…
…*Bonne nuit*…*overdue.*"

Suah pressed Jaxon's hand and Claire's hand together. As he took his hand away from their joined hands, he came out of trance. He took a step back from Jaxon and whispered in his normal voice.

"It doesn't matter what Hawa says. It's more important what you and Claire say to each other."

Jaxon looked back, confused. "Is that it?"

Suah turned to go. "I'm going to go back to sleep…"

Jaxon broke the hand connection with Claire to stop him. "No, wait. Can you stay here, just a little while longer? I think we were close…so close."

"OK…" Suah sat back on the end of Jaxon's berth.

Jaxon got up off his knees and sat back too. It was hard to know what to say. He couldn't very well ask Suah if a miracle had been performed. But

Jaxon didn't see how what had happened was anything like other healings Suah had done. Suah hadn't worked over Claire directly. She never responded in any way or showed any signs she'd been affected at all. All that Suah had done was put their hands together and Suah had touched Jaxon's hand far more than Claire's.

Jaxon's excitement waned and was steadily replaced by doubts. Even though Suah had spoken in trance, what he had said hardly seemed like miracle material compared to what Jaxon remembered from other healings. It didn't sound like Hawa at all; at least not Hawa in healing mode.

Jaxon and Suah kept a steady vigil in the dark for a while. Jaxon remained tormented. Trying to decipher a deeper meaning for the words spoken in trance was growing more elusive by the minute.

Jamais vu referred to a peculiar state of mind when a person momentarily does not recognize something that he or she already knows.

Presque vu was the familiar tip-of-the-tongue phenomenon that everyone had experienced at one time or another.

Everyone had heard of *Déjà vu*. How the three terms related to Claire was obscure. But most of what Suah said in trance was like that. To try to find a literal translation was meaningless. As with *Suah's Prayer*, the translation was only helpful when analyzed in context and given an interpretation.

Maybe he should ask Suah directly. Would Suah even remember what he had said? It was never documented whether or not Suah was aware of what he said or did while in trance. If nothing else, it would be a good way into a conversation that might shed light on what had or hadn't happened.

Jaxon turned to speak but caught himself and said nothing. Suah had slumped back and fallen asleep. He was contorted in a half-sitting position with his head slung back between a cushion and the bulkhead.

Jaxon felt the anticipation of the moment drain away; with it went the charge of hope from moments before. He was certain now. There had been no miracle and there would be no more conversation until morning. By then, everyone would be awake and the deeper, more sensitive discussions he hoped to have with Suah would have to wait until they got to the ranch.

Jaxon stood and carefully repositioned Suah's body into the berth he'd been using. He put a blanket over the boy and stood a minute, reviewing the lost opportunity and what it meant. Was Hawa trying to tell him something? Had what he expected of Suah's healing ritual distracted him so much that he'd missed a clear-cut message right in front of him? Answers and any healing would have to wait, no matter how fast time was flying by.

CHAPTER 45

London at night spread out beyond the picture window. Perry enjoyed the elevated view of Chelsea Bridge and strolled his West End flat in pajamas. In pursuit of a cocktail refill, he speed-dialed his sister along the way and listened with a wireless earpiece until a familial female voice answered.

"Dollie?" Her name was Dorothy but an elfin brother was never enslaved by such droll formalities. "Tell me I caught you at a good time."

"You know it's always a good time when I hear from you, Perry." Sibling sarcasm was expected. "And what kind of good time *are* you having?"

He paused at the wet bar long enough to refill his old fashion glass with ice and spirits. "I'm happily crucifying myself with a few Rusty Nails."

"Are we going heavy or light on the Drambuie?"

Perry sipped. "For your tastes, I'd say I'm leaning on it."

"Oh, we're feeling sweet tonight. What's the occasion? Getting ready to cruise King's Road?"

"Here we go with the snobbery again. My postcode may not be W8 Kensington but I'm not exactly slumming it."

She opted to be patronizing. "I know. The flat is simply a pieds-à-terre until construction completes on your primary residence in Knightsbridge."

"How did you know?"

"What else would you do with all the quid you're raking in off Jaxon Muse?"

Perry considered the lights of the skyline. "I'll have you know I work bloody hard for my measly ten percent. If it was up to him to manage who he was, he'd be nobody."

"You don't say…" Dorothy floated an air of incredulity.

"I need a new job title, that's what I need," complained Perry. "I'm much more than an agent, really. I'm publicist, master of ceremonies, researcher, wet nurse, you name it. That reminds me, did you get my post?"

"I assumed that's why you rang me up."

Perry acted crushed. "You didn't want to hear about the endless party I'm having over here?"

"I'm so jealous already, what's the point?"

"Well, I'm glad you have things in perspective. Now, about that post, could you make hide or hair of it?"

"It was clear enough, although I can't imagine someone like Gianna

Chase worrying herself over wooden effigies. I guess when one gets to that level of stardom, we can expect to see all sorts of wonky indulgences."

"That may be true, but don't spread it around." Perry grew more serious. "I don't have to remind you about client confidentiality."

"Oh, is Gianna my client now?" Dorothy's surprised innocence was thin.

"I'm referring to Jaxon and me as you're quite aware."

"Let me get this straight; I'm bound by your agreements?"

"You know what I mean."

"Yes I do. At least one of us understands…"

"What?"

"Why talk about clients at all? What happened to family? Brothers and sisters do favors for one another; why bring this up like it's business?"

Perry strolled his flat like a caged animal. "Jaxon Muse *is* my business. Sorry if I appear insensitive to family ties; then again, you could pull your knickers out of your arse and just tell me what you think."

Dorothy demurred, "About you or the wooden effigies?"

Perry chuckled, "I already know you think I'm a wanker; why go there?"

"At least we got that straight."

"So what about it?"

"I'm not sure what you want to know? Should Gianna Chase have one of these wooden statues made up for Suah? Is that it?"

"That's the bottom line, I guess. You're the psychologist; you tell me."

"You forward me one post and expect an answer just like that?"

"Why not?"

Dorothy laughed. "If what I do is that easy, I should set up a drive-through therapy booth."

"Jaxon Muse isn't asking for a diagnosis, just an opinion."

"And if somebody takes action based upon that opinion, who's liable?"

Perry ran his hand back through his hair. "Bloody hell, why do you insist on making the simplest things so difficult?"

"Since when was a little bit of prudence so difficult?"

"Brilliant. One minute you're in a snit about me not acting like family and the next minute you're giving me a lecture about professional malpractice."

"I'm just leery of giving snap opinions in these matters when I know so little about the situation."

"You know enough. You've got ample experience and gut feeling about how these things work. If it was up to me, I'd carve the thing and be done with it. I don't see what all the fuss is about. If her boy likes it and it makes the villagers where he came from happy, why not do it?"

"You could be right," concluded Dorothy. "Then again, what if you're not? What if Suah Chase is truly a prodigious savant with a rare and special gift? No one knows how that comes about or how long it will last. Messing with that now could have unpredictable results."

"I didn't know savants could stop being savants."

"It's happened before."

"And what about this thing they say about his soul being unbalanced? As a rather serious psychologist, you can't be buying into that."

"Many cultures believe that twins share a special bond. It's reasonable to think that a surviving twin might be affected if something happens to sever that connection. Some cultures make a bigger thing out of it than others."

"So it's not whacked…"

"Of course it's not *whacked*!"

"So you're saying it could be a good thing to make the wooden effigy…"

"It might let Suah feel some closure or help him adjust to the world around him—but it could also affect his gift."

"How so?"

"It's quite possible that Suah has his gift partly on account of the death of his twin sister."

"You lost me…"

"A pearl will never form if the oyster isn't exposed to the proper irritant. Likewise, the boy's perceived unbalanced state may be part of the psychological dynamic that generates the savant reaction—his gift."

"But his sister is dead; no one can fix that."

"Honestly, no one knows. Some people think savant abilities are the result of unique damage to the central nervous system. Such damage could have happened during a traumatic birth process. But if there are no organic causes, the only thing left may be the one thing we'll never be able to pin down."

"So what's the bottom line?"

"It's possible that tampering with Suah's psychic make-up with a soul-balancing effigy could help him be more well-adjusted…"

"You mean more normal."

"If you want to use that word, OK; I'm not going to have that argument with you. On the other hand, the fact is, he may be special with extraordinary gifts precisely *because* he's different. If they do anything to take away that difference, his gifts may diminish as well."

"So what am I supposed to tell Jaxon?"

"Truth is," admitted Dorothy. "Going through the whole effigy thing now could do a lot of good or it could be very bad. No one knows."

"That's great. The expert opinion is—it could be good or bad."

"I told you why. There might be a way to satisfy the superstition without ruining his savant gifts but there's no way to predict or engineer such a thing. I wouldn't want to try. There'd be no way to predict the outcome."

"Well, in that case, why even go there?"

"Precisely. I see no driving need to satisfy the people of Suah's village, at least not anything worth risking Suah's future over. What would you do if Suah was your child? Would you risk making him worse or him losing his savant gift for a million-in-one shot that he *might* become a normal, well-adjusted child?"

"Many people would. They'd say to do anything else would condemn him to a life that's less than what they had hoped for him. Every parents wants their child to have the fullest life possible."

"But is there only one kind? Who are we to say?"

"There you go again—claiming to be a psychologist but itching to be a philosopher. Spare me the parlor wisdom."

"You got my point; I know you're not *that* dense."

"All right, enough of this. Do me a favor—send me back a post that says you'll need a couple of days to get back to me on this."

"Why?"

"I suspect Jaxon Muse knows a bunch more about what's going on with Ms. Chase, Wyatt Dumashe, and who knows what else. I'd like to know more of it as well but if I answer him too quickly, he'll have no reason other than business to correspond with me."

"Sounds like a gauge of your popularity. OK, fine. Consider it done."

"Oh, and copy Jaxon on your note too. I want him to get the news of the delay from you, not me."

Dorothy had a smile in her voice. "You're right—that would make it much more credible."

"You're so sweet…"

"Not as sweet as those Rusty Nails you've been pounding back."

"Oh yes, that reminds me, the evening is young. I must be going…"

"Behave yourself on King's Road."

"Failed as a philosopher; now failed as a comedienne. Whatever are we going to do with you?"

"Thank heavens, that's not up to you."

CHAPTER 46

The gleaming jet glided out of the clouds and down to earth on a spot of land in a turquoise sea. Jaxon Muse and his motley group had flown into tomorrow only to discover it was 7 a.m. local time. The flight attendant woke up everyone a half hour early to prepare for landing. Some of her passengers were more eager to open their eyes than others.

Suah, Hailey, and Leah were easy to convince to rise and shine. Brody, Jaxon, and Claire needed some extra gentle persuasion. Only one in the group had been up and active without any wakeup call; that was Gris-Gris.

After touchdown, the roar of air-braking soon faded away. Suah scooted across the aisle to see the better view. "Look, a new island to explore!" Kneeling on a couch, he pressed his nose to a porthole.

Brody rubbed his beard's graying stubble then pushed the brim of his faded Fedora up from his eyes. "If I had half your energy, I'd be a danger to myself."

The flight attendant was quick to her duty. "For your safety, please stay in your seats until the plane stops moving."

Suah turned around and sat down; he looked more sheepish than guilty.

Leah smiled and petted Gris-Gris as she watched. "After ten hours in the air, you can't blame him for being anxious."

The flight attendant retained her casual elegance. "Yes, it's going to be a beautiful day for exploring." She stepped away.

"Where exactly can we explore?" asked Hailey of no one in particular. "Do we have to stay on the ranch?"

Brody was amused. "Call me crazy but somehow, 750 acres of prime Caribbean real estate might be enough to satisfy me."

"You don't want to go into town?"

"If they have a town, it's probably there to sell trinkets to cruise ship passengers. Why get into that mess?"

"You never know," countered Hailey.

Brody noted her mischievous smirk. "I know enough to find a nice hammock and a bottle of rye and let my daydreams be all the trouble I get into."

The reference went over Suah's head. "You have trouble with your daydreams?"

Brody flashed Hailey a glance before leaning into Suah. "Yeah, the trouble is, they're only daydreams."

Farther back in the cabin, Claire faced the scenery. "It's so beautiful."

Jaxon leaned in closer at her side. "How did you sleep?"

"Fine. The sleeping pill helped."

"This is the last day I have with Suah; I'll be preoccupied for most of it. I promise, we'll have time starting tomorrow to do whatever you want. Wyatt told Gianna we can stay the whole week."

"I understand."

But Jaxon was conflicted. Suggesting that he needed to wait a day to spend his full time with Claire ran contrary to the fact that their time was running out. There was no way he could do both.

"I don't know why Suah can't stay longer. I only have two days with him and half that time is gone already."

Claire smiled. "Just the other day you didn't think you'd get to see him at all. Now you have a whole day with him."

The jet rolled to a stop and Jaxon relaxed. "You're right; I shouldn't complain. I need to focus on what we have."

She reached out to him to help her up. "Let's go enjoy the ranch."

After a "thank you, bye" to the flight attendant, Suah and Gris-Gris were the first to exit the jet and head down the stairs. Hailey was next followed by Brody holding Leah's arm and helping her to slowly negotiate the steps. Behind them came Jaxon, helping Claire.

At the bottom of the stairs stood a distinguished-looking middle-aged man and woman dressed in casual whites. Behind them were two Range Rovers waiting with open doors. The couple introduced themselves as Henri and Eugénie Sinclair, resident caretakers of Wyatt's ranch. They would also be butler, maid, cook, and chauffeur during the group's stay.

"Welcome," offered Henri. He shook Jaxon's hand as Eugénie smiled and acknowledged Claire with a slight bow of the head. "We have a drive of twenty or thirty minutes, then we'll get you settled in and prepare whatever breakfast you'd like."

Jaxon, Claire, and Leah got in the first car with Henri; Suah, Brody, Hailey, and Gris-Gris went with Eugénie in the second car. The drive through town and into the countryside had everyone checking out the sights.

In the first car, Jaxon and Claire had an interesting discussion with Henri about the ranch's fabled history, purportedly involving pirates. When prompted, Henri volunteered a few veiled references to his own checkered past working as a French merchant marine; but that was eighteen years ago, before he fell in love with Eugénie and became a landlubber.

In the second car, Eugénie enjoyed describing the amenities and possibilities for activities on and around the ranch. Hailey perked up when she heard that ATVs were available for getting around. Suah was charmed by the suggestion that horseback riding might be the way to see the sights in some of the more beautiful and remote sections of the ranch not readily accessible by car.

As they entered ranch property, Suah was the first to notice grazing sheep in the distance. "You have animals here?" he asked.

"Oh, yes," answered Eugénie. "We have quite a few sheep."

"What kind are they?"

"This breed has many names. We call them West African. In Barbados they're called Wiltshire. In other places they're called Pelona, Rojo Africana, or Colombian Woolless."

"How many do you have?" asked Brody.

"Two or three hundred, I think. I lose count."

"Wow," gasped Suah. "You and Henri take care of all of them?"

"No, no..." laughed Eugénie. "There's a livestock foreman and he hires seasonal ranch hands to take care of the sheep. Actually, over the past couple of weeks, they've been rounding up some for sale; it's the seasonal thinning of the herd. Henri and I don't follow it that much; we stay pretty well occupied about the house for the most part."

And what a house it was. Perched on a tabletop viewpoint, it would be underwhelming and inaccurate to call such a marvel a ranch house. Three stories in places, with spires and balconies and character to spare, Wyatt's custom residence on the island was a showpiece of inspiring architecture and the kind of ready comforts permitted only when cost wasn't a consideration.

The Range Rovers pulled around the entryway courtyard and parked near the central fountain. As everyone got out, Eugénie led the way into the house while Henri tended the luggage.

Brody nudged Suah and pointed out a large lighthouse-like appendage jutting up from the end of the house that faced the ocean. "You won't see that at the Ritz Carlton."

Suah gazed up at it. "You think it lights up at night?"

Brody considered the bevel etchings and curve of the 360° windows. "I bet it'll do whatever you want it to do."

One by one, Eugénie showed everyone to their rooms. It didn't take long to settle in when it meant acclimating to such luxury. After breakfast, each went their own way to explore the parts of the house they hadn't seen. There was the Great Room overlooking the back esplanade with pool and spa. For quiet reflection, there was the study and library with its wide solarium sitting room. And on the second floor was the party room, one end of which featured an elaborate spiral staircase that led up to the top of the lighthouse, the highest point in the house.

Coming back from the solarium, Jaxon and Claire passed Hailey on her way out. Jaxon noticed she had made a quick change into shorts and bikini top. Hailey's eagerness to be out and about after the long flight was understandable; still, Jaxon was interested to know what she was planning.

"Where are you going?"

"Did you look at the map of this place? There's a beach cove just down the hill from here. I'm going to take one of the ATVs and check it out."

"Is the cove part of the ranch?" asked Jaxon.

"Yeah, sure, it's on the property. It's private. Eugénie says it's beautiful."

"All right," agreed Jaxon. "But no off-road hotdogging, OK? It's easy to turn over on those things."

"I'll stay on the trails," promised Hailey. "I'll be fine."

Hailey started to scamper off but Jaxon called after her, "Have you seen Suah anywhere?"

Hailey called back, "Last I heard, he had roped Brody into riding horses."

Before Jaxon could ask more, Hailey was gone.

His frustration was evident to Claire. "What's wrong?"

Jaxon's aggravated stroll led them back to the Great Room. "Why does Suah have to do that now?"

Claire took a seat by the picture window. "He's excited. He just got here. There's plenty of time to talk to him about what went on at the conference."

"No there isn't," insisted Jaxon. The urgency in his voice belied deeper concerns, ones that Claire now saw completely. Seeing him try to hold back so much emotion, she surmised their limited time only meant one thing.

"This isn't all about me, is it?"

Her question went to the heart of the matter. Jaxon felt too raw to carry on with any other excuse for why he had brought her so far from home when the issues confronting them were as near as ever.

"Jaxon, tell me…" she insisted. "Are you trying to get Suah to help me somehow? Why are we really here?"

Jaxon stood at the picture window, convicted. "If there's any possibility, we should take it."

"We came all this way, expecting miracles—for me?"

"Why not? Something is happening with Suah. Haven't you ever wondered why it's happening around us now, at this time? There has to be a reason for it."

"You dragged all of us 6300 miles to have Suah do a healing for me?"

"I had to try!"

"But why this way?"

"It's the way Gianna wanted it. It was convenient for her."

"And what about Brody, and Leah, even bringing the dog? Don't you see how crazy this is?"

"I told you, Suah wanted them to come. Gianna said I had to meet his conditions. It's what I had to do if I wanted to talk to him."

"What else did you have to agree to?"

"What does it matter? I agreed and that's fine; I'm not complaining. But now that we're here, I want to get on with it and try to get you some help."

Claire looked weary and shook her head. "Oh, Jaxon, I appreciate the thought—I really do, but all the same, don't you see how sad it is?"

Jaxon dropped down next to her. "Why? It gives us hope."

"Really? Like the hope the advanced protocol gives us?"

"It's not like that at all," insisted Jaxon.

"When Vincent first suggested the protocol, you were against it—I know why. I'm not blind. You're against it because you think it's admitting defeat; it's grasping at straws. It's saying that nothing else can be done; the only thing left is an experimental drug, a shot in the dark."

"The drug is unproven but we've seen Suah heal more than once. Turning to him for help is not admitting defeat."

"Hoping for miracles isn't admitting defeat? Would you have gone through all of this to get me here if we weren't grasping at straws?"

Jaxon said nothing because he couldn't answer honestly.

Claire patted his hand. "Bring me my morning pill. It's time."

Not knowing what else to say, Jaxon stood and left the room. He climbed the stairs and went into the en suite bathroom adjoining their bedroom. There he unzipped his toiletry case, took out an aspirin bottle and got one aspirin.

He stared up at himself in the mirror for a minute and considered the options left. Claire reasoned that banking on Suah's healing powers to save her was a hopeless last resort. Jaxon thought the same about the advanced protocol. Maybe both were so, but he had to have hope in something.

He took her the aspirin.

CHAPTER 47

Brody was first to reach the ridgeline and found the view well worth the trip. He pulled back on the reins and his ambling horse came to a halt.

"Let's stop here." Not waiting for an answer, he dismounted.

Suah brought up the rear on a smaller horse with Gris-Gris tagging along. He stretched up in the saddle to see what Brody was seeing.

"Whoa! Look at all of them…"

Rolling pastures spread out below, leading to the sea. Upon a fertile carpet of green grazed dozens of sheep. Many of them stood perfectly still with heads bowed into the grass. Others moved slowly or in small groups. The faint sound from bells hanging around their necks drew Suah's attention.

He chuckled, "They like music when they eat."

Brody helped Suah off the horse. "Sheep music; it's mildly pleasant but monotonous. That's why we don't see any of them dancing."

Suah laughed, "I'd like to see dancing sheep; how 'bout you?"

"It certainly wouldn't be the two-step, now would it?" Brody took off a small backpack filled with water and snacks and set it on the ground.

Suah stepped to the ridge with Gris-Gris by his side and took in the pasture's full expanse. "It's good they don't have to grow food here…"

"The sheep are food," Brody corrected.

"If they grew plants, the sheep would eat them," explained Suah.

"You're talking about a farm. This is a ranch."

Brody unzipped the backpack to get bottles of water. He gave one to Suah who sat down cross-legged and took a swig. Suah leaned over and checked the backpack for a pad of paper he had put in there earlier.

He handed the pad to Brody. "You know what I would really like?"

"Can't imagine."

"A drawing of the horses. Could you draw one for me?"

Brody took the pad handed him but was uninspired. "Right now?"

"I could take a picture if I had my camera but a picture isn't like a drawing. A drawing shows more than a picture."

Suah's reasoning appealed to Brody's veiled artistic sensibility. He relented, "Oh, all right, but nothing fancy. Two horses on the hill; that's it."

"Great!" smiled Suah. He turned to the view. The open range connected with him in ways that said home. A reverie of a far away past came over him.

"We grew things when I was little, but it wasn't a farm. My job was to keep the birds and goats off the plants we were growing."

"How would you do that?"

"I'd run into the fields and scare them away. I did that all day."

"Sounds about as boring as what I do most the time," answered Brody.

"Hawa and I made a game of it."

"Hawa?" Brody glanced over at the horses and sketched away.

"Yes, she's the same age as me. We'd run and see who could scare away the animals first. We did that a lot."

"Who usually won the game?"

"I did. The birds and goats would ignore her or she'd stop too much to watch other birds in the sky. She played other games by herself while she played the game with me. She giggled too much; the goats didn't take her seriously."

Brody grinned and sat on the ground nearby. "How old were you?"

"Four, five years old."

Brody adjusted the hat on his head and lit a cigarette. After a long drag, he squinted at the horizon. "You're lucky; I was never that young."

Suah looked back from the view. "You had to be."

"Not in this universe." Brody's retort was curt.

Suah's mouth gaped. "You're from another universe?"

"No," snapped Brody. He leaned in closer to Suah. "*You* are."

Suah tried to fathom it. "What happened?"

"Wouldn't we all like to know…"

"Don't you know anything?"

Suah's innocent question and its alternate meanings gave Brody pause. He considered other answers before settling on one less telling.

"All I know is, a long time ago, when I was in my twenties, something happened and I wound up in your universe." He blew smoke at the clouds. "Nothing's been the same since."

"What is it supposed to be like?"

Brody flicked ashes into the breeze. "It's hard to explain."

"But it should be different," reasoned Suah.

"Oh yeah, way different." Brody sunk into the feeling.

"That's OK," Suah brightened. "It doesn't take long for *that* to happen."

"For what to happen?"

"Something different. Look at us; yesterday we were 6300 miles away and you were just wasting time." Suah grinned, "Now we're here, wondering if the sheep are going to dance. That's something different. I bet you didn't expect that yesterday."

"You got me there." Brody held his cigarette out and watched it burn.

Suah had fun running with the thought. "Maybe the only way we could get here was going into *another* new universe."

"I don't know about that..." Brody restarted the sketch, filling in landscape around the horses he had drawn.

Suah's wonder was amused. "Maybe every second we're picking which universe we want to step into. If you don't like this universe, then wait a second and step into another one!" Suah laughed.

"Yeah, we should all be able to decide how it works." Brody ground the cigarette in the dirt and changed the subject. "Why did you bring me and Leah on this trip? You even brought that stray dog; that's pretty wild."

Suah's giggle faded with reflection. "I started my adventure with all of you—so I wanted to finish it with all of you."

"What do you mean *finish it*?"

Suah looked to the ocean. "Tomorrow, I'm going back with my mom on the concert tour. We'll be back to the way it was."

Brody chuckled, "I don't know if it's ever going back to the way it was; not after everything that's happened. Not after everything they're saying about you and what you can do."

Suah was pensive. "Why are people surprised when they see things the way they're supposed to be?"

Brody had seen enough news about Suah to know what he meant. "Well, you see, it's this way. When you see something broken, you don't ever expect to see it fly back together again. It's just not the way things happen. It's like time; you can't go back, it's always moving forward."

Suah strained to understand. "Is wasting time the same as other kinds of time. Is there only one kind of time?"

"As far as I know..."

"I heard my mom tell somebody once they were wasting time. She said it was like sitting in one place and what she was trying to do couldn't move forward until they stopped wasting time. That sounds like wasting time is not moving forward. If you're not moving forward, it's a different kind of time."

Brody grinned, "That's a whole lot of confusing right there..."

"If there *are* different universes, why not different kinds of time?"

"If Jaxon Muse was here, he'd tell you anything is possible. Of course, anyone believing that should be riding on the wildest *nutzo-crazy* adventure ever. That's why I don't think any of them really believe it 'cause they seem to be wasting time as much as me. They're sitting around wondering about the way it should be like the rest of us."

Suah felt his reverie deepen; as it deepened, he felt Hawa approach.

"Making things the way they should be doesn't make things fly back together again."

"But that's the way it looks to people," explained Brody.

"Maybe people only think they see things flying back together because they're watching it from the outside and they're moving too. They're caught in *their* kind of time. They don't see what flying back together again *really* is—it's a new moving *forward*, not backwards."

Brody eased back. "You know how I told you thinking too hard about wanting an adventure was a sure way of making it not happen?"

Suah was barely distracted from his thoughts. "Yeah—the more I try to grab it, the faster it squeezes out of my hand."

"You got it. Well, I should have told you—thinking too hard about anything is a sure way of confusing the shit out of yourself. I wouldn't recommend it. It's like trying to grab hold of something that's bigger than your brain."

"Whoa!" The visual had Suah amazed.

"The more you try to grab it, the faster it squeezes out of your head."

"No way!" laughed Suah.

"You'll only get yourself all flummoxed and contradicted…"

"Contradiction…like a *pair-of-socks*?"

"Whatever. The main thing is, you'll look like a sorry pretentious ass while you're doing it. Look at me, I don't try to figure it all out and the world leaves me alone on account of it." Brody handed Suah the finished drawing.

Suah's eyes lit up. "This is great!"

Brody tossed the pen into the backpack. "Some people order up pancakes; you order up two horses on a hill."

Suah handed it back. "Could you name it at the bottom?"

"Name it? Whatever for?"

"All the pictures in the art gallery have names," noted Suah.

"So what?"

"It makes it official."

Brody reached for the pen. "What do you want to call it—*two horses on a hill*?"

Suah knew right away. "No, call it *Reaching Near*."

Brody took back the drawing and added the title at the bottom. "That's an odd name. What does that have to do with two horses?"

"It's the journey they took—a journey from far to near."

"If you say so but it looks to me like they're just standing there." Brody finished it off and handed it back. "There you go."

Suah gazed at it a minute before asking, "How did you figure out you were in a different universe?"

The question came as a surprise to Brody but he fielded it right away. "That's easy. Just look around. Look at what you're doing and not doing every day. If you get a creepy feeling that none of it is what it should have been, that's it—that's when you know it; you're in a different universe."

"Wow," gasped Suah. "I never thought of that before."

"Thought of what?"

"It's not just things here or there that can fly back together the way they should be—a person's whole life can do that too. It would happen to you if you got back to your universe."

"Maybe so; some people get lucky I guess. Stranger things have happened. Look at you. Everyone says that you have a gift, something so special that people can't even believe it."

Suah was astonished. "They can't believe it *because* it's special?"

"That's about it, I suppose."

"But *all* gifts are special; that's why they're given as gifts."

"I don't think they're talking about birthday gifts," grinned Brody.

"What's the difference?" quizzed Suah.

"Don't make me squeeze my brain. Remember what I told you; it'll get messy."

Suah proudly held up the drawing. "You have a gift too. You can do this. I couldn't do this."

Brody scoffed, "That's nothing. You have a real gift, something everyone wants to be a part of."

"It doesn't matter what everyone wants. When I get a birthday gift, I enjoy it no matter if other people like my gift or not. The gift is for me. If someone else doesn't like the gift I got, it doesn't mean I can't keep it and like it, does it?"

"Yeah…so?"

Suah looked down at the drawing. "So if I have a gift, you have a gift too. It's like my birthday gift; it's special even if no one else thinks so. Anyway, you're the one who gets to unwrap it. It's yours. The only way it isn't special is when you don't think it is."

Brody got up and stretched. "Sounds like you've been hanging around with Jaxon Muse too much. You're starting to talk in riddles. Come on, let's head back."

They mounted their horses and settled into a leisurely pace going back down the trail. Gris-Gris trotted around them, sniffing and enjoying the wide open exploration of the open fields. By the time they got back to the ranch house, Suah had talked himself into wanting to go down to the beach.

He had to see if this sand was like the sand on the island back home. Over the years on journeys with Gianna, he'd seen pink sands and black sands, gritty sand and other sand that felt as soft as oatmeal flakes. The more he described it to Brody on the ride back, the more he got himself enthused at the idea that this island might have a new kind of sand to be found.

Brody and him split ways after leaving the stables.

A little while later, Jaxon stopped Brody on his way to the solarium.

"Have you seen Suah?" asked Jaxon.

Brody stepped to the window and pointed at an ATV driven by Leah with Suah on the back, just heading out. "There he goes right there."

Jaxon rushed to the window, gripped with anxiety. "Where's he going?"

"The beach. He wants to study the sand."

"How in the hell did he get Leah to take him there?"

Brody noted Jaxon's dismay with some humor. "I know. Weird, huh? Looks like another miracle."

"No really, how is she even driving that thing in her condition?"

"That's not even the strangest part," added Brody.

Curious, Jaxon turned to Brody as a prompt for an explanation.

Brody rubbed his beard for effect. "From what I hear, she hates the ocean. Won't even look at it. A guy I know back home who lives in the park, he says Lolo comes there every day to have her lunch, but she always sits facing the mountain, never the ocean."

"Does anyone know why?"

"Well, yeah, don't you know? She got crippled—diving into the ocean."

Jaxon looked back out the window and watched the ATV recede. "It's so easy to get stuck on things we think we can't change."

"There's a hell of a lot we can't change. That's the way it is. No one wants to look at their failures or their fears. Who wants to look at pain?"

"Even if it's the one thing we need most?" asked Jaxon.

"People need a lot of things. It never ends." Brody shrugged and walked away, leaving Jaxon standing at the window, waiting for Suah to return.

CHAPTER 48

The dusty trail wound its way down a gentle but constant slope to the sea. The farther Leah and Suah travelled on their ATV, the more lush and dense the foliage filled in on either side of them.

Coconut palms and exotic bushes and flowers had overgrown and narrowed the trail, leaving them with less room to navigate. The lush constriction only added to a feeling of being remote and isolated.

Leah had been taking it slow all the way from the ranch house but now she backed off the accelerator even more. "It's like a jungle down here."

Straddling the seat, Suah sat behind her. The softening of the ATV engine allowed more to be heard. "Listen!" he exclaimed. "I hear the ocean…"

Then and again, the tossing rhythms of the restless surf could be heard even if they couldn't be seen through the trees. Leah followed a curve only to find the end of the trail dead ahead. It was nothing more than a rounded-out clearing and not very big. To their surprise, two other ATVs and a two-stroke motorcycle were already parked there.

"Looks like a popular spot," commented Suah.

Leah slowed to a stop and cut the engine. "Yeah, except this area is part of the ranch. I wonder who's here."

"Maybe it's the neighbors," guessed Suah. He hopped off the ATV and looked around.

Leah made slow and deliberate progress climbing off the ATV and then settled back on it more comfortably. "I don't know; it's a long way for neighbors to come."

Then Suah remembered something. "I know. It must be the ranch hands that take care of the sheep."

"Ranch hands?" Leah sized up the other ATVs; they looked to be the same make and model as the one Suah and her were riding.

"Eugénie told us about them in the car. They're thinning the herd."

"How pleasant," remarked Leah, sarcastically.

"It could be their lunchtime," surmised Suah. He stepped to the edge of the clearing. "This must be the path to get down to the beach. Are you sure you don't want to come along?"

Leah sat, immovable. "No, I told you I'd take you down here but that's all. You want to see the sand, go see it. I'll wait for you here."

Suah sized up the tree-shrouded path snaking its way down. "It really doesn't look that bad. I'll help you if you want."

"Just go," ordered Leah. "And don't take all day. I don't know why you had to do this right now, anyway."

Suah stretched and rotated his arms in play. "I told you. I was talking to Brody and I started thinking about sand. I couldn't stop thinking about it."

"What's the big deal with sand?"

"There's lots of different kinds."

"That doesn't mean you have to see it right now."

Suah stood and listened to the sounds of the breeze and the surf meld together like a voice coming from afar. "*I know...I know*...but when I think that much about something, I know I have to listen to it."

Leah groaned, "I don't know how you talked me into this. I don't even remember what you said. Just go, do whatever you need to do, but hurry up."

Suah thought about saying more but something held him back. He gave Leah one last glance then turned and started down the beach path. The downward slope was dry and well-worn, so much so that repeated footfalls had beaten obvious stepping places into convenient steps.

A jaunty Suah, full of the wonder of exploring, made short work out of the descent. Nearing the end of the path, he finally saw shifting water and glistening sand through the trees and bushes.

The full extent of the cove, as it came into view, was spectacular; it was a crescent gem of turquoise water sheltered by a set-back rise of jagged cliffs. The wide, arching strip of protected beach was eggshell white and perfectly smooth from the action of insistent winds and endless waves.

Only one spot on the pristine beach was interrupted by any signs of life. Not far from the end of the path, a beach towel had been laid out. T-shirts and a pair of shorts lay in playful disarray nearby where they'd been dropped. Next to them, two bottles wrapped in paper bags were halfway buried in the sand.

Suah reached the beach, clear of all the foliage, and the sound of laughter caught his ear. At first he thought it was a bird call or Hawa singing. Reacting, he looked up from the beach towel and saw three forms frolicking in the waves, two men and a woman.

One man was larger and older than the other, but both men looked to be in their twenties at most. The woman was partially obscured by a white-capped wave as she bounced in and through it. When she came out on the other side of the spray and turned around, Suah could see it was Hailey.

Suah stood enraptured and watched for a while as the three of them played in the surf. First it was a jumping game, each seeing how best they could leap and clear the brunt of the next incoming wave. Once, when Hailey turned her back to the ocean and got blindsided by a rough breaker, the larger man caught her from being swept away by the undertow and helped her back up.

That led to the second game. Even though Hailey had been helped up, she was still unsteady and took time recovering. When the next wave came, the larger man held her steady by the arms until she could catch her breath. Laughing at the silliness of being so blindsided, Hailey's humor signaled she was all right and ready for more play.

When the next wave came, the larger man took hold of her under the arms and lifted her high so her head and shoulders would clear the wave. She got such a kick out of the lift and being able to enjoy the waves so effortlessly, she invited the lifting to continue. It didn't take long until the two men were competing, taking turns lifting her to see who could lift her the highest.

Back and forth the men traded her off between them. The larger man naturally had the advantage on the smaller man. The large man could lift Hailey easily and swing her with ease. The smaller man couldn't compete, which was a delight to the larger man and emboldened him. Keeping Hailey to himself, he started lifting her from behind, but now his hands shifted forward, letting his fingers clutch her bikini top during the lifts.

The first time he did it, Hailey showed a mixture of surprise, amusement, and discomfort. After repeated lifts flipped her bikini top up, exposing her breasts, Hailey started squirming with surprise and discomfort on her face. After one wave knocked them both off balance, she broke away from the larger man and struggled frantically through the water to get to shore.

He chased her out of the water and caught her in a dead run crossing the sand. Clutching her from behind, he dragged her over to the beach towel. Their struggle intensified so rapidly that neither of them noticed Suah standing back by the path watching them.

"Let me go!" clamored Hailey, writhing on the towel as he held her down.

The smaller man sloshed out of the water and jogged up to them. "What are you doing?" he asked the larger man.

"Leave me alone!" ordered the larger man. Pinning Hailey's arms back, he fought to position himself on top of her.

Sensing nothing but trouble, the smaller man took off in a run. He ran right past Suah and tore up the path. Soon after, Suah could hear the two-stroke motorcycle revving up and zooming away.

Suah was left facing the beach and the violence unfolding before his eyes. Hailey was too shocked and distressed to have any voice left to yell. Her efforts to break free were punctuated only by her grunts and panicked whimpers. The large man held her on her back with one hand while he worked on untying his board shorts with the other.

"Come on, you like to play," he heaved over her. "Let's play. Maybe you need more rum to get in the mood."

"Stop it!" was her only response, repeated but ignored.

Suah had an impulse. Without knowing what he intended to do, Suah somehow knew that the time to step forward was now. He walked out on the sand and approached the beach towel. Standing next to the struggling pair, he stood and focused a blank gaze on the face of the larger man.

"Who the hell are you?" the man roared. "Get out of here."

Suah held his ground, his gaze unblinking.

"Did you hear me?" shouted the man. "Leave or I'll mess you up!"

Without moving, Suah maintained eye contact with the man. Suah's insolence enraged the man so much that he jumped up and lunged at Suah. With the full force of a body blow, the man pushed Suah back across the sand with the punch of both hands against his chest. As Suah flung back, Hailey scrambled to her feet and aimed herself for a getaway up the path.

With Suah recovering in the sand a good distance away, the larger man took off after Hailey. The chase was brief. He caught her just as she reached the path, bear-hugged her from behind, and carried her back to the towel.

Dropping her on her hands and knees, he scraped at the small of her back and pulled her bikini bottoms down. Opening his board shorts, he dropped down behind her and brandished his arousal; his impulse to be satisfied became all-consuming. Hailey fought to crawl away but the man held her by the hips. Nearing his goal, the man paid no attention to what Suah was doing.

Suah scampered over to the bottles half-buried in the sand and unscrewed the tops. In one coordinated flourish, Suah upended both bottles and emptied them over the mans' head. Streams of rum poured down over the man's face and into his eyes. As soon as the liquid hit, the man realized what was happening and turned in a blind rage to attack Suah.

Suah spun around and ran down the beach with the man struggling with half-lowered board shorts to follow. Pulling them up, he ran after Suah at top speed. There was no way Suah was going to outrun him. Suah turned to see how close the man was getting. In the background, Suah could see Hailey running up the path and getting away.

Suah had no choice. The man was between him and the path to the parking area; he was bound to catch up if Suah stayed on the beach. There was only one thing to do. It was time to take a leap of faith and trust in the rising feeling that everything would work out.

Suah ran at full sprint with a wild and happy abandon. He aimed himself at the water, giggling out loud at the adventure of it, and jumped into the waves. It was a leap for joy that Hailey had gotten away. It was a bounding release of moving forward in time, trusting his instincts. It was a soaring expression of gratitude that he could feel himself flow forward so effortlessly into a different kind of time.

He plunged into the water and arrived, it seemed, in another universe. He had no way of knowing if the angered man would follow him into the water. Suah had to assume he would but the eruption of liveliness coursing through Suah assured him he needn't pay it any attention. He sensed a source of rising energy, a power he could tap into for whatever he needed. Diving down, he swam under the waves and out towards the open sea.

Quickly passing the area where the breakers churned the water white and foamy, Suah held his breath and opened his eyes to another world. It was the same world Hailey had introduced him to on their snorkeling trip. Kicking his legs like a scissors, he swept the water aside with a breast stroke and headed between outcrops of reef. His heart was pounding as the push and pull of the tide jostled the world around him. It was like nature herself was breathing alongside him, enfolding him into her arms.

The feeling was electric. And then Hawa whispered in his ear.

"Don't worry...this day is like no other day...just like all the others...
I know...I know you know how to play...Don't hurry...
I-and-I can dance...enjoy yourself to find the way..."

As the tender words resounded, Suah cleared an outcrop of coral and beheld a marvelous sight. It was so marvelous he almost forgot he needed to hold his breath. He wanted to shout and laugh out loud.

There in front of him, perfectly in sync in tandem glide, swam two enormous turtles side by side. All at once, they were as much a revelation as a spectacle. The mottled beauty of their shells, the gentle swish of their flippers mesmerized and shot tingles of elation through Suah. He halted underwater and watched them, astonished by their timely visitation.

He had always wanted to see a turtle close up, for real. As much as he'd tried on the snorkeling trip with Hailey, as much as Lucas had promised that the area they were in was ripe for turtle watching, nothing had happened that day. How peculiar and wonderful it should happen now. He watched them glide away into the dark of deeper waters.

About to burst from holding his breath so long and unable to contain his excitement, Suah rushed to the surface and gasped enough air so he could shout and laugh at the sky. Gulping air, he giggled as he treaded water then turned back to look towards shore. There was no sign of the angered man anywhere; not on the beach, not in the water. Taking it as a good sign, the beach towel was gone. Suah felt it was safe to swim back to shore.

Up above, in the parking area, Leah consoled a traumatized Hailey. Shaking and dizzy with shock and the aftereffects of shots of rum, she needed a calm and compassionate friend to understand and be there for her.

Leah held her arm around Hailey as they sat side by side on the ATV.

"That's it, let it out…deep breaths; try to relax, it's all right now."

Hailey closed her eyes and bowed her head, borderline hysterical. "Oh my God, that was crazy. What was I thinking?"

"It's over now," stressed Leah. "It wasn't your fault."

Hailey started to cry. "Everything was OK for a while…"

"It usually is," noted Leah. "It doesn't take long for things to go bad, believe me. But don't think about it now. Just relax."

Hailey's head jerked up and her eyes opened. "What about Suah! Where is he? I should go down and find him."

"You're not going anywhere," ordered Leah. "Especially down there right now."

Hailey looked down at the tracks from ATV tires in the dirt across the way. "I can't believe he walked right by us. I thought he was going to get both of us for sure."

"He's dumb but not that stupid," sneered Leah. "It's not as private up here, plus it wouldn't be much fun trying to control two of us."

Just then, Suah appeared at the top of the path. He was dripping wet and looked exhilarated. Upon seeing the girls, his excitement turned into concern.

He stepped up to both of them and asked Hailey, "Are you all right?"

Hailey nodded but averted her eyes.

Suah wasn't sure what to say next. He handed Hailey her bikini top and shorts. For the first time since meeting her, she looked embarrassed. She put her top back on and held her shorts in her lap. Shudders of emotion rippled through her breathing.

"Thank you for what you did down there," she offered.

Suah looked around. "Is everybody else gone?"

Leah answered for Hailey. "Yeah, they ran by here and took off."

"Good." It was simple and direct and all Suah really had to say.

To lighten the mood, Leah eyed him up and down and noted the obvious.

"Looks like you took a swim."

"It was a good thing to do..."

Hailey mumbled, "You're not kidding."

"No, really," brightened Suah. "You'll never guess what I saw."

"Where?" asked Hailey.

"Out along the reef. There's turtles out there!"

The change of subject was enough of a distraction to get Hailey to stop shivering. "You went out that far?"

"Like I said, it was a good thing to do!"

Hailey shook her head. "That's just crazy..."

"Going out that far or seeing turtles?" asked Leah.

Hailey murmured, "You don't know the half of it."

Suah explained, "We were on a boat together once. I looked for turtles all day and couldn't find them."

Leah's sneer became a grin. "Of all times, huh?"

Mention of it soured the mood. Leah glanced at Hailey then back to Suah. Leah was just talking; she didn't mean it the way it sounded.

Hailey hugged herself. "Don't say anything about this, OK?"

"You can't be serious." Leah shifted towards her. "Those guys need to be put in jail."

"I don't want my parents to know," confessed Hailey. Her tears started again. "My dad would go ballistic, probably on me, and my mom is too sick—I don't want to worry her with this right now."

"Those guys should get what they deserve." Leah's tone was less forceful, more opinion than a call to arms.

Hailey stood and pulled on her shorts over her bikini bottoms. "It's not worth what it would cause. Please, just let it go. Nothing happened, really."

Leah hesitated then stood and hugged her. "If you say so..."

Suah took Hailey's hand and held it. Slowly, lightly, he patted it with long, sliding touches. He did this for a while before he spoke.

"Will you come back with me sometime and see the turtles?"

Leah expressed her concern. "You expect her to come back here?"

Hailey looked up at Suah. A calm came over her.

Her smile, weak at first, broadened before she nodded.

CHAPTER 49

The ranch house was large enough to swallow up a group of people and still give each person a private alcove for play, study, or solitary reflection. In Hailey's case, the library offered a secluded spot to settle her nerves after the ordeal on the beach. She found the room quiet, with a great view. To top it off, it had one of the most elaborate fish tanks she had ever seen.

Watching the exotic fish was hypnotic and soothing. More importantly, it gave her an excuse to be by herself while sorting out her feelings. The initial shock had worn off but now she needed time to think it through.

The nightmare episode with the ranch hands had left her shaken and unsettled. It became more difficult to avoid the hard questions. What were the limits she'd go to assert herself? Were there any? What was she willing to do to mask whatever feelings she needed to put aside? How could she answer herself when she wouldn't even face the truth of what it all meant?

With Hailey lost in thought, it would have been easy for most people to enter the library without her noticing. But Leah was different. Her slow and methodical limp was too iconic not to catch the ear.

Hailey looked up to confirm she had company.

"I thought I might find you here," announced Leah.

Hailey looked back to the fish tank. "Why?"

"Oh, I don't know; it's a nice place…"

Hailey felt awkward being with anyone. "Checking up on me?"

Leah's pace slowed. "Maybe a little; just wondering how you're doing."

"I'll be OK." Hailey stared at one particular fish.

"I know you probably don't want to talk to anybody now, but when you do, you can talk to me."

"Thanks." Hailey's memory flashed back to the path leading up from the beach. Terrorized and gripped by fear at the visions of terrible violation that could have happened, Hailey's only saving grace had been finding Leah's comforting arms and reassuring words. She had been so nice to her; Hailey felt ashamed. "By the way, I'm sorry," she started.

"Sorry for what?" asked Leah, confused.

"Oh, you know, we didn't talk much on the airplane."

"That's all right."

"No, it was really bitchy of me; I shouldn't have ignored you. I'm sorry."

"I understand," offered Leah. "You didn't know me. Why should you talk to me? It's not like anyone introduced us or anything."

Seeing that Leah held no grudges, Hailey relaxed a bit. "It was kinda strange, you know, with all these different people coming on the trip."

Leah laughed, "Yeah, I read about these celebrities who take a bunch of their friends off on some elaborate vacation and then, all of a sudden, I'm doing it. It's really weird, I mean, who would think this would happen."

Hailey was not quite ready for so much talk. She shied away and began looking at the fish tank again. "I guess anything can happen…"

Hailey's tone belied thoughts of other, more serious things. Leah changed the subject. "This aquarium must have cost a fortune." She examined the recessed way it was inlaid into the bookcase. "I wonder how they fill it."

"Buckets of water from the kitchen." Hailey's flip answer attempted to be droll but fell flat.

Leah couldn't help but zero in on the inaccuracy of the statement. "Oh, they would never fill this with potable water. This is a saltwater tank."

The snap correction got Hailey's attention. "How do you know that?"

"Because these are saltwater fish." Leah pointed them out one by one. "Just look at the variety: Yellow Tank, Chromis, Clownfish, Butterflyfish, Dottyback, Sweettip, oh, and there's a Brackish one over there…"

"Do you have an aquarium at home?"

Leah grew more somber. "No, Mrs. Gorst doesn't like that kind of thing."

"Who's that?"

"The lady I live with. She thinks fish tanks take too much maintenance. I told her I'd take care of it but she worries the thing will bust and ruin her antique carpets. If you ask me, they could use a good washing."

"So where'd you learn so much about fish?"

"At school. In another life, I was going to be a marine biologist."

"Sounds like you still could be; you lit up naming those fish."

"Maybe in another universe," mused Leah, defensively. She rushed to make light of Hailey's suggestion. "I'm waiting for someone to invent a new kind of space or time travel first."

"What does that have to do with it?" asked Hailey.

"Oh, it's a long story. Some things you don't want to talk about; you know how it goes." The reference to Hailey's recent experience was obvious in a way that expressed shared pain and a mutual need to respect each other's privacy in some matters.

Hailey let it go. "I was thinking of going outside, maybe trying out the pool. Wanna come?"

The suggestion of being near any kind of water into which one could dive induced automatic panic in Leah. She flinched, "Oh, no, I don't think so."

"You don't have to go in or anything," negotiated Hailey. "I just really would like some company right now, if you don't mind."

"Well, maybe…maybe some other time."

"You said you'd talk to me when I felt like I wanted to talk."

Leah remembered her promise. "OK, I'll think about it."

"Great. I'll get changed…" Hailey started to go.

"Why do you have to change?"

Suddenly awkward, Hailey stumbled over her answer. "Ah…I wanna wear a different suit. I'll meet you back here."

Before Leah could ask more or excuse herself from going to the pool, Hailey had hurried from the room. Leah was left in the empty library with the ebb and flow of her thoughts. It was telling that Hailey wanted to change bathing suits. Avoidance was a tactic Leah knew all too well.

Leah turned back to the fish tank. She betted herself that Hailey would never wear that swimsuit again. It might only be a simple cut-out of fabric; it made no difference. Some energies, once evoked, simply had to be shunned.

A restless Jaxon Muse roamed the ranch house's second floor. The sound of racked billiard balls breaking into a run on a green-felt tabletop punctured the silence. Jaxon changed direction and headed for the party room. There he found Brody standing in his usual daytime uniform: flip flops, khaki shorts, and a dingy, loose-fitting shirt. For once, the Fedora hat was not on his head; instead, it adorned a pair of animal antlers hanging from the wall.

"Is Suah around?" asked Jaxon.

"That boy is unbalanced," declared Brody. He wielded a pool cue like a natural appendage and sized up another game of solitary eight-ball.

After waiting during hours of horseback riding, Jaxon had little patience. "What did you do with him?"

Brody chalked the tip of his cue then pointed with it. "The lighthouse. You have to be unbalanced to pass up a game like this to climb up there."

Jaxon hurried on by. "Thanks."

Brody took note of Jaxon's lack of island cool. "Don't mention it."

At the other end of the expansive room, the spiral of the lighthouse steps led up into a well of light that jutted through the ceiling. Despite any frustrations and worries, this was Jaxon's first climb into the lighthouse and he couldn't help but be impressed with the attention to detail and the sheer novelty of such a feature in the house.

At the top of the stairs, Jaxon found Suah looking through a telescope. Besides relief at finally finding the boy, Jaxon took a second to be amazed at the marvelous structure around him. Added to that was the incredible view beyond the 360° windows.

Brass-plated fixtures and beveled glass panes ringed Jaxon and Suah in splendor. Above where the curving steps ended, the central core of the spiral staircase was topped by what looked like a legitimate lighthouse light, one that could easily reach ships at sea at night if it was ever turned on.

"There you are." Jaxon announced his presence after forcing a calm.

Suah turned from the telescope. "Hi, Jaxon!"

"This is quite a place, isn't it?"

"Lots of fun. You should have gone horseback riding with us."

Jaxon was anxious to get on topic. "I would've liked that but you know, Claire can't do things like that. I wouldn't want to leave her here by herself."

"It's nice the house is so big. There's lots to do even if you stay in the house."

"That's for sure." Jaxon gazed into the view. "So what are you seeing out there?"

"Lots of things. I like looking at the boats the best."

Jaxon sized up the telescope's power. "Any nice ones?"

"Here, take a look." Suah stepped aside.

Jaxon leaned down to the eyepiece and surveyed the distance until a boat with full sails came into view. "You aren't kidding; this thing's great."

Suah gazed down at the pool cabana in the yard below. "But it's no good for things in the yard." Suah laughed, "Looking at somebody down there would be like looking up their nose."

"Oh, yeah, the yard would definitely be too near for this…" Through the lens, Jaxon watched as a man brought a woman a drink while she sunbathed on deck. "…But far away stuff, wow—this is amazing."

"So you think it's OK to use it?"

"Sure, why not?"

Suah considered the distance. "I don't think the people on the boats know we're watching them; they're so far away."

Jaxon raised up, hit by a twinge of moral ambiguity. For the sake of Suah and the avoidance of a much too involved conversation, he rationalized. "It's not like they're in their own houses; they're out in public."

"Don't some people live on their boats?"

"Yes, but that's not what I mean."

"I like to people-watch," admitted Suah. Innocently enough, the statement incriminated Jaxon for what he was just doing.

Jaxon claimed the elder ground. "Everyone does. We like the variety, the differences we see in others."

"Why? Are we trying to figure them out?"

"No, that's not the main reason. Strange as it might sound, our differences remind us how we're all connected."

"How does that work?"

"Well, we think we're attracted to the differences between us. But once our attention focuses, we start to see below all of that. In a deeper way, we realize how much alike we really are."

"You think we're all alike?"

Jaxon couldn't help but fall into his philosophy of life. After so many years lecturing and writing books on such topics, it was natural to draw upon his professional reservoir of understanding. "Yes, we're all connected. We share a common nature, a universal energy of spirit that binds us to eternity."

"You sound like you're back at the conference," grinned Suah.

Jaxon snapped back to casual mode. "I guess you're right. Sorry."

"It doesn't bother me. It's just a lot to remember. Maybe if you said it slower."

Jaxon nodded. "Good idea. I'll have to try that."

"When Lolo—I mean Leah and I heard you talk, I really tried to listen. It's good you talk through speakers. It helps, but only with some of it."

As always, Claire surged to the forefront of Jaxon's thoughts. "I'm not sure you need to hear any of that. You seem to understand so much without needing to put it into words. Look at the way you helped that woman."

Suah considered it. "*You* were the one talking about *the way things should be*. I'm surprised you're surprised by it."

"Faith is a funny thing," confessed Jaxon. "Reaching for something is never the same as being certain what you reach for is really there."

Suah looked confused. "So which one? Are you certain or have faith?"

Jaxon wavered; he felt exposed, as if inadvertently Suah had turned the telescope onto him and a private side of his doubts was there for all to see.

Vulnerability drove him to be honest. "Maybe I'm not certain I even have faith. With some things you have to be certain, it's all part of it, otherwise when you reach, nothing will be there. It's what they call a paradox."

"Oh, I know all about those," Suah was quick to agree.

"Maybe that's where hope comes in. I still hope for Claire. I hope I will see her tomorrow and the day after…"

"Hope is the easy part," declared Suah. "At least that's what my teacher used to tell me."

"She talked about hope?"

Suah nodded. "She said hope is more perfect than any wish could ever be. The heart can be fooled, but the place where hope comes from is never wrong and never selfish. It's not like making a wish after blowing out the candles on your birthday cake. It's so much better."

Jaxon was amused. "And your teacher said it's easy."

"Oh, yeah. It's like what you said that day at the conference."

"You remember something from that? I thought I spoke too fast."

"Most of the time," Suah qualified. "One thing I remember. Maybe because when I heard it, it came through like I'd heard it before."

"What is it?"

"You said *we are the magic we're looking for.*"

"That's right," agreed Jaxon. "I remember saying that."

Suah shrugged. "Well, that's why hope is easy. My teacher said it comes from us and it's always with us. Like you said, we are the magic."

Jaxon stepped closer. "But you have a different kind of magic. Your magic heals."

"Hawa told me once that magic is like a flashlight. You can make it shine on different things, but it's always the same light making you see."

Jaxon grew impatient. "What does that mean?"

A calmness came over Suah; it was a kind of knowing serenity that often heralded a communion with Hawa. Suah looked up at Jaxon in wonder. A rushing cloud moved on in the sky and sunlight returned. Through the many bevels in the surrounding glass, dozens of pinpoint rainbows flooded the lighthouse chamber. Suah dropped into trance.

"You shine your light on hope and keep it there,
no matter how far away you have to reach for it.
You hold it there, when the light you make is so very near.
You miss so much that's possible in the surrounding darkness,
when all you have to do is follow yourself to find the way."

The words, the rainbows, the moment lost to emotion were too much for Jaxon. Silently, he cried. "All I want is for you to help Claire. You've done so much already, so effortlessly. You make miracles!" Reaching out, Jaxon took Suah by the arms and cried out, "Can't you make one for her?"

"Your wish is for a miracle?" asked Suah.

"That is my hope—my prayer. I know you can do it. I have faith in you."

"Maybe hoping for something isn't the same as being certain what you hope for is really there. Can you have faith in anything else?"

"You're talking in circles," exclaimed Jaxon. "This isn't a game of semantics. A life is at stake! Claire will die if she doesn't get help."

Suah's honesty was unintentionally unmerciful. "You're the one everyone goes to for *Helf Selp*. I don't feel it's my place."

"But I can't do this!" shouted Jaxon. "I can only do what I do, no more."

"I'm sorry you're sad but everyone is like that."

"Like what?" demanded Jaxon.

"Everyone can only do what they do. Everyone's magic is their own."

"But how do you heal? If you can't or you don't want to heal Claire, at least tell me how it's done! This is her one chance. I can't let it slip away."

"How can you say there's only one chance?" asked Suah. "Isn't that living with a belief that is far less than what's possible? I thought you called that *the near-life experience*."

The reference hit Jaxon at a place that left his mind blank but his heart full. The verdict had come down. Could it be he was acting out the perfect example of what he had warned the world about in books and lectures?

It didn't make sense but Jaxon had to keep the conversation going; he could see that Suah was still in trance. Who knew what person or thing Jaxon was really talking with. Was it Suah's savant subconscious coming through as a lucid daydream? Was it Hawa being channeled from another realm? Maybe it was something far more exotic and improbable? It didn't matter in the moment. Jaxon wanted answers but more than that, he needed help.

Before Jaxon could regroup, Suah became uncharacteristically eloquent and lyrical once again. As he spoke, Jaxon realized another part of Suah's gift. It was his ability to penetrate the fog of knowing with the clarity and infinite potential found in a rational yet empty space of mind.

"On TV once, I saw a show about a beautiful island," started Suah. "It has peaks and valleys, beaches and tall mountains. In the tall mountains, there are gigantic waterfalls so high that the water evaporates as it falls. By the time it gets all the way down, there's no water left to hit the ground. People stand under this waterfall and don't get wet. The island really exists. It's in the Marquesas. It's called Mystic Island. The native people call it *Nuku Hiva…*"

Jaxon chilled at being startled. The name *Nuku Hiva* was familiar, too familiar. It was the name of the room at *The Manuia Resort* where he'd given his conference. How could Suah know so much about that? How had he ever made the connection? A strange attractor of synchronicity was at play.

Suah continued, "...You are standing here and not even getting wet. You think there's only one chance. But miracles are happening everywhere all the time; they're flowing down constantly from above. I can't be everywhere doing them; somebody else must be doing them too!"

"What are you talking about?" frowned Jaxon.

Suah pointed down into the yard. "Look..."

Jaxon turned to the glass. In the yard below, Hailey and Leah were laughing and splashing in the shallow end of the pool.

Jaxon gasped, "Leah hates the water, she won't even look at it."

"And Hailey has a new friend," added Suah. "From a distance, somebody else might not see the miracle that is—but we know different, don't we."

Jaxon watched the girls play. "That's crazy. What's got into them?"

"Some want to be healed; others need to be cured. Only we see the difference when we're near enough to reach it."

"I just want Claire well again. I need to understand how to make that so."

"A sunrise doesn't need any explanation, not if all you want to do is reproduce it."

Transfixed on the action in the pool, Jaxon sunk back into his doubts. "I'm not talking about a sunrise, damn it!"

"So why shine your flashlight into one?"

"What does that mean?" Jaxon gripped the brass railing. "You're lost in too many symbols. After a while, *none* of it makes sense."

Suah laid his hand on top of Jaxon's hand and held it there. "When it all falls away, then you'll be ready."

"By then, Claire will be gone. I'll have nothing left."

"You talked about Lao Tzu. Remember what he said?"

Jaxon thought back to the conference. The quote came back to him. "'If you realize that all things change, there's nothing you will try to hold on to. If you're not afraid of dying, there's nothing you cannot achieve.'"

"That's right."

Jaxon's eyes flooded with tears. "But *I'm* not the one dying!"

Suah stepped away and started down the steps towards the party room. As he made his descent, the words trailed off. "It only seems that way."

CHAPTER **50**

Evening passed into night as a fading memory of desperate last hopes for a miraculous resolution. The last day with Suah was gone. In the morning, Suah would pack all hope of saving Claire with him on his journey to Rome. There was little else to do but let go of the day and sleep.

But there would be no rest for Jaxon Muse.

With everyone else asleep in their rooms, Jaxon prowled the upstairs suite and balcony where Claire fought through a dazed and fitful exhaustion. She was neither awake nor asleep but lost under a haze of pain and sleeping pills. Her condition had taken a turn for the worse in the past two days. Jaxon couldn't escape the self-loathing of thinking that the stress of the very journey meant to save her might have somehow hastened her decline.

He paced the darkness. The surrounding night beyond the balcony was unfamiliar in so many ways. Its blackness led to foreign spaces, but even more disturbing, it pressed on him, reminding him of a relentless passage of time that was slowly tugging Claire into it. Soon she would disappear. If one listened to the night, everything Jaxon heard whispered such was inevitable.

Tomorrow would come; he couldn't hold it back. What would he do then? What *could* he do? What was left? The advanced protocol? A wing and a prayer and more aspirin? Despair had a way of robbing meaning from everything. If he couldn't find meaning in any of it, how would he ever find his way out? How would he face the hardest question of all—how would he go on without Claire?

The strain of another long trip, one that took them back home, might be too much for her—it *would* be too much for her, he was certain of that now. Wyatt had given them the ranch for a week. Now that Suah was leaving, now that the miracle had passed them by, their options were limited.

Claire liked the natural beauty of the ranch. If nothing else, they would have that as some comfort. Reacting to the thought, Jaxon fumed. Him trying to cherry-pick positives out of the situation was worse than dishonest; it was pathetic. Jaxon felt sick. Regardless what his whole life's work had told him, despite the messages veiled in Suah's trance, practical wisdom now said that all hopes for something glorious happening wouldn't survive the new day.

Jaxon stood at the end of the balcony and stared into dispassionate night enveloping the ranch. Nothing in his life had prepared him for this. There was no one to turn to, nothing more to be said. This was the end.

CHAPTER 51

A night without sleep took the edge and the energy out of Jaxon. Unspoken preoccupations not only tormented him, they left him in a state close to sleepwalking. He barely spoke through breakfast. He carried trays up to the suite so Claire could eat in bed but he picked at his food and said little as Claire dallied among light conversation topics. She didn't want to talk about what was happening even if Jaxon couldn't stop thinking about it.

Henri had Suah packed for an early flight. They would have to leave for the airport not long after breakfast. Jaxon knew he needed to say goodbye but after their encounter in the lighthouse the day before, he found it too awkward to approach him and find closure.

After all the plans had fallen through, what else could he say except goodbye and have a good trip? It was so superficial and meaningless to go there but anything deeper would be impossible. Trying to avoid the obvious would be the most noticeable thing of all.

And yet, good manners demanded he say goodbye.

Jaxon sought out Suah to have last words before he took off. He found him on the back esplanade, kneeling and petting Gris-Gris goodbye.

"And so the adventure ends…" Jaxon wondered which part of that sad double entendre did he mean more—Suah returning to a life governed by au pairs or him seeing his hopes for Claire evaporate before his eyes?

Suah looked up from face licks from his good luck charm. "Maybe not; getting a new nanny is going to be a whole new kind of adventure."

"What's her name?" asked Jaxon, keeping it superficial.

"Sandy."

Jaxon shoved hands in pockets and paced over the tiles and into the sunlight. "Oh, you'll have no problem; Sandy's a good name. All the Sandy's I've known have been really nice."

"You've known a lot of Sandy's?" Suah was amazed.

"I meet many people travelling around."

"Like my mom. People are always wanting to meet her."

"You're going to find the same thing. You know that, don't you?"

Suah went back to petting Gris-Gris. "I don't know, maybe."

"You're right about miracles," admitted Jaxon. "They probably happen all the time. The problem is, most people can't see them."

"And if you can't see them, just like magic, they don't happen."

"Maybe so. Maybe cause and effect with miracles works backwards."

"You mean like broken things flying back together again?"

"Perhaps. The point is, there's a lot of people who want to meet you. They need to know what you know, but they don't know how to get there."

"Like you?"

"Yeah, like me." Jaxon thought better of lapsing into a lecture. They didn't have time and he didn't have the energy. "Just be careful out there? I want the best for you. Watch out around crowds, OK?'

Suah nodded. "I had a dream last night. You were in it."

"You sure it was a dream, not a nightmare?"

"It was a nice dream. Really, it wasn't my dream. In my dream, Hawa told me about *her* dream."

"So it was Hawa's dream?"

"Yes. She tells me all her dreams. She thinks there're stories in them, stories that couldn't be told any other way."

"So what was the story last night?"

"We were all with Maadoops, making music. Maadoops is a friend of mine in Jamaica."

"Who was there?" asked Jaxon.

"All of us, but you and Claire were dancing."

Jaxon's chest tightened as he stood in place. He wanted to interrupt and put an end to it but he didn't. Instead, he listened.

Suah continued, "...Maadoops was tired and wanted to stop making music but my grandfather wanted you and Claire to keep dancing."

"So what happened?"

"Hawa isn't sure. She fell asleep."

"But this was her dream..."

"*In her dream* she fell asleep. My grandfather was on one side of her and Maadoops was on the other side. My grandfather whispered in her ear, '*you should see them now.*' After that, Maadoops whispered in her other ear, '*now is the time for Life Everliving.*' She never woke up—until she woke up, if you know what I mean."

Jaxon swallowed on emotion. "That's quite a dream. I can see how Hawa might find stories in it." Jaxon knew Suah didn't mean to be insensitive; it was just a condition of the way he was, a way that was as much different as it was special. So much could be forgiven when one knew the intent was pure.

Henri appeared just as Suah started to say more. "It's time; we better go."

Suah hugged Gris-Gris. "Someday we'll go exploring again. I don't know where; it'll be our surprise. OK?" The tail wagged in full agreement.

All the superficiality Jaxon had promised himself melted away when the moment to depart arrived. He stepped forward and gave Suah a hug. "No matter what happens, it's meant so much to me to have you here."

Suah hugged him then stepped back. "Thanks for ending my adventure in a way that didn't make me try too hard."

"Why would that matter?" asked Jaxon.

"Ask Brody; he'll tell you."

"So Brody is the wise one now." Jaxon forced a grin.

Suah headed for the door with Henri leading him. "Oh yeah, like he told me yesterday, don't believe everything you hear, especially when you're talking to yourself.'" Suah gave a wave. "Bye!"

Jaxon was left alone, standing on the tiles, bathed in sunshine. The warmth of the new day seemed a cruel mockery, a tantalizing reminder of good days and better times that weren't possible anymore.

On his way out, Suah enjoyed hugging and chatting with Leah, Hailey, and Brody. Each in their own way had been touched by the experience of his adventure; in his explorations each had found new territory in themselves.

"I wish you could stay longer," said Leah.

Suah agreed, "Me too. The next time we find a ranch like this, we'll have a reunion party. I'll bring the fireworks."

"Whoa! I can't wait," she grinned.

Hailey stepped up and gave him a hug. As she hugged, she whispered in his ear, "Thanks for being there for me." She stepped back, "We were supposed to go see the turtles; you owe me a turtle trip, remember that."

"Oh, yeah," gasped Suah. "I'll find a way to do that..." He looked up at Brody. "...It's not good to disappoint a mermaid."

Brody's eyebrows raised. "Mermaid, huh?"

Remembering their boat trip, Hailey laughed and even blushed a little, "That's right. I'm the mermaid and he swims like a fish."

"OK, stop there..." Brody held up both hands. "That's getting into too much information, although it explains one thing."

"What?" asked Suah.

"It explains why you walked around for a week, carrying a snorkel and mask and didn't know what the hell to do with it. Fish don't use snorkels. It makes perfect sense now!'""

Suah laughed and the rest caught the giggles.

Brody gave him a slap on the back. "You're a damned fine protégé."

Suah got wide-eyed. "A proto what?"

"A protégé. My initiate in aquatic adventures and beyond. On this last trip together, you've come into your own. You've achieved greatness."

"Wow," beamed Suah.

"That's right. You've mastered the art of wasting time. May it serve you well."

Suah was excited. "Does that mean I get paid for it too?"

"Don't stretch your luck, kid."

Henri stepped in and broke up the conclave. "Sorry to interrupt but it's time to go."

With one last smile and wave, Suah dashed off and got into the waiting Range Rover. A new day had begun but the adventure had ended.

As the excitement of Suah's parting faded, everyone wandered off to find a leisurely way to adjust to what their vacation had become without Suah around. Without Suah to pal around with, Brody found himself tagging along with Hailey and Leah in the direction of the esplanade. The general consensus was that a relaxing discussion out by the pool would be the best way to decide what to do with the day.

On the way there, a fretting Jaxon passed the group. "Has anyone seen my phone?"

Leah and Brody gave shakes of the head but Hailey spoke up.

"I've got mine," she offered.

Jaxon halted but wasn't satisfied. "I don't need to make a call; I'm expecting a message. It's important. Of all times to lose it!"

"I'll call you and see where it rings. I'll find it."

Hailey scampered off, dialing Jaxon's phone as she went. As Jaxon retreated, lost in thought, Leah and Brody continued out to the pool area.

From dining room to kitchen, from party room to library, Hailey marched around the house dialing and listening. It wasn't until she arrived in the solarium and stood perfectly still that she finally heard a familiar buzzing. She found Jaxon's phone wedged between cushions of a wicker couch.

Turning to leave, she paused. The temptation of checking her dad's phone was enticing, especially since he said he was expecting an important message. What if it was from Mom's doctor? Was Jaxon hiding the truth about Mom's condition or treatment options? Maybe it was about Suah or Wyatt Dumashe and the real reason why everyone was hurried to this island.

Seduced by how easy it would be, Hailey rushed Jaxon's phone to a niche in the solarium where she trusted she'd be alone. Quickly, she navigated the phone and noticed an unopened message. Without opening the message, she forwarded it to her own phone then deleted the sent reference to cover her tracks. She switched to her own phone so she could read the message.

She scanned quickly but the mystery only deepened. The message was someone called Dorothy. It was short and didn't say much, just that she'd need a couple days to get back to him on what he wanted.

But what he did want? Who was Dorothy? Hailey had never heard her father mention anyone called Dorothy before. Hailey scrolled down to find there was more to the email thread. Below Dorothy's message was another message Dorothy had received. The second message was about Suah.

Hailey read the short note. It described Suah's dead twin sister affecting him and how a native carving, a twin effigy might be able to heal or bring closure and balance back to him. Should Suah's mother have such a carving made? That was the question for Dorothy.

Hailey paused. This was nothing like what she expected in one of her father's important notes. Was Suah brought to this island in an attempt to heal him somehow? Is that what her father was trying to do? It didn't make sense. All the news said it was the other way around—*Suah* was the healer.

Sensing the other way around shot through Hailey. A revelation hit her. It was now so obvious. In her distracted crusade to ignore her parents and find the latest and wildest fun, Hailey had missed the reason for it all. The message was about healing Suah, but it was now clear that Suah was brought to the ranch to heal Claire. It suddenly made sense; her father's behavior, his preoccupations and passionate need to find and talk with the boy.

Tears clouded Hailey's eyes. The desperateness of her father's quest to reach out to Suah only proved what had been shielded from Hailey up to now. Claire's condition was far worse than she'd been led to believe. Her mom was closer to leaving her forever than she'd ever imagined. All the talk of doctor's and treatments was window dressing hiding a stark and final truth.

Hailey's restless thumbs scrolled the message aimlessly, hopelessly to distraction. As they scrolled, the bottom of the second message came into view. For the first time, she saw who had initiated the email thread, the person who sent the original message to Dorothy. The name popped out, recognizable. It was Perry, her father's agent in London.

As Hailey stared in sadness, another revelation caught her sight. It was barely there but it hit her like a slap in the face. The message to Dorothy had been sent with Perry's personal email address, not the usual work address.

Next to his signature, a small icon personalized the post. It was a stylized version of the letter "P" as a lightning bolt. She recognized it immediately but in a far different context. The "P" stood for Phantom, the nickname of one of the online game players that liked to play *private rules* with her. The last time she had seen that avatar, she had just sent him a winning photo she had taken of herself in her bedroom.

The intense sadness about the revelation about Claire now turned into anger at the intimate intrusion she'd unwittingly invited. She had met Perry on occasion a couple of times, in passing, while on family trips to England.

He was always pleasant; in retrospect, maybe too nice. Now the revulsion was immediate. Added on to everything else, it left her emotionally drained. Focused on herself, Hailey missed the fact that Leah had entered the room.

"Did you find it?" asked Leah.

Startled, Hailey jerked. "Oh! It's you…"

"Are you OK? What is it?"

After the beach ordeal, Hailey had shared much with Leah and she with her. Normally, Hailey wouldn't be this open with anyone but given the circumstances, she couldn't hold back.

"Oh my god…this is bad," confessed Hailey. "I just found out something. It's pretty creepy."

Leah saw the two phones in Hailey's hand and assumed why she was hiding in the solarium. "You read your father's message?"

"It's from my dad's agent. It's not much, something about Suah having a twin who died."

"What's creepy about that?"

"No, it's not that. It's Perry, the guy my dad works with. He's been pretending to be someone else…" Hailey hesitated to say more.

"What? Is he cheating your dad or something?"

"No," admitted Hailey. "I've been playing a game online with him. I didn't know it was him. He's one of the guys I let play by private rules…"

"Private…" Leah said no more. The inference of the word was enough.

"If I win, he sends me money. If he wins, I send him pictures."

"You mean…?"

"Yeah. Stupid, huh?"

"You said you didn't know it was him."

"Sure, but still—he's got those pictures. You should see this guy…"

"You met him?"

"A couple times with my family, at his office. He's an older guy; oh, it just creeps me out!"

"Would it creep you out less if it was somebody your own age?"

"Well, yeah! What do you think?"

"I think it's creepy either way."

"Oh, like you've never sexted before."

Leah was conciliatory. "No, I haven't, but I guess it's no big deal if you keep it anonymous. Is that it?

"It's a game site, what can I tell you..."

"How many people do you play private rules with?"

"I don't know, a few."

"Equally unidentified, I suppose..."

"What is this, the Inquisition?"

"All right, so what happens now?"

Hailey paused. "Right now...I give my dad his phone."

"Is that it? You're not going to tell him?"

"Tell him what, that I snuck into his phone and read his messages?"

"No, tell him about this guy, Perry."

Hailey laughed. "Like I'm sure! Hey Dad, guess what? Your agent's a perv. I know because I send him naked pictures." Hailey started to storm away. "Give me a break."

Leah tried to follow but working her walking stick with her limp made it impossible to keep up. "I didn't mean to upset you."

On the verge of tears, Hailey halted and turned back. "Promise me you won't say anything."

Leah caught up to her. "I promise."

They shared a moment, a look, and understanding between friends.

Hailey went into the bathroom and dried her eyes and waited until her composure returned. Then she found her dad and casually gave him the phone. He was in his bedroom suite, talking to Claire.

"It was in the solarium." She handed him the phone and then turned away quickly to face her mom and give her a kiss. "Hi, Mom."

Claire smiled and raised her hand to touch Hailey's arm. "Another day to have fun, huh?"

Hailey forced a smile. "Yeah, there's lots to do on the ranch."

Claire glanced towards a balcony glowing with morning sunshine. "Maybe later I'll get up and join you. I'd like to see you swim in that pool. I heard you out there yesterday."

"Oh, was I too loud?"

"No, no, no," Claire assured her. "You were fine. I like hearing your laughter. You were with Leah, weren't you?"

"We were just being silly." Hailey glanced back. As she and her mom talked, Jaxon was reading the message on his phone.

Claire lowered her arm back to the top sheet. "Right now, I think I should rest."

Hailey kissed her on the forehead. It was all she could do not to break down and cry. "OK, I'll see you a little later." She hurried from the room.

Claire shifted her gaze onto Jaxon. "Important news?"

Jaxon looked up from his phone then stuffed it in a pocket. "Ah, no, nothing much. Just more delays."

"I think I'll take a nap. Then I want to go down by the pool."

"All right, I'll have Eugénie make you up a nice shady place out there."

Claire grinned, "Trying to make me the shady lady?"

Jaxon got up and kissed her hand. "You're too sweet for that."

Claire tensed as a wave of pain shot through her. She closed her eyes a moment. When she opened them again, her smile was gone. "I'd better take my pill now. I don't know how long I'm going to sleep."

Jaxon made strides across the room. "I'll be right back."

In the bathroom alone, Jaxon opened a drawer and took out his toiletry case. He looked at it for a while before zipping it open. The routine motions came automatic. He reached in, pulled out the bottle of aspirin, popped open the top, and shook one aspirin into his open palm.

It was a hopeful habit repeated many times over the past couple of days. But now with Suah gone, it became an empty ritual. Now it was nothing but a symbol of what a mockery hope had become.

He tossed the aspirin back into the bottle and jammed the cap back on with unnecessary force. Dropping the bottle back in the toiletry case, he zipped it closed. Then he reached farther back in the drawer and pulled out another pill case, one with a prescription label on it.

He held the advanced protocol case in his hand for a while, long enough to wonder in a thousand ways why it had ever come to this. His heart sank to open the lid but after he did, the genie of no return seem to escape from the bottle. The feeling of it grated around him and left him raw. Nothing in his life had made him question himself and what he believed more than the simple action of opening that one prescription bottle.

He shook a single pill of advance protocol into his hand.

As he stared at it, future time and the glorious Earth all slipped away.

CHAPTER 52

A rising chaos was in view from any window of the Royal Suite or adjoining rooms occupied by the concert entourage. Gianna Chase stared down into the *Piazza della Repubblica* and listened as her business manager lost patience with yet another city official riled into yammering on the phone.

"I'm quite aware of your situation; I would hope you would consider mine." Olivia paced with phone pressed to ear and hand on hip. "No, I don't have that information. Ms. Chase has limited staff. Most of them are at *Olympic Stadium*, preparing for her concert…"

The man interrupted her with another tirade. Olivia halted and watched Gianna give her an irksome glance. Back at the window, Gianna watched below as a throng of people clogged city arteries. Both eager fans and solemn pilgrims gathered at the *Fountain of the Naiads*. By sheer numbers alone they had occupied it as their base of operations for an ongoing vigil.

Word had gotten out. *Suah the Healer* had arrived in Rome. He was being rushed under heavy guard to a reunion with his adopted mother. By now, media outlets had leaked the location where they'd be staying: the *St. Regis Grand Hotel*, in the heart of the city surrounded by busy historic sites.

The fact that Suah Chase was seen getting off Wyatt Dumashe's private jet at *Leonardo da Vinci-Fiumicino Airport* only intensified the frenzied speculation. Especially when cell phone video taken by a baggage handler was bought by a local television station and confirmed the story.

"That won't be possible," snapped Olivia into the phone. "All I need is your assurance that a police escort will be provided for Ms. Chase from the *St. Regis* to *Olympic Stadium* within the hour."

For a moment, Olivia held the phone away from her ear in a show of frustration boiling into resignation. Having enough of her plight, Gianna marched from the window and reached out.

"Give me that." Gianna snatched the phone from Olivia and strutted back to the window. Olivia sat down. Already exhausted, with the concert still hours away, she was content listening to Gianna's side of the conversation. In between outbursts, there were only a few electric pauses in which Gianna allowed the man to speak.

"Who am I talking to? That's right, this is Gianna Chase. I take it you have some problem with all the attention your city is getting. I find it unconscionable you have the blatant insensitivity to complain about a mother wanting to be with her child. That's what's going on here..."

Gianna marched to the window and flipped the curtain back so she could see out. "The dreadful behavior of the people in your city is not my responsibility. Neither is your lack of preparedness. You knew well in advance that my concert was coming to town. Unless you are deaf, blind, *and* dumb, you also know the media is creating a circus around my son. Why aren't you on the phone, complaining to them? They're the ones who've pumped this up to be ridiculous..."

Turning back to the suite, Gianna paced by sumptuous antique furniture plush with opulent silk brocades and gilt edges. Her silence was brief.

"I'm surprised, for a city official, how you can be so unstable *and* shortsighted. I would think you'd realize how much revenue the concert and all this publicity means for the city and be thankful..."

Nearby, a hand-painted fresco depicting one of the monuments of the Eternal City adorned the wall. Gianna gazed into it but only saw red.

"If your attitude and the situation don't improve immediately, I'll be forced to direct my business manager to ignore Rome and make Florence my destination for future concerts. I won't be bashful letting the world know why. I leave for the stadium within the hour. I realize it's six kilometers away; that can't be helped. Unless you want a riot on your hands, I suggest you provide an escort."

Gianna listened as she walked the phone back to Olivia. This time the pause was longer. "Very well. I appreciate a man who can be reasoned with. This is difficult for all of us but everyone has something to gain. Before you know it, we'll be gone. Then you'll be courting us to come back..." For the first time, Gianna grinned. "*Affare fatto. Grazie!*"

The conversation ended, apparently well. It was a surprise to everyone.

Olivia knew enough Italian to translate Gianna's last words into *it's a deal, thanks*. She accepted her phone back from an energized Gianna.

"So what's the deal?"

Gianna was still worked up. "He'll pull his head out of his ass if we minimize our public appearances; basically, he wants us to stay put in the hotel after the concert."

Olivia slumped to one side. "That's what we were planning anyway."

Gianna sat down. "He doesn't have to know that."

"In a way, you can't blame him," admitted Olivia. "No one expected the pandemonium going on outside. The *Piazza* is completely blocked, it's a mess around the stadium, and the motorway from the airport is shut down with cars crowding on hoping to see the motorcade."

"They aren't still going that way, are they?"

"They can't. That's what's taking so long to get him here. Alternate routes are turning out just as bad. It doesn't take long to tweet somebody a new location. Spectators are tracking the thing minute by minute."

Unable to stay in one place, Gianna jumped up and paced. "I just wish he'd get here. I'd want some time with him before we leave for the stadium."

"Where's Sandy?"

"Prepping the Imperial Twin guest room for him."

"How's *she* reacting to all of this?"

Gianna looked to the ceiling for deliverance. "It must be like getting all dressed up with your hair just right and being pushed into a wind tunnel?"

"That bad?" smirked Olivia

"The first day at work, from hell."

"Look at it this way. If she survives her initiation over the next few days, you'll have one hell of a nanny. She'll be ready for anything."

"You think all of this will be over by then?"

Olivia dropped her gaze. "No, but maybe she'll be used to it."

"Like us? We'd better learn from this and prepare for Paris."

"If anyone's wiser, I hope it's the Parisian authorities."

"Tomorrow afternoon isn't far away. They don't have much time."

Gianna stepped to the doorway into the next room. Amidst frescos and delicate brocades, a flatscreen TV showed live news reports from helicopters following Suah's motorcade. As the scene shifted to Steadicam shots from motorcycles giving chase, Gianna's mood darkened. Her murmur was private but loud enough to be heard. "Am I doing the right thing?"

"Don't second guess yourself now," answered Olivia. "The time for that is at the top or bottom of the hill—not while racing down."

"I knew it was going to be different, but not like this. This is nothing like before." Gianna's flat statement intimated something newly realized.

Olivia knew Gianna well enough to worry if her mood fluctuated too much before a concert. "We can't judge everything by right now; we knew this would be the roughest part but it can't be helped. Hiding away would only make things worse."

The scene on the TV changed. Police had closed down the street out in front of the hotel and cleared it for Suah's arrival. On the bottom of the screen, the hotel's location was clearly shown—*Via Vittorio E. Orlando*.

Gianna watched as a reporter worked the barricades with microphone in hand and elicited comments from the impatient crowd.

"I want him with me but how is this going to work out for him?"

"You're doing everything, providing the best," answered Olivia.

"But he and Sandy won't be able to go out or do anything, even if they take the guards. He can't spend the rest of his life locked in hotel rooms, no matter how large and lavish they are."

Olivia's phone rang. She ignored it long enough to answer Gianna. "The teaser tour has less than two weeks to go. By the time the larger summer tour rolls around, things will have calmed down. You'll see."

As Olivia answered her phone, Gianna noticed that Sandy had entered the room. She turned to talk with her.

Sandy was a bright and cultured woman in her mid-thirties who enjoyed combining her passions for children and service as a full-time au pair. Despite a professional bearing, it was obvious that finding herself in the eye of a media hurricane was unnerving, and this was before Suah's arrival.

"How's everything?" asked Gianna, projecting expectations of positives.

"The connecting suite is all ready, just as you wanted," answered Sandy.

"Suah's personal effects in place?"

"Yes, ma'am."

"He'll come up the diplomatic entrance. They'll use the private elevator to this suite." Gianna forced a calmer, more casual tone and smiled. "I know he's excited about meeting you. You'll be great."

Sandy relaxed a bit. "Thank you."

Gianna could tell how much the woman was overwhelmed at what she had gotten herself into but also how determined she was to make it work.

Gianna touched her arm. "Let me worry about the craziness outside; you concentrate on Suah. If you need anything, don't hesitate to contact anyone on my staff. Did you sync the contact list to your phone?"

"Yes but I'm still memorizing everyone's security call sign. I'm worried I'll mix up the code words and get the guards mad at me."

"Oh yes, on each tour they come up with something new. As long as you get the code for Suah right, that's the main thing. What is it again?"

Sandy answered right away. "*Sirius.*"

"Right. It's easy to remember; Sirius is the brightest star in the sky."

Sandy's opportunity to flatter didn't go wasted. "I should think that would be *your* sign."

"Oh no," corrected Gianna with a smile. "Everything may revolve around me, but Suah will always be the brightest star. I know my place; it's *Polaris.*"

Gianna led Sandy across the room. "They tell me the private kitchen is all stocked. Have you had a chance to check it out?"

"No, not yet. I was thinking of making cookies with Suah after you leave for the concert. Something fun for the two of us to do together."

"Great idea," agreed Gianna. "Go ahead and do whatever you need to do; it's right through there." She pointed the way as Sandy dashed off.

Olivia stepped up, her phone call complete. "That was Ava. They had a security breach at the stadium. A photographer snuck in posing as a worker. One of our crew found him taking pictures inside *The Box*."

The Box, Gianna's private area backstage, was for her rapid costume changes and anything else she needed during a performance. For someone to penetrate so far through three layers of security—Rome police, stadium guards, and Gianna's own staff, only demonstrated how great the rewards had become to elicit such cleverness and determination.

"How are they ever going to manage things when the doors open?" asked Gianna. "Eighty thousand people will pour into that stadium."

Olivia knew it didn't look good but had to sell the intrusion as an aberration. "*Olympic Stadium* handles crowds like this all the time…"

Gianna cut her off. "Then it has to be a problem inside. Someone on our staff may be selling favors. Check into it. Find out anything you can before we get over there."

Olivia concurred by hurrying off.

Gianna's phone rang once before she answered it. "Yes, what is it?"

"Gianna…Wyatt Dumashe. Do you have a minute?"

"Oh, Wyatt, are you watching what's going on?"

"Who isn't? I thought I might catch you before Suah gets there; I know you won't have time later."

Gianna couldn't help but express frustration. "By the time he gets here, I'll have to leave to prep for my concert."

"I know, it's incredible," commiserated Wyatt. "The ride from the airport is taking longer than his flight from the island."

"Did you get through to Muse?"

"No, he hasn't answered the phone. Henri, my man onsite, says he asked for privacy. I think it's best to respect that. He hasn't called you, has he?"

Gianna retreated into the *Royal Suite's* bedroom and sat down on a corner of the bed. "No, only a text message saying he'd be in touch later."

"I thought I should let you know as soon as possible. I got a report back from *The Protoprime Society*. I won't go into all of it now but they are recommending you go ahead and have the twin effigy made. They don't see any real downside to it."

"I appreciate their work and all you've done to coordinate it, but I don't have time for anything other than what I'm dealing with right here."

"Understood. If you want, I can have them research next steps. I can handle the rest of it from there."

"You don't need to get that involved."

"I want to," asserted Wyatt. "I'd be honored to do so."

"I don't mean to sound ungrateful, but why? Why take such a personal interest in this?"

"I'm not sure we have time for me to fully explain. I'll say this. I've been talking with a brilliant man, a scientist. He consults with *The Society* sometimes. He has me wondering if some rumors about Suah may be true."

"Which rumor; there are so many."

"The one about Suah being a new kind of prodigious savant."

"Even if he is, why would that mean so much to you? There are other savants, aren't there?"

"The professional literature documents about one hundred savants classified as prodigious. And yes, finding another one would be exciting, but what's really remarkable concerns the prodigious *talent*. Suah's abilities, if they are what they seem to be, go far beyond what's called 'splinter skills.'"

"It's his level of ability you find fascinating?"

"Actually, no. I'm told most prodigious savants have abilities that go well beyond normally organized and coherent skills. The mind-blowing thing about Suah is the unique category of his talent."

"Which is?"

"He's a *healer*. Imagine that. It's not just rare; it's unprecedented. Fifty percent of all savants have musical talents. Most others have great powers of memory or calculation. But there's never been a documented savant whose unique talent was to heal people. You realize what that means?"

Wyatt's awe and enthusiasm captured Gianna's attention. "What do you think it means?"

"Zeroing in on that is why I got in touch with the consultant at *The Society*. He agrees with me. If we can be certain that healing is Suah's unique savant talent, that might prove that the power to heal is a potential ability within all of us, just like music or math or feats of memory."

"But no one knows how or why savant talents switch on or off."

"No, but we still recognize the talents as natural to the human mind. The level of talent may be extraordinary, but everyone can do a little math or hum a tune or remember their shopping list. In the same way, maybe the power to heal is latent in all of us, something we could develop and master just like we learn to play an instrument or get good at figuring calculus."

Gianna paced around the room. "People have claimed that forever. They're always talking about a grand New Age. There's no science to it."

"Theories need proof. Proofs are the result of rigorous study."

"I'm certainly not going to turn Suah over to some laboratory."

"But to see this in a savant; it could be a sign. If we follow up and give it the right attention, we might be able to shift the whole topic away from something mystical to formalizing it as a true discipline of mind."

"Lots of things sound great. The difficulty is that Suah is a boy who deserves the happiness that a normal life offers."

"Except, what's happening outside is trending the wrong way."

"I'm doing whatever I can to insulate against that."

"And I have resources that can help you with that. The ranches and jets are only some of them."

"Excuse my bluntness but I'm not surrendering Suah to anyone's agenda. He'll tell me what he wants. If it falls in line with what you're saying, fine. Let's give it some time and see where it goes."

"All right, but learning from Suah doesn't have to preclude him having a normal life. *The Society* and I have the means to ensure that. I'm willing to take as long as required, do whatever is necessary, and go at his pace."

"Privately *and* publicly?"

"Yes, I feel that strongly about this. I believe Suah's legacy could be transformative."

"For whom?"

"In the short term, for our understanding of savants and what happens when someone is healed. In the long term, there are those who believe the potential is there to transform the planet."

"I'm not prepared to buy into that. I'm sorry."

"Fair enough. Your son is precious whether he has this gift or not. I'll always respect that. But just like you share your music with the world, Suah should be allowed to share his gift with the world—if he so wishes."

Gianna paused to consider the comparison. She couldn't deny it but she wasn't willing to confirm it either. "Let's see what Jaxon Muse has to say. He had two days with Suah. They were together when all of this started. I don't believe you know how personal the trip to your ranch was for Jaxon."

"In which way," asked Wyatt.

"Jaxon's wife is very sick."

"So that's it. He was trying to get Suah to heal her?"

"Yes. He gave me the impression they had run out of options."

"I'm sorry for them but you must see how incredible that could be! Their time at the ranch could jumpstart everything I've been talking about."

"I'm trusting that you'll respect Jaxon's privacy."

"Of course."

Gianna reacted to sounds from the other room. "I really must go."

"We can talk about this later. I'll work on next steps with the twin effigy. I'll find the best way to have it done. By the way, I heard Jaxon is going to donate two-days' earnings to the village where Suah was born."

"How did you hear that?"

"Does it matter? I only bring it up because I wanted to tell you—I've decided to match whatever he gives."

Gianna halted. "Thank you. I know the village wants to refurbish their school; that will help."

"We might be able to do better than that," added Wyatt. "A community center and some better water management facilities might be a nice addition, don't you think?"

"What makes you say that?"

"The researchers I sent there reported back on the conditions of things."

"If you do that, the village would be so grateful, as would I."

"I'll have plans drawn up. I'll let you know what we come up with."

Gianna smiled. "Now, there's something we can agree on right away."

"Have a great concert. Say hello to Suah for me."

"Will do. Bye." Gianna pocketed her phone and hurried into the adjoining room to see what the commotion was.

Led by hopeful sounds of welcome, Gianna found Suah standing in the foyer surrounded by Olivia, Sandy, and two bodyguards.

"Suah!" cried out Gianna. She hurried in his direction.

He turned and smiled, then ran to her. "Mom!"

"It's so good to see you? Are you OK?"

He hugged her and stepped back. "The ride in the car was long but there was a lot to see. I think I've seen more of Rome than Julius Caesar."

Gianna chuckled then asked, "Did you have fun on the ranch?"

"So much fun! I rode a horse and saw a turtle. I went in the lighthouse and looked at the boats through the telescope. I even rode on an ATV."

"Wow, that sounds great!" smiled Gianna.

One of the bodyguards whispered something to Olivia and she nodded.

"I hate to break up the party," she started. "But your escort is here."

Gianna looked up. "Now? But Suah just got here."

Olivia looked tired. "We really should be getting over to the stadium."

Gianna kept Suah close and stepped towards the new nanny. She asked Suah, "So, you've met Sandy?"

"She showed me my room. All of this looks like some movie set."

"Yes, it's pretty fancy, but that is what's fun about it. You know, I hear you might be doing something in the kitchen pretty quick now."

Suah smiled. "Sandy already told me. We're making cookies."

Gianna squatted down and gave Suah a parting hug. "I wish I could stay and be with you but I've got to go. It's almost time for the concert."

"Can I watch it on TV?" asked Suah.

"No, this one isn't on TV. But I'll be back right after. You have fun with Sandy and I'll see you then."

As Gianna moved towards her guards, Suah stepped back to Sandy.

"OK, Ciao!" waved Suah.

Gianna and Sandy laughed to hear the Italian salutation. A moment later, Gianna and her entourage disappeared into the private elevator.

Sandy took Suah by the shoulder. "Ready for some fun in the kitchen?"

"In a minute," answered Suah. "I want to check something in my room."

"OK. I'll meet you in the kitchen when you're done."

Suah toddled off surrounded by sumptuous luxury, the best the St. Regis could offer. Passing through Regency and Louis XV furnishings, he barely noticed the intricate flower arrangements and the Murano glass chandeliers.

In the car, his guard had told him how a procession of movie stars and dignitaries, including royalty, had stayed in the *Royal Suite*. Now it was Suah's turn, although none of the opulent trappings really impressed him.

He passed them all to make his way back to his room. There he stepped to the side of his bed, back to where Sandy had been instructed to place one of his personal effects.

There on the nightstand he found his kaleidoscope toy, the same one he kept by his bed at home. He picked it up and then hurried over to a wardrobe door and opened it. Taped to the inside of the door was the pencil sketch done by Brody, the one Suah had labeled with the names *Suah* and *Hawa*.

He closed the door and looked around the room. No, it wasn't home; it wasn't even close. But it was nice to have some things near.

CHAPTER 53

The solarium was lit by moonlight and decorated with stars. After lounging back alone for a while in the late night hour, Hailey had seen only one shooting star. There must have been more but she hadn't the awareness to notice them. What some would see as the grandeur of the universe on display, to her was a shroud of uncertain night. All of it appeared cold and far removed from the cares of a girl shaken within herself. Lost in the feeling, she barely reacted to the sound of someone entering the room.

"Hailey…" Jaxon Muse startled to find his daughter sitting in the dark. "I thought you'd gone to bed."

She gave him a glance. "No."

Jaxon wavered. Her presence preempted plans for his own solitary retreat. He wasn't sure if she wanted to be alone; neither was he sure he wanted to join her. But the moment had its own momentum.

"Mind if I join you?" he asked.

"Go ahead." The reply was weak and noncommittal.

Jaxon took a seat across the way. A row of clear panels along the outer wall of the solarium had been retracted and a fresh-air breeze flowed through the screens. Jaxon sat a few moments and let the soft night air caress his face, even if he found little comfort in it.

The two of them sat awhile, not saying a word. Night was a meditation and the solarium had become its temple. To speak might puncture the fragile state of mind that wanted nothing more than to reduce a bitter world to contemplation. Then again, to stay quiet might mean a troubled heart would find no relief in its quest to secure answers for its cares.

Today was the first day that Claire hadn't gotten out of bed.

Even when visited in her room, she barely had spoken to anyone.

Hailey could hold back no longer. "How bad is it for Mom?"

For Jaxon, Hailey's words rattled the stars above. "You know she's sick."

"How sick?" she shot back.

Jaxon started to answer and swallowed instead. He dropped his gaze to moonlit tiles and struggled to say out loud the very thing that continually flashed across his brain. "It looks like it we're going to lose her."

Hearing it confirmed poured pain on Hailey's anger and rising hopelessness. "Why didn't you tell me before?"

Jaxon confessed, "Saying something like that makes it seem so final."

"*That's* why you didn't tell me?"

Jaxon raised his voice above a whisper. "I didn't think it was final."

"You mean you didn't want it to be," snapped Hailey.

"Yeah, you're right. I didn't want it to be. Guilty as charged."

"You should have told me how bad it was," cried Hailey.

"I didn't see any reason to. The doctors had faith in the treatments."

"And then what?"

Jaxon lowered his voice. "There were other things to try."

"You made me think everything was going to be all right."

"I didn't want you to hurt..."

"So now the hurt is worse!"

"I never meant it that way."

"And that's all that matters, the way *you* think it should be. It's all so very clear; anyone can read about the way it's *meant to be* in one of your books! Because *you* know how *everything* should be! No one dare question the wisdom of the great Jaxon Muse!"

"I'm sorry. I only wanted to protect you."

Hailey's tears turned to chuckled sarcasm. "How's that working out?"

"I saw no point in putting you through what I was going through."

The silence between them built up into an unbearable, expectant charge.

"Why are we really here?" asked Hailey.

The answer touched a nerve that wouldn't let Jaxon speak.

"It's all about Suah, isn't it?" Hailey watched her dad's reaction. In the moonlight, details were blurred but his despair was palpable nonetheless.

Jaxon leaned forward. "We can only do what we can do."

"What's that supposed to mean?" Hailey sat up.

"Like I said, there were other things to try."

"Did you bring Suah here to do some kind of hocus-pocus healing?"

Jaxon stared into space. The glory of the overarching sky left no room for evasive voids. "Yes. I thought I believed incredible things were possible..."

Hailey shook her head, dazed in disbelief. "You dragged all of us all this way just to set up some kind of miracle?"

Jaxon threw up his arms. "What can I say? In my case, I guess desperation gave the illusion of inspiration. I had to at least *try* with Suah."

Hailey stood. "Suah's gone. So what are we doing the rest of the week? Flying to Fatima? Or maybe we're filling the pool with water from Lourdes? I can't believe this!"

Hailey stormed out of the room leaving Jaxon alone with his universe.

Sheltered by darkness and suddenly alone, he couldn't hold on. Like a giant wall giving way, he let down all façade of inner strength, all pretense of personal certainty and cried in a way that wrenched the child from him.

For someone who knew and had so much, there seemed precious little to hold onto. The feeling was rootless, shifting, sinking, closing in upon itself. Very quickly, the darkness of his spirit found a density that warped reality away from it. Ambiguity became the only absolute. The only grace—the fact that nothing, even his hopelessness, could last if everything was negated.

How had it come to this? His family in shambles, his beliefs shaken, why was there nothing in all he knew to hang onto to guide his way? His own words from the conference came back to haunt him.

"It's not enough to focus on potentials and possibilities. We must move towards them and have confidence in the way things should be…"

A thousand wise sayings paraded through his mind, bloated by years of repetition. Now when he really needed to hang onto to at least one of them, they rang hollow, sounding empty and cliché. To slap a positive face on what was happening wasn't just irrelevant, it was dishonest.

But these had always been the sage offering of the ages, eternal truths found across all cultures, the same things he'd tell anyone that came to him for help. Why were they so ineffective now when *he* needed them the most?

It would be a cruel joke of creation if fear and grief had suddenly become fundamental forces of nature. What must he do to get back on the right path, if indeed one existed? What form of forgiving, cleansing, praying, meditating was necessary? What ritual or venerated mantra could restore his once enlightened and assured place in the cosmos?

He wept into his hands and felt himself falling, not from up to down but from distant to close, and then from close to nowhere.

His jumble of thoughts lost traction and all of the painful anger and unavoidable aphorisms self-annihilated each other. At his lowest point, Jaxon Muse impacted a place that collapsed inward and shrunk to a point infinitely small, so small he couldn't take his Earthly self with him.

What remained was undefined but whole, ageless and clear of any need for experience or ideas to define it. It had no concept of enlightenment and it had no need to be assured of anything. All had been stripped away.

Suah's words, spoken in trance on the plane, came back to him. They were the last thing on his mind but the first thing to hold his attention. Now they held a tinge of prescience, as if a golden thread had been strung from a hopeful past into possible futures. A lifeline when the time was right.

"...Jamais vu...passing through...
...out of the blue...Presque vu...
...seeing through...Déjà vu...
...Bonne nuit...overdue."

Tormented into action, Jaxon headed upstairs into the bedroom he shared with Claire. Along the way, a vibration radiated into his nerves from the infinitely small still-point inside of him. He heard Suah again as an emerging memory, fresh and new, but this time Jaxon could hear himself answering Suah. Blending with the memory of Suah's French, Jaxon spoke his own obscure refrain in trance. Back and forth they traded expressions of wonder.

Jamais vu...
> *I know where I am should be familiar,*
> *but it doesn't seem to be, to me...*

Presque vu...
> *I know the answer is near, on the tip of my tongue;*
> *if I only had a deeper breath of life to go that far...*

Déjà vu...
> *I know I've been here before, or so it seems;*
> *it's the way it should be, if wishes were dreams.*

Only when he heard himself say the words did it feel as if they had meaning. Afterwards, a rising part of him discounted them as gibberish.

He approached the bed slowly. Claire lay on her back, shrouded in darkness with a top sheet pulled up to her shoulders. Her arms looked lifeless outside the covers. In the dark she lost definition. She lay only as a pale impression of the wife Jaxon once knew.

Already it felt as if part of her essence was no longer in the room.

These were the final hours; Jaxon knew it. A higher power must have brought him to her side so he wouldn't miss his chance. Saying goodbye wasn't something he had ever prepared for, even if facing the moment had occupied his thoughts for so long. Now that the time for saying goodbye was near, he felt humbled and lost, unsure of himself yet unwilling to surrender.

He didn't fight his tears. He reached for Claire's hand and pressed it between both of his, the same way Suah had done to them on the airplane. Her fingers were cold, her pulse weak. He squeezed her hand and in doing so, crushed the passion out of himself.

"I'm here, my love…"

He leaned closer, whispering more to himself than her. "I'm holding on. I don't want to let you go. You can't go. I need you so much…"

Unexpectedly, his words echoed back and shamed him into silence. In the quiet of the room, it seemed anything he said reflected back as desperate, even pathetic. He was so confused, so at a loss to center himself.

What could he try next to cajole empathy and compassion from the fates? As true as they were, all of his words fell flat. A pang of earnestness hit him. No amount of self-interested bargaining disguised behind a tissue-thin sincerity would save Claire for him. And that's all it was. If there was no way to fool himself, how would he ever fool the grander destiny now unfolding?

If there was any truth left, it wouldn't be words that came from him.

There was nothing else to do. The doctors had failed; Suah was gone. Shedding all remaining pride and worldly common sense in what he had always believed, he reached into his pocket and took out a sheet of folded paper. On it were printed lines of text he had copied from a webpage.

He held the page out and let moonlight provide all the illumination he needed. As if from a bottom of a well, he raised a desolate voice, reciting the lines over and over as a rote escape into meditation—a surrendering of self that forfeited the last vestige of his earthly power and will.

"Imamu, Skudakumoochooowte,
Bote, Alma Bote, Ananta Bath,
Obarati Ochee Afikomen Banafrit,
Sikera Bote, Alma Bote, Subito Fröhlich Kutamba."

Over and over, the words passed Jaxon's lips as nonsense murmurs. They flowed until he had memorized them and didn't need to read from the paper. Dropping the printout to the floor, he once again held Claire's hand between both of his. Pressing warmth over and around her cold fingers, he couldn't help but fall into a sense of defenselessness. The feeling of loss was tangible in all the ways her hand failed to respond to his.

Suddenly, a stab of insight forced a rushed confession up from his gut. He was nauseous and doubled over towards the bed. The truth of the situation filled the room with a blinding light that left the darkness intact. Nevertheless, it showered Jaxon with pins and needles of revelation.

There was only one person needing to be healed. It wasn't Claire.

Echoes of Suah's words came back to him.

"...when it all falls away, then you'll be ready..."

It was all about *Jaxon*. It had always been about *him*. *He* wanted Claire healed so *he* wouldn't be alone, so *he'd* have the comfort of loving continuity in *his* life. Never mind an afterlife without pain, a joyous hereafter that meant Claire's reconnection with the creative, loving force embodying the universe. Why would Jaxon plead for Claire to stay if it was truly her time to go *there*?

He wanted Suah to work his magic regardless of the boy's natural instincts. No matter what Suah told him, *he* wouldn't take no for an answer. *He* even orchestrated the elaborate trip to Wyatt's island, just so *he* could corner Suah into something that Suah didn't feel was his place to even try. Why would *he* pursue Suah that way if *he* really believed in letting nature take its course? Why was *he* trying to force his will on the world around him? Why must *his* wisdom about *'the way it should be'* be everyone's?

Distanced from himself for the first time, Jaxon saw his selfish behavior and found it repellent. He wanted the comfort, company, love, and validation that others could provide, regardless what was in anyone else's best interests.

So much of how he defined himself was lost in shaping the world to fit his desires. This from a man who had spent his life telling others many things in contradiction to the life he led. If he was ever to be the man he claimed to be in his books and lectures, first it was he who would have to be healed.

Above all, he needed to be free of all anxiety and pain at having to say goodbye to Claire. The desire to release from the anguish of it was so great that he felt himself adrift and then fading. A yearning vibration started as an ache and then erupted into an energetic trance that shuddered through him.

"Help me, Claire!" he called out. "I don't know who else to turn to. You're closer to the source than I am. You're so full of love, you always have been. Heal me! Please help me let go of you..."

"...Jamais vu..."

His breath quickened.

"Help me accept whatever gifts may come, in whatever form they take! If you must go, help me to allow it into my life and see that whatever blesses you, also blesses me..."

"...Presque vu..."

His hands grabbed Claire tighter.

"Help me accept whatever happens to us as foreshadows of bliss! Our love is a joyful entanglement! It makes no difference who lives or dies, who's near or far, nothing can ever separate us!"

"...Déjà vu..."

Jaxon expanded through an altered state from meditation to trance to selfless transcendence. He was willing to let go unconditionally, not only of Claire but himself. Unbounded by a state of allowing, he was free to perceive and receive the energies swirling around him, a silent tornado of quintessential possibilities deafening all extraneous thoughts.

In the moment of expansion, he heard a clear but distant voice. It was fresher than a memory but nearer than any moment he had lived. It was Claire's voice, bright and playful, singing to him in that way she always did, a way that teased him to sing along with her.

"Did you ever see a fishie on a hot summer day?
Did you ever see a fishie out swimming in the bay?
With his hands in his pockets and his pockets in his pants.
Did you ever see a fishie do a hoochie-coochie dance?"

Jaxon smiled through his tears and joined in, completing the refrain.
"You never did - you never will!"
Again, Claire's voice sang out, this time with even more giggle she couldn't hold back. It was just like that day on their date so long ago when it seemed they'd be swamped by fear going down the whitewater rapids. Coming together with a playful song had pulled them through. Reliving that distant memory, Jaxon once again heard her voice clear and so very near.

"Did you ever see a fishie on a cold winter day?
Did you ever see a fishie out frozen in the bay?
With his hands in his pockets and his pockets in his pants.
Did you ever see a fishie do a hoochie-coochie dance?"

"You never did - you never will!" The joy of singing again with Claire filled Jaxon up. He imagined the smile on her face as the whitewater spray shot over them. He saw her leading the way out of the boat and dashing up onto shore. She ran and danced with the thrill of surviving the treacherous waters. Jubilation replaced fear and her playfulness was the spark that ignited their love. Showering around them now, the sparks became a waterfall.

Visions of *Nuka Hiva* flooded Jaxon. They were standing under the waterfall and not getting wet—for it wasn't water showering down. As they stood and embraced, voices on either side of them whispered to each other.

"...you should see them now...now is the time for Life Everliving..."

Without warning, Jaxon was slammed back into his body with incredible force. The showering sparks of the waterfall whipped into a tornado around him and sucked inward to his still-point deep inside. With a flash, the upstairs ranch house bedroom blasted dark around him. A total silence consumed all thought. The starkness of normalcy left him feeling disassociated from his role in the flow of time and where he found himself.

Dazed and lightheaded, he felt less of himself but finally whole.

Before him, Claire laid on the bed gasping for breath. In total surprise to Jaxon, she was convulsing. As her head arched back, her chest jerked upward, sucking in air. But no matter how deep she took it in, her body craved more. Her hands were hot and clammy. She had to be running a fever.

It was unbearable to see her in such discomfort. If this was to be her time to go, Jaxon wanted it to be as easy on her as possible. If there was anything medical science could do to ease her way, it had to be done now.

Jaxon jumped up and scooped her up into his arms. Into the hall he ran. He called out for Hailey until she appeared from her room.

"Get dressed!" she shouted at her.

"What's wrong?"

"We have to get to the hospital! Hurry up! I'm getting Henri!"

Tearing down the steps with Claire in his arms, Jaxon shouted for Henri at the top of his voice. The yelling woke up everyone in the house.

Brody staggered out of his room rubbing his eyes. "What's all the shouting about?"

"Get Henri for me," begged Jaxon. "I need to get Claire to the hospital!"

Brody ran off in boxer shorts to find Henri. Within minutes, Henri was driving them off the ranch headed for town. Jaxon sat in the back seat with Claire's head on his lap. Shivering with frightful anticipation, Hailey sat up front as Henri had them flying down familiar roads in the dark.

The Range Rover raced to a stop outside the hospital's emergency room. With Henri's help, Jaxon got Claire out of the car. Cradling her in his arms, Jaxon scurried into the admittance lobby with a stunned Hailey in tow.

"She needs help right away!" implored Jaxon.

Hospital staff directed him to set her down on a nearby gurney. They asked what was wrong with her.

Dazed from the trance earlier in the bedroom, Jaxon said the first thing that came to his mind. "Nothing's wrong with her!"

"What sickness does she have?"

Jaxon was calm and direct. "She's dying."

Assuming he was delirious from being inconsolable, they turned to Hailey for basic information. In her state, Hailey offered minimal help.

"My…my mom's name is Claire Muse…" she stammered.

"What happened to her?" they asked Hailey.

Jaxon answered for her. "She has a rare cancer. Where are they taking her?"

"Just down the hall."

"I need to be with her!" Jaxon took off down the hall.

"Excuse me…!" The nurse started after him. "You really need to stay in the waiting room."

Henri followed alongside the nurse and spoke to her in the native island dialect. "Let him go. It's all he has left."

The nurse hesitated and Hailey ran after her dad.

"It'll be OK," Henri assured the nurse. "They won't get in the way."

Down the hall, Jaxon found a series of medical work spaces divided here and there by hanging curtains that could be pulled around the patient's bed. It was easy to spot the space where Claire had been taken. It was the one place where doctors and nurses were concentrated and rushing around.

Hailey caught up and halted beside her dad. Noticing she was with him, he put his arm around her and they stepped forward, closer.

Claire was being worked over from both sides of the bed. Monitoring equipment began to beep and shine with moving readouts. Oxygen was administered as were fluids through a needle in her arm.

The medical staff were so busy trying to stabilize her, they weren't aware how close the family members had drawn. The doctors talked freely in front of Jaxon and Hailey. None of their concerns were hidden or softened.

"Her vital signs are all over the place!" one doctor called out.

"There's no way we can treat her until we have her stable!"

"Doctor, look at this temperature; this can't be right!"

"Hold onto her! We can't have her jerking off the bed!"

The more they heard, the more Jaxon and Hailey held each other closer. In minutes, Claire's convulsions settled down but her vital signs didn't. The doctors argued about how to treat her. Given the wild fluctuations of basic readouts, it was hard to know what exactly was the correct course to take.

At one point, Jaxon and Hailey turned to each other. Nothing was said, no one initiated it. It was simply time. They hugged each other and wept tears of sadness but also tears of joy. They hadn't hugged each other for over a year. Leave it to Claire to find a way to heal the rift between father and daughter.

CHAPTER **54**

The insensible gulf of night passed by in the ER waiting room. The drag of passing hours was like an errant ghost of happier days gone by, paying one last visit before crossing over, never to return.

Between the glare of fluorescent ceiling lights and dull scuff marks on the floor, Jaxon and Hailey passed the time of not knowing slumped together on a battered couch. Surrounding them, native people from the town came and went throughout the night. Each focused on their own cares, their own vigils. Nothing was said between Jaxon and Hailey and little word came from staff.

All they knew was that Claire's condition needed to stabilize. Everything was being done that could be done considering that a firm diagnosis was hard to settle on. There was nothing to do but wait. No one could have guessed when all of this began that the wait would last until morning light.

The nurse entered the waiting room but Jaxon barely paid her any attention. So many nurses had come and gone from the room to speak with other people. Jaxon had become numb to the wait and expected little else.

"Mr. Muse? The doctor would like to see you now."

Jaxon shook the drowsiness from his eyes. "You mean me?"

"Yes…"

Hailey was hunched at Jaxon's side, curled into him for comfort and warmth. She rousted awake. "What is it?"

"The doctor wants to see me." Jaxon kissed her forehead then asked the nurse, "Can she come?"

The nurse stepped away. "The doctor only mentioned you."

"I'll be right back." Jaxon patted Hailey's hand.

Hailey sat up and rubbed her eyes awake. Before she could fathom what was going on, Jaxon and the nurse had scurried away.

Along an antiseptic corridor Jaxon was led. The nurse stopped at an office doorway and ushered Jaxon forward. "In here…"

Jaxon entered the room to find one of the doctors from the ER the night before getting up from his seat to welcome him.

"Sorry to keep you waiting but it couldn't be helped."

Jaxon shook his hand and sat down. The office was cramped and cluttered and it appeared that several people had to share it at different times.

"What's going on?" asked Jaxon.

The doctor closed a file folder on his desk. "We're discharging Claire.

She's stable enough now."

"How is she?"

"Her vital signs have settled down. She's breathing better. There's nothing more we can do for her."

The suddenness of the news took Jaxon off guard. "I know this isn't a hospice, I don't expect extended care, but how can you turn her out like this? It's such a quick turnaround."

"I can see how it must seem abrupt. The staff should have kept you more apprised of the situation throughout the night. The fact is, this hospital only has so many beds. We really must prioritize how we fill them."

"Triage…" bristled Jaxon.

"Well, yes," admitted the doctor. "We really must apply our resources where they can do the most good."

Jaxon was angered at the man's flippant attitude. "So what you're saying is, she isn't worth any more care."

The doctor was quick to counter. "She's received care throughout the night. We gave her breathing treatments, the same kind we use to treat severe asthmatic attacks. We administered fluids to help with her mild dehydration."

Jaxon stood up. "What about something to ease the pain? Something to ease her last hours? Isn't there anything more you can do?"

The doctor leaned back from his desk. "I'm not sure what pain you're referring to. As I said, her breathing has returned to normal and her vital signs are stable. She's ready to go home."

"How do you know she won't have another one of these attacks?"

"We don't—but we don't treat future illnesses. If such a thing happens, you should bring her back. Right now, there's nothing wrong with her."

Jaxon shouted, "Of course there's something wrong with her! She has a rare brain cancer! After being with her all night, you never noticed that?"

The doctor stood and motioned with his hands to pacify the situation. "OK, let's be calm about this."

"You don't understand what's she's going through. How can that be?"

"When you brought her in last night, her vital signs were extremely erratic, so much so that a diagnosis was difficult to pin down. In order to help her, we had to check out everything. It took all night. I can assure you, if your wife had such a severe condition, we would know about it…"

Jaxon froze "What are you saying?"

"I'm saying we're discharging her. She's well enough to go home."

"You're not discharging her because she's terminal?"

"Of course not!" The doctor came around the desk, incredulous. "Your wife is fine. The fact is, we don't keep healthy people in our beds."

Jaxon felt ascendant and nailed to the floor all at once. Was it possible that somewhere in the night he had missed a miracle? Could it be that at the very moment he'd made peace with letting Claire go, she'd returned to him?

The doctor led Jaxon out of the office. "I know it's been a long night. The best prescription I can make is for you and your family to go home now. Enjoy the day." He took Jaxon's hand and shook it again. "We'll be here if you need our help again."

Jaxon entered the hallway as if passing into another universe. Time moved more slowly than before and space suddenly contained hidden dimensions curled up with energies ever present yet rarely tapped.

He turned to look down the hallway and had his sight rewarded with a view that was beyond belief but cured all doubts he'd need anything else.

At the end of the hallway, Hailey was wheeling Claire toward him in a wheelchair. Both of their faces were beaming. Hailey's tears had set her face aglow. Claire was intent upon her man. She looked refreshed and a renewed light sparkled in her eyes.

Jaxon set out in a run and rush towards them. Dropping on his knees, he slid into the wheelchair. He pulled Claire towards him and hugged her for dear life. "Oh my God! How is this possible?" he cried.

Overcome with having her family so close, Claire laughed for joy as she wept into Jaxon's shoulder. "You of all people shouldn't have to ask that."

Jaxon pulled back and enjoyed taking in the rekindled vitality on her face. "I can't believe this…I don't understand…!"

"Maybe we're not supposed to—not in any way we can explain."

"How do you feel?" asked Jaxon. It wasn't that he was desperate for another form of confirmation; he just wanted to hear it from her.

"I feel fine, better than fine." Claire looked up and caught Hailey's smile.

The spectacle of their reunion and the energy they brought to it drew people to watch. Some gathered around. One of the attending nurses walked up to alert them. "Your ride is here, he's waiting back by the ER."

"Thank you," answered Jaxon. He turned back to Claire and took her hands in his, just as he had done the night before, just as Suah had showed him. He looked to Hailey then back to his wife.

"We're going to have a great day…"

Claire squeezed his hand. "Just like every other day we've ever had."

Jaxon blinked away happy tears and felt humbled. "I know…I know…"

CHAPTER 55

It was a new day. That meant another city and another concert for Gianna Chase. On this day, it meant Paris and the *Stade de France.* Standing on her center mark on stage, she absorbed all she could from the moment. Cavernous and impressive, the gigantic stadium spread out in front of her.

The stage was a huge platform located at one end of the field. Colossal LED screens formed a curving wall behind her. As craft workers busied themselves with equipment and staging details, colored lights turned on and off in tests of proper sequencing. An electric, expectant energy was in the air.

For Gianna, the thousands of empty seats drew her attention; the expanse of open lawn out in front even more so. Soon, both areas would be filled with nameless but unique people, all sharing a common love of celebration and music. Tonight, it would be all about *her* music.

Centering herself in the feeling, she found the quiet space inside of herself. It was time to complete one of her most treasured concert rituals. Before the gates opened, before any of the people rushed in, she cherished standing in the place where it would all happen. There she listened to the wishes of the fans on their way to see her. She drew energy from those wishes. She liked to say those were the desires that powered her to be kinetic.

This time as she stood and listened, a stitch of intuition pulled loose and reordered itself in her mind. She reached for the small control pack on her hip and switched on a headset link to the control room.

"Matthew, are you still there?" she asked the air.

After a brief pause, a familiar man's voice answered. "Right here."

Gianna turned and surveyed the upper seats. "I want to make one change for tonight."

"Ah, the hour's pretty late. Are you sure you want to do that?"

"I know it's past failsafe but it's important. I want to try something out."

"What do you have in mind?"

Gianna turned and stepped towards the giant screens. "I want a different encore song. I want it to be *Make The World Well Again.*"

"You're putting your number one song at the end of the show?"

"That's right. I have a feeling that'll work better with this crowd."

"And how would you know that? Have you been taking a poll of their wishes again?"

Gianna smiled. "You know me so well."

"You know what I'm going to say. There's a lot of staging we'd have to move around…"

"Nonsense," objected Gianna. "It's just the choir and they'd be better out of the way until the end, don't you think?"

Matthew chuckled, "If you weren't a singer, you'd be in sales. All right, a new encore it is. I'll pass the news along."

"Thanks for indulging me. I feel so spoiled," smiled Gianna. She expected the customary *Matthewesque* witticism in quick order but paused when she heard only silence. She waited but Matthew's voice didn't come back.

"Matthew?" she called out. She checked her control pack. "Is this thing working?"

Suddenly, Matthew was back on. "Sorry, Gianna. I got distracted. We've got the news on in the control room. Something's going on…"

"What is it?"

"There's some bulletin. I heard Suah's name…"

Gianna turned about face and froze. "Suah!"

"They've got Nathan Mackey on. They're interviewing him. It's wild."

Gianna turned back to face the curving wall of LED screens towering at the back of the stage. "Can you put it on the screens out here?"

"Just a second."

A few moments later, the gigantic LED screens lit up with the news report. Nathan Mackey was being interviewed on an airplane. The sound of the interview reverberated throughout the empty stadium. Gianna stood in the middle of a bare stage, transfixed by the huge display before her. A split screen showed a reporter in studio and Nathan in his first-class airline seat.

"…how did you first hear the news?" the reporter asked.

Nathan spoke into a streaming feed from his smart phone. "From *The Protoprime Society*. They were contacted by someone on the island."

"Is that where you're headed now?"

"Yes," confirmed Nathan. "I want to meet some of the people I've already talked with."

"Members of the hospital staff or are there others?"

"Mainly hospital staff right now. They're the ones who were kind enough to share what happened."

"Again, for those just joining us, what exactly did happen?"

"It's quite simple but extraordinary," commented Nathan. "The hospital has documented evidence that Claire Muse, the wife of Jaxon Muse, was taken to the emergency room in the middle of the night. Jaxon told staff she was dying. Eight hours later, she was fine and they released her in perfect health. Jaxon swore to them that she had a rare form of brain cancer going into the hospital but medical staff could find no signs of such a thing."

"Has anybody corroborated Jaxon's story about this brain cancer?"

"Yes. Dr. Vincent Halstead. Come to find out, he's been Claire's oncologist for the past year. He claims that she's been secretly taking an experimental medicine, and yet some of Halstead's colleagues have serious doubts that the trial formula could be responsible for her remission. They claim she hasn't been on it long enough and even if she had been, the reported dose was so marginal, effectively it was little more than a placebo."

"Well, if the remission wasn't caused by the medicine, what could it be?"

Nathan speculated. "ER doctors on the island believe it's a case of *spontaneous* remission. As we've heard before in other cases of people being healed, the doctors say such cases are extremely rare but not unprecedented."

The reporter glanced aside and read the latest notes on his prompter. "We've also got word coming in about an energy worker name Faith. She works at the *Nani Ahi Pua* Yogic Retreat on the Muse's home island. She says Claire Muse had an energy treatment with her at the North Shore retreat. So there you have it. It seems there's as many explanations for what's happened as there are people wondering about it."

Nathan interrupted, "But one explanation, I think, is most compelling. As I said before, it's come to light that Suah Chase spent time with the Muses just one day before the remarkable remission."

"So you think this is another miraculous healing by Suah Chase?"

"I'm saying the circumstances can't be ignored."

"How did you ever learn that Suah was on this island?"

"A migrant worker recognized him and came forward. He saw Suah on the beach one day after the worker finished herding some sheep."

From the side of the stage, Ava walked up near Gianna. They glanced at each other but kept their attention fixed on the news report.

The reporter pressed Nathan. "You still haven't explained why you think Suah's presence on the island is so compelling?"

"Review the facts. He wasn't with his mother on her concert tour. He didn't join her until yesterday, the same day the healing took place. Why else would Suah Chase and Jaxon Muse be on the same island—an island six thousand miles from his home and nearly half that far from his mother?"

The reporter's most provocative question was set up. "What do you say about rumors that Suah and Jaxon were actually staying on a ranch owned by someone I think you know—Wyatt Dumashe?"

Nathan deflected it. "I've heard that too but I can't comment on it now. Maybe after I get to the island and start to verify some things…"

Gianna's phone rang.

It was Wyatt with an opening line, "The herd of cats is out of the bag."

Gianna motioned for Ava to have the news feed cut from the LED screens. "This mess keeps getting deeper."

"An embarrassment of riches, I would say," added Wyatt.

"More like mention the devil and all hell breaks loose. There's no way anyone's going to contain this now."

"Agreed. Maybe we shouldn't bother. The idea that we ever could was probably our greatest folly. Nothing's going to settle down as long as Suah keeps leaving miracles in his wake."

"That's not certain," countered Gianna. "There's doctors and energy workers coming out of the woodwork to claim a piece of this one."

"They'll all fade away and you know it. The facts will support Suah being the one responsible."

"What makes you so sure?"

"You have intuition; I have my gut. My gut is never wrong."

Gianna turned to see hand signals from a stage manager thirty paces away. "Suah's with me now and I have a concert to perform. Those two things fill up my space right now. I can't worry about anything else."

"You don't have to," Wyatt assured her. "I have Nathan. He'll keep on top of whatever we need. Go hug Suah. Sing your songs. I'll handle the rest."

"I've got to go. Thanks." Gianna pocketed her phone. Immediately, she turned to Ava, her concert assistant. "Where's Suah?"

"At the hotel, with Sandy."

Gianna made strides towards the rear of the stage. "This is the worst time for this. I don't want to be separated from Suah. Bring him here."

Ava worked to keep up. She didn't hide her concern. "To the stadium?"

"Yes, I want him here. I want us to be close. It's the only way we'll be able to react quickly should anything happen tonight."

"But isn't the hotel more contained than here?"

"He can stay in *The Box* under constant guard. I can visit him between numbers. I'll feel better having him close. Do whatever—make it happen."

Gianna marched on. Ava stopped and made a call. On the other end of the line, Olivia Platt heard Ava sigh, "You're not going to believe this…"

CHAPTER 56

The ride back to the ranch from the hospital was tranquil. Throughout the trip there was an peculiar calm and silence. The Muse family had nothing to say. The moment was too perfect, their shared love too obvious. Nothing had to be added or taken away. Everyone rode along in a steady daze of delight.

It would take some time for the shock of what had happened to settle in. Of course, the way things were now was *the way it should be*, but the wonder of it was, *the way it should be* went far beyond anyone's idea of normal good fortune. What had changed went far beyond a cure for Claire.

Rolling along, watching the scenery, everyone harbored a surreal feeling of having just arrived on the island. It pervaded the car and made everything seem new and fresh, especially themselves. There was simply nothing better to do than sit back quietly and enjoy the shared view. Even Henri, behind the wheel, felt something and respected the silence.

Arriving at the ranch house, they found Eugénie had breakfast ready for everyone. Gathering out on the esplanade, the whole group sat down in the rising light of another morning like no other. Brody and Leah had heard the news of what had happened and radiated their own elation at being fellow travelers in the Muse family's joy.

Jaxon took a moment to look around and appreciate the soulful feast.

"It's quite a day," he sighed.

Hailey caught his eye and smiled. "The best!"

Claire sat nearby, amazed at how miraculous a normal day could be.

Jaxon made eye contact with everyone. "It seems so perfect that all of us are here." He laughed, "I have to admit, when Suah first told me what he wanted for this trip, I thought he was crazy…"

Brody chewed away as he spoke. "That boy taught me a thing or two about *nutzo-crazy* adventures, that's for damned sure!"

Hailey's thoughts raced from snorkeling trip to her ordeal on the beach. "Too bad he couldn't be here today."

Leah noticed Gris-Gris lying down by an empty chair. "I think Gris-Gris thinks he is…"

"The dog may be right." Jaxon's gaze settled on the empty chair.

Claire glanced back. "Suah is near in our hearts and thoughts; that's the main thing."

Brody pushed his empty plate away and turned to Claire. "So, have you made any plans on how you're going to spend the big day?"

Claire chuckled as she considered a flood of options not within her reach a day before. "Oh, I don't know..." She grinned at Hailey and Leah. "I've heard so much fun going on around this pool, It might be fun to try it out."

"That's a great idea," exclaimed Hailey.

"Watch out for this one," warned Leah with a grin. "She likes to splash."

"Oh, I know," agreed Claire. "She's been doing that since she was a baby in the tub."

"Mom, no!" pleaded Hailey. "No baby stories. You start that and I'll tell stories about when you and Dad were first dating."

The mention of first dates rang true between Claire and Jaxon and resounded in a crystalline place reserved in a special way for them and them alone. They looked at one another and the moment slowed and expanded.

Claire had been unconscious and Jaxon lost in trance the night before. The warmth of rising impressions from their newly shared experience caught them unprepared. They weren't even aware they could remember it.

Now the surprise of it drew them towards each other in spirit, as if all the distance that was possible between them was far away. Now they settled at a limitless point that existed only because they had allowed it to be near.

They looked to one another in a knowing way and wondered how to comprehend it. Between them, a shared thought occurred at the same time. Even though they never said it out loud, somehow they knew the other one shared it as well. All they were left with was an inner urge to sing and dance. That and telltale echoes of the one shared thought: *"Bonne nuit...overdue."*

The sound of laughter from the group around them resonated from far off and snapped Jaxon and Claire back into the moment. They turned towards the others to find they had missed someone's comment about their shared silent moment. Apparently, their timeless ecstasy was mistaken for a simple loving glance. Full of the fun of it, Jaxon grabbed his glass and stood up.

"A toast!" He raised the glass. "To every one of you and the day ahead. It truly can be anything we want it to be."

The others joined in with their glasses.

Claire pushed back from the table. "Well, I need to see if Eugénie can conjure up a bathing suit for me. I certainly didn't bring one."

Leah got up as well. "I saw some suits out in the cabana. I'll go check."

Brody downed the rest of his papaya juice and donned his hat. "While you're doing that, I'm going to work off this big breakfast in the hammock."

The group split up, going different ways to enjoy the day. Jaxon went over and petted Gris-Gris for a while and then followed Claire upstairs. Minutes later, he found her coming out of their en suite bathroom.

She was holding a bottle of pills.

"I found these on the sink…" She held the bottle out in her open hand.

Jaxon instantly recognized the pills as advanced protocol. In his anguish the other day, he had taken them out and forgotten to put them back.

"It's your prescription," admitted Jaxon.

Claire opened the bottle and shook a few of the pills into her palm. "I counted them…" She looked up as if blackout curtains had been pulled back and she'd become unexpectedly weightless. "…They're all here."

There was no need for a confession. As much as Jaxon felt ashamed for lying to her, he couldn't mask his joy at the outcome. He stood as if awaiting sentencing for his crime. There was nothing he could say to justify the person he had been except to insist he wasn't that man anymore. But that he would never do. That was something he needed to show, not say.

Claire calmly put the pills back into the bottle and closed the lid. Confronting the evidence that medicine had nothing to do with her cancer's remarkable remission was an affirmation of things she had heard from Jaxon for so long but never truly believed.

Maybe she didn't believe in them because she was so close to Jaxon and felt he didn't quite believe in them either, not really. The change in both of them, after all they'd been through, stripped all that away. What was left was undefined and a bit frightening, but it was something to build on.

She stepped forward and put her arms around him. She hugged him close and said nothing. Her silence found harmony with his. It would take quite a while to process all that had happened in the past few days. Neither had any desire to start analyzing the rainbows in their life.

And this minute was a rainbow.

Downstairs, in the hallway, Hailey was eager to change into her swimsuit for a pool party with her mom and Leah. As she rushed past the study, she heard the ringtone from Jaxon's phone. She detoured to fetch it for him and in the process, discovered who was calling. On impulse, she answered it.

"Hello, is this Perry? This is Hailey. I just wanted to let you know. It's game over, Phantom. I've got *new* private rules. You match my dad's contribution to Suah's village or I'll tell him what you've been doing."

Content with the stunned silence on the other end, she hung up.

CHAPTER 57

Ava led the way with four guards encircling them. Sandy hurried along with Suah at her side. The roar of the crowd and the blaring music provided the perfect backdrop for the funhouse maze they had to run through to go from limousine to the sanctuary of *The Box*.

Welcome to the *Stade de France*.

For Suah, after a day shuttered away in the hotel, he imagined the rushed maneuvers would be a welcomed jolt to the system. As long as the guards and handlers knew what they were doing, he might as well enjoy the sudden thrust into the carnival of action. The lights, the sounds, the many faces and interesting little places along the way were so overwhelming at first, he didn't have a chance to be frightened by them.

"*The Box* is now a lockbox," announced Ava. She turned down the final walkway that led under the unused stands directly behind the stage. "I'll feel much better when we get in there."

Transit guards met door guards and signaled their handoff of *Sirius*.

Ava stood in the hallway and made sure only Suah and Sandy were admitted to Gianna's special place behind stage.

Suah hurried in but immediately slowed to conduct a meandering inspection. *The Box* was nothing like he had imagined it. It was much smaller and austere. Its structure was makeshift and functional with a place for everything needed and no space wasted. Except for area lights embedded in work spaces, the place was also dark and gave the feeling of being heavily padded and insulated.

Ava closed the door behind her and introduced Sandy and Suah to Gianna's hair, makeup, and wardrobe team. Each of them gave a wave and a quick smile but stayed dutifully ensconced in their respective cubbyholes. Surrounded them was a dazzling array of appurtenances ready for their craft.

"It's really noisy back here," exclaimed Suah.

Ava rushed forward to shush him. "We have to be quiet…"

Suah's whisper was loud. "Who can hear us?"

"We never know when everything will go quiet on stage," explained Ava. "When it does, we don't want to be heard back here."

"Does Mom know we're in here?"

Ava pointed to her head. "They told her through her headset, yes."

"It took a long time to get here. Are you sure we aren't back in Rome?"

"No," Ava assured him. "This really is Paris."

Sandy looked around for places to sit. "How far into the concert is it?"

"The second number." Ava thought in program sequences, not time. "You were supposed to get here before the whole thing began. Gianna was upset."

"It couldn't be helped," offered Sandy. "That uproar leaving the hotel made us late. That guy laid down right in the street to stop us; then his partner took pictures through the window…"

Suah added, "The crowd got loose and we couldn't get started again."

Ava checked concert statuses on her tablet computer. "It doesn't matter. Part of the job is anticipating the unexpected."

"I never expected to come here," added Suah.

Ava looked up. "And I never anticipated that. I'm not liking this pattern." Ava turned to leave but Sandy stopped her.

"One other thing…" She drew near enough to Ava to guarantee their conversation wouldn't be overheard. "Olivia told me you had something to tell me in private once we got here."

Ava gave a nod. She watched while Suah wandered away to inspect the swivel makeup chair positioned before a bank of mirrors and lights When she was certain his attention was focused there, she took Sandy to one side.

"There's nothing you have to do; this is for your information only. We believe someone on our staff is selling favors to the press."

"What kind of favors?" asked Sandy.

Ava didn't want to go into all of it. "Helpful information, mainly. The hotels we're going to be staying at, the routes we plan to take by car…"

"How do you know it's someone on the inside?"

Ava didn't want to elaborate. A simple example would suffice. "Look at what happened tonight. How did that photographer and his buddy know Suah and you were leaving? Moving you here was a spur-of-the-moment thing. You can't tell me that was a lucky guess."

"What should I do?"

"Keep your eyes open and be ready for last-minute changes. They're harder on us but the only way to keep one step ahead of this."

With that, Ava rushed out. Sandy and Suah were left so close to the stage, it was like hearing the concert as a performer. And yet, cloistered in *The Box*, they could see none of the action.

A ribbon of bright light shining through a split in blackout curtains was the only hint of the sights on stage, the projections on the vast LED screens, the faces of fans in the packed stadium beyond. Through that ribbon of light is where Gianna made most of her entrances and exits from the stage.

Suah and Sandy waited until, after two more numbers, Gianna needed a costume change and dashed through the curtains. Immediately, she searched for Suah and rushed to him. Dressed in tailored silks dotted in crystals, she effused the glamour, passion, and energy of her live performance.

"There you are! How are you doing?" She leaned down and hugged him.

Taken aback by the burst of her radiance, Suah gasped. "Whoa! You're super-duper pretty!"

She smiled, "You've seen me dressed up before."

"Not at a concert." Suah was starstruck.

"You know, you're right..." The notion hit Gianna as odd. "You've never been to one of my concerts, have you?"

"I saw one on TV..."

"Well, you're here now..." Gianna pointed to the curtain. "Next time, we'll get you a seat out front so you can watch everything."

"In the middle of all those people?" Suah was apprehensive.

Gianna stood and let her wardrobe lady start unfastening her dress in the back. "We'll find the perfect place. You'll like it."

Suah stood in place and watched as Gianna disappeared into her dressing area. As fabrics swished and transition music played on stage, each one of her team processed her through *The Box*. A minute later, she was transformed and with a blown kiss and a smile, she dashed away.

Over the next hour and a half, three more costume changes necessitated more rushed conversations and frenetic doting on by her staff. The guards ushered in production assistants frantic to deliver this or that. A general crush of organized chaos reigned and left Suah with no place to hide.

By the time Gianna was ready for her last set before the planned encore, she noticed that Suah looked overwhelmed. The excitement had become bedlam and the adventure had become pandemonium. Amidst the endless commotion backstage and the powerful anarchy of a roaring crowd, there was no way Sandy could insulate him from the turmoil and uncertainty that passed for reality behind the scenes at a concert as big as this.

Before passing through the curtains one last time, Gianna paused to look back. She could see a rising anxiety in Suah's eyes.

Her rushes on and off had to be abrupt, but she knew now it must be even more unsettling to a child like Suah. Regret mixed with worry as she remembered the fact: he had never been to one of her concerts. This level of electricity, action, and noise might be too brusque an experience for him. She fretted about leaving him at the hotel, but now she worried how well he was adjusting to a location so central to the madness.

"I'm almost done, sweetie," she called back.

He looked to her hopefully and smiled with his eyes.

The last song before the encore played. During parts of it, the crowd joined in and sang the song with Gianna. The sound of thousands of live voices, all coming together to share a feeling and a message, was powerful.

Suah listened and felt his heart race. It was all so confusing. The singing sounded so full of hope and solidarity, and yet the massiveness of the crowd felt so imposing and daunting, wild and unpredictable.

How could his mother's one voice command such an unwieldy force? How did her presence wield so much influence over something that could roar and gyrate like a distressed monster? He never realized before how significant one person could be. Her example was awe-inspiring.

As he sat and listened, Sandy reacted to a buzz of her phone. She grabbed it quickly and read a text message. She sent a quick message back, asking for confirmation, and immediately her phone buzzed again with the answer.

She stood, suddenly anxious. "We've got to go."

Her announcement took Suah by surprise. He sat, unsure what she meant.

She took him by the arm. "We need to move to another location."

Suah followed along but asked, "Why?"

"Last-minute changes."

"But Mom isn't done yet."

"It doesn't matter. She'll meet us right after."

Sandy opened the door and confronted the guards. She showed them the text message. "You're supposed to move us right away."

"I have no orders of that," the guard protested.

"I just got this message," Sandy insisted. "You'd better check."

Sandy and Suah entered the hallway as one guard turned to access his communicator. Just then, the other guard was distracted by a fight that broke out on the other side of him. Moving through the fight, two other men rushed towards them.

"What the hell?" The guard reacted and slammed a man against the wall.

Jumping aside to avoid being tackled, Sandy and Suah had to shift several steps farther away from the door to *The Box*. As the second guard called for reinforcements, two more men rushed him.

With their path back into *The Box* blocked, Sandy and Suah had few options. She grabbed his hand. "Come on! This way…"

Running away from the fight, Sandy led Suah further down the hallway.

"Where are we going?" yelped Suah.

"I don't know but we can't stay here!"

"Where are we supposed to move to?"

"The message said the guards would know."

"The one at the door didn't."

"Maybe he wasn't the right one..."

The hallway ended in an elbow that took a right turn. Sandy followed it and exited through a door. Bursting through it, they found themselves outside at the side of the stage at ground level. Waiting for them as an impenetrable wall was an anxious pack of photographers and reporters, obviously tipped off that Suah was on his way.

"Oh, no!" gasped Sandy. Startled, she turned around in a frantic attempt to lead them back inside the hallway.

The press of the mob pushed her into the hallway and closed the door behind her. Suah was caught outside on his own.

All at once, a shower of popcorn flashes from cameras taking shots at Suah burst at ground level on that side of the stage. The concentration of flashes was so great that eyes everywhere in the stadium were attracted to it.

Surrounded, Suah had nowhere to turn to run away. He stood frozen at the center of attention and absorbed the sharp light and shouts from those clustered around him. He'd been herded to this spot and now it was time for the feeding frenzy.

"Suah! Over here! Look this way! Say something!"

The disruption was so noticeable that it attracted the attention of everyone performing on stage, including Gianna. Worried by her instincts as to what might be happening, she stopped singing in the middle of her song and craned her neck to see what was going on below at field level.

Soon after, the music stopped and a rippling murmur passed through the crowd. Gianna's steps were slight at first, just a step or two out of curiosity in the direction of the flashes. Then she began to walk and the walking soon turned into a run. As she ran, her motion attracted the determined response of a dozen security personnel positioned around the stage.

Onto the stage rushed Gianna's personal bodyguards. They followed her in her run to one side. There, she could finally see what was going on. There she ripped off her headset mike and tossed it aside as she yelled—"Suah!"

Ignoring all safety protocol and not waiting for her guards, she scurried along the edge of the stage and down the side steps. As she progressed, she attracted another rain of photoflashes aimed her way.

With guards powering their way to her side, Gianna lost it and shouted at the mob around Suah. "What are you doing! Back away from him!"

The more the situation deteriorated, the more interest got generated in recording the action. Fans in the stands and on the field joined in as thousands of phones were raised overhead in an attempt to capture the melee.

Muscling a path through the crowd, the guards shoved and punched their way en route to Suah. Their blunt force opened up a narrow lane for Gianna to rush through until she had Suah in her arms.

Suah was stiff and shaking when she got to him. He was temporarily blinded by all of the close-up flashes that had gone off in his face. With streaks from tears on his cheek, he buried his head on Gianna's shoulder as she hugged him. Clutching each other in the center of the storm, she cried out loud but in the din her shouts could only be heard by the one she held near.

"Oh Suah! I'm sorry, I'm so sorry!"

Raho, Gianna's security manager, opened up the door that led back into the hallway. "Go this way!" he yelled.

Gianna reacted. Clutching Suah to her side, she ran with him into the hallway. Three of the guards came with them. Two ran ahead to ready the path and one stayed monitoring the door.

Gianna knelt down and hugged Suah to her. He wouldn't stop shivering no matter how much she tried to comfort him. It was all so imposing and daunting, wild and unpredictable. He had experienced firsthand how much the distressed monster could roar and gyrate. It only made him respect the power his mother wielded that much more.

"What happened?" she gasped. "How did you get out there!"

It was a desperate question. Suah couldn't answer.

More stadium guards came running around the elbow in the hallway. Seeing that the situation was under control, they slowed to a stop. Respecting Gianna's and Suah's privacy, they kept their distance.

"It's all over now," promised Gianna. "It's OK, we're going to be all right. I have you; I'm not letting you go."

Shaking and with his gaze fixed on nothing, Suah was without words.

Gianna began to cry. As she cried, she got angry. The very thing she was most determined to avoid had happened. It seemed there was no safe place for them. There would be no safe way to do this no matter how many precautions she took. She had been so worried that something like this would happen at the hotel, she had brought Suah to the stadium to be close to her.

But there was no way to keep him near enough, no way to shut out the world.

She had to put it from her mind. Suah needed her now. This was no time to make things worse by flying off in a rage or retreating into herself. Suah was the one who needed help now. She wasn't sure how but they'd find a way together to get him whatever help he needed.

Kneeling in front of him, holding him by the shoulders, she fought back her tears and said the first thing that came to mind. "What do you want, Suah? What would you like to do? What do you need? If you could have anything in the world, what would it be?"

Around the corner came Ava and Sandy. On seeing Gianna and Suah together, they waited with the guards. Beyond the nearby door, the sound of the crowd grew restless. Gianna refocused and asked her question again.

"Tell me, Suah. I'm here for you. What do you want?"

For the first time, Suah looked up and into her eyes. He didn't want to talk, she could tell, but the promise of a wish fulfilled managed to find a way through the trauma that enveloped him.

His voice was weak. "I want to talk to my grandfather."

"Your grandfather?"

Suah nodded.

Taken by surprise, Gianna wavered. With all her money and influence, this wasn't the answer she expected. She was prepared to do anything for him, but this was an unknown.

"Is there anything else?" she asked.

His gaze dropped with a shake of the head.

"All right," offered Gianna. "We'll try to do that. But some things I can't be sure of. When was the last time you talked with your grandfather?"

Suah's eyes kept downcast. "Right before I went to live at the school."

"The boarding school in your village?"

He nodded. "They said he couldn't take care of me anymore—but one day I would see him again."

"They said that?"

Suah nodded.

"OK, well, we'll try to do that. I promise you."

Ava stepped up, anxious about interrupting but needing to anyway.

"I'm sorry Gianna...they need to know what you're going to do about the show."

Lost in thought, the concert was the farthest thing from Gianna's mind.

"The show?"

Stressing to the point of collapse, Ava stepped nearer. "Yes, the crowd doesn't think it's over. They're not leaving. Are you going to do the encore?"

Gianna sat back on her legs. The prospect of going back on stage seemed out of the question. She hadn't the energy or the emotional strength for such a thing now. But she also knew the pressures that would come to bear.

"I don't know," she stalled. "I don't think so."

"Olivia sent me to tell you it wouldn't be good to cut it off now. The stadium people are worried. They think the crowd is unpredictable."

Gianna looked up into Suah's eyes. They were so expressive and soulful, so hopeful and moving. She reached up and held his hands.

"What do you think I should do? Should I sing or not?" she asked him.

Suah glanced around to check out the others waiting up and down the hallway on either side of them. Then he looked back to Gianna.

"I like it when you sing to me."

Gianna smiled. "That's right. You do, don't you?"

Suah nodded. With his nod, Gianna gathered strength.

She glanced over at Ava. "OK...I'll sing." She looked back in Suah's eyes. "But I'm singing to Suah."

Not certain what that meant but delighted that the show was going on, Ava rushed to send word on her headset. "Prep the encore. *Polaris* rising."

Gianna stood and walked with Suah back down the hallway. Along the way, Gianna passed Sandy and gave her a look. "We'll get into this later."

Distraught at what had happened, Sandy nodded and followed.

Back in *The Box*, Gianna quickly changed into her street clothes.

Olivia rushed in and thought Gianna had changed her mind about performing. "You're not going on?" she asked, assuming the worst.

Gianna stood in a pullover cashmere top and blue jeans. "I'm going on like this."

"Why street clothes?"

Gianna walked over and picked up two wooden stools. "Because I'm leaving right after." She turned to Ava. "Have the car ready. And tell Matthew I'm going to do the encore a cappella."

Ava froze. "What about the music and the choir?"

"I won't need them."

"What are you doing, Gianna?" asked Olivia.

Gianna turned to Suah. "Come on...I want to sing you a song."

Suah was wide-eyed. "Where are we going?"

Gianna made eye contact with Olivia and Ava, then looked back to Suah to answer him. "We're going onstage."

Olivia started to say something but Gianna held up her hand to preempt it. Gianna handed Suah his stool. "Here, it's just you and me out there. OK?" Suah hesitated but then gave a tentative nod.

Gianna led him through the blackout curtains and out from behind the wall of towering LED screens. The crowd knew something was coming because the lighting had changed and a choir, dressed in red robes, had taken their position in tiered rows upstage. The house lights around the stadium had dialed down and all of the stage presets for the encore had shifted in color.

The rumble of eighty thousand people became thunderous applause as Gianna first appeared back on stage. Added to the applause was shock and rising excitement when Suah appeared toddling after her. Each of them carried a wooden stood. Both of them never left each other's side.

Gianna led Suah to her central mark downstage. It was the same mark where she always stood before a concert and listened to the wishes of the fans who would show up later. But now, for this song, she'd only listen to the wishes of one precious boy. It was his time, his wish, and she was singing for no one but him.

The rest of the world could watch if it wanted. Let them take their pictures and cell phone videos. Let them watch from above with zoom lenses from helicopters. Let everyone have a look. Finally, maybe then, after the song was over, they'd feel something different about themselves and the kind of world they were creating every day. Maybe then, everyone would stop and hear what the song was saying and not just listen to it.

Getting set, she pulled a radio hand mike out of her blue jean's back pocket. Turning briefly to the choir, she motioned she wouldn't need them. They could stand silently by and listen to Suah's song like everyone else.

Positioning the stools side-by-side, she and Suah sat down and faced each other. As the crowd quieted down in anticipation, her gaze swept the stadium until everyone silenced even more. Then she turned on her mike.

Turning back to Suah, she took his hand in hers and reached down deep for the strength and breath to complete what she wanted to do.

Sensing her struggle, Suah put his other hand over hers. Slowly, lightly, he patted her hand with long, sliding touches. He did this for a while. He did this until his mom, with no music or choir, started to sing to him.

The encore began. Gianna's voice was clear. The sound system amplified the words so everyone in the stadium and could hear. Immediately, everyone recognized the song—Gianna's number one *Make The World Well Again*.

"There's a place in all our hearts
Where everything that's good between us must start.
There's a window in the prison
Where all the things we locked away
Find the light of a brand new day that has arisen.

If we only mend our hearts
Love will make the world well again,
Make the world well again,
Make the world well again."

There's a way to get us through,
And it's all about a new and beautiful view
Of who we are…and what we do,
Of making love…not making do,
Of lending a hand…and pulling through,
No longer wasting away…when it's wiser to renew,
No longer needing to be right…when it's easier being true,
Finding a peace in a time…so long overdue.
A better me…loving a better you.

If we only mend our hearts,
Love will make the world well again,
Make the world well again,
Make the world well again."

Throughout the song, Gianna kept focused on Suah. Suah wasn't nervous about being on stage at all. Why should he be? His mom was singing his favorite song to him—and she had the power to control any size crowd.

By the second verse, the crowd started singing along. Thousands of lighters, phones, and lit matches were raised in harmony with the moment. Suah and Gianna hardly saw them but for a silent choir moved to tears, it was quite a sight to see.

When the song ended, the crowd erupted like never before. Gianna and Suah hugged at center point downstage, bathed in the roar of approval. Then they walked away, arms around one another. When they walked away, arms around one another, the twin wooden stools stayed at center point, twin effigies marking a special time in a very personal space.

CHAPTER **58**

For most people, the sensational headlines said it all.

POP STAR AND MIRACLE HEALER ESCAPE INTO THE NIGHT.

It was a night that had the whole world talking and watching endless replays of the spectacle at the stadium. But the night also felt transitional, a blazing signpost at the start or end of something. For Gianna and Suah, the night's events ran deeper and forced more far-reaching consequences.

Returning to their same hotel was out of the question. Emergency plans had to be invoked and one of several backup locations was chosen as a safe house. Crafty but typical limo diversions were employed to confuse trackers. The tireless pursuers never knew their chase didn't matter.

Gianna and Suah actually left the stadium incognito in a special taxi. They were shuttled unceremoniously to an office building nearby where guards whisked them to a helipad on the roof for a helicopter flight to safety.

Safety was to be found at a friend's chateau a distance out of town. The friend was yachting in the Mediterranean and had made his empty place secretly available to Gianna should she need it. In the countryside, the tour entourage might be able to grab a few hours of the peace and seclusion they'd need to recover and regroup for whatever lay ahead.

Set back on acreage, the modern interpretation of a French provincial house was guarded by the latest sensors and cameras tied in to a security firm's rapid response network.

As if that wasn't adequate, Gianna brought her own guards to patrol the grounds and monitor the main country road that gave access to the property. After what had happened, it would take time to restore a sense of security. If any place afforded them a good start at it, this was it.

While Suah took a bath upstairs, Gianna attended to business in the living room downstairs. She wanted to keep all disruptive details of what they were going through far away from Suah's ears. He had been traumatized enough; there was no way she would worry him further by hashing out business in front of him. Everyone else was ordered to do the same.

The large fireplace was lit, the setting was designed for comfort, but the atmosphere in the room sweated out of everyone as if they were trapped in a contentious corporate boardroom.

Gianna was not happy with bottom-line performance and it was Olivia's and Ava's jobs to stand and take the fire. After Gianna had a chance to launch a barrage of incriminations and threats on how she intended to dismiss her entire staff, she eased up long enough for Ava and Olivia to reiterate how things had gotten away from them.

"We really can't blame Sandy," Ava asserted. "I told her to be ready for last-minute changes…"

Olivia sat hunched and brooding. "This bastard is clever, whoever it is. They used our need to respond quickly as a ploy against us."

"The text message came from one of the guard's phones," added Ava. "Somebody swiped it from him. Honestly, we can't fault the nanny. Yes, she made the wrong choice but she did it to protect Suah."

"The source is definitely inside. They knew our latest codes."

Gianna paced before the fireplace with energy that burned hotter. "If this can happen, then anything can."

"Yes, it turned out bad, but it really wasn't a clever plan," braved Ava.

Gianna turned to snap at her but Olivia spoke forcefully to make a point. "All they did was set up a situation, an opportunity."

"That's all they needed!" shouted Gianna.

"They weren't sure if anything would happen. The way it played out…it went against us."

"Is that it? Is that your excuse? They got lucky?" An upsurge of feeling choked Gianna's words. "…Tell me your plan for guarding against that!"

After a half hour of yelling at them, Gianna was spent. She held a hand to her forehead and turned towards the mantle. She showed them her back. She wanted to stay mad, needed to be mad. This was no time to weaken and break down. She seethed with rage, hurt, and disappointment. And yet, she couldn't get the image out of her mind. Again and again the memory forced her to relive Suah under siege, all alone and afraid by the side of the stage.

With her back still turned, she gathered last words to impressed upon them the importance of new unfinished business. "Suah and I need to make a trip to Africa…to his village…"

The news shocked Olivia and Ava to drop all excuses and listen.

Gianna explained, "…it may be preposterous to ask for, given the level of competency around me, but I need this trip to be kept private."

"How long of a trip?" asked Olivia.

"I don't know. A couple days, I imagine. We'll need guards, of course, but everybody else should move onto London as if the tour is unaffected."

Ava sat down. "And what about London?"

Gianna took a minute to consider it. "I can't say right now."

Knowing Gianna wouldn't see her reaction, Olivia grimaced and added, "If you're back by the third day, we could go on with the current schedule."

Gianna said nothing.

Olivia pressed the issue. "We don't have the same luxury of time between London and New York. We'll need fair warning…"

Gianna cut her off. "Make the arrangements for Africa." She turned around and stared at them. "Now leave me alone."

The two of them stood and made strides in retreat out of the living room. Gianna was left standing with little but the lavish chateau around her for relief. But it was no relief at all. She stepped to a nearby couch and sat down. She crossed her legs and stared into the fire.

Ten minutes later, her phone rang on the coffee table before her. Looking over at it, she could see the call was from Jaxon Muse. At first, not wanting to talk to anyone, she let it ring. A moment before it transferred to voicemail, she snatched it in hand and answered.

"Hello…" The salutation was a statement of many things besides a greeting. A mélange of anxiety, fatigue, and annoyance was there.

Jaxon heard all of it. "My God, how are you holding up? Are you OK? How's Suah?"

"We'll be all right. Congratulations on your news. You and Claire must be walking on air."

"That's a perfect way to express it. We're so blessed. I can't thank you enough."

"Don't start with that," sighed Gianna. "It isn't necessary."

Jaxon was ebullient. "I know what happened to Claire had Suah's help. He wasn't there at the time but all the same, something flowed through me. It's almost as if he did it this way so Claire and I *both* could be healed."

"Why did you need to be healed?"

"Claire's body had a sickness but for me, my illness was in my spirit. Somehow, Suah must have sensed what we both needed. It was the strangest thing; hard to describe."

"It usually is. Then again, you're a professional at that, aren't you? The mystical is just another day at work for you."

"Just like the magic of performing is for you," countered Jaxon.

"It's no secret; the power of music is mystical to me. That I understand."

"We're both in the business of understanding and moving the human spirit. You do it by reaching people's hearts. You did that tonight with your encore."

"I was singing to Suah and no one else. If anyone overheard me, it was purely incidental."

"Pure is a good way to describe it, just like what I've been through."

"It was that powerful?"

"You have no idea. I'm so grateful for this trip. Spending time at this ranch has given me time to think."

"I'm surprised. I thought thinking was your stock in trade all the time."

"No, not like this. Here I've experienced a different kind of thinking. It's more like listening and allowing, really. It's changed me."

A mild chuckle lightened Gianna's tone. "Sounds like you've found your way to get into the zone. As a musician, I can relate to that."

"I realize what you've gone through makes this a touchy subject, but I have to say it—I can't help but believe that the journey Suah took over the last couple of weeks was the best thing possible for him."

"I appreciate the intent, but don't go there…"

"No, really, hear me out. In its own mysterious way, maybe it was a good thing that Suah was cut loose by Blake Fry and left to wander around town. It gave Suah experiences that opened him up, introduced him to the world on his own terms for the first time in his life. It allowed him to flow with his instincts and listen to the potential of his higher self."

Gianna rested her head back and closed her eyes. "I'm glad you've had your epiphanies but I'm sorry. Right now, I can't see a sugar-coated world."

In his enthusiasm, Jaxon persisted. "It's not unreasonable to say that Suah discovered an independence and confidence unlike anything he ever had before. It's not sugar-coated to say that he was given opportunities to interact with people and in doing so, began to use and develop his gifts."

"I know you're a convert. You think Suah's the great healer…"

"You still doubt that?" Jaxon was incredulous.

"I don't know what's been going on. I'll leave it to people like you and Wyatt Dumashe to figure that out—but none of it will be at the expense of Suah having a normal and happy life."

"If Suah is special in so many ways, do you think that's possible?"

"There's only one way to find out—I'll do everything in my power to make it so? There's no other way."

"But if he really has these gifts, these remarkable powers to heal, shouldn't he be allowed to use them? Why deny the world something that might revolutionize medicine and the whole way we think of human abilities? A door has opened; how can we ignore it?"

Gianna paused. She thought back to the melee at the stadium and the feeling she had clutching Suah to her as the horde of photographers and fans pressed in on them. "The world isn't ready for a gift like his."

Her statement, if true, was crushing and final. But it wasn't something that Jaxon would ever accept. He answered her with equal energy.

"Sure it is! It has to be! Just look around—it's *more* than ready."

Gianna's energy deflated. "That's no endorsement. The fact is, the world's always been ready only because it's been screwed up forever. My son isn't going to change that."

"How do you know?"

Gianna opened her eyes and stared at the ceiling. "The same way you know there will always be an audience for your next self help book. People like you tell everyone you have the answers, but if that was true, your whole industry would have collapsed long ago."

"There's always work to do…"

"Not when the work is simply recycling the answers that the great minds have told us for thousands of years. What's the point?"

"Just because it's never happened doesn't mean it's impossible."

"That's a nice sound bite for your next book…"

"Or lyrics for your next hit song."

Gianna sat up. "The difference is, I do what I do for entertainment. Are you willing to say the same thing?"

Jaxon didn't answer, directly. He could hear the bitterness and sarcasm rise up in her voice. He didn't want to alienate her. He decided to let it go and switch to more pressing matters.

"I have news about the twin effigy question you asked me to research."

Gianna went with the flow. "Anything interesting?"

"I take it you already have a lot of the details about the custom, its meaning, and how it relates to village life…"

"Yes, I've heard all about it."

"Then I'll get to the heart of it—how it relates to Suah in particular."

"That was the idea…"

Jaxon began. "My sources are ambivalent about going through with it."

"Making the effigy?"

"Yes. They admit it might have a balancing influence for Suah, but they warn it could have an adverse effect also. The chances are pretty even between the two."

"What kind of adverse effect?" asked Gianna, suddenly more interested.

"The gifts of a prodigious savant, if that's what Suah is, are mysterious, even to medical science. Tampering with those gifts could make them go away."

"Go away? How does that work?"

"No one knows. The psychology of it is complex; the end result up to chance. If given the effigy, Suah might find a more normal balance within himself, become more adjusted, or maybe not. Changes to the dynamic between Hawa and him could upset him—in ways no one can predict."

Gianna's thoughts went right away to *The Protoprime Society's* recommendation. "I know other experts that claim there's no downside to it. Who should I believe?"

"You've been talking to Wyatt?"

"Yes, he has his resources too."

"I'm sure he has. Now that Claire is well, he'd like Claire and me to join his list of resources."

"Why not? Like you, he wants to find out what is going on."

"Oh, I'm sure of it. He sent me a note to that effect. The man who runs the place here, Henri, gave it to me. Wyatt definitely shares my excitement for Suah's gift. In his note, he mentioned a lab in Finland that can do brain scans. He was quite excited about the fact that the scans were non-invasive— no big, claustrophobic machines to get into; it can be done sitting in a chair."

Gianna got up and paced back to the mantle. "How interesting…"

"You'll have to make the call about whether to do the effigy or not. Anyone competent will tell you—it could go either way."

"So once again, as usual, the experts can't come to a consensus. Why am I not surprised?"

"That's always the way it is with a new field of study."

"Knowing that doesn't help me. Meanwhile, what am I supposed to do?"

Jaxon paused. "If you want Suah to stay the same, exactly the way he is now, I'd say do nothing. It's the one way that's safe."

"Do nothing. Even if he never gets closure with Hawa?"

"Strange as it may sound, that open wound may be the exact reason why he has this power to heal. He might be what they call an *acquired savant*. His gift is the result of overcompensating for some damage he's suffered. Usually, it's central nervous system damage. But in his case, it could be some sort of psychic damage that goes all the way back to the womb."

"Theories don't help me, Mr. Muse. I have to go. I'm tired."

The call ended, leaving Gianna more unsettled than before.

CHAPTER 59

The caravan of three SUVs moved as one racing east from the airport directly into the African morning sun. In time, the wide highway became a two-lane road. Sometime later, the road turned into a dusty path through parched fields. The world out here was wider, the sky larger in a way that left no doubt that a resilient Nature was still in charge.

The drivers were locals but everyone else on board belonged to Gianna's team. Olivia was in the lead car with one of the guards. Suah and Gianna followed in the middle car with a second guard. That left the remaining two guards trailing with supplies in the third SUV.

In the distance, the broad savannah was festooned with majestic Baobab trees. Even from far away, the towering height and breath of these ancient wonders could induce awe and a sense of inimitable beauty.

Seeing them in person, Gianna could see why they were called the *tree of life*. With a trunk reaching fifteen meters in diameter and crinkled white flowers that lasted only a single day, it was easy to understand why these splendid giants were the source of so many native superstitions.

The caravan slowed past huts and scattered livestock as barefoot children ran alongside the vehicles. They waved and smiled and offered handmade trinkets for sale but no one stopped.

Suah strained against his seat belt to watch them as the car rolled past.

Sitting next to him in the backseat, Gianna noticed how his face changed with interest. "Look familiar?" she asked.

Suah glanced over and nodded, then pressed his nose to the window again. They were on the outskirts of his village. Its main buildings and one intersection were yet to come. The whole place wasn't that big but it took seeing it up close to jog memories and fill in the blank spaces in his mind.

Suah hadn't been back since the adoption four years before. Such a gap in time might not make that much difference to an adult but for Suah, leaving when he was only five-years old, the impact was substantial. So much was recognizable and yet everything was so foreign to the life he was now living.

The caravan stopped for pedestrian traffic before passing through the main intersection. It gave Suah and Gianna a snapshot impression of the pace and variety to village life today. A short time later, the three SUVs turned into the frontage space outside the village's one school building.

The school was one story and the most basic of architectural styles. Next to it was a plot of land where planned new construction was being surveyed. From the looks of it, the planned additions would triple the school's size.

Gianna and Suah got out and stretched from their long ride as the four guards took up positions and watched the perimeter around the group.

Right away, a school administrator and a teacher came out to greet them. Village elders knew the visit was coming, even if for security reasons few details about the circumstances necessitating it had been shared.

"Welcome!" A lanky man in his thirties approached. "My name is Zokaya. I'm the school administrator." He turned to the older woman next to him. "May I introduce Mabasi…"

The woman rushed forward and met Suah halfway before they hugged. Obviously, she needed no introduction.

She smiled at Gianna, "I was Suah's teacher."

Suah looked back. "Mabasi taught me to sing songs."

"Oh! Very happy to meet you," beamed Gianna.

Mabasi shook the pop star's hand. "The honor is mine. We share a love of singing and it's well known you do great things with your music."

"You bring the joy of singing to children; there's nothing greater than that."

Zokaya agreed, "Yes, everyone, no matter how little they have, can make music with their voice."

Olivia stepped up and Gianna introduced her. "And this is Olivia, my business manager."

"You've had a long trip," noted Zokaya. "Come, let's go inside, out of this sun."

Once inside, Suah and Mabasi broke off in one direction so Suah could reconnect with the old place. Gianna and Olivia followed Zokaya on a stroll elsewhere. Soon, they approached a central yard where children played.

With Suah out of earshot, the school administrator saw an opportunity to handle business. "I must tell you, we received your request just this morning but I'm afraid fulfilling it will not be possible."

"Which request?" asked Gianna. "Are you talking about Suah's grandfather?"

Zokaya halted and turned to them. "Yes. You've come a long way. I hate to disappoint you but the grandfather you're searching for died years ago."

"He died?" Gianna's heart sank with the news.

"I'm afraid so. He took seriously ill shortly after Suah started school here. The man was old and not well. He had also become quite unstable. With no other family, we thought it best to give Suah fulltime care."

"Pardon me, but there's one thing I don't understand."

"Yes?"

"Suah said he was told he'd see his grandfather again..."

"That is correct. I asked Mabasi about that. Regrettably, it was misunderstood. Suah was told he'd see his grandfather again as part of a religious teaching. It was meant to express an ultimate joining in the afterlife, nothing more."

"Why wasn't Suah told his grandfather died?"

Zokaya looked troubled. "At the time, Suah's state was fragile. He had no one else except his imaginary friend..."

"His sister Hawa."

The man nodded. "We thought it best not to disturb him. He had so little; he was already so withdrawn. There was no reason to burden him further."

Aching for Suah's loss, Gianna took a moment to blink back tears.

Olivia spoke up to cover for her. "Is there anyone else here that Suah was particularly close to—in the same way he was close to his grandfather?"

"No, not in the same way. For five years they were together. It was not a stable life but they did share love. Some didn't see it but Mabasi and I could tell. We let it go a long while; some say longer than it was good for the boy. We didn't see it that way. It was true; life in the school was more normal for Suah, yes, but it couldn't compare. No way."

A few moments of silence passed among the three of them. As Gianna gazed out at the children in the play yard, Zokaya thought through next steps.

"How would you like Suah to find out? Do you want Mabasi or myself to tell him?"

Gianna shook her head. "No. Thank you, I'll tell him."

"Very well..." Zokaya reached into his pocket. "We did find this. You should have it. It's not the grandfather in the flesh but maybe it will help."

Reaching out, Gianna accepted a snapshot on worn paper.

Looking down on it, she was struck by what she saw. It was Suah with his grandfather; they were sitting side-by-side. Suah's arm was around his grandfather's shoulder and Suah was smiling broadly. Even though the grandfather wasn't smiling, he was looking at the camera with happy eyes.

Gianna smiled and showed Olivia the photograph. "Thank you," she said to Zokaya. "Thank you so much. I know this will mean a lot to him."

"There are others who really deserve the thanks, not me."

"Who do you mean?"

"A week ago, a pair of researchers came here. They said they worked for *The Protoprime Society*. They interviewed many people. They are the ones who found it. You should thank them."

Gianna tucked the photo away. "I will."

"Good. Now, as far as your schedule, you tell us what your plans are and we'll see what we can do to accommodate."

Gianna gave it some thought. "Right now, I think it's best I told Suah. I know he has a lot of anticipation around his grandfather."

Zokaya nodded. "Suah is fortunate to have such hard news softened by a mother's love."

The three of them walked back and found Suah and Mabasi catching up on what had happened with each other over the past four years. Gianna tempted Suah away by asking him to show her where he used to live. Olivia stayed behind with Zokaya to square away sleeping arrangements for Gianna's group. With two guards trailing steps behind, they set off.

Once outside, Suah turned to the north and followed a footpath.

"Did you have a nice visit with your teacher?" asked Gianna.

"She *used* to be my teacher when I was *this* high…" Suah held his hand out by his waist.

"I never knew she was the one who taught you how to sing."

"Well, that's not really right," Suah corrected. "I always could sing; I just didn't know any songs. Mabasi knows lots of them."

The distinction made Gianna smile. "So you used to sing in class?"

"Every day. We had to sing after we came in from the play yard. She said it helped settle us down."

"Oh, so that's it. She had you sing to calm you down."

"Not always. Sometime we sang to fill up with the spirit. She said some songs would help us feel what a little bit of heaven was like."

"Do you remember one of those songs? I'd like to hear one."

Suah walked along. "You want me to sing it now?"

"If you want…"

The cadence of Suah's steps changed as he began to rock back and forth. His song started as humming and the humming grew stronger until the repeating notes were replaced with words he sung out.

"…*This little light of mine*
I'm going to let it shine
Oh, this little light of mine

I'm going to let it shine,
This little light of mine
I'm going to let it shine
Let it shine, let it shine, let it shine …

Everywhere I go
I'm going to let it shine
Oh, everywhere I go
I'm going to let it shine
Everywhere I go
I'm going to let it shine
Let it shine, let it shine, let it shine. "

The song returned to humming but Suah kept stepping along at the same pace with the tempo of the music.

"That was wonderful!" praised Gianna.

"It's funny singing it out here. I never sang in the field before."

"So how does everything look? Does it look the same?" asked Gianna.

Suah toddled along. "Just about, except for the new things they're building."

"Some of that is being paid for by Jaxon Muse, did you know that?"

Suah shook his head. At a fork in the trail, they took the branch to the left.

"I'm glad he's happy now," said Suah.

"His wife Claire isn't sick anymore. That's big news."

"I know, I saw it on TV."

"Jaxon thinks you had something to do with that."

Suah shrugged then slowed to study the fields on his right side.

"We all had something to do with it."

As Suah halted, Gianna stepped up alongside. "What do you mean 'we all had something to do with it'?"

Suah gazed out over the field as if it was another time and place. *"Like the air around us, it touches everyone at the same time."*

Gianna had never seen Suah drift into trance. After years together, it was not an experience that they'd ever shared. In fact, Gianna had only heard about such a thing recently. The video of the Jaxon Muse conference claimed to show it but, for a nonbeliever, it wasn't convincing. Witnessing it firsthand, Gianna found the change in him unsettling yet strangely persuasive.

Despite the hot sun, a chill went through her. She looked out to the distance where his attention was fixed. "Is this a special place for you?"

More of the regular Suah returned and overlaid his daze. "This is where my grandfather grew things. Hawa and I spent many days together out here. It was our job to scare away the birds and goats."

"So they wouldn't eat the crops…"

"We made a game out of it."

There was never going to be a good time to break the news to him about his grandfather; no easy way to start. Part of her regretted having volunteered to be the one to tell him. Another part would have it no other way.

Gianna crouched down and put her arm over his shoulder. "You know, sometimes the things we want the most just aren't possible. You know that, don't you?"

The non sequitur didn't faze Suah. "I know lots of people believe in magic. Some even think *they're* the magic. They say with magic, anything's possible."

"Maybe so, for some people. Maybe they have the secret, but I'm not like them. There's some things, no matter how hard I try, I can't make happen."

Suah turned his head to look at her. "Jaxon Muse told me the same thing. He said, 'I can only do what I can do.'"

"Yes, that's the way it is for most people. Maybe we don't believe enough, or try enough…maybe something with us didn't happen just right, but for whatever reason, the only magic we have…is the love we share. And I love you…" Tears welled in her eyes. "…but I can't take you to your grandfather. No one can…I'm sorry."

Suah stood and absorbed the blow. The sadness on Gianna's face explained everything he needed to know. He was left with more melancholy than grief. Maybe the grief would come later, but right then, he was more disturbed than anything. He didn't like to see his mom cry.

Suah had to ask, "So, will I see him again some day?"

Gianna had no way of knowing the answer to that question but for Suah's sake, she lied and nodded her head. "Yes, some day, but not here." She pulled out the old photograph and handed it to him. "They found this for you. It's the closest thing I can give you for what you want."

Suah took the picture and held it in hand. He stared at it a long while and cocked his head to one side. A little grin crept onto his lips as a tear fell.

Wanting to give him something, anything, to ease his pain, Gianna reached out and held him, then asked him, "What do you want, Suah? I'm here for you. You can have anything you want."

As soon as she said it, Gianna felt sickened by the lie. What was she doing? She had just proved to him he *couldn't* have anything he wanted. Now, here she was, once again, promising him the same again.

Suah glanced into her eyes and then back to the photo. Back and forth he looked between them as he thought. Finally, he looked up and out, into the fields. "I'd like to stay here…"

Gianna's heart fell, the bottom dropping out of it. "In the village?"

"Yeah…" The answer was slight, barely a whisper, but monumental.

Gianna couldn't believe what she was hearing. "You want to live here?"

Suah nodded.

The possibility was remote but just the thought of losing Suah shook Gianna to the core. She hugged him close so he wouldn't see the torment on her face. What would she ever do without him?

She raced to explain it away. He was just sad about losing his grandfather. Perhaps this was his way, in his grief, of feeling close to the one he'd lost. The reaction was understandable but she shouldn't read too much into it.

To stall her panic, she kept asking questions.

"What would you do here?" As soon as she said it, she regretted it. Asking such a thing was not meant as a denigration of village life but it certainly could be taken that way. She rushed to cover it over with another question. "How long would you want to stay?"

"I don't know. Maybe long enough to do something…"

"Like what? If you could do anything, what would it be?"

Suah went deep in thought for a while before looking back to her.

"Maybe I could be a *Helf Selp* person. I could do that here like Jaxon Muse does everywhere else."

Gianna didn't understand. "What does that mean? What would you be doing?"

Suah puzzled to explain it. "I don't know; not yet. I guess I'd have to stay here a while to find out."

He had been promised anything he wanted. She never should have asked him such a question if she wasn't prepared for what he might say.

If there was any way to take it all back, she wondered if she would. Would it be selfish or was she only be feeling the full force of the love she had for him? How could she ever deny the expression of love she felt?

With curiosity, he watched villagers walking in the distance.

Gianna tried to reason with him. "But Jaxon Muse travels around the world doing what he does. He doesn't stay in one place."

"I know, but he's a lot older. I have to start somewhere."

It was hard to argue with that. "That's right. You do."

Gianna was at odds with herself. If the greatest love was unconditional love, how could she ever put conditions on giving him anything he wanted?

Flash images of eighty thousand fans cheering for her moved across her field of vision and melted away into the parched fields. In all the world, Suah was the only one she had, the only personal love she could call her own. How would she ever be able to let him go? Must she share him with the world too?

Suah strolled off the path into the tall grass. "If I lived here, Hawa and I could play together again like we used to."

Gianna followed along. "Can't you and Hawa play anywhere?"

"We can dance anywhere but we only play here."

"Why is that?"

"All we need is music to dance but to play we have to be out chasing the birds and goats."

Gianna let the image rest with him. She could tell he was lost in the thought of days gone by playing in these fields.

They walked on. In time, their steps turned back down the path towards the school. They walked back in silence. Gianna wrestled with what to do.

She had just told him how sometimes the things we want the most just aren't possible. How could she ask of him what she wasn't willing to apply to herself? Despite wanting him all to herself, perhaps that was just not possible. To her heart, the thought of letting him stay in the village was out of the question. All the while, her mind wondered.

Nearing the school, Suah ran ahead. Other children ran up to him and frolicked around. They kicked a soccer ball back and forth by him in a game of keep-away. He smiled and tried to follow the action whirling around him. He didn't join in even though his eyes danced with amusement.

Gianna stopped and watched from a distance. She enjoyed seeing children play. As far as she knew, Suah had never played a game of soccer. There were so many things he had yet to do. So much of life was in store for him.

A pang of loss jolted through her as she remembered Suah's words.

"I have to start somewhere."

CHAPTER 60

The children had fun giving Suah their version of a village tour. For the most part, it was little more than gathering around, getting acquainted, wandering off, or running to look at something when the suggestion came up.

They met him with excited smiles and curious looks, some trying to engage him right away, but most tagging along to see what the excitement was all about. A couple of the older kids obviously remembered him. To most others though, he was a curious stranger who had arrived by caravan.

Gianna let him run off and explore the immediate area around the school and orphanage dormitories. He was not quite blending in but it was clear he wondered what it would be like once he did. Gianna turned away and shuddered. She told herself it was the effects of thirst and the heat of midday but her heart knew it as separation anxiety.

Given what Suah had asked for, she couldn't help but let a moment of jealousy pass through her. The feeling was unreasonable and yet, no matter how good or bad her feelings had ever been, they never had to pass a test to see how rational or realistic they were. Raw emotion rose up automatically, inevitably, most times without a doubt and often times without recourse.

To anyone else it would look like simple play but a needy side of her saw it for what it really was—a subtle seduction that might convince Suah to stay in the village. What he had asked for in a moment of grief could be given credence by those children's smiles. Either way, she needed to prepare for the eventuality that was most likely, even if it was the last thing she wanted.

She ambled back towards the schoolhouse. Along the way, Olivia hurried up to her, fretful and needing to settle something right away.

"Did you know Wyatt was coming here?" Olivia looked aghast.

Gianna was jolted from her reverie. "No…"

"Mabasi said he should arrive any minute. She thought we knew."

"I don't know what gave her that idea. I know your history with Wyatt. I certainly wouldn't surprise you with such a thing."

"He obviously wants to be here when we're here. How did he know about our trip? Did you tell him?"

"We talked about whether it made sense to have a twin effigy made; that's all. He said he'd take care of it."

"Apparently, he's doing more than that. Mabasi said he has plans on expanding their community center and upgrading water facilities in the area."

"Yeah," admitted Gianna. "He told me that—but nothing about a visit."

"It can't be a coincidence," charged Olivia.

"Probably not," Gianna admitted. "We'll just have to wait and see what he has in mind. Right now, there are more pressing things to consider."

"Why? What's going on?"

Gianna led her on a slow stroll. "Suah told me he wants to stay here."

Olivia read the seriousness on Gianna's face. "You mean live here?"

"I told him about his grandfather, gave him the picture, then asked him what he wanted. That's what he said."

Olivia had none of Gianna's emotions. "We didn't see *that* coming."

"I promised him anything he wanted." Gianna chuckled and looked to the sky. "It was so stupid…"

"Now, wait; don't be so hard on yourself. You've always said your main priority is giving him a happy and normal life. The only question is—who gets to decide what that should be? You or him?"

"Some would say he's too young to know what's good for him."

"People are going to talk no matter what you do. Magnify that a thousand fold since the world knows he's a special needs child."

"Maybe my failure is never finding out what that special need really is. I thought love would handle anything. Maybe I was wrong."

"You're not wrong," asserted Olivia. "Suah's had a good life with you; it's matured him in many ways."

"And held him back in many others. I can't see giving him up for any length of time but it's clear to me—there are some things he'll only get from the rest of the world. It doesn't seem wise to leave the decision up to him and yet, I don't know what to do."

Olivia halted and turned to her. "There's one way to find out. Let him stay here—temporarily, for just a visit. It could work out for everyone."

"How?" Gianna was limp with bewilderment.

Olivia drew close. "After Rome and Paris, you've said it yourself—taking Suah on the road right now looks pretty much impossible. And that was before Claire Muse had her remarkable recovery. Now it's unthinkable."

"I don't know…" Gianna stepped away and forced Olivia to follow.

"If you let him visit here—just until we finish the teaser tour, he'll get the visit he wants and you can finish your tour dates without the kind of hysteria the two of you had to endure at the *Stade*. It might be the best thing to do."

Gianna shook her head. "Why is all this happening? It all started with this tour! I shouldn't have left him home with Paige to begin with. Now we end up here. I can't help but wonder if this will be something else to regret."

"Don't think of it that way," urged Olivia. "You want to make Suah happy and he wants to try this out—so let him."

"And what if he wants to stay!"

"He won't," Olivia assured her. "It's natural for him to be curious about his village. But really, how could he give up his life with you for this? Don't worry about what people might say; you're not abandoning him. If anything, we'll stress how important it is for him to get in touch with his cultural roots. How can they call that anything but politically correct?"

"I don't care what people say. You don't get it!"

"Yes, I do. But it's not forever. You'll still be his mom. The day after the tour ends in L.A., he can join you on the island. Sandy will be there. The two of you can go on like it was before."

A bitterness descended over Gianna. "You make it sound so easy, almost like this is a lucky break for everyone concerned. Why do I distrust that?"

Olivia could read between the lines of Gianna's suspicions. "Maybe because you've been listening to Nathan Mackey too much."

"It's hard to ignore some things he says. I suppose if it's lucky for *everyone concerned,* that includes you."

"Gianna, I shouldn't have to go into this. I'm not the same person I was years ago. Whatever I did then doesn't define who I decide to be today. Nathan has a theory and he went looking for facts to support it. You know how it works. Assembled together just right, fragments of the past can lead one to believe all sorts of things."

"You can't fault me for having doubts, not when the facts are so clear."

"After ten years together, do you really think we're that unhealthy and codependent? Jesus! If anyone's a drama queen, it's Nathan Mackey."

"I can't help but wonder sometimes about your motives. Some facts stand on their own. The passage of time doesn't obscure what they are."

"And I guess no matter how misguided I was years ago about some things, there's no redemption—no chance to change and move on."

"I'm not saying that..."

"Then what *are* you saying? I'm not trying to sabotage all your relation-ships so I can keep you to myself! OK? I thought you knew me well enough not to buy into that. *You're* the one who brought up the pressing business of Suah wanting to stay here. I didn't suggest the idea to you—*he* did!" Olivia was visibly shaken.

"You're right. He did." Gianna's bitterness abated. "I'm sorry. Everything the past few days…it's too much for me. No wonder we're all on edge."

"Whatever you want to do is fine with me," concluded Olivia. "Tomorrow morning we fly out of here with or without Suah. You decide. Just let me know so I can give a heads up to our people in London."

"I told you; I don't know what to do," confessed Gianna. "If he did stay here for a visit, how would it work? Who would he stay with? I think he should stay with a family. I can't see him living in the dormitory, going through what it was like to be an orphan again."

"Let's go ask Zokaya. He might have some ideas."

The two of them walked back to the schoolhouse and found Mabasi.

"Where can we find Zokaya?" asked Olivia.

"He's over at the community center," answered Mabasi. "He's preparing for the visit by Wyatt Dumashe. Can I help you?"

Gianna spoke up. "I was wondering. If Suah wanted to stay here for a short visit after we leave, would that be possible?"

Mabasi was surprised. "Suah said this?"

"Yes," admitted Gianna. "I think he misses his grandfather and wants to spend a little more time here. Unfortunately, I cannot stay. I need to be in London tomorrow afternoon."

"He would have no guardian staying with him?"

"Not for the visit, no."

Olivia added, "We'd probably leave one guard here, just to be sure Suah and the village wouldn't be bothered by anyone from the outside. "

Mabasi was pleasant. "I'm sure something could be arranged."

"I would really like him to stay with a family," insisted Gianna.

"A family? All the boys in the dormitory are like a family."

"I'm sure they are, but Suah has special needs. It's taken four years for him to open up the way he has. The central issue facing him has always been the loss of his family. I wouldn't want him to feel like an orphan again in any way. I'm sure you understand…"

"Yes," nodded Mabasi. "I understand you are fearful for him—but there is really no need. All the adults in the village are parents to all children as if they are their own."

"That's beautiful, a lovely way to live, but you see, Suah's had a home ever since he left here."

"How many are in your family?" asked Mabasi.

In comparison, Gianna felt exposed. "It's the two of us, Suah and me…"

"Two can be a family, this is true, but I do not think you should be fearful for him here. His misses his grandfather but he never knew his mother or father so he won't miss them the same way he would if he lost them now."

Gianna fought back tears. "He could still miss them. He might even miss me."

"Of course he would miss you!" asserted Mabasi. "But that's not what I mean. You said the loss of his family is the main issue. That family is his birth family. Except for the grandfather, they are something he didn't know. Others miss something they did know. We have older children who lost their mother or father to disease or in the war. They remember their parents very well. Some saw their parents die or be killed right in front of them. These children find a home here too. You see, no one is outside the family village. You need not worry about Suah no matter how much he stays inside himself. We'll surround him with a good outside."

Olivia drove home the point. "I think it's staying in the dormitory we want to avoid…" She turned to Gianna for confirmation, "Isn't that right?"

"Yes," confirmed Gianna. "If we could avoid that, I think it would be best for him."

Seeing how intractable Gianna was on the point, Mabasi smiled. "If this would give you peace of mind, it's a little thing, easily done. Suah could stay with me at my house, if you'd like. He would sleep there at night and during the day join the other children."

"That would be wonderful. Thank you." Gianna caught herself and wondered what she was doing. She had started with a simple question whether or not a visit by Suah was feasible. All of a sudden, the arrangements were made. How had it gone that far?

Around a corner came Zokaya. On seeing the three of them, he hurried over. "There you are! I've been looking for you. Wyatt Dumashe is here. He wants to meet everyone over at the community center."

At the mention of Wyatt's name, Olivia got defensive. "Why over there?"

"That's where he's going to start the new construction. He has something to show you."

Gianna gave Olivia a way out. "If you have work to do regarding London, go right ahead. I'll go over and see what it's all about."

Olivia's weak smile was stoic. "No, that's all right. I'd like to go and see what he's up to."

Zokaya pointed towards a group of children in the distance. "Wyatt asked that Suah be there too."

"What for?" asked Gianna.

"He didn't say."

Gianna called out across the yard. "Suah!" She waved him over.

Out of breath, he came running up. "Is it time to eat?"

"Why do you ask that?" laughed Gianna.

Suah pointed behind him. "They've been working in the outdoor kitchen. I heard they're making cassava root and rice. I'd like to try it."

"Maybe in a little bit but right now, we're all going over to the community center to see something."

"What are we going to see?"

"I don't know. It's a surprise."

"Like a birthday surprise?"

"No, I just mean we don't know what it is."

The group began the walk in the direction of the center. Suah was full of tidbits of information he had gathered from the other children.

"Do you know why they have their kitchens outside?" he asked Gianna.

"No, I don't. Did you find out?"

He sauntered along at her side. "Yep. They cook outside so the buildings stay cool on the inside. Is that why we barbecue outside?"

"No," corrected Gianna. "We do that to keep the smoke outside."

"Oh, that's right. We've got air conditioning, but it's a lot hotter here than where we live."

The members of the group, other than Suah, exchanged awkward smiles and glances. The innocence of children had a way of putting things in focus.

Gianna put her arm around Suah's shoulder. "That's right. It is…"

As the group neared the community center, they could see Wyatt's own caravan of vehicles parked near the entrance. Off to one side in an adjoining field, a team of surveyors and engineers went about their tasks.

Flanked by a pair of personal assistants, Wyatt Dumashe interrupted his conversation to turn and notice the approaching group. His ready smile beamed almost as wide as his broad shoulders. He set out at once to meet the group halfway.

Everyone knew each other and yet some had never met in person. As Wyatt acknowledged everyone, his salutations extended from guarded to effusive. He zeroed in on Gianna and Suah right away.

"Gianna!" He gave her a hug. "It's so good to finally meet."

Reacting to his size and powerful presence, Gianna chuckled. "It's true what they say; you really are larger than life…"

Wyatt tapped his chest with an open palm. "I'm a healthy boy. " He gave

Olivia a quick glance. "Hello, Olivia."

Olivia stood polite but resolutely restrained. "Hello, Wyatt."

His attention diverted immediately. "And this must be Suah!"

Suah looked up wide-eyed at the big man.

Wyatt crouched down and shook Suah's hand. "I'm very pleased to meet you too. My name is Wyatt."

Suah grinned, "You have a ponytail."

Wyatt laughed, "That's right! Isn't that a hoot? At my age, I'm so happy to have hair, I can't part with any of it."

"You kinda look like a pirate."

Wyatt stroked his close-cropped beard. "Some people say I act like one too—but don't believe them."

"What do you do?" asked Suah.

Wyatt stood up tall. "I travel the world making good things happen."

"Wow! Do you know Santa Claus?"

"I wish I did. I could learn a thing or two from him about worldwide distribution, don't you think?"

To be agreeable, Suah nodded.

Zokaya added, "You are making good things happen here."

Wyatt looked back at the survey team in the field. "I couldn't let Jaxon Muse hog all the publicity, now could I? We've got a glorious competition going. Whatever Jaxon and his agent build onto the school, I need to do something even bigger over here at the community center. The nice thing is, whoever wins, the village wins. That's the kind of competition I like."

"You are very generous," offered Mabasi.

"I'm also very excited about showing Suah his surprise."

Gianna and Olivia looked to each other, perplexed.

Suah's ears perked up. "A surprise for me?"

"I hope you don't mind," explained Wyatt. "As long as you're here, I thought I might as well swing by and give it to you."

Gianna raised a hand and showed Wyatt by her facial expressions that she needed to talk to him in private. He was caught mid-excitement and had to shift gears. He shifted around and nudged Suah by the shoulder.

Wyatt spoke to Zokaya. "Why don't you take Suah over and show him what we have planned for the community center expansion. I know he'd like to see some of the surveyor equipment."

Zokaya caught on. "Good idea." He led Suah away with Mabasi and Olivia following. Gianna and Wyatt were left alone.

Gianna was concerned. "I didn't even know you were going to be here. Now this? What surprise are you talking about?"

"I should have told you," explained Wyatt. "But it was quite spur of the moment."

"We have to coordinate these things. Now you've already told Suah he's getting something."

"I'm sorry. I thought that's what you wanted."

"Are you talking about the effigy?"

"Yeah, I think I've found the perfect thing…"

Gianna groaned, "I should have told you."

"Told me what?"

"Jaxon had somebody research the topic. They think the effigy could harm Suah just as much as it could help him."

"Harm him?"

"We can't be sure what effect it might have on him."

"*The Society* did research too. It's a standard village practice, one that Suah must be aware of. This area of Africa has one of the highest concentration of twins in the world."

"I know. That isn't the point. You believe Suah has a gift, something that is savant-like. Jaxon's researchers think there's a chance that his gift is tied up with Hawa, the dead sister."

"Why does that matter?"

"They think fooling around with his relationship with her might affect his whole psyche. It could affect his gift."

"In what way?"

"It's unpredictable. There's even a possibility that the issue he has with his sister is the very reason why he has the gift. If that issue gets solved, his gift could go away."

Wyatt took the news in somber silence for a few moments. "It looks like an impasse. The research doesn't agree. I think we'll find as many professional opinions one way as another. The truth is, no one knows."

"It's odd," noted Gianna.

"What?"

"Something you told me before about Suah's grandfather. You said villagers told your researchers the grandfather got it in his head that an effigy would mess up the mystic nature of something unique going on here."

"I also said that little of what he said made any sense to them."

Gianna let it go. So what's the surprise? Did you have an effigy made?"

Wyatt turned and gazed back towards the existing community center. "No. I didn't have one made, because I think I found something better."

"Better? In what way?"

"Better for Suah, something he can connect with personally. Something he's already chosen."

"How can that be?"

"When Nathan Mackey went to your island initially, his team scoured the place, looking for anyone who had any interaction with Suah. As you know, not all of that research made it in to Nathan's documentary."

"What did they find?"

"Something that Suah wants. We don't have to say anything about the effigy thing if you don't want. We can give it to him to enjoy for what it is."

Gianna wavered. "Are you sure of that?"

"You decide." Wyatt took steps away. "Come on, I'll show it to you. If you have any reservations at all, then we'll think of something else to be the surprise. OK?"

Gianna nodded and followed him to the community center's doorway. Right inside the small lobby, a space had been cleared for the presentation. It took only a few moments for her to see the surprise and decide. A minute later, Suah and the others were called to the center too.

Suah hurried into the lobby expectantly, the thrill of anticipation lighting up his face. "Is that it?"

Wyatt nodded. "That's it!"

Suah's steps halted before a short table. On the table, a drape as tall as he was covered something bulky. That something was his surprise.

"Go ahead," urged Wyatt. "Give it a yank!"

Suah reached out and tugged on the shimmery silver material. Like a run of satin over glass, the drape slid down from the object and fell to the table with a swish.

Suah gasped, "Oh, wow! It's *Far Reaching*..." There before him was a sculpture in Brazilian black soapstone, the very same one he had admired at the art shop in town by his home.

Wyatt chuckled, "I think it's called *Reaching Far*."

"Is this really for me?"

"Yep, it's yours. You can do whatever you want with it."

Suah reached up and slid his fingers gently over the stone. "Whoooo!"

Stunned, Olivia leaned close to Gianna. "What is this?"

Gianna whispered back, "Something Suah found on his adventure around town. Mackey's team interviewed the art gallery owner. She remembered Suah coming in one day and wanting to take this piece home."

"No wonder," gasped Olivia. "It's amazing; the two of them leaning back like that…"

"I know," smiled Gianna. "It looks like Suah already picked out his perfect twin effigy."

Suah's gaze followed the lines of the sculpture up from where the twin figures were joined at the base then split apart mid-thigh. As they reached up and back they stretched farther away from each other while sharing a common base.

Gianna stepped up and put her arm around his shoulder. "That's quite a surprise, isn't it?"

"It's big; it's as big as me!" He looked to Wyatt. "Thanks a lot for my surprise."

"I'm glad you like it, but then, I knew you would!" Wyatt laughed.

Mabasi inspected the smooth stone. "Where are you going to keep such a beautiful thing?"

Suah ran his fingers over the brass name plate. "I told the lady at the art store I wanted to keep it in my room—or maybe my closet."

"You must have a very big room," mused Mabasi.

"It's big, but not big enough to get lost in."

Wyatt chimed in, "That sounds like the world around us."

"The world is a lot bigger than my room!"

"Bigger but the world is round like a circle," offered Wyatt. "No matter how far you go, you'll always wind up near some place you started from. That's why it's so fun to explore. That's why we can never get lost from each other, not for long." Wyatt gave Gianna a glance."

"You like exploring too?" asked Suah.

"Every day in every way." He pointed to himself. "The fun thing is, there's as much to explore on the inside as there is outside."

"How do you do that?" quizzed Suah.

Wyatt caught a glance from the others. "Somehow, I think you already manage that. So, is it going in your room or your closet?"

Suah looked around. "Maybe I could keep it here for a while…"

Zokaya stepped around to inspect the piece. "That's a great idea. When everyone comes to the center, they can walk by and enjoy your surprise."

Suah took a step back and looked at the piece. "I'd like that."

With mixed emotions, Gianna hugged his shoulder. "Me too."

CHAPTER 61

Morning came quickly on the flat African plain. For Gianna Chase, after a fitful rest in unfamiliar surroundings, the first light of day brought a mixture of relief and foreboding. It was passing relief to have the sleepless night of second-guessing herself over and done with. Now came the dreaded worry for what the day would mean going forward.

Gianna crept out of her group's makeshift quarters in the community center before anyone else was awake. She needed time to herself to think, to come to terms with what was happening. She prayed for strength and the peace of mind that comes when one is sure what they are doing is right.

Searching a bright and clear sky, she found nothing new, only blue.

Arrangements had been made. Suah would be staying in the village. One guard would stay with him. Mabasi had generously offered to open up her home to him. The villagers had kindly embraced Suah again as one of their own. He would stay here until he wanted to leave or until after the last concert date in Los Angeles one week away—whatever came first.

A week without Suah on the road, given the temperament of the media storm around him, probably was the best way to handle things. In that, Olivia was right. And yet, a nagging notion needled away at Gianna's resolve.

What if this wasn't temporary?

What if Suah asked to stay here for good? What would she do?

For now, she forced the idea out of her mind, even though it had kept her awake all night. There was enough to think about and do without tormenting herself with future possibilities that might never come to pass.

In less than fourteen hours, she had to hit the stage full-throttle in London for another concert performance. By then, she needed the plains of Africa and her personal troubles equally remote. If she ever hoped to have the energy and attitude to perform, she had to get through the next couple of hours with her soul and her spirit intact.

After a while, the sun rose higher and the village stirred with activity. Everyone had breakfast and most went about the lives they knew. For Gianna and Mabasi, it was time to take a stroll into the fields where Suah played.

When they got close enough to see him but far enough away not to disturb his private time, they stopped and shared a deep and parting communion with each other. They were the only two women ever to give Suah motherly advice and comfort. In this, they sensed their bond and their common goals.

"You have done so well by him," offered Mabasi. "Just look at him. He has so much happiness inside of him."

Gianna watched as Suah wandered in the far field. He was alone as he played but he didn't act that way. He watched for birds and spoke to the sky.

"It's hard to let him go," confessed Gianna. "Even for a visit."

"He did not come from you but he's in your heart the same way. I understand."

"I never knew exactly what he needed—so I tried to give him every-thing."

"There's no fault in that," stressed Mabasi. "He has his special ways, no one understands."

"Except maybe his grandfather."

Mabasi rocked her head back and forth. "That could be. But he's unlike his grandfather. If his grandfather was the seed, Suah is the tree. Suah does with no effort what his grandfather struggled with his whole life."

"Do you believe in any of the mystical things?" asked Gianna.

Mabasi thought a second. "I know with Suah, there's no way to confine him—no definition for what he is. He needs what he needs and only he can say what that is. His route may not be normal, but his destination is sound."

"What do you think that is?"

"You want to know what I think or what I feel?"

"Is there a difference?"

"Oh yes," confided Mabasi. "I feel he has the ability to touch lives."

"What makes you say that?"

"I remember his grandfather talking about his birth. He said when Suah was born, he heard compassion in the baby's cry. This was not the cry of a normal child. This child could feel the world around him and know what was well and not so well. His grandfather knew right then—a rare and good magic had happened; something of the unseen world was among us."

"But I thought everyone in the village said the grandfather was unstable."

"Yes, he was," agreed Mabasi. "That doesn't mean he was wrong!"

Taken aback, Gianna had no comment.

Mabasi added, "The seed and the tree. Suah gravitates to people who are wounded because he identifies with them so much—because he's wounded too. Like his grandfather, Suah is also unstable. But unlike his grandfather, he has an outlet to express for others what he can't do for himself."

"I know he misses Hawa even though he's never met her."

"Who are we to say? If you ask him, he will tell you he *has* met her. Look at him out there. Who do you think he's playing with?"

"An imaginary friend. All the doctors say he made her up to help him cope with being an orphan."

"Is that all you think it is?" asked Mabasi.

"I can't say for sure but it's the simplest explanation."

"Why do you think that's simpler than his story? He knows he shared his mother's womb with Hawa. There's nothing imaginary about that."

Gianna gazed out in the field and watched him run and twirl around. "I've been told if his wound ever heals, then his healing powers might go away."

"Maybe so. He's drawn to certain people, I know that. There are things no one can explain. He could not even explain to us what he does. It would be like asking a tree how it designed its blossoms to look different from the blossoms of every other tree. The tree simply knows without knowing how."

"That's what you feel. Now tell me what you think."

Mabasi took hold of Gianna's hand. "I think we are both mothers. We love our child unconditionally. All of the rest of it—we'll never know. If it makes us feel better, we can have hope or faith that our child turned out the way he did because there's a greater purpose for it."

"That's too open-ended," countered Gianna. "A greater purpose that's never defined tells me nothing."

"Many believe it *has* been defined. Long ago, words were spoken to describe it. Just because we've never lived up to the promise of those words doesn't mean the purpose is unachievable."

"What words were spoken?" asked Gianna.

Mabasi squeezed Gianna's hand and recited from memory. "*...Most assuredly, I say to you, he who believes in Me, the works that I do he will do also; and greater works than these he will do, because I go to My Father.*"

Gianna recognized the Bible verse.

Mabasi added another, "*...Heal the sick, cleanse the lepers, raise the dead, cast out demons. Freely you have received, freely give.*"

Gianna despaired at the easy answer. "That's all well and good but you teach at a missionary school. What else could you say?"

"You asked what I think and feel. I can say nothing else."

"It was kind of you to share with me," offered Gianna.

Mabasi started away. "I'll leave you some private time to say goodbye. I know you have little time before you have to go."

"Thank you, for everything." Gianna stepped after her and gave her a hug.

Mabasi hugged back. "I will be good to Suah. He will have a good visit."

With Mabasi stepping away, Gianna was left alone at the edge of the field. She called out to get Suah's attention and he came running. As he ran, he laughed. As he neared, his laughter softened into an embarrassed chuckle.

"What's so funny?" asked Gianna.

Suah pointed to the gap where his two missing teeth should be. "Every time I open my mouth, Hawa giggles…"

"Well, tell her to enjoy it now because we're going to get that fixed."

"She thinks it makes me an *incredibly unique specimen.*"

"You're unique enough already," smiled Gianna. She held her emotions in check the best she could. "Hey, I'm getting ready to go. I wanted to take your picture."

"Here? In the field?"

"Yes, here, where you and Hawa like to play."

He smiled and fidgeted about. "Where do you want us?"

Gianna pointed at a place not far away. "Just stand out there."

He hurried through the tall grass. Along the way, he snatched a single blade of grass in his hand and waved it back and forth to the side of him.

"That's it. Now turn this way." Gianna squatted down and framed the shot. Through the viewfinder, Suah appeared. As he waited, the mischievous smile faded from his face. In its place, a steady and expressive gaze came over him. For a moment, Gianna thought he might be going into trance.

"Hold it right there…"

Suah mistook her direction as applying to the piece of grass in his hand. Eager to comply, he brought the single blade of grass up in front of him and held it there. An instant later, the shutter released and the picture was captured. Gianna stood and held out her arms.

Suah came running once again.

"I'm going to miss you so much," she cried. She held him and hugged him close.

"I'll miss you too."

"You and Hawa have lots of fun, OK?"

"We will…"

"I wish I could stay longer today but my plane is ready to go."

"Sounds like we both have more to explore."

"That's right. No matter how far we're apart, our adventure continues, remember that. If you need me, just let me know. If you get tired of your visit here, your home with me will be waiting for you."

"OK." Suah pulled a piece of paper from his pocket. "This is for you."

"For me? What is it?"

Suah shrugged. "I wanted to give you a surprise. It's the best thing I have right now."

Gianna opened the folded paper to find a ink drawing of two horses on a hillside. At the bottom, the title was written—*Reaching Near*. It was signed *Brody Mud*.

"Where did you get this?"

"Brody drew it at the ranch. I like it a lot. I think you should have it."

"This is wonderful. Thank you."

"I'm glad you like it too."

"Very much. Now I'd better get going…goodbye, Suah. I love you."

He gave her a kiss on the cheek and hugged her one last time. "I love you too, Mom. Goodbye."

She stood up. "Now you better go play. Hawa's waiting for you."

He smiled, gave a wave, then turned and meandered off. Ever so often, he would turn to see if she was still there. On seeing her, he'd smile again and give another little wave. The pattern repeated several times.

Gianna watched him go. As he shrank into the distance, the feeling came over her—chances were good he'd never come home with her again.

As she stood there, unable to pull her eyes from him, Zokaya walked up.

"Sorry to interrupt, but everyone is ready to go. They say it's time."

Gianna nodded. "Thank you." She paused for one last look. "I wonder when I'll see him again…"

Zokaya read her emotions. There wasn't time for discussion. The best he could offer was a word to comfort her. "Imagine the man he'll be some day."

"It's hard to think that far ahead."

"You don't have to. The core of his manhood is already there, near to his spirit. You have helped him get in touch with that a great deal."

"It's nice of you to say that, but I wonder…"

"You are afraid he will want to stay in Africa."

"Yes." Admitting it out loud was a stroke of pain.

"Maybe this is where it needs to start."

"Start what?" Hurting, Gianna had little patience for platitudes.

"I think you know what I mean."

Gianna considered it briefly. "Sorry, but I'm not a believer."

"You don't think it's possible?"

"It's not even about that."

"Imagine when he becomes a man. Imagine his gift spreading through this place and beyond, to the rest of the continent. Just imagine—what you've started here today could one day reach the whole world."

Gianna could only process her hurt and loss; the rest was aggravation.

She donned her sunglasses to hide her tears. "Meanwhile, life goes on."

She brushed passed him with nothing left to say.

EPILOGUE

"I know that you can do anything, and no one can stop you."
Job 42:2 (NLT)

It was prime whale-watching season and Lucas and Gavin were doubling up catamaran runs out of slip number nine. They now offered whale-watching tours as well as their regular snorkeling jaunts to reefs near and far. Business was booming for *Island Aquatics and Adventures*.

Hailey turned off the main highway in a Jeep that had its top off. Open to the morning sunshine, Leah sat windswept and smiling in the front passenger seat. They drove down the side street that bordered the harbor on one side and the park with the big tree on the other.

"You want to come along?" asked Hailey.

Leah gazed past her. "You go ahead. I'm going to check out the park."

"All right," grinned Hailey. "But no climbing trees this time, OK?"

"Yeah, right." Leah laughed as they both got out.

Hailey called back as she scooted away. "I'll come look for you."

Leah acknowledged her with a wave as she crossed the street.

Hailey bopped along, heading for the hawker stands in the harbor. At the sound of a ringtone, she was quick to answer her phone.

"Hi, Dad. What's up?"

"Hey, sweetie, I wanted to let you know. Mom just got off the phone with Gianna. Suah's plane has been delayed in Atlanta. He'll be a couple hours late."

"What about the party?"

"It's still on but Gianna wants us to get there at seven instead of five. Could you pass the word around and see if that works for everyone?"

"No problem. Oh, and Dad, I'm about to make the reservations. Are you sure you can't come along?"

"Oh, I don't know. I'd really like to but there's still so much I have to do before the San Francisco conference."

"Yeah, but tomorrow's our last day here."

Jaxon hesitated and allowed his focus to shift. "You're right. OK, count me in."

"Great! That'll be much better for Mom. She'll have some serious company while Leah and I are being silly." Hailey chuckled.

"The way your mom's been acting, I may wind up with The Three Stooges. I've got to go; catch you later."

"OK." Hailey stuffed the phone in a pocket of her shorts and aimed in the direction of *Island Aquatics and Adventures.* The regular signup booth was still there behind the store but now alongside it was a new encampment under a large and brightly-colored umbrella.

As Hailey approached, Brody's back was to her. He was sitting in front of an easel, sketching a tourist who sat and posed in a chair while family members gathered around and watched.

Hailey gave a wave to Kip, the new guy who was manning the signup booth, then halted behind Brody for a minute and watched his process.

Brody saw the woman who was posing for him move her eyes to check out someone behind him. He glanced back to see who it was then continued to sketch with a steady gaze passing just beneath the rim of his hat.

"Thar she blows!" he announced in reference to Hailey. "She's the rarest of all quixotic creatures, a cross between a sprite and a mermaid." The spectators chuckled. "What salty dog have you come to charm today?"

Hailey loved the attention but was a bit embarrassed. "I've come to watch the whales."

Brody scanned the small crowd of spectators. "This beauty is obviously confused; she thinks she's in Vegas!"

After the laughter subsided, Brody finished his sketch with a flourish and handed it over to the woman. His face lit up as much as hers when she saw the finished product and reacted with delight.

After paying him, the woman rejoined her family and they went on their way. Brody sat down and offered Hailey another folding chair.

Hailey stood. "Thanks, but I can't stay long. Leah's waiting for me."

"Palling around with miscreants again, I see…"

"I came to see you, didn't I?"

"What kind of corrupting influence are you being to that poor girl today?"

"We're going to the aquarium."

"You mean that big tourist trap."

"Yeah, the place with all the fishies. I talked with a friend of mine who works there and he's going to get Leah in as a volunteer."

"Are we talking about Lolo Leah? Never-look-at-the-ocean Leah?"

"That's not her name but yeah, if she works out, there's a good chance they'll add her on as an intern."

"What for? She can't be *that* crazy about feeding fish."

"She wants to be a marine biologist. She knows a bunch about it already."

"To each his own…"

"So how's business?"

"What business? I'm having fun. Are you serious about whale-watching?"

"Yeah, I need to make reservations for four."

Brody pointed in Kip's direction. "Better see the man over there pretty quick. I hear the prime times are filling up fast."

"Another thing," Hailey added. "You're coming to the party tonight, aren't you?"

"I never miss birthday cake…"

"I heard Suah's going to be late getting in. We all need to be there at seven, not five. Is that going to work for you?"

"It works out better. I can sit here a couple more hours. The sunset crowd are suckers for portrait sketches. You know, the hopeless romantic type."

"Yeah, I know, just like the people who like to sketch them."

"Hey, watch your mouth." He pointed at her menacingly then settled back. "So, how old of a man is Suah going to be?"

"Ten, I think."

Brody looked into the blank page on his easel. "Wow. Ten years go by in a flash." He pulled himself back from a deeper mood. He grimaced at her, "You're not even *two* flashes yet."

"A *year* ago is a long time to me," noted Hailey. "In fact, one *month* ago seems like an eternity."

Brody scratched his beard. "That's the way it is with alternate universes."

Hailey smiled, "Oh, here we go…"

"Go ahead, laugh, but I know what I know. So, what did you get Suah for his birthday?"

"My family's giving him a solar-powered ATV. You should see this thing; it's wild! It's got its own compact charging station and everything. We're having it shipped to his village so he can use it when he gets back."

"What the hell does he need that thing for?"

"He wants to explore around, maybe go to neighboring villages."

Brody pushed back his hat and shook his head. "The whole thing's kinda *nutzo-crazy* if you ask me. He's going to live *there* but vacation *here* a couple weeks out of the year? Seems bass-ackwards doesn't it?"

"Not if you're from there," countered Hailey.

"You have a point…" Brody leaned towards her. "…a weak one!"

Hailey remembered something. "Do you know what Leah's giving him?"

Brody checked around then whispered, "It can't be diving lessons."

"Shut up!" grinned Hailey. "You're so bad."

"So what is it?"

"She asked my father and he's going to have Gris-Gris sent back with Suah to his village."

"Damn! What else is being shipped to Africa?" Brody sat up and looked around his chair. "I'd better check around here and see what's missing."

"I think it's sweet," commented Hailey. "So what are *you* giving him?"

For the first time, Brody's wisecracking shell showed signs of surrender to the sentiment of the moment. He dropped out of character long enough to let Hailey see another, larger side of him.

"I didn't know what to give him," he confessed. "It's pretty big what's happened to me in the last month. One thing's for sure: I know Gianna didn't want a copy of that horse picture leaked to the press."

"The one you did at the ranch?"

Brody nodded. "It's a strange world. For Gianna, the leak was nothing but trouble. For me, it got me my very first showing in the gallery here in town. Nothing's been the same since."

Hailey tried to make him feel better. "That's all right; I don't think Suah expects anything from us."

"Oh, I got him something."

"I thought you said…"

"I said I didn't know what to give him. And that's right. There's only one thing to do when that happens."

"What?"

Brody was back in character. "Give money, of course!"

"Pardon me, but I didn't think you had any money."

"Nope, I don't, but I can draw and apparently all of that news hoopla about that horse picture turned out to be good for something after all."

"How's that?"

"I drew a picture for Suah."

"Oh! He'll love that!"

"Wait, that's not all." Brody leaned forward in his chair. "I didn't give the picture to Suah. I gave it to some fancy auction place in New York City."

"They auctioned it off?"

"Yep. And guess who bought it for half a million dollars…" Brody waited as Hailey's eyes widened. She shook her head, then he told her, "…Wyatt Dumashe."

"Wow," gasped Hailey.

"Best of all, Wyatt bought the thing but he's giving it to Suah, tonight."

"So you just scored half a million dollars!"

Brody choked back his emotion. "No. That's going in a trust fund for Suah to use however he wants. He gets that—and the picture from Wyatt."

Hailey leaned down at gave Brody a hug. "That's wonderful," she cried.

Brody struggled with humor to maintain composure. "I thought so."

Hailey stood up, suddenly curious. "So what's the drawing? What is it?"

"Well, I didn't have any horses to put on a hill," explained Brody. "So I put Suah and Hawa there instead. It's the two of them, playing."

Hailey laughed as she cried. "And I thought the ATV was cool…"

Brody noticed a family approaching his encampment and reprimanded Hailey. "Hey, no crying around here; you'll drive away my business."

Hailey wiped her cheek. "I better make those reservations." She sidled off to the signup booth to talk to Kip.

Brody sat back with casual friendliness and greeted the people. "Hello there! Nice day for something, isn't it? I still haven't figured out what…"

The young couple had three children; two were old enough for school and a third must have been three or four years old. They all looked fascinated by the drawings displayed as samples and lingered long enough for Brody to offer them his services.

"You tell me how good you want to look and I'll draw it." He smiled. "I'm *that* good."

The couple chuckled. The man asked, "How much to get the kids done?"

"All together or separately?"

"All together."

"Single sketch price is right there on the sign. Best of all, there's no surcharge if the little munchkins pick their nose and fidget around."

The couple smiled then looked at each other as the woman nodded.

She told her husband, "Yes, let's do that. Just the kids."

The man herded them closer. "Where do you want them?"

Brody stood up to direct traffic as Hailey returned from the signup booth.

Just then, the three-year-old stumbled and face-planted on the pavement. A wail of shock and pain rose up from the tyke like an emergency siren.

Brody was closest to the child and hurried to pick him up and set him right on his feet. Hailey rushed in too but Brody got there first. The child screamed as the parents rushed in but Brody already had him well in hand.

Talking to the child, Brody stroked his hand back along the side of the boy's head. "There, there, big guy, it's going to be all right. Everything's OK." With long, slow passes of his hand, Brody patted the child.

Incredibly, the child stopped crying and looked up at him.

Hailey crouched down and saw the look on the child's face go from anguish to a place curious and serene. She looked up at Brody at the same time he looked at her. The change in the child was dramatic to both of them.

Hailey and Brody shared a moment of understanding and wonder. Each glanced at Brody's hand. They had seen another hand move like that over people who needed help and they'd been awed by equally quick turnarounds.

It was too wild to think the same thing was happening. But what was it?

They stood up and the parents rushed in to claim the boy.

Brody and Hailey stepped back and let the mom and dad dote away.

There was nothing to say that wasn't already understood. Hailey waved goodbye. "I gotta get going. See you tonight."

Brody raised a hand and nodded, then turned back to his customers.

Invigorated by the electric feeling of seeing Brody with the child, Hailey's steps quickened away from the harbor. She crossed the street and hurried into the park. It didn't take long for her to find Leah.

She was sitting on a bench, wistfully looking out to sea but turned as Hailey approached. "Everything all set?" asked Leah.

Hailey plopped down next to her. "A whale of a time guaranteed."

Leah groaned, "Tell me they didn't say that."

"They didn't say that," parroted Hailey. "Oh, the party's at seven, not five. Is that OK with you?"

"Sure, but I don't know about Gris-Gris. He's *so* particular." She laughed. "Did you see Brody?"

"Yeah, happy as a clam, camped out under his umbrella."

"What a life." Leah sensed Hailey's energy. "And how are *you* doing?"

Hailey thought back to the encounter with the little boy and looked out to sea. "I'm fine…" She turned back to Leah and smiled. "I'm *more* than fine."

Hailey jumped up. "Come on, let's get going. I want to get there before all the fish swim away."

Leah stood. "I'll race you to the car."

Hailey looked perplexed then accepted the challenge. "You're on!"

Leah turned to go and announced right away, "I won!"

"What! We haven't even started…"

"Maybe *you* haven't," grinned Leah, her limp lighter than ever before. "But I've been there and back; you missed it. It's not *that* far away."

*"I know that nothing is better for them than to rejoice,
and to do good in their lives."*
Ecclesiastes 3:12 (NKJV)

M. C. MILLER is the author of the epically bizarre
apocalyptic spectacle **PW2 2012: The End of the Beginning**,
the Sino-American techno-thriller **Islands of Instability**,
the cautionary tale **The Leaves In Winter**,
the inspiring whimsy of **The Girl From An Alternate NFAR Universe**,
the science fiction short story anthology **Prefetching Self,**
and the seriously zany black comedy **Uberwoot!**
He lives in the Pacific Northwest with his wife Deborah Joy
and enjoys hiking, kayaking, food adventures in the kitchen,
and what-if speculations about the near future.

www.mcmillerbooks.com

www.ingramcontent.com/pod-product-compliance
Lightning Source LLC
Chambersburg PA
CBHW031414240626
47154CB00001B/36